THEIR DEADLY TRUTH

A Jake Cashen Crime Thriller

Declan James

This is a work of fiction. Names, characters, businesses, places, events, and incidents are either the products of the author's imagination or used in a fictitious manner

Author's Note

This story contains themes of suicide, murder, and mental illness. While these elements are part of the fictional narrative, I understand they may be difficult for some readers.

If you or someone you love is struggling, you are not alone. Help is available.

In the U.S., call or text 988 or visit 988lifeline.org for free, confidential support.

To view full content warnings for all books in this series, visit https://declanjamesbooks.com/content-warnings/

One

Thirty-one years, eight months, sixteen days, two hours, and thirty-nine minutes ago ...

On the last day of her life, Sonya Cashen hated her shoes. Such a stupid thing to care about, she knew. But as she ran through the yard toward the house, her heel broke as she stepped into a small divot in the front yard. Her ankle bent sideways, and she went down hard. She heard a crunching sound, and a spear of pain shot from her ankle all the way up to her heart.

It cost her a few seconds. She would wonder if it would have made a difference. If she'd worn the navy-blue flats she put out last night instead of these ridiculous strappy things her mother liked. The tears came as she ripped both shoes off and flung them behind her.

"Jake!" she cried out. Or maybe she should be silent, not let him know she was here. Would it matter? Would catching him off guard make things better?

Her heart aching as she tried to catch her breath, she ran toward the house. She could see the light still on in the kitchen, glowing through the tiny window on the side of the door.

He was here. Thank God. He was here. It would be okay. She'd made it in time.

She twisted the front doorknob. It wouldn't turn. She'd left her purse on the front seat of her car, parked across the street.

"Jake!"

He wasn't answering. God. She knew what it meant if he didn't answer. She reached down, fumbling for the fake rock they kept beneath the meticulously landscaped bushes. With shaking fingers, she slid open the secret compartment and pulled out the single key. She jammed it into the lock and flung the front door open.

She didn't know her fall had created a tiny tear in the tendon of her ankle. She felt nothing. Just desperate fear. Jake was nowhere.

A square pink piece of paper from the phone pad sat on the counter. She picked it up. She read the first line, and it felt like her lungs turned to mud. She couldn't draw in air.

"Jake!" she grunted, her voice sounding like it was coming from someone else's mouth.

She heard movement. A crash. It came from the basement. The door just off the kitchen stood ajar. She never liked it that way. Jakey had a set of drums Grandpa Max had given him last Christmas. Payback of some sort for whatever ruckus his own son, Jake, had made her in-laws suffer through twenty-five years ago. With the basement door shut, he could bang the things to his heart's content.

A moment later, Jake stepped through. Her heart flooded with relief so heavy, she felt her knees buckle. She clutched the note against her chest.

"Jake," she whispered. "Baby. I was worried. We've been looking for you."

He turned to her, staring at her with bloodshot eyes that made the blue of his irises stand out as if they'd turned to pure ice.

"Baby," she said, taking one step forward. He raised his right arm.

That's when she saw the gun. Time slowed. Sonya's head swam and she saw double. Jake put the barrel of the gun against his own temple.

"Go," Jake said. "Get away from me."

She wouldn't. She couldn't. In her mind's eye, she watched him pull the trigger. Over and over. Every time she tried to reach for him. Stop it. Hold him.

"Jake. Listen to me. It's going to be okay. I'm here. We're going to get through this together. Remember? I told you. Just listen to my voice. I'm here. It's me. I'm real, Jake. Just me. Just you. No doctors. I promise. We're done with that."

He pulled the gun away from his temple, at least. But she knew the cold expression on his face. As if his muscles had turned to granite.

"You can't talk your way out of this," he said. "You lie and you lie and you lie. They all do. You're just like them. You want to kill me. Poison me."

"No," she said. "Jake. No. It's me. It's you and me. Remember what you told me? Remember what we promised? If I say it, it's the truth. Hold on to me. Follow me, Jake."

He pursed his lips and shook his head furiously from side to side. He knocked the gun against his own head three times as if he were trying to shake something loose inside his skull.

His tears came.

"You're not here. You're not real. I know where you are. I know you want him."

"No," she said. "I'm real, Jake. And I'm the only place I ever want to be. With you. With the kids. Our kids, Jake. They'll be home soon. Here." She took another step toward him and reached for his hand.

He raised the gun again. Only this time, he pointed it at her. Something happened inside her. Not fear. It was as if she were seeing everything from above. Like she'd floated to the ceiling and saw Jake and herself facing each other.

She remembered it. Seeing him. Seeing herself. A strange déjà vu. Or a dream she'd had. How did it end?

"I love you," she whispered. "Jake, listen to me. I love you."

"No," he said. "No. No. No."

The last time, she thought. What did I say to him? She'd found him in the corner, curled up under his workbench in the basement. She'd crawled beside him, sat with him. He let her pull his head into her lap and quietly wept there as she caressed the back of his neck. As she grounded him and brought him back to her.

He needed to touch her. She hadn't said anything. It was just her simple touch.

"Shhh," she said as she took another step toward him. He was only a foot away. She could smell him. He dripped with sweat, reeked of body odor.

"I love you," she said again. She kept saying it. He lowered the gun. A wave of calm went through her. She floated back to the ground. His eyes changed. He looked at her, not through her.

"Give me your hand," she said. He let her touch him. She brought his left hand up and pressed it against her breast. She let that awful pink note flutter to the kitchen floor beside her.

"It's me," she said. "Feel me. Touch me. Come back to me, baby."

God, he was beautiful. Lashes so thick they didn't look real. The curve of his full mouth, giving him that mischievous expression that always made her feel like they shared some secret. His chiseled jaw that she was always telling him not to clench when he worried. And his hands. Strong. Calloused. Before the babies, he could span her waist with them. His gentlest touch still heated her, made her feel safe, protected, loved.

Her broken boy. Scared. Lost. Clinging to her. They said she gave up everything for him. But they didn't understand. He *was* everything. He could build anything with those hands. An artist. Seeing shapes and connections in things others couldn't. He'd filled up his father's pole barn with beautiful cabinets, coffee tables, and birdhouses. All custom pieces. Each one a work of art.

She ached for him. Missing his arms around her. Her protector. Like nothing could ever hurt her as long as he was around. The world could fall away but they would survive, thrive, together. He was all she ever needed. And their babies. Their beautiful babies. Jakey, who she could look at and see her husband as a little boy. His carbon copy. Gemma with her fiery spirit and Cashen temper. Fearless. Or feral, as Grandma Ava liked to tell her. In just a few short years, she would give her father a run for his money. And Sonya couldn't wait to see it.

"It's okay," she said. "Just give me the gun. Let's put it away. Let's go upstairs. How about a bath? The kids won't be home for a couple of hours. We can talk. Or we can just ... be. You and me. Jake, I've missed you so much."

"God," he whispered. "I've missed you too. It's only quiet when you're here."

"I know," she said. "Believe that, Jake."

It happened then. The change. One moment he was with her. Seeing her. She felt his love for her in every halting breath he took. In the tiny pulse she felt in his wrist as she held his hand against her heart.

Then the clouds came in. He ripped his hand away from her. His eyes went cold. Dead. Sonya instinctively took two steps back until she had her back up against the counter.

He raised the gun again. A breeze kicked up. It cycled through the house and made the door to the basement slam behind him, loud as a rifle crack.

"No!" Jake cried. "Go away. You can't have her."

He was no longer looking at her. Sonya felt her skin crawl as Jake looked beyond her at the screen door leading to the backyard. The wind caught it too, making it bang open, then shut.

"It's only me, Jake," she said. "And it's only you. How could you think anything else? You're mine, Jake. This is me. Don't you know? Don't you feel it? It's always been you. Us. Always."

She saw that blasted note on the ground. She wanted to tear it to pieces in front of him.

"Sonya," he said. "Don't turn around. Just run."

She could feel something behind her, but didn't dare turn.

"No," she said. "Look at me, Jake."

"Get out!" Jake yelled. "I told you not to come here. Why are you here? I told you I'd kill you before I let you touch my wife again."

She felt something tickling between her shoulder blades. As if someone were standing behind her, ready to reach out and touch her there.

"Jake," she said. "Who is it?"

He murmured something. She couldn't make it out.

The basement door slammed shut again, louder this time. The sound of it stung her heart. Stole her breath.

Jake's eyes went wide. He wasn't looking past her anymore. His eyes locked with hers. So intense was his gaze, it got hard to breathe. She felt the room spin.

He came to her. God, he was strong. She reached for him, needing his strength now. Her knees buckled.

The wind howled. It was as if autumn turned to winter in no more time than the rapid beat of her own heart.

"Stay here," Jake said, his voice deep, commanding. He would take care of her. Always. It would be all right if he stayed with her.

So tall above her. So hard to reach. She could hear the screen door fly open again. This time, Jake ran toward it.

"No," she said. But she couldn't hear her own voice. She looked down. The yellow dress she wore turned red. So strange. She tried to wipe at the stain. Her hand turned red too.

"Jake," she croaked. But he was gone.

The wall phone was just a couple of feet away from her, but Sonya couldn't make her body move. She felt stuck in tar. She took a halting step forward, gripping the counter to keep her balance. She grabbed the receiver but the effort of it was all she had left. She sank slowly to the kitchen floor, the phone clutched in her hand. A moment passed.

"Help," she tried to scream. Hoping the operator would come online. Where was the damn operator? She could no longer reach the keypad. All she heard was the infuriating hum of a dial tone.

She saw her daughter's face swimming in front of her. Her son.

"Gemma," she whispered. Her eyes went to the side of the refrigerator. She had two 5x7 photos of the kids. Last year's school pictures. Jakey's hair stuck straight up on one side. He had a cowlick that refused to lay flat and he'd caused such a fuss about getting a haircut, Sonya hadn't found it worth the battle. Jake found it hilarious. He said Jakey looked just like Dennis the Menace, which was fitting. Jakey. Her baby.

And Gemma. She refused to smile in the photo. She was stunning anyway. Everyone said she looked just like Sonya. She did, in her way. But Gemma was so like her father in every other way.

So like her father ...

Gemma. Gemma. Sonya tried to reach for her. Tried to call out to her. But Gemma simply stared silently at her from that photograph, eyes blazing. Stubborn. Fierce.

The room grew dark and cold. Sonya held on to Gemma's eyes.

"Help him," Sonya whispered. "I'm so sorry. Take care of them all."

The basement door slammed shut one last time, sounding just like a gunshot.

Two

Present day ...

Gemma sat beside him, her blonde hair whipping around her face. Jake stole a quick glance at her and smiled. She kept a cool eye on the back of the boat. Her chin jutted out, her jaw set slightly off to the side.

Jake heard yelling, but couldn't make out the words over the boat's engine. "Signal!" he shouted. He told his sister half a dozen times. She was looking at the wrong thing and it was about to make things dangerous.

Jake circled and ran through his own wake. He heard his nephew Ryan's laughter behind him.

"Gemma!" Jake shouted. "Is she down?"

Gemma shook her head and circled an index finger around her head. Jake nodded. He made a wide-arcing turn toward shore. From the corner of his eye, he saw the ski rope go slack. His skier waved; she jumped the wake easily and coasted gracefully to the sandbar.

"She's good!" Ryan said, beaming as he pulled up the rope slack. Jake aimed toward the dock. By the time he got there, Peyton had already tossed her skis and hopped up, ready to grab the dock ropes.

"She grew up on a lake," Ryan said. "Devil's. Up in Irish Hills. Michigan."

Jake nodded. Gemma went to the back of the boat and helped Peyton tie it off as Jake cut the engine. Ryan jumped off and joined his girlfriend. They were arm in arm as they walked up the dock toward Virgil Adamski's house.

Virgil sat on the porch under the shade provided by the second-floor balcony. He lived alone now. His son and daughter had moved across the country. He told Jake to think of this place as his own. He didn't use the boat much except for fishing.

Jake got up and worked the ropes on the starboard side. Ryan and Peyton were already on the porch, talking to Virgil. Ryan hadn't removed his arm from around Peyton's waist. Gemma made a noise. A scoff. Then she plopped back in the passenger seat, staring hard at her son.

"What?" Jake asked, knowing he'd regret it.

"He's all over her," she said. "Like he's afraid she's gonna float away if he doesn't keep his damn arm on her ass."

Jake laughed. "It's not that bad."

"That bikini covers nothing," Gemma said. "It's like three Post-it Notes."

"Gemma, come on. She's what, twenty? You wanna know the truth? She looks a hell of a lot like you did at that age. Grandma and Grandpa used to tear you a new one every time you came down in bathing suits that looked pretty much just like that one.

She seems like a nice kid. More importantly, Ryan's good with her. Respectful. He opens doors for her. Carried her bag in."

"He's following her around like a puppy," Gemma said. "He needs to focus. It's gonna be a tough season. His coach is depending on him to be a leader now that he's gonna be an upperclassman."

"Name one thing that girl has done to offend you besides turning your son's head?"

Ryan and Peyton disappeared inside Virgil's house. Virgil gave Jake a wave.

"Will you talk to him?" Gemma turned to Jake.

"About what?" Again, Jake figured he'd come to regret asking.

"Do you think they're ... um ... sleeping together?"

Jake had to swallow a laugh. "Gemma, come on."

"No. I know. Of course they are. He's almost twenty. I mean, really. How many times does a kid his age think about ... you know?"

"Are you a prude all of a sudden?"

"Jake!"

"All right. All right. Yeah. I don't know. A lot."

"Well, then you have to talk to him."

Jake stepped off the boat onto the dock. He held out a hand to his sister. She took it begrudgingly, but planted her feet in a wide stance, arms crossed. Jake wasn't going to be able to make a clean getaway from this conversation.

"About what?"

"You know what!" Gemma managed to shout and whisper at the same time.

"He's almost twenty. He's been away at college for two years. Don't you think that particular ship sailed a long time ago? You mean to tell me you haven't had the talk with him?"

"It's different. I'm his mother. He needs it man to man."

"For Pete's sake, Gemma. You want me to tell him to wrap it? He already knows."

"It's not just that," she said. "I just want him to ... you know ... like you said ... be respectful."

All her bravado vanished, which was pretty rare for his sister. It had been her default setting since they were kids.

"He's a good kid, Gemma," Jake said, his tone gentle. "You raised him right. He's not like his dad."

That too was a sore subject. Ryan's dad, Gemma's first husband, hadn't really been in the picture. Jake had been away during most of her relationship with him. But Gemma was a dirtbag magnet when it came to men. Her second husband, Dickie Gerald, had laid hands on her before Jake came back to Blackhand Hills. Ryan had been around that.

He put a hand on her shoulder. "I'll check in with him," he assured her. "But don't worry about him. I'm not. Not in this area. And Peyton seems sweet."

He was right that she reminded him of Gemma at that age. At least physically. Dazzling bright eyes, a killer smile. Personality-wise, Peyton couldn't be more different. She was sweet, polite, maybe even a little gullible. A kid. Gemma hadn't been a kid since she was twelve years old. She'd been forced to grow up overnight when they lost both their parents.

"Thank you," she said. "I just don't want him to do anything stupid."

"Anything you did?" Jake teased. She shot him a murderous stare. It was true though. Gemma had been a wild child. Rebellious. Headstrong. She'd driven their grandparents crazy. The chaos agent in their lives.

Jake put his arm around his sister and led her up to the house.

"How's it running?" Virgil asked. Peyton came out the sliding door. She'd wrapped a skirt around her waist and twisted her hair up into a knot. She had deep dimples in both cheeks as she handed Virgil a fresh, tall glass of lemonade.

"Can I get you anything else?" she asked him as she stood beside him and put her hands on his shoulders. "I made some cowboy caviar. I can bring you a plate with some tortilla chips. The kind you can scoop."

"They're telling me I gotta watch my salt," Virgil said, bitterness in his tone.

"I got low-sodium chips," she said. "The dip's all healthy stuff. Beans, corn, salsa. Ryan said you're watching what you eat. I made it just for you. I really appreciate your letting me spend the day here. I'll grab you a plate." Peyton leaned in and kissed Virgil on the head before springing back through the sliding door. Virgil blushed.

"That girl's an angel," Virgil said. "A keeper."

Gemma snorted. Jake gave her a gentle backhand to the arm.

"He could do worse," Virgil said, catching Gemma's resting bitch face. "Hell, you *did* do worse."

"Okay!" Jake said, seeing the first signs of Gemma's erruption.

"Gemma, go in and grab those patties out of the fridge. I'll get the grill going."

She eyed him, but took the cue. She grabbed her black swim cover-up off the clothesline beside the porch and slipped into it. With an angry eye on Jake, she went inside.

"Whooo, boy." Virgil laughed. "That is one keyed-up Mama Bear. Can we trust her to behave?"

"I think so," Jake said. I hope so, he thought to himself.

To Jake's memory, Ryan only had one other girlfriend in high school and it hadn't lasted very long. Peyton was definitely different. Gemma was right that he was clinging to the girl like Velcro.

"The girl's got the right idea," Virgil said. "Kill her with kindness."

The slider opened. Virgil went quiet as Peyton stepped back out carrying paper plates with chips and dip. She handed one to Virgil and the other to Jake.

"Thanks," he said.

"Cold beer in that blue cooler you're about to sit on," Virgil said. Jake reached in and grabbed a bottle. He picked out a water for Virgil and got the stink eye when he tossed it to him.

Ryan came out carrying a tray of burger patties. "I'll get the grill started," he said cheerily. Peyton followed him over to the side yard.

A moment later, Jake heard tires crunching on the gravel driveway behind them. He lifted his hand to shield his eyes from the sun as a car door slammed.

"Who's that?" Virgil asked.

It was Birdie. Jake's friend and fellow detective. She was wearing a suit and had her badge hanging around her neck. She had a somber expression as she walked up.

"Hey, Virge," she said, stepping onto the porch. Like Peyton, she leaned over and kissed him on the cheek. "You look good. Like you're putting some weight back on."

Birdie stole a chip from his plate.

"What's up?" Jake asked. She gestured with her chin. Whatever it was, she didn't want to talk about it to anyone but him. Which meant it wasn't good news.

Jake put his plate down and followed her back to her car. He was off for the next four days, but Birdie was working a make-up day.

"I'm sorry to come grab you," she said. "Max said this is where I'd find you. I tried to call."

Jake's phone was currently in the glovebox of his truck.

"We just got off the boat," he said.

"I figured. Look. There's been an incident out in Navan Township. Deputy Bundy called it in about thirty minutes ago. He was first on scene."

Jake sighed and blinked with heavy eyelids. "What have we got?"

"Two victims," she said. "Married couple. Both with gunshot wounds. Their dog walker found them. From what Bundy said, it sounds pretty gruesome. Landry wants you on it."

"Yeah," Jake said. "Of course."

Gemma came around the front of the house. Brow furrowed, she looked at Birdie.

"Sorry, Gemma," she said. "I don't mean to disrupt your day."

"It's okay," she said. "Does he have to leave?"

Jake turned to her. "Looks like I do." He walked over to his truck, reached in, and grabbed the keys from under the visor. He tossed them to his sister. She caught them one-handed.

"I'm their ride," he explained to Birdie.

"Will you be back?" Gemma asked. He turned to Birdie. With pursed lips, she gave him a quick headshake.

"Might be pulling an all-nighter," he told his sister. "I'll call you in the morning."

"Can you at least get him home in one piece for me?" Gemma asked Birdie.

Birdie smiled. "Roger that." Then she slapped Jake on the back and nudged him toward the passenger side of her car.

THREE

Jake was relieved to see crime tape when he pulled up. Two patrol cars blocked off the entry to 624 Mill Pond Drive.

"Who's on scene?" he asked Birdie as she parked behind one of the cruisers and they got out. Jake slid his sunglasses up his nose.

"Tom Stuckey and Matt Bundy," she said. "Responded to a 9-1-1 call from the dog walker. She's just a kid. Eighteen, nineteen."

"Good job," he said under his breath. Three years ago, when Sheriff Landry promoted him to detective (and more like conscripted), crime scene management had been a serious weakness for Worthington County deputies. He was glad to see that people were starting to pay attention to him.

They walked up to a small brick ranch with black shutters and cheery yellow flower boxes under the windows. Well-tended pink geraniums swayed in the breeze as Jake headed for the front door. He spotted Tom Stuckey in the side yard, doubled over and spraying his lunch all over the lawn.

Birdie went to him. She put a hand on his back. “Better out than in,” she said.

Stuckey put a hand up and nodded. He straightened. Blushing with embarrassment, he walked over to Jake.

“Sorry,” Stuckey said. “I thought I had it under control.”

The front door swung open. Deputy Matt Bundy walked out. Jake was glad to see he wore blue latex gloves and booties over his shoes.

“Whatcha got?” Jake asked.

“Two victims,” Bundy started. “White male, white female. Both are in their mid-twenties. No formal IDs yet but it’s Cameron Katz and his wife, Rianne.”

Jake had a pair of gloves and booties in his pocket. He put them on. Birdie followed suit. From the front door, they walked straight into the living room. The first victim sat with his back to them, slumped on a couch facing the kitchen.

Jake walked around the couch to get a better look. The man’s face was mostly intact, with an obvious gunshot wound to the right temple. He stared straight ahead. If Jake followed his line of sight, he could see part of the second body, her legs sticking out behind a kitchen counter.

Jake noted a black semi-automatic handgun on the ground a few inches from the male victim’s dangling right hand.

“Looks like he shot himself,” Birdie said.

They walked into the kitchen. Blood had seeped through the grout on the gray tile floor. Jake carefully sidestepped it and came to the other side of the counter.

Stuckey retched again.

“Do not blow chunks in my crime scene,” Jake said.

"I'm okay," Stuckey assured him. "I've got nothing left."

Jake could guess what had Stuckey so rattled. The female victim was young, beautiful. Her thick red hair fanned out beneath her. Her head was turned slightly. She died staring out of her brilliant green eyes toward the living room.

"They were looking at each other," Birdie whispered.

The victim wore cutoff shorts and a yellow tank top with a daisy decal on the front, matching yellow flip-flops, though one had fallen off and lay next to her toned right leg. She had a deep tan and a mani-pedi with yellow polish to match the flip-flops.

"God, she's young," Jake said. She barely looked older than Ryan's girlfriend Peyton. But this girl had a diamond ring on the fourth finger of her left hand and a matching wedding band.

"Does it look like anything was taken?" Jake asked Bundy.

"Not from what I've seen so far. We cleared the house of course, but were careful not to touch anything."

"That's good," Jake said. He turned back to the male victim. He too wore a tight tank top. His was black, showing off massive biceps and solid shoulders. He looked like a bodybuilder. He wore a large gold chain around his neck. Whatever happened here, neither victim had been stripped of their jewelry. This wasn't a robbery. It was way worse. It looked like the guy killed his pretty wife, then killed himself.

"If that's real," Birdie said, pointing to the woman's wedding ring set, "that's gotta be seven or eight grand."

"Who found them again?" Jake asked.

"Dog walker," Bundy said. "Her name's Marne Kowalski. She's out back sitting at a picnic table. I wanted to keep her out of sight. Some of the neighbors are starting to gawk."

Jake turned and looked out the kitchen window. A young woman with curly black hair sat on a glass-topped table, holding a little white dog in her arms.

"She lets herself in through the mudroom off the back door. She's got a key," Stuckey said.

Jake looked down at the pool of blood surrounding Rianne Katz. She lay on her side in a loose fetal position. She clutched her cell phone in her right hand. The screen was cracked.

In the kitchen. On her side. She had the phone in her hand.

Jake's vision warped. For an instant, he felt as if he'd shot backward, like he was viewing Rianne's body from fifty feet away instead of just inches. He closed his eyes and sucked in air. When he looked down again, he was back in his body.

"I need to talk to the neighbors," Jake said.

"Stuckey and I tag-teamed, split up and did a cursory canvas as soon as the second crew got here," Bundy said. That too impressed Jake. "Stuckey will write it all up. But I've got both of our notes. The neighbors on either side and the two right across the street. Nobody's home at the east-side neighbor's house. On the west, it's a single guy. There's a big privacy fence between the houses. The guy had the day off, but he's been working in his basement. He's finishing it. He said he didn't hear anything, but the power tools he's running get pretty loud."

"That's good work," Jake said. "Anything usable from the others?"

Bundy shook his head. He flipped through his notepad. He had loose scraps of paper in it, likely some of Stuckey's notes as well. "Directly across the street is an older lady. Her name's Esther Gorley. She's sort of a shut-in. She gave us an earful about Cameron Katz. Says the dog's a yapper and Katz doesn't cut his lawn enough. But she hasn't heard or seen anything unusual in the last twenty-four hours. Next to her are the St. Johns. Jim and Kelly. They've got kids in high school. She works from home. Jim's a real estate agent. Says he sold the Katzes this house. Anyway, they didn't hear or see anything either. Nadya Louden also lived across the street. She was out with her cat late, knew Rianne a little. Didn't see or hear anything either."

"Good," Jake said. "That saves me some time. Make sure Stuckey gets everything in there. I don't care how useless a detail you both might think it is."

Bundy beamed at the praise. He was a good, solid cop, in Jake's opinion. So was Stuckey. He couldn't have asked for two better to be first on scene, despite Stuckey's weak stomach.

"Let me talk to Ms. Kowalski," Jake said. Bundy led him to the backyard. Marne Kowalski had her nose buried in the little white dog's neck.

Bundy made the introductions.

"I'm sorry to keep you," Jake said. "I know you've already talked to my colleague here, but would you mind telling me what you saw again?"

"Sure," she said. "This is Zephyr. She's only six months old. She's a Maltipoo. They got her from a rescue a couple of weeks ago. I walk her three times a day while the Katzes are at work."

"Where do they work?" Jake asked.

"Rianne works for an interior designer in Logan. That's what she went to school for, I think. Cameron's a personal trainer. Katz Latz?"

She said it as if Jake should know what that meant. He shook his head. "Sorry, doesn't ring any bells."

"Ladies Love Katz Latz? He's got a pretty big following on social media. And I know he's got some kind of software company or an app he invented. I don't know. He works from home mostly. There's a full gym in their basement where he records his videos and live streams."

Marne was in shock. She had a detached look and a dreamy quality to her voice.

"Tell me what happened today, Marne," Jake said.

"They crate Zephyr at night. She's still learning how to go potty outside. Cam is usually running live streams downstairs on Saturday mornings. Rianne was supposed to be at one of those Parade of Home shows. They asked me to get Zephyr at noon and bring her over to my house. I live two streets over. I have a little doggie daycare. When I got here, she was howling in her crate. She'd messed inside of it. She never does that. I don't think anybody let her out."

"From last night?" Jake asked.

"I don't know. But I took her out and walked into the kitchen to get her some biscuits. Rianne keeps them in a cookie jar. That's when ... Rianne was just lying there. I ... I called 9-1-1."

Marne started to cry.

"It's okay," Jake said.

"They just got married," she hiccuped. "I mean, two weeks ago. I was at their wedding! Rianne hasn't even got the professional photos back from it. They were in the Bahamas all last week. I had Zephyr with me. They got home four days ago. They haven't even opened all their wedding presents. They're in the spare bedroom down the hall."

"It's okay," Jake said. He gestured to Birdie.

She mouthed, "I've got it."

Jake nodded and led Deputy Bundy around the side of the house where they could talk out of Marne's earshot.

"I feel really bad for her," Bundy said. "She's like seventeen years old."

"We need to find their families," Jake said. "Quick. If Katz is some kind of influencer, this might already be on social media." He gestured with his chin toward two teenagers standing right outside the police tape, recording on their phones.

"Stuckey!" Bundy yelled. Stuckey sprinted around the side of the house. He saw where Bundy pointed.

"On it," he said, and made a beeline for the teenagers.

Birdie reappeared. "Marne's mom is on her way. She's gonna take the dog with her."

"Good," Jake said. "I need to put a call into Agent Ramirez and get Dr. Stone out here."

"You'll call BCI on this one?" Bundy asked, his tone eager.

"Absolutely," Jake said.

"He killed her," Birdie said. "Then, himself."

Jake nodded. "Looks that way. Bundy, I need you to start a log."

Matt Bundy's face split into a wide smile. He went quickly to his car and came back with one of the crime scene logbooks Jake created just after Landry promoted him. For three years, Jake had been working to get them in the hands of all field crews.

"On it," Bundy said. "Nobody goes in or out without me writing down who and when."

"Good," Jake said, patting Bundy on the arm. "When BCI gets here, you do whatever Ramirez tells you, got it?"

Bundy nodded with enthusiasm. Jake had heard through the grapevine that both Bundy and Stuckey had ambitions to make detective. Bundy, at least, was off to a good start.

"For now," Jake said. "Back Tom up. Keep the looky-loos out of here."

Birdie followed him back toward the front of the house. Jake scanned the windows. Everything was locked up. The air conditioner was running inside.

"Nothing's broken," Birdie said. "Doesn't look like there were any signs of forced entry. Though I suppose there wouldn't be. But I checked it anyway."

They walked into the living room. Jake stood in front of Cameron Katz's body. He couldn't stop looking at how the man seemed to be staring at the kitchen. At what was left of his wife.

He shot her. Then, he sat down and watched her bleed out before turning the gun on himself. Jake followed Katz's sight line, walking back to the kitchen.

"Who was she talking to?" Birdie said. "Or who was she trying to call? If she managed to dial 9-1-1, they would have had to come out, even if she couldn't cry for help."

Jake froze again, feeling that strange tunnel vision. Who was she trying to call? Who could have helped her?

He reached out, gripping the counter to keep from losing his balance.

"Jake?"

He shook his head.

"Jake, what is it?"

From the corner of his eye, he saw Birdie turn white. "Oh. Oh, good God, Jake. I didn't think ..."

He put a hand up. "Don't."

"Jake, I've got this. You should get some air. There's nothing left for you to do here. Ramirez will handle everything. Let me take you back to the office."

"I'm fine," he snapped. Though he felt anything but.

She was on the floor in the kitchen. He heard the words, but in his head, they were spoken by Gemma. She was on the floor in the kitchen and she had the phone in her hand.

As he looked down at Rianne Katz, his vision became a kaleidoscope. It was Rianne, her red hair fanned out beside her. Then it shifted, turning blonde. Her green eyes morphed to blue. She reached for him, as she did so many times in his nightmares. The ones he'd finally pushed away decades ago. For a split second, he stared at Rianne Katz's body, but he saw his own mother.

She died on the kitchen floor, with a phone in her hand, from a bullet wound Jake's father had put in her. Then, his father walked outside and shot himself.

Four

At six a.m. the next morning, Roger and Pam Timiney were informed their daughter and only child had been murdered. At noon, Jake had no choice but to question them. They lived in a luxury home in Terrace Park, just under a two-hour drive from Blackhand Hills.

All things considered, the Timineys remained remarkably composed. They sat in the living room of their newly built condo. Pam held a tuxedo cat on her lap, gently stroking its back as she looked Jake straight in the eye. Roger Timiney had a bottle of gin next to him on the table. He sipped a gin and tonic throughout the interview and poured a second midway.

"Cam killed her," Roger said. "Can you tell us that much?"

"Understand it's an ongoing investigation," Jake said. "But it looks that way, yes." A tremor went through Roger and he took a sip of his cocktail.

"When was the last time you spoke to Rianne?" Jake asked.

"Pam talked to her more regularly than I did," Roger said. "You know. Mothers and daughters."

Pam blinked. "The day before yesterday," she answered. "I called her in the morning before she left for work."

"Did she sound normal? Did it seem like she was upset about anything?"

Pam shook her head. "She was annoyed. But that wasn't unusual. She was in a rush to get to work. She was always on me to text her instead of calling her. But I hate texting. That's why she was annoyed. But it wasn't anything serious. We hadn't seen her in almost two weeks though. They went to the Bahamas for their honeymoon."

Pam quaked with silent tears. "Her wedding dress is hanging up in the next room. I was supposed to take it to the dry cleaner today to have it preserved and boxed for her."

"They were married on the 14th?" Jake asked.

"June 14th, yes," Roger answered. "I haven't even gotten the bill from the caterers yet."

"I'm so sorry," Jake said. "What can you tell me about Cam? About their relationship?"

Roger and Pam shared a quick glance. Each had a sour expression on their faces.

"You didn't approve of the match?" Jake asked.

Pam reached over and took Roger's drink from him. She downed the rest of the glass and slammed it on the coffee table in front of her. Roger picked it up and poured two fingers of gin back into it. Straight.

"You wanna know the truth?" Pam said. Sensing a shift in her mood, the tuxedo cat jumped off her lap and darted under the couch Jake sat on.

"He was trash, okay? A con man. Big ideas. Get-rich-quick schemes. When they met, he was selling some kind of protein shakes. That was his entire job."

"An MLM," Roger added. "A pyramid scheme."

"That went on for a few months," Pam said. "He lost his shirt, of course. He was working part time at some big gym chain in Logan. That's how they met, actually. It's on the same block as where Rianne works. She started working out on her lunch breaks."

"Where did Rianne work?"

"Designs by Delilah," Roger answered. "Delilah Grossjean is her boss. That's what Ri went to school for. Interior design. She graduated two years ago and Delilah hired her right away. Someday, Rianne wanted to open her own firm. Delilah's been a good boss to her. Taken her under her wing. Before all of this, before she hooked up with Cameron, Ri was going to go to New York. We were going to help her. But everything changed once she met Cam."

"She couldn't stop talking about him," Pam said. "Cam this, Cam that. My daughter is level-headed. Practical. But she seemed to swallow every line of BS Cam fed her. His latest is this software start-up. He went into business with some friend."

"Cam started getting a following on social media," Roger said. The two of them had a sort of rhythm to their narration, going back and forth, one starting a thread, the other picking up on it. "Workout videos. A couple of them went viral. He started making a little bit of money off that."

"Which shocked me," Pam said. "Cam isn't exactly charismatic. He's ... I'm sorry ... I've always found him sleazy. I know I shouldn't say that. I know what it makes me sound like ..."

"Who cares what we sound like?" Roger snapped. "He killed our daughter. Every single thing I've ever thought about that monster turned out to be true. I knew he was going to ruin Rianne. She was going to end up supporting both of them. Worse. Cam was going to take every red cent she saved and blow it on whatever his next scheme was. He wasn't a serious person like Rianne is ... was. He walked around thinking the world owed him something. I tried. I swear to God, I tried talking her out of marrying him. I should have tried harder."

"You couldn't have," Pam said. "Rianne was stubborn. Not rebellious. She never gave us any trouble. But she didn't always attract the best men."

"She was too nice," Roger muttered. "Too trusting. Naïve. I don't know where that came from. I feel like Cam saw her as an easy mark. He tried to get me to invest in several of his businesses. And I'm talking the second time I met him, he started in. It's like he took one look at us, figured we had money, and tried to sink his claws in."

"I didn't know that," Pam said. "Why didn't you tell me he asked you for money, Roger?"

"What does it matter?"

"I should have told Rianne!" Pam shouted. "Maybe it would have helped her see what a loser Cam was."

"It's all right," Jake interjected. "Neither of you could have predicted what happened. I can't pretend to know what you're feeling, but this isn't your fault."

"He's a damn coward!" Roger shouted. "If he didn't want to live, fine. I don't care if he blew his brains out. I'd have given him the damn gun! But he took her with him. Our sweet angel. He dragged her down with him."

"Did Rianne ever say she was scared of Cam?" Jake asked.

Pam shook her head. "No. She made plenty of excuses for him. But it was always about finances. Not anything physical. I had no inkling that she was in any kind of physical danger from him. I knew he had a temper. He yelled. He didn't like it when Rianne disagreed with him in front of other people. But I never had a sense he was hurting her. Rianne was pure, like Roger said. But she wasn't stupid. She wouldn't have stayed with someone who was abusing her like that. I'm sure of it. I just can't imagine what happened."

"Did you know Cam owned a gun?" Jake asked.

"Yes," Roger said. "But it was Rianne's. A couple of years ago, she got it. She had some friend take her to the range and show her how to shoot it. I would have. But she never asked. But yes, Cameron took it out and brought it to me. I've always owned guns. I was fine with my daughter having one for protection. I belong to a members-only gun range nearby. He asked and I took him with me a couple of times. My God. I wanted to make sure he knew how to use it."

Roger hung his head and cried. Pam put a hand on his back and touched her forehead to his.

"It's not your fault," she whispered. "He was going to have access to that gun with or without you."

"I can't," Roger said. "I'm sorry, Detective. I don't know what else we can tell you. Cam was trash. He was beneath Rianne. But she loved him, and nothing we said was going to dissuade her from marrying him. And we didn't want to lose our daughter over it."

He choked on the last sentence.

"It's okay," Jake said. He rose, hating to put the Timineys through any more trauma today.

"When can we have her back?" Pam asked. She'd collected herself, turning stoic while her husband fell apart beside her.

"It shouldn't be more than a few days," Jake said. He pulled his card out of his pocket and placed it on the coffee table. "I'll be in communication with the medical examiner later this week."

"We have to make arrangements," Pam said. "And I don't want anyone from Cameron's family or circle of friends there."

"I understand."

Pam Timiney rose with him and walked him to the front door. Behind them, Roger Timiney started drinking straight from the bottle. Pam walked Jake outside and closed the door on her husband.

"Please keep us informed," she said. "Anything you need."

"I appreciate that, Mrs. Timiney. I am so sorry for your loss. There is one thing. Do you know who Rianne's close friends were? The people you think she might have communicated with the most? We'll have the data from her phone, but that will take some time."

"She has two," Pam said. "Lucy Vane and Shantal Watson. They were sorority sisters. They were her bridesmaids. Another one was Mia Casey. Rianne wasn't as close with her. They met more recently. I don't know how to get ahold of Mia. But if you give me a piece of paper, I can write down Shantal and Lucy's numbers. I have them in my phone. Oh God. I'll have to call them."

"Do you want help with that?"

"Murder-suicide," she whispered. "It sounds so awful. This is a nightmare. How do people get through something like this?"

She searched his face. It hadn't occurred to Jake that she might know his own family history. She couldn't. There would be no reason why someone from Terrace Park would know the small-town lore of Blackhand Hills.

"Thanks again," Jake said, unsure how to answer her. "I'll be in touch. I wrote my cell phone on that card. Don't hesitate to call me. No matter what it is."

She rubbed his arm, almost as if she were trying to comfort him instead of the other way around. It felt awkward. Jake patted her hand, then walked briskly back to his car.

Roger and Pam Timiney lived in a different world than the one Cameron Katz came from. His parents were dead. But his older brother, Grady, lived four blocks from the house Cam grew up in just outside of Maudeville in the northwestern part of the county. The line between the Katz family and the more affluent citizens of Blackhand Hills ran straight along Brown Creek. Just fifty yards separated the Haves from the Have-Nots.

Jake walked up the cracked sidewalk, overgrown with weeds. A child's bicycle leaned against the porch steps. A rusted-out Chevy pickup sat in the side yard. The mailbox attached to the loose siding beside the front door was stuffed with letters. A past-due utility bill sat on top, its hot-pink paper showing through the envelope's plastic window.

Before Jake could knock, a young girl opened the door, peering at him through the ripped screen door. She was maybe ten or eleven, with dirt on her face and a tee shirt torn at the collar. She had haunted brown eyes that Jake instinctively knew had seen far more than a kid should.

"I'm looking for Grady Katz," Jake said, as kindly as he could. "Is he your dad?"

The girl just stared at him, her face blank. A moment later, a man appeared behind her. Tall, with a reddish beard and unruly brown hair.

"It's okay, Keeley," he told the girl. "Go in the back room and watch TV. We'll order some pizza in a little while."

"I'm sick of pizza," she said, not taking those saucer-shaped eyes off of Jake.

"Go!" the man insisted. Keeley darted behind him and disappeared, reminding Jake a little of Pam Timiney's cat.

"You're the detective I talked to?" the man said.

Jake put his hands on his hips, spreading his suit jacket, making his badge visible. "Jake Cashen. May I come in, Mr. Katz?"

"Grady," he answered, opening the screen door. Jake walked into a living room with a beat-up recliner and two mismatched couches. It was dark. No lights were on.

Grady led Jake to the kitchen and sat at a small square table with four green vinyl chairs that had to be from the fifties or sixties. Grandma Ava used to have a set just like it in the basement.

"You care if I smoke?" Grady asked, grabbing a box of cigarettes from the table. He had an ashtray next to it with at least a dozen butts.

"Your house," Jake answered.

Grady deftly lit a cigarette and puffed smoke from the side of his mouth as he sat down.

"You want a water or something?" Grady asked.

Jake put a hand up. "No, thanks. Grady, I'm very sorry for your loss. Thanks for coming down to the hospital to make the ID. I'm sorry I missed you."

Grady scratched his chin with the hand holding his cigarette. "I still can't believe it. Like it's not even real."

"Were you and your brother close?" Jake asked. "You're listed as his emergency contact."

"I don't know why," he said. "That should have been Rianne, right? God. What am I saying? Yeah. I mean, no. We were brothers. He's my little brother. But we're seven years apart. Our mom died, gosh, ten years ago now. Cam was only sixteen. Our dad? He wasn't in the picture much after Cam was born."

"When was the last time you saw or spoke to your brother?"

"The wedding. It's been pretty tough these last couple of years." As he said it, Grady rested one arm on the table. Jake saw the track marks. Grady caught him looking and jerked his arm back to his side.

"I'm clean," he said. "Almost thirteen months. No booze either. Just these." He waved his cigarette.

"Good. For her sake." Jake nodded toward the basement steps.

"Yeah," Grady agreed. "She's all I got. Her ma. She's in a hole she can't dig herself out of. She OD'd a year and a half ago. She was supposed to be in rehab down in Sarasota. Last I heard she bolted. I got Keeley out of foster care six months ago. It's just the two of us now. Rianne was so good to her. This is gonna kill her."

"You haven't told her yet?"

Grady shook his head. "Doesn't even seem real to me. I don't know how to do it. How can I tell that kid her uncle killed her Aunt Ri and then himself?"

"Did you have any reason to suspect something like that could happen? Did your brother ever talk to you about being depressed?"

"Naw. Nothing like that. Though I don't know if he'd have told me. We didn't have heart-to-hearts. It wasn't that kind of relationship. I mean, we only started talking again after Rianne came along. She forced it, you know? She didn't understand why Cam wasn't talking to me."

"Why wasn't he?" Jake asked.

Grady shrugged. "Cam was always really intense. When we were kids, he got into Taekwondo and it was all he could talk about. Then he got on a clean-eating kick. He was the kinda guy who'd try to push whatever he was into on other people. Judgmental, like. It was hard to be around him. Lately, it's been this fitness crap. And look, I get it. I've been a mess for a lot of the last ten years. Cam didn't want to get dragged down. But Rianne? She's just ... kind. Like an angel. And she took time with Keeley. Took her to get her hair done. Her ears pierced. The kind of stuff her ma couldn't pull herself together enough to do."

"It's my understanding Cam and Rianne were only married for a couple of weeks."

"Yeah. They got together not even two years ago. It was fast. But that's what I mean. When Cam's into something, it takes over his whole life. And he was into Rianne from day one. He moved her into his house after they'd only been dating maybe a month. But she was into him too. I didn't get any kind of negative vibes from them. Not ever. He loved her, man. And she was good for him. Kept him focused. Kept him on track. Cam had a habit of bouncing from one idea to the next. No follow-through. But Rianne was starting to settle his shit down."

"Rianne's parents said Cam was involved in some kind of software start-up. What do you know about that?"

Grady rolled his eyes. "Rianne was nothing like her parents. Those two have sticks so far up their asses. They looked down on Cam. Like he was dog shit they had to scrape off their shoes. Me too. Though, in my case, I probably deserved it most of the time. But they acted like Cam was ruining their daughter. Bringing her down to our level. It was not a good vibe. I know Cam got into it with them more than once. At one point, Rianne was so upset, she wanted to cancel the whole wedding and just elope. But everybody calmed down and came around."

"So you had no inkling Cam was in any kind of personal crisis?"

Grady ground his cigarette butt into the ashtray. "I don't know. I know things weren't going so great with this new business of his. He didn't give me all the details, but I know money wasn't coming in. I heard him on the phone with his partner. Maybe a month ago. Something about some loan not coming through. I heard only Cam's side of it. But it sounded like this partner of his was blaming Cam for it. I don't know. You'd have to ask him."

"Do you have a name?" Jake asked.

"Pfeiffer. Guy's first name is Troy? Toby? Something like that. When they first got into it, Cam talked about him all the time. Like he was smart like Bill Gates or something. He's some kind of computer nerd. Cam was getting some traction doing home workouts. Live streams. He was starting to make good money selling ads on 'em. Anyway, this Pfeiffer. He and Cam went to college together. Same dorm, I think. Pfeiffer built some software that made it so Cam could stream his workouts to multiple platforms at the same time. He told me he could quadruple his viewership all at once. A lot of it went over my head. But there was money in it. Cam and Pfeiffer started going all over the country selling this thing to other muscleheads."

"But you're saying the bottom was starting to fall out?" Jake asked.

"Yeah. The money was drying up. Just like every other time Cam started something. I told him he had a reverse Midas touch. Everything he touched turned to shit, not gold. I can't tell you specifically what was going on with this one. You'd have to talk to Pfeiffer."

"Do you know where I can find him?" Jake asked.

"Why? I mean ... you really think something like that had something to do with what happened?"

"I don't know," Jake said. "But if your brother was in financial trouble, that could have put a lot of pressure on him. And a strain on his marriage."

"I just don't get it."

"I know. And I'm sorry."

Grady shook his head. "God. I know what this is gonna sound like. But I have to ask. Do you know whether my brother left a will or anything? Or life insurance? I know that house is in his name."

Jake tilted his head. "I don't."

"Don't get me wrong," Grady interjected. "It's not me. I know that sounds gross of me to ask. But it's Keeley. I'm trying here. I want to give her a better life. A stable one. She's been through a lot. I know my part in all of that. But I told you. I'm clean."

Jake believed him. He also believed Grady Katz was holding on by a very thin thread.

"Grady," Jake said. "There isn't a single light on. You've got past-due bills in your mailbox out there. If your electricity is shut off, you're one home visit away from CPS taking Keeley back."

"I know. I know." Grady hung his head. "I get paid next week. I'm going to take care of it. You can't rat me out."

"I don't want to have to."

"I'm not perfect. I get that. But foster care is worse. You're a cop. You know I'm telling the truth."

He did. He'd only just met Grady Katz, but Jake sensed he was sincere.

"I don't know about any life insurance," Jake said. "Or anything else. If there is anything, you'll probably have a fight on your hands with the Timineys."

"Those people," he said. "They have everything."

"They don't have their daughter," Jake answered.

Grady squeezed his eyes shut for a moment. "Yeah. Son of a bitch. Yeah."

"Thanks for your time," Jake said.

Grady met Jake's eyes. "I don't even know what I'm going to do for him. For Cam. I can't afford to bury him. I'm embarrassed to admit it."

Jake wanted to assure Grady Katz that everything was going to be okay. Of course, he couldn't. He said goodbye and headed out the front door. He turned one last time toward the house as he slipped his sunglasses on. Keeley Katz stood in the doorway staring at him. She was an eleven-year-old living the life of a fifty-year-old. She didn't have the luxury of being a regular kid. And she was about to find out she'd lost maybe the only person who tried to give her some of that childhood back.

It was hard not to think the Timineys were right about everything. But that's exactly what his own mother's family had believed when his father took her away from them too.

FIVE

"The deeper the squat, the better it feels, ladies. We want those legs to burn. We want you aaaaaall the way down."

Birdie sat at her desk, staring at her large computer monitor. As Jake walked in, he saw Cameron Katz on screen, in a room painted deep purple with full-length mirrors on all four walls. It made it look like there were four versions of Katz squatting almost to the ground from every angle.

"He's like every gym creep I've ever met in my entire life," she said. As Katz dropped to the mat in front of him and started doing one-armed push-ups, dozens of heart emojis and thumbs up floated across the screen.

"This is a recording of a live stream he did just last week," Birdie said.

"People like this?" Jake asked.

"I don't know if they so much like it for the workout part of it. But I see the attraction."

Jake didn't. Katz was showing off more than anything else. Blatantly aware of his own reflection.

"It's like a hate-watch," Birdie explained. "A train wreck. You know you should look away, but you just can't."

She pulled up the comments. Most of them were laughing emojis. There were quite a few words of encouragement. A couple of "douche-tastics" floated up.

"He made money doing this?"

"He's got close to two hundred thousand followers," she said.

"What are they saying now?"

Birdie froze the screen, catching Cameron Katz mid push-up, every vein in his neck popping out.

"I went to his socials," she answered. "People are starting to ask if rumors are true that he killed himself. His people might want to put out some kind of formal statement. How'd it go with next of kin?"

"No real surprises," Jake answered. "He's got a brother out near Maudeville. Guy's barely hanging on by a thread himself. Asked me if there was a life insurance policy."

"Nice."

"And her folks pretty much hated Katz. Said he was beneath her. But no suspicions of any kind of domestic violence."

"He just snapped," Birdie asked. "One day he comes home and just loses it to the point of ..."

She stopped. Jake sat at his own desk. When he touched his keyboard, his monitor came to life. He had crime scene photos open from the Katz house. Rianne's body on the kitchen floor turned him cold from the inside out.

"Jake ... I'm sorry ... I ..."

"Don't!" He put a hand up. "Birdie, I'm not some fragile flower. Yeah. I get it. There are similarities between these two and Jake and Sonya. They were gunshot victims. Are you falling apart in every case because of what happened to Ben?"

The moment he said it, he hated himself for it. It was a cheap shot. She was worried about him. She was trying to check up on him.

"Sorry," he said.

"It's good, Jake. It's a fair question. And a solid point. No. I can compartmentalize just fine. Weird as it sounds, I don't put these things in the same box. Ever."

"Well, there you go." Even as he said it, his eyes kept going to the image on his screen. He'd never seen the photos of his own parents' kitchen after it happened. Gemma had been the one to find them. She'd only been twelve years old. But over the years, he'd asked her questions. Sometimes, she'd answer.

"I'll be glad just to close this one out," Birdie said.

"Me too. Katz's business partner is coming in today. Any minute, actually. We need to talk to the wife's boss. Maybe a friend or two. But the reality is, we're probably never going to know what went on between those two in those final moments."

She still fixed that motherly, worried look on him.

"I've already reached out to Delilah Grossjean. She's in Chicago until tomorrow night. But she's keeping an hour free the morning after next if you don't mind talking to her at her office."

"Thanks," he said. He reached into his backpack and pulled out his notepad. He had the two names Pam Timiney had written down for him when Jake asked her about Rianne's closest friends. He tore the sheet off and handed it to Birdie.

"You think you can run these two down?" he asked. "I just want to know if Rianne might have told her friends about any worries or fears she had about her husband."

"Done," Birdie said. "Oh. The gun Katz had on him was registered to Rianne. But Cameron had a concealed carry permit. It looks like Rianne bought the thing a little over two years ago."

"That tracks with what the father-in-law said. The poor guy said he's the one who taught Cameron how to shoot the thing."

"He can't think it's his fault," Birdie said.

"People are gonna go down the what-if hole for the rest of their lives when stuff like this happens."

Jake's desk phone rang. He hit the speaker button. "Yeah, Darcy?"

"Your witness is in interview room one," Darcy Noble, one of Worthington County's longest-serving civilian dispatchers, said. "Seems like he's in a hurry."

"The business partner," Jake said to Birdie. "I'll be right down, Darce. Thanks." He hung up.

"You want me to sit in on this one?" Birdie asked.

"No. Let's divide and conquer. You track down those girlfriends of Rianne's. The sooner we cross the t's, the better. Is Meg breathing down our necks yet?"

"Not so far," she said. "She's still at that conference in Miami. She'll be back at the end of the week."

"We're gonna start getting a lot of questions if this guy had the kind of social media following you said. I don't want randos camping out in front of the Timineys' house."

"That would be awful," Birdie said. She grabbed her bag off the desk and slung it over her head, carrying it cross-body.

"Agreed. We'll compare notes later today. But I'm not expecting any surprises."

Birdie took her leave. Jake grabbed his suit jacket off a hook near the door and headed across the hall to meet Troy Pfeiffer, Cameron Katz's business partner.

Pfeiffer and Katz could not have looked more physically opposite. Katz had stood over six feet, packed with corded muscle. Pfeiffer was about five foot two as he stood to shake Jake's hand. If he weighed one ten, Jake would have been surprised.

"Mr. Pfeiffer," Jake started.

"Call me Troy," he said. "Mr. Pfeiffer is my dad."

"Understood. And likewise. Call me Jake. Thanks for coming down. I have a few questions for you. And I suppose you have some for me."

Troy's whole body seemed to deflate with relief. "Nobody would tell me anything. Our website's getting bombarded with messages. Some real whacky ones. Somebody said Cam cut Rianne's head off. Is that true?"

Jake let out an exasperated sigh. He knew it wouldn't take long for the online rumor mill to churn.

"No," he said. "That is absolutely not true."

"But he killed her," Troy said. "He killed Rianne."

"It looks that way, yes. There will be autopsies. And I'm sorry that there are some things I won't be at liberty to say. Cam's next of kin ..."

"Grady," Troy chimed in. "He's got a brother. I've met him a few times. He was kind of a thorn in Cam's side over the last few years. He's a junkie."

"I'm aware," Jake said. "Troy, tell me about your relationship with Cameron."

Troy shrugged. "We're friends. Partners. We went to college together. OSU. I got my degree in computer engineering. Cam was exercise science. He got there on an academic scholarship. That's what people don't get. Cam wasn't stupid. I mean, he was an idiot in his own way, but he wasn't stupid. He lived across from me in the same dorm. We kept in touch."

"When did you start your business together?"

"Just a couple of years ago. Cam was doing these cheesy workout videos. They kinda blew up on TikTok during the pandemic. Anyway, we got together for lunch one day and he was talking about how he wished he could streamline things. He wanted to be able to stream simultaneously on a couple of different platforms from his phone. There are plenty of apps for that, but he was looking for something that was mobile-first and better integrated. I wrote some software to help him out. He really liked it. I started thinking maybe I could sell it to other influencers. Cam was my in for that. The online fitness community is smaller than you think. We worked out the bugs. Then started booking trade shows and conferences. The thing took off pretty quickly."

"That's exciting," Jake said. "How's it been going recently?"

Troy's face darkened. "Bad. Awful. I've had to take a day job again. We had some growing pains. Kinks that had to be worked out with the way followers were being displayed. Cam figured out a way to fudge things. Duplicate followers from multiple platforms. I wasn't happy about it. We needed capital so I could fully get us out of beta. There was some bad PR over Cam cooking his follower numbers. Things started to dry up. We were in the process of winding down."

"But Cameron was still making videos," Jake said. "His last one was posted the day before he died."

"Probably."

"So is it fair to say the last few months have been pretty stressful for the two of you?"

"I'd say. I mean, I'll be all right. It's not that hard for me to find work. Cam, though, he doesn't have a lot of marketable skills. Also ... his work ethic wasn't great. That was the main source of friction between us. And I know Rianne got frustrated too. She was supporting the two of them."

"Did you get a sense they were having issues in their relationship?"

Troy shook his head. "No! Nothing out of the ordinary. I mean, they were only married two weeks ago. Ri was crazy about Cam. It was the same with him. Cam was pretty wild until Ri came along. She sorted him out. Gave him some structure."

Jake rubbed his chin. "Cam was pretty jacked. Which stands to reason in his line of work. But I have to ask, were you aware if he was using performance-enhancing drugs?"

"You mean like 'roids?" Troy asked.

"Whatever you know could be helpful."

Troy's nostrils flared. "I mean, sure. You saw what he looked like. I can't say I ever saw him take anything. I didn't eyewitness that. But it was kind of understood with guys like him."

"You understand rage can be a side effect of some of those drugs. Did you see him display anything like that? Anything disproportionate to the situation?"

Troy let out an uncomfortable breath. "When he drank, yeah. He flipped out a few times."

"What do you mean?"

"We were at a conference once. You gotta understand, these guys are proprietary about their stuff. Cam got bent out of shape that this other influencer had copied some of his videos. I mean, I didn't think so. Like how many ways can you do a push-up, right? Anyway, Cam confronted him at the tiki bar and it got ugly. Cam took a swing at him. Luckily, other people stepped in pretty quickly before it got completely out of hand. But it was a zero-to-one-hundred kind of situation. It wasn't the norm with him, though. I just saw it one or two times."

"How well did you know Rianne?"

Troy flipped his palms upward and shrugged. "I knew her. Cam brought her to dinner with us a few times. She was always around if I came over to work on something with Cam. I liked her. She was sweet. Genuine. I told Cam more than once he hit the jackpot with her."

"How did he respond to that?"

Troy gave Jake a puzzled look. "He agreed. See, that's the thing. Cam was crazy about Rianne. And protective. That's the other time I saw him fly off the handle. We are at a bar and some guy bumped into Rianne. It was packed. It was an accident. But Rianne got jostled pretty hard. She dropped her drink. Cam went ballistic. Pushed the guy up against a wall. Again though, the bouncers got into it pretty fast and broke it up before Cam could do anything too stupid. They did throw us out though. Rianne was pissed. Embarrassed. But it was nothing. Just ... a thing that happened. I just can't believe any of this. I don't even know what to tell people."

"You don't have to tell them anything for now. The Sheriff's Department will put out a statement in a day or two once we have the final report from the medical examiner."

"Good," he said. "What about ... Cam's things?"

"What do you mean?"

"I mean, did he leave a will or anything? Since Rianne's gone too, where does that leave things? Was there life insurance or something?"

Jake frowned. That was the second time someone close to Cameron Katz had asked that question.

"I really don't know," Jake said.

"It's just, Cam owed me some money. I loaned him some stuff from the business. He didn't pay any of it back. God. I don't mean to sound like some kind of vulture. I just don't know what to do. Or say. I've never really dealt with anything like this before."

"I get it," Jake said. "But sorry. I don't have any info that could help you with that. You'd have to talk to an estate lawyer, maybe."

"Yeah. Yeah. Okay. That makes sense."

Jake pulled out his business card and handed it to Troy. "I don't foresee having to talk to you again," Jake said. "But you can call me if you have any other questions. I'll do my best to answer them."

Troy took the card. He fingered the edge for a moment, then his face fell.

"My God," he said. "What about a funeral? Cam's brother certainly isn't equipped to handle anything like that. He doesn't have any other family. He had Rianne. Do you think her folks will take care of it? I heard they have money."

"I can't say. Although, I don't think Rianne's parents are concerned about Cameron's arrangements just now. They're trying to come to terms with having to bury their own daughter."

"God," Troy said. "Of course. They've got to think he's a monster. I don't know. You think ... oh man ... maybe I should do it. Maybe I'm the only one who can. Cam could be a lot to handle. But he was a good-hearted guy. He'd do anything for you."

"Those videos," Jake said. "I've seen a few. And I've seen the kind of comments he got. A lot of it seemed like a hate-watch." Jake recycled Birdie's phrase.

"Oh, for sure," Troy agreed. "I said his stuff was cheesy."

"Intentionally so?" Jake asked. "Do you think he was in on the joke?"

Troy's face went hard. "God, it's bad of me to say stuff like this now. Cam's gone. But I don't know. That's the honest-to-goodness truth. Between us, no. I don't think Cam was in on the joke. I think he was being totally serious. That's kind of how he was."

"Was Rianne in on the joke?"

Troy pursed his lips. "Yeah. Most definitely."

"How did she feel about that? Her husband being the butt of jokes he didn't get."

"She didn't like it. She got angry with me once, worried that I was trying to exploit Cam. She was just as protective of him as he was of her. I told her I had nothing to do with Cameron's content. All I did was make it so he could make it as widely available as possible. Cam was Cam. He was hoping he'd get acting gigs out of this whole deal. Or some talk show appearances. He was writing his autobiography. He showed me a draft. It was ... ugh. I feel like a jerk now. But it was not good. I talked to Rianne about it. It was obvious she never wanted that thing to see the light of day either."

"Did they argue about it?"

Troy shook his head. "I really don't know. I can't see Rianne saying anything to Cam that would potentially hurt his feelings. See, well ... you said you saw his videos, right?"

"Just the one."

"Okay. Well, Cam got popular, but not for the reasons he thinks."

"What do you mean?" Jake asked, though he already had a pretty good guess.

"Like I said. They're cheesy. Almost like a parody of the worst workout videos you've ever seen. But Cam was sincere. I don't think he realized people were kind of watching more for how outrageous Cam could be rather than to get fit, you know? But it didn't really matter. His platform was growing. He thought he was going to be able to sell that book. Who knows, maybe he would have."

"Got it," Jake said. "Troy, you've been really helpful."

"I have?"

"You've helped me see a better picture of what Cam was like as a person. I've gotten the sense that he didn't have many close friends in his life. I'm sure you were important to him."

From what Troy described, Cameron Katz was an insecure, probably volatile guy. If he thought his own wife didn't believe in him, that horrific scene out on Mill Pond Drive made a certain tragic sense.

For the first time, Troy Pfeiffer teared up. He covered quickly and shook Jake's hand with vigor when both men stood up. Troy pocketed Jake's card.

"I just can't believe this. If I haven't made myself clear, I cannot believe Cam would do something like this. He loved Rianne. He'd do anything for her. I don't know what happened, but I'm sure of one thing."

"What's that?" Jake asked.

"Cam had to be out of his mind in those last few minutes. He *had* to be. Cam would never have hurt Rianne unless something pretty crazy happened. Like he lost his mind for some reason. Rianne was the most important thing in the world to him. Whatever happened, that wasn't Cam. I know it. He just would not hurt her like that, let alone kill her if he were in his right mind."

Troy showed himself out. Jake stood there, staring after him, his words ringing in his ears.

He would not hurt her like that. He loved her more than anything. It wasn't him.

So many times, he'd heard those same words about his own father. And it never helped.

Six

"That one's Ernestine; you gotta keep an eye on her," Grandpa said. "She tried to take a chunk outta Aidan's rear end yesterday."

Ernestine the Offender coolly eyed Jake as she munched on a clump of grass. She was a Spanish goat with a crooked left horn and an attitude. Her sisters, Bernadette and Fern, grazed downhill, one spotted, one white. Ernestine was a brown-and-white mix with one black leg.

"Aidan's gonna have to show her who's boss," Jake said as he bolted down the trough to the wooden platform he built. "I'm not gonna be the one coming up here every other day to refill this trough and clean out their water."

"They'll drink from the creek," Grandpa said.

"Not in the winter they won't," Jake said. "I'm gonna have to find some time to fix up that old barn for them so they have shelter and a heated waterer."

"Aidan can learn how to do that too," Grandpa said. "He's ten. It's time. Past time. Gemma spoils that one rotten. He's not a baby."

Jake smiled. He couldn't help but think of his youngest nephew as anything but a baby either. He was growing fast. He'd started wrestling with the local youth club team last winter. From what Jake had seen, Aidan was a natural athlete. More gifted than his brother had been at that age. More gifted than Jake, even. But a lot could happen between now and high school. The trick was to make sure he didn't grow to hate it.

"I'll get him sorted," Jake said.

"He should be here today."

"He went to Cedar Point with a couple of friends. He's a kid. He's allowed."

Grandpa grunted. "This was Gemma's project anyway. I didn't ask for goats."

He was right that this was Gemma's scheme. One of her bar regulars had to re-home these goats and Gemma had a soft spot. Long ago, Grandma Ava had started a little hobby farm for herself out on the property. Jake was raised with goats, chickens, and even an angry sow for a while. Grandma named her Suzannah. Until Suzannah got so unruly, she knocked Grandma down and bit her ankle. She became pork chops and bacon not long after that.

"It's actually one of her better ideas," Jake defended his sister. "You can't mow down here anymore. They'll keep everything from getting overgrown and save me some work. You're right. Aidan will learn how to take care of these ladies. I'll make sure of it."

Jake wiped the sweat from his brow with a blue bandana he kept wadded in his back pocket. Grandpa sat in the passenger seat of the four-wheeler. His eyesight was too poor for him to make it out to this part of the property alone, but not so poor he couldn't oversee and bark orders as Jake tried to do anything. He didn't mind though. Grandpa's bark had always been worse than his bite.

Jake walked over to the four-wheeler and hopped in the driver's seat. Grandpa reached over and snapped his seatbelt. Then he turned to Jake. "You coming with me today or you just wanna drop me off?"

It was Saturday. Every week when the weather allowed it, Grandpa wanted to visit the family cemetery just over the next hill. Jake rarely went with him. In recent years, Gemma or one of her boys took Grandpa down. Today, it would fall to him.

"I don't want you trying to walk back up to the house by yourself," Jake said. He put the vehicle in gear and sped over the hill and down to the wooden bench Grandpa had hand-carved twenty years ago. He'd built it right in front of Grandma Ava's headstone. As soon as Jake parked, Grandpa hopped out and grabbed the bouquet of wildflowers he'd picked and tied with a piece of twine.

Jake stayed in the four-wheeler, giving the old man some privacy as he knelt in front of his wife's grave. His lips moved in silent prayer. He placed the flowers at the base of the marker and ran his hand lovingly across the curved stone.

The cemetery was here before Grandpa Max was born. The Cashens had owned this land since the 1890s. Patrick and Siobhan Cashen emigrated from County Cork along with the wave of their Irish kinfolk. But Patrick had something the others didn't—a bit of money in his pocket. At one time, the Cashen tract of land encompassed almost one thousand acres. They held it for two generations before Max Cashen's father had to sell off the bulk of the tractable land during the Great Depression. In Jake's opinion, what remained was some of the most beautiful ground in Blackhand Hills.

When Patrick died, Siobhan picked out this very spot to bury him. From here, you could watch the sunset over the largest hill on the property. Grandpa's house sat just behind it on a smaller hill. The creek gurgled to the south. That, and the cool breeze rustling the surrounding oak trees, created a natural sound bath.

Grandpa struggled to get back on his feet. Jake got to him just as the old man was about to tip sideways.

"I'm fine," Max barked. But he let Jake help him over to the bench. Max positioned himself to leave room beside him for Jake to join him. Reluctantly, he did.

They sat in the quiet for a few minutes. Grandpa kept his eyes closed, seeing the people he lost behind them, probably. He always did that. A peaceful smile would come over his face. Sometimes, he would lose himself so deeply in the memory that he would start conversations with ghosts.

Jake could never do that. He could never conjure the memory of people he barely remembered. There was Grandma, of course. The woman who dropped everything to raise him the moment her son died. But his parents? Jake had only fleeting memories of either of them. Though his memories of those first few months without them and everything after remained vivid. It was as if his personal timeline started the moment Jake Sr. and Sonya Cashen went into the ground. But his mother wasn't here. Her family had refused to allow it.

He let his eyes wander to his father's headstone. The man had been just twenty-nine years old when he destroyed everyone he was supposed to love.

Jake tried to do what Grandpa did. He closed his eyes and tried to think of him. He remembered that his father had yellow hair. He'd grown a mustache once that tickled Jake's cheek when his father kissed him. He remembered his parents dancing in the kitchen.

His mother had thrown her head back, laughing as his father circled his arm around her waist and pulled her closer.

But that memory quickly faded. In its place, he saw his mother lying on the kitchen floor, her chest covered in blood. Except it wasn't his mother at all; it was Rianne Katz. His eyes snapped open. He felt his grandfather's hard stare. He took a beat. A spike of electricity shot through his heart. He almost didn't speak. When he did, it felt like someone else was asking the question for him.

"When did you know he was sick?" Jake asked.

Grandpa kept his eyes locked on Jake. If the question caused him distress, he didn't show it. After a moment, Grandpa turned his gaze back to the headstones.

"Most of the people here died too damn soon," Grandpa said.

"You're right," Jake said.

Along with his young father, Grandma Ava had only been sixty when cancer claimed her. Between her grave and his father's, Jake's only niece had died two hours after she was born.

Grandpa said nothing for several minutes. Jake assumed his lack of an answer was his answer. Max Cashen didn't like to dwell on the past.

But finally, he looked at Jake again. "I don't know," he said. "Not really."

"You never noticed him acting differently?" Jake asked.

"I didn't say that," Max answered. "But ... maybe I didn't. It was your grandmother who got worried."

"Why?"

Max looked at the ground. His whole posture changed. He

slumped forward and braced his hands on his knees. "I don't know how to make anyone understand."

"You don't have to make me do anything."

"He was fine," Grandpa said quietly. "Not sleeping very well. They kept switching up his shifts. He'd earned his spot on days. But there were a couple of guys with a little more seniority who just wouldn't retire. So your dad got flipped to afternoons. He hated that because he didn't get to see you and Gemma as much. That was hard on Sonya. She was alone a lot. Isolated."

"Okay," Jake said. "But this was more than just sleep deprivation."

"You can say that now."

"What did Grandma notice?"

Grandpa went silent again. Then he asked a different question. "This case of yours. It's rough, isn't it?"

"What?"

"Gemma told me. Then I heard some talk at the barbershop the other day. Nasty business. It was like your parents, yeah?"

Jake didn't want to answer. He half regretted bringing any of this up.

"Yeah," he said.

"Was he sick? This man?"

"I don't know. I mean, of course he was."

"Hmm."

A black squirrel hopped down from the nearest tree and started eating acorns a few yards away.

"Did she ask you for help?" Jake asked. "What did my mother say about it?"

Max picked a stick off the ground and started pulling the bark off it. "She loved your dad. And we loved her. But Sonya kept to herself a lot. She wasn't a complainer. Not a woe-is-me kind of woman. Your grandmother loved that about her. So did I."

"But what about Dad?" Jake asked, his frustration growing. It always went like this. Grandpa talked in circles. Deflected.

"I don't know what you want me to say. Yeah. Something happened. That summer, your grandmother noticed he'd lost a lot of weight. Your dad was the kind of guy who could never sit still. He was always busy. Always working on something. But it got strange. Sonya said he'd be out in his garage workshop all hours of the day and night. Random stuff. He built about fifty birdhouses and stacked them all up against one wall. Those that he thought were worth keeping. There were dozens more he thought were crap. Those piled up in the fire pit. A mountain of them."

"Manic," Jake said. "You noticed he was manic."

"Something. Yeah. Then … he …"

"What?"

"He took a swing at me."

"For what? Why?"

Grandpa shrugged. "I thought he was drinking. That's what it seemed like. He acted drunk sometimes. So I called him out. Told him to get his act together. That Sonya didn't need that around you kids. So, Jake got angry and tried to have a go at me. That's when Sonya said he needed help. But it wasn't alcohol. She thought maybe he was manic-depressive. So I did what she asked and helped her talk him into seeing a doctor."

"But you didn't think he needed one?"

"He was never sick like that. He didn't need a shrink. He was good. Solid. Level-headed."

"Until he wasn't."

"They gave him some blasted pills. I don't know what it was. They made him worse. I didn't like it. I thought Sonya was pushing stuff he didn't need. I thought if I could just have him out here with me for a few days. Help him work through whatever was making him so nervous. He begged me."

"Begged you what?"

"He said that poison was making him sick. I thought it was too. Then, a couple of weeks went by and we didn't see him. Didn't hear from him. I figured things had calmed down. I figured Sonya would reach out if something else was wrong. She didn't. Then, Grandma and I went away for the week. First trip we took together in years. I get a call and you know what happened. He was gone. They were both gone."

"Yeah," Jake said quietly. "I know what happened."

"I wish I could tell you what you want to know."

"I don't know what I want to know."

"You want a neat answer. There isn't one. There never will be. And I know you think I should have done more to stop it."

Jake jerked his head toward his grandfather. "I never said that."

"But you've thought it."

"You didn't make Dad sick. You weren't there in the house the morning he did that to her. To himself."

Grandpa rubbed his forehead with his right hand. "I shoulda been. I could have talked him down. Kept him from doing something stupid. Those pills weren't working. They were only making him crazier. If I'd listened to him. Taken his side, maybe it would have been different."

"Nobody blames you. Nobody has ever blamed you. I haven't."

Max looked back at his son's headstone. Then his wife's. He didn't say anything, but Jake got the eerie sense Grandpa was asking for forgiveness from Grandma Ava. Had she blamed him for what happened? He'd never heard her say anything like that. But no one truly knows what goes on in a marriage except for the people in it.

He felt sympathy for his grandfather he hadn't before.

"Come on," Jake said. "Let's let the dead rest for today."

Grandpa let out a haughty laugh. But he didn't argue. He waved off the arm Jake extended to help guide him.

"I'll walk back up to the house," Grandpa said.

"I can drive you," Jake said.

"I don't need help, Jake. I don't need eyes to walk this path. I've known it my whole life."

He turned his back on his grandson and left him standing among the ghosts.

Seven

Deputy Tom Stuckey leaned against the brick wall facing the parking lot. He'd kicked a bad smoking habit but replaced it with vaping. As Jake approached his cruiser, he went to him.

"Good job the other day," he said. "You and Bundy handled that scene so well. I got a call from Ramirez at BCI saying the same thing. You made his job easier."

Stuckey smiled for an instant, then his face fell. "It was a rough one."

"Yes, it was," Jake said.

Matt Bundy came out to join his partner. Jake repeated what he'd told Stuckey about Ramirez's praise.

"I appreciate that," Bundy said. "I just wanted to do right by those two."

"I can't stop thinking about her," Stuckey said, his gaze going spacey.

"You have to," Jake said.

"Is there anything else we can do?" Bundy asked.

"No," Jake said. "This one is pretty much wrapped up. I'm on my way to talk to Rianne Katz's boss. Detective Wayne is following up with two of her best friends. Then it's just Dr. Stone's summary."

Bundy nodded.

"I don't think I could do what you do," Stuckey said.

"You could," Jake said. "After what I saw the other day, both of you could."

Bundy beamed. Jake had heard through the grapevine he'd put in for Birdie's job. Based on seniority alone, he had to have known he'd be a long shot.

"Keep doing what you're doing," Jake said to him. "It gets noticed."

He slapped Bundy on the arm as he headed for his car. There were still plenty of idiots in the department, but those two had real promise. They would be at the top of the list of any crew, including a handful of others Jake would ask for.

He pulled out of the lot and headed for Logan. Once he hit the highway, he told his smartphone to give him driving directions to Designs by Delilah.

Delilah Grossjean had a little shop along the main drag in downtown Logan. She was sandwiched between a bakery and a pub. The heavenly scent of baking donuts made Jake's stomach rumble. Delilah had a closed sign in her window, but he knew she was expecting him.

Before he could knock, a young woman sprinted toward the door and turned the knobs to three different locks. It was overkill, as her front door was mostly glass.

"Detective Cashen?" she asked brightly. She had jet-black dyed hair that hung to her shoulders. Thick, straight bangs framed her pale face. She wore huge cat-like false eyelashes and flaming-red lipstick. Her dress looked straight out of the 1940s with a swing skirt and puffy sleeves.

"Call me Jake," he said.

"I'm Delilah," she said. "Come on back to my office. If people see me in the window, they're going to want to come in. I get more walk-in traffic than you'd think. Even though my signage says by appointment only."

"Good to see your business is thriving then," Jake said.

"We just participated in a parade of homes," she said, leading Jake down a short hallway into a small office painted bright pink with mint-green trim. To Jake, it looked like an ice cream parlor. He couldn't imagine hiring her if these were her tastes. Though Gemma liked to point out regularly that he had no taste when it came to decorating, so what did he know?

"I don't know if you're the one to ask about this," she said. "But do you know if there have been any arrangements made for Rianne yet?"

Delilah took a seat behind her white desk with gold trim. Jake took the chair in front of it. It had mint-green upholstery with big white dots all over it.

"I can't say," he said. "She hasn't been released from the coroner yet. I'm sure her family will put something together soon enough. Are you in communication with them?"

Delilah shook her head. "Afraid not. I never met them. Though Rianne talked about them all the time."

Delilah teared up. She grabbed a tissue out of the shiny gold box in front of her. "I'm sorry. I'm still trying to process it all. I've been hearing a lot of rumors. Is it true Cam had her tied up in some sort of ... um ... BDSM contraption?"

"What?" Jake sputtered. "No. Where did you hear that?"

Delilah's face went even paler. "I'm sorry. Oh, I'm not trying to gossip."

"Good," Jake said. "Small towns are frustrating in that way. But no. Any of the more outlandish things you've heard are lies, I can tell you that. Though the reality is dark enough."

"It sure is. I just can't believe it."

"When was the last time you talked to Rianne?" Jake asked.

Delilah pulled her phone out of her desk drawer. She scrolled through it. "We texted that Friday evening. Eight o'clock. She was going to pick up some fabric samples for me before coming in the next morning. I was out at our model home. The parade started at noon on Saturday. But as you know, she never showed. I texted her a few times, but I had my hands full. I was angry with her. It wasn't like her to just flake out on me like that. By the time I was able to come up for air and try tracking her down, it was evening. That's when ... well, a friend of mine let me know she'd passed."

"A friend of yours?" Jake asked. "Where did the friend hear it?"

"I don't know."

It angered Jake. He knew it was very likely someone from the department. But he supposed it didn't matter now.

"Did Rianne ever mention any issues she was having in her marriage?" Jake said. "Did you know her husband?"

"Oh, of course I did. Cam was here all the time. He'd pick Ri up sometimes. Take her to lunch."

"What did you think of him?"

Delilah shrugged. "Kind of a lovable lunkhead. But he seemed pretty devoted to Ri. You know, like he couldn't believe his luck that she wanted to be with him. It was sweet. I know a lot of people didn't understand what she saw in him. But I think it was that. He was nuts about her. She told me once how good it made her feel to be with someone who thought she was *it*, you know?"

"That's hard to argue with," Jake agreed. "So that leads me to my next question. You had no sense she was afraid of him or anything like that?"

"No."

"What was her mood the last time you saw her?"

"That would have been the day before. Friday. We were swamped getting everything ready for the home tour. I worked pretty late. But she left around six. Like I said, she was going to run to a couple of stores for me and get the fabric samples I needed. I couldn't tell you what time she got done with all of that. It might have been as late as ten o'clock."

"That was okay with her? With Cam, as far as you know?"

"As far as I know. Like I don't think he was calling her a lot asking where she was. I assumed he knew. And Ri wasn't acting like she was in a hurry or had to be somewhere. She would have pulled an all-nighter with me if I asked her. She has before."

"Got it," Jake said.

"I'm sorry," Delilah said. "I don't suppose this is very helpful."

"It's fine. I'm just trying to dot my i's and cross my t's. Trying to get a sense of who Rianne and Cameron were."

"Ri was just the sweetest girl you'd ever want to meet. I think she had potential. She had a good eye. But she lacked confidence. She had a raging case of imposter syndrome. And she didn't give herself enough credit."

"She was submissive?" Jake asked.

"Most definitely. That was my biggest frustration with her as an employee. She always needed to check in with me about things. She had a hard time trusting her own instincts. I told her many times that was going to be the thing that held her back in this profession. You can't be meek. You'll get eaten alive. Working with design clients takes a certain kind of fortitude. You need a thick skin. And you need the ability to assertively convince people of what they really need, instead of what they *think* they need. Ri struggled in that area."

"Her parents said something like that too," Jake said. "That she was too trusting of other people."

"That's true. But it was more that she didn't trust herself and looked to other people to tell her what she was supposed to think. And I know she was frustrated with me. She wanted more responsibility. She just wasn't ready for it. Her real talent was in client relations. She put them at ease. She was warm. Unfortunately, she tended to back down easily when confronted with a strong-willed, opinionated one."

"Is it fair to say Cameron dominated her, then?"

"To some extent, yes. I suppose that's true. He took care of her. Made all the decisions. I personally couldn't have lived like that.

But she wasn't meek with him. She spoke her mind to him. To me. She just needed time. Maturity. A little more life experience. She would have come into her own."

Delilah grabbed another tissue. "I'm sorry. Is any of this helping?"

"It is," Jake said. And it was to some degree. Whatever happened with Cameron Katz, it appeared he'd just snapped. So far, none of the people close to Rianne reported any marital discord. Nothing that would have precipitated the kind of violent end the Katzes met.

"Did you ever see Cam get angry with Rianne?"

Delilah shrugged. "I mean, maybe I saw him get annoyed with her. But he doted on her for the most part. Called her his princess. Or his queen. One of the two. I don't know. We didn't hang out socially. I mean, not with them as a couple. Rianne and I went to lunch together all the time. We grabbed drinks after work frequently. Especially after finishing a big job. We'd celebrate. You know? But that was all work people. I have a receptionist and a personal assistant. I work with builders and subcontractors. It's a small world in my business. Rianne was well liked by everyone. I just don't understand what she could have done that would have turned Cameron like that. I never saw any sense of that."

"You never really know who people are behind closed doors," Jake said.

"Was he on drugs?"

"I ... I can't really discuss that. And we don't have the full picture from his autopsy."

"But steroids," she said. "It had to be that, right? I never asked Rianne about that stuff. But it was obvious. You don't get that kind of physique without performance-enhancing drugs. I was an athlete myself. Played basketball all through college. I know that can really mess with someone's head. Do you think that played a part?"

"We just don't know yet," Jake said. "And we may never know."

"It's just so awful."

Jake rose. "Thanks for your time. I won't keep you anymore. But please, if you think of anything else that might be useful, don't hesitate to call me."

Delilah rose and shook Jake's hand. "Of course. It's just ... I was at her wedding. It was two weeks ago. She was so happy. Excited to start her life with Cameron. She was talking about wanting to have babies right away. It's all just too much."

"I'm sure," Jake said, thanking her again. He showed himself out as Delilah started to cry. As he walked to the front door, people peered in the window. Pointed. He heard the trailing conversation of one couple.

"... heard he pumped her with so much lead she had no face ..."

Jake swore under his breath. Rumors. Rubberneckers. Questions and gossip he'd heard so many times about his own mother. He found it a small blessing that Rianne and Cameron Katz hadn't been parents themselves. As he thought it, he halted mid-step.

If they'd been parents, it would have put Jake in the position of having to inform children of their parents' deaths. He had a flash of memory as Grandpa Max sat him down in the middle of Ben Wayne's living room almost thirty-two years ago and uttered the sentences that altered the course of his life.

They're dead, Jake. They're not coming back.

Jake remembered asking his grandfather when he could go back to his own house. Grandpa said never. It wasn't his house anymore.

That he and Gemma would live with him and Grandma now. His grandfather hadn't cried. He was stoic. Calm, clear-eyed. And he'd stayed that way ever since.

EIGHT

Sheriff Meg Landry sported a deep tan. She had "raccoon eyes" where she'd been wearing sunglasses. After a week in Miami for a conference, she looked rested and ready for Jake's report. She waited for him at Birdie's desk as Jake walked in Monday morning, coffee in hand.

"You look good," he said. "Learn anything?"

Meg rolled her eyes. "The con itself was mind-numbing. But it was nice to get away. And we got a college visit on the way down. The University of Florida."

Jake whistled. "Are we there already? Paige is a baby."

"She's only got two more years of high school. She's made it abundantly clear she wants to pick somewhere far, far away for college."

Jake set his coffee down. "She might change her mind."

"I'm not sure I want her to." Meg laughed. "Not that I want her gone. But I don't mind if she leaves, if that makes sense."

Meg's teenage daughter was of the particularly sullen kind when it came to her mother. She doted on Meg's husband, Phil. She was also pretty fond of Jake himself. She was a good kid.

"I get it," he said. "She reminds me a lot of Gemma, strong-willed. She drove my grandparents up the wall. She turned out all right."

Meg nodded, then turned her attention to the crime scene photos Jake had laid out on the table behind her. He'd stacked them before he left the office last Friday. Meg had clearly rifled through them.

"Pretty awful," she said. "Is there anything I can share with the public yet? There have been a lot of inquiries. Cameron Katz was more famous online than I realized."

"Probably by tomorrow morning," Jake said. "I expect a call from Dr. Stone by the end of the day. Then we can close things out."

Birdie walked in with a file folder under her arm.

"Morning, Sheriff," she said. "You look great. Did you make it to the ocean?"

"Sure did," Meg said. "Had a bona fide cabana boy and everything. Jake was just getting me up to speed on the Katz case."

"How'd it go with Delilah Grossjean?" Birdie asked.

"Nothing we didn't already know. Rianne was on the quiet, submissive side. She and Cameron were crazy about each other. Rianne's boss had no inkling of any trouble between them."

"So he just snapped?" Meg asked. "Kills her, then turns the gun on himself? Ugh. What a tragedy. At least they didn't have any kids, I guess. That's the only blessing."

Birdie's eyes widened as Meg said it. Meg caught her expression and her own face fell.

"Yikes," Meg said. "Jake, I'm sorry. That was insensitive of me."

"Forget it," he said. "What'd you learn from Rianne's friends?"

"About the same as you. They've been close with her since they started college. Six years. Sorority sisters, actually. Lucy Vane and Shantal Watson. They're both married now. They didn't get together in person much lately. Both women have kids under two. But they had a group text and kept in daily contact."

"What was their read on Cameron?" Jake asked.

Birdie shrugged. "They didn't much like him. Thought Rianne was too good for him. But they could see that he doted on her. And that she was over the moon for him. They were both bridesmaids in the wedding a few weeks ago. Shantal's theory is that Cameron was on the sauce and maybe it was some kind of testosterone-fueled rage."

"We'll know soon enough. Stone texted me yesterday saying he expected toxicology by this afternoon. Then he can finish his report."

Birdie's desk phone rang. Meg rose out of her chair to let her answer it. She walked over to the photos and spread them out further. She picked up the one of Rianne lying on her kitchen floor.

"Do you have phone forensics back? Have we been able to figure out who she was trying to call?"

"Not yet. Ramirez will have his full report back to me this week too. Then hopefully we can close everything out."

"Gotta go," Birdie said as she hung up the phone. "There's been a robbery at the Dollar Kart over in Navan Township."

"Anybody hurt?" Meg asked.

"No," she answered. "Probably just a shoplifting gone bad."

She grabbed her cell phone off the desk and waved to both Meg and Jake.

"How's it going with you two?" Meg asked.

"She's good. But we knew that. She's been a big help on Katz. It'll allow me to close this thing in half the time it would have otherwise taken. Actually, everybody's been at the top of their game on this one. Bundy and Stuckey did a great job out at the scene."

Meg nodded, impressed. "Glad to hear it. You know Bundy has ambitions to make detective."

"He's still green," Jake said. "But he's moving in the right direction."

"It'll be a while anyway," Meg said. "You know how I had to wrestle with the budget for Erica's shield. I don't imagine I'll be in a position to bring anyone else up for two years or so."

"He's got time," Jake said. "I'll keep an eye on him."

Meg put the photograph down. "How are *you* doing with this one?"

"Fine," Jake said, shorter than he wanted.

"I am sorry about what I said before."

"Don't sweat it. And you sound like Erica. I don't need a work mom or a work sister on this one. This isn't my family. I know the difference."

"Well, it would make sense if this one stirred things up for you. I'm just saying ... if you need help, can I trust you to ask for it?"

"I don't need help."

Meg put her hands up in surrender. "Fine. Uncle. You want me to back off. I get it. But ... just ... be careful, okay?"

Jake felt every muscle go rigid. He was holding on to something tightly. He knew if he let go, everything Meg was worried about might just happen.

"I'm fine," he said, softer this time. "Really."

"Okay," Meg said. "I'll let you get back to work. Come find me when you know what Stone knows. I'd like to put out a press release no later than tomorrow afternoon."

"You should be able to," Jake said.

Meg stood in his doorway for a moment, the look of concern still written on her face. But she did what she said she would and let Jake get back to work.

Birdie had left the interview summary she wrote up for Lucy Vane and Shantal Watson. He thumbed through it, impressed but not at all surprised by Birdie's thoroughness and attention to detail. She'd met the women together at a coffee shop. Of the two of them, Lucy Vane had been the most visibly shaken. Birdie noted that she was in tears throughout the whole interview.

They loved Rianne. Shantal had actually lived in an off-campus apartment with her for a year. She'd been there the day Rianne met Cameron at the gym. Shantal had come down for a visit. Cameron had actually hit on Shantal first. Shantal never told Rianne. But the takeaway for both of them ... they never saw any signs that Rianne and Cameron's lives would end this way.

Jake clipped the notes into the three-ring binder they kept on the Katz file. He grabbed his own notes from his interview with Delilah Grossjean and slipped them in right behind Birdie's.

He went over to the table and gathered the crime scene photos. One by one he slipped them into a manila envelope that he'd three-hole punched as well. Birdie had backed everything up on a flash drive, but they both preferred working with physical copies of everything.

The last photograph in the bunch was the one Meg had been holding. It was a wide shot of Rianne Katz as she lay in a partial fetal position on her own kitchen floor. Jake sank into a chair and placed the photo in front of him.

It was the expression on her face that stuck with him. Her furrowed brow frozen in permanent shock. It didn't look like fear. Jake closed his eyes and tried to imagine Rianne's last moment as her own husband lifted the gun. He'd aimed for center mass, blowing two holes in her left upper chest. With the amount of blood loss, Jake guessed Dr. Stone would tell him the bullet penetrated her abdominal aorta.

Was it quick? Did she know? Was there pain?

Jake clenched a fist, unwittingly crushing the photo.

Of course, there was pain. Brutality.

He tried to smooth the creases out of the photo and then put it in the envelope with the others.

It got hard to breathe. The room began to spin. The light flickered in an almost strobe pattern.

Did she know? Was there pain?

There was another binder not far from here. It contained its own three-hole-punched manila envelope with photographs inside.

Jake had known it was here. At least on an intellectual level. Of course it was. It was three floors below him in the basement archives. The Crypt, as everyone liked to call it. But not once had

Jake ever thought about it. Ever felt drawn to it, almost as if it called to him.

Until now.

Jake walked over to his computer and ran a quick search. He grabbed a pen and wrote a number down on a sheet of paper beside him. He folded it and tucked it into his pocket.

He made no conscious choice to stand. To walk out of his office. To board the elevator and punch the basement button.

He pulled out his phone and made a call. Deputy Karen Altman answered right away. Jake heard himself talking, but it was as if someone else said the words. He heard her answer.

"I'm two doors down," she said. "I'll meet you there."

As the elevator doors opened, Jake felt sweat trickling down his back, even though it was ice cold down here.

No windows. Just more flickering fluorescent lights. One of them buzzed no matter how many times maintenance tried to fix it. Jake always thought it would be slow torture to work down here listening to that all day.

His footsteps echoed on the old tile floor as he made his way down the hall. He passed the maintenance closet. The second hallway led to the property room, where former Sergeant Jeff Hammer spent his days in purgatory after lying about his personal involvement with a victim in a murder case.

Jake kept on going. The offending buzzing light hung just above him as he stood in front of the door to the Crypt.

He opened the door. True to her word, Deputy Altman had beaten him here. She unlocked the giant cage to the Crypt.

"You have the file number for me?" Altman asked.

He pulled out his folded piece of paper and handed it to her. "You're lucky," she said. "We haven't gotten to that section yet. It should be right where it's supposed to be. We're in the process of digitizing everything going back to 1970. I don't have enough help. I'm only up to 1978."

Altman disappeared further into the cage. Two minutes later, she reemerged, rolling a single banker's box on a handcart.

"Double lucky," she said. "It's just the one box."

She rolled it out of the cage and locked the gate behind her. Jake picked up a clipboard on the counter next to him.

Altman walked over to him and pointed to the right line. Jake signed and handed it back to her. She wrote the file number and date next to his signature.

"Thanks," he said.

"You can take the handcart," she said. "If you think you need it. It's not that heavy. I'm just careful with my back these days. I had a pretty terrible sciatica flare-up last year. I was off my feet for two months."

Jake reached down and picked up the box. She was right. It wasn't heavy. "I've got it," Jake said.

She went over to the computer at the end of the counter and started typing in the info from the clipboard. She stopped. Frowning, she looked at Jake.

"Are you sure about this?" she asked.

Jake didn't answer. He was already heading out the door.

Two minutes later, he was back in his office. He cleared some space on the table and set the box down. It was sealed shut with packing tape. He grabbed the Swiss Army knife he kept in his desk drawer. Odd that. It had belonged to his father.

Jake sliced open the tape. The label was stuck to the top of the box.

RB#00592-92 – HOMICIDE
VICTIM: SONYA CASHEN
SUSPECT: JAKE CASHEN
DISPOSITION: CASE CLEARED

He smoothed his hand over her name. A part of him knew this was a mistake. It changed nothing. But he couldn't stop now.

He curled his fingers under the lid and started to pull it off. Before he could, his cell phone rang on the table beside the box. The caller ID read, "Dr. Ethan Stone."

Jake let out a hard breath and pushed the lid back on the box. He picked up the phone.

"Cashen," he said.

"Good," Dr. Stone said. "You haven't left yet."

"I'm here."

"Jake, you better meet me at my lab. I've finished with the Katz couple."

There was an urgency in Stone's tone. "Is something wrong?"

"Just get here. But before you do, shoot the sheriff a message. Tell her not to talk to the press."

Nine

Dr. Ethan Stone met Jake in his office. As usual, he had a cigarette dangling from the corner of his mouth as he wrote furious notes on a yellow legal pad. He acknowledged Jake, lifting the index finger of his left hand in the air, gesturing for him to wait.

Jake took a chair in front of Stone's desk. The man had a deep scowl on his face as his fingers flew across the page. He concluded his notes by stabbing a period with a dramatic flourish, then tossed the pen on the desk hard enough it bounced once and settled, teetering on the edge.

"You're in a bad mood," Jake said.

Stone responded by sliding off his readers and rubbing the bridge of his nose.

"Sorry to pull you away from whatever you were doing. But I know this county. I swear, the mice in the walls talk. This'll get out. You and Landry are going to need as much lead time as possible."

"You have mice in your walls?"

"Don't joke," Stone said. He rose from his chair. "Sandra! Can you type this up for me!"

Sandra Ketcham, Dr. Stone's long-suffering office manager, came to the open doorway with a withering frown. "Put a cork in it. There's not a single person down there who constitutes an emergency. And if there was, then you're supremely bad at your job."

Jake suppressed a laugh as Sandra walked to the desk and grabbed Stone's legal pad. "Hello, Jake," she said. "Ignore his caterwauling. He's trying to quit smoking again."

Jake looked back at Ethan Stone. Though the cigarette was still in his mouth, Jake realized it wasn't lit.

As Sandra left the room, Stone got up. "Come on," he said. "Better if I show you than tell you."

Jake found himself hesitating as he realized he had no desire to see either of the Katzes again. He'd investigated plenty of unnatural deaths. He wasn't squeamish. But this was something different.

He followed Stone down the hall to his lab. Two bodies lay on cold metal tables, covered in white cloth. The size difference between them made it obvious that Cameron Katz lay closest to Jake. Stone walked around him and went to Rianne's body.

"Pretty straightforward with the female victim," Stone said. "Two shots. First one alone was fatal. Shredded her aorta. Second one passed dead center through her heart. Shooter knew what he was doing."

"God," Jake said. "Her own father took the husband out to the range. Taught him how to shoot."

Stone raised a brow and then tossed his unlit cigarette into the trash.

"She's clean," he said. "Only thing in her toxicology was birth control pills."

"No sign of pregnancy then?"

"Nope," Stone said. "This girl was probably religious about taking them. She was shot from about six feet away. Would have gone down pretty much instantly. I'd like to say she died instantly, but probably not. She knew what was happening to her. Looking 'em dead in the eye."

Stone started to pull back the shroud over Rianne's body.

"It's okay," Jake blurted. "I'll take your word for it."

Stone gave Jake a curious look. "You okay?"

Jake didn't answer. Then Stone's face fell. "Shit. I'm sorry, Jake. I didn't think. This one hits kinda close to home for you."

"I'm fine," Jake said. "People need to stop worrying about that." As he said it, realization settled over him. Ethan Stone had been the county ME for decades. He would have performed the autopsies on his parents. His report was sitting in that banker's box on Jake's desk.

"Good," Stone said as he moved over to Cameron Katz's body. "Because you're gonna wanna buckle up for this one."

He pulled back Cameron's shroud. The body was white and waxen, all blood drained from it. His face looked unblemished. He stared at the ceiling. It was only when Jake walked over to the body's right side that he could see the gaping hole in Cameron's temple.

"I've done a lot of suicides," Stone said. "More than I care to remember involving semi-automatic pistols. You always find certain hallmarks. Muzzle imprints for one. A guy holds the gun to his head, you get a depression that matches the shape of the muzzle on his skin."

Stone grabbed the tablet on the cart next to him. He pulled up an image and handed the tablet to Jake. It was a close-up of a man's head with a wound almost identical to Cameron's. Jake could clearly see a circular pattern just above the victim's ear.

Stone took a pen out of his pocket and pointed it at Cameron's temple. "It's not there, Jake," he said. Jake put the tablet down.

"There's no soot deposit around the wound," Stone continued. "That image you had. That's what the dark ring around the wound was." Again, he pointed his pen at Cameron Katz's head wound. It was clean.

"You're gonna expect to see a seared, blackened color around any entry wound that was a contact or near contact shot. This guy doesn't have it."

Stone put a pair of latex gloves on and turned Katz's head, revealing even more of the wound where Stone had shaved off the hair. He pointed to small red and brown marks near the hole in his head.

"We've got stippling, or tattooing. That's caused by powder burns. The pattern on your victim shows that the kill shot was fired from several feet away, Jake. This isn't like any contact or near contact shot I've ever seen in over forty years of doing this shit."

Every point Stone made seemed to hit Jake in the chest like kill shots of their own. "He didn't shoot himself," Jake said.

Stone shook his head. "Not unless the guy had ten-feet arms. The gunshot residue test on his hands came back negative. This guy didn't fire a gun that day. This isn't a suicide."

It was a stupid question, Jake knew. But he asked anyway. "You're sure. You're absolutely sure?"

Stone pulled off his gloves and tossed them in a medical waste container a few feet away from him. "No doubt whatsoever. You've got a homicide."

Jake took a step back. "A double homicide."

"Yeah. Sorry. I know it's not the news you were expecting."

"You were right," Jake said. "This is gonna catch fire quick. Meg doesn't need to be ambushed on the steps of the Public Safety building. And I need to inform the families."

"You heard anything from Ramirez?" Stone asked. "Ballistics will help paint a fuller picture. I didn't find any evidence of defensive wounds on either victim. They didn't have a chance to fight. I don't think there's gonna be any blood at that scene that doesn't belong to these two, but there's always that possibility."

"He's supposed to get back to me in a day or two. Can you send a copy of your full report to him by the end of the day? It'll help if he knows what he's looking at."

"Already told Sandra to make that a priority."

"You told me about Rianne's toxicology. What about him?"

Stone grabbed another cigarette from the pack in his breast pocket. His fingers shook with the urge to light it.

"Screw it," he finally said. He went over to the counter, opened a drawer and pulled out a lighter. He lit the cigarette and took a drag. Euphoria settled over his face as he let out a long puff of smoke.

"How long did that last?" Jake asked.

Stone smiled. "Day and a half. The hell with it. We've all got to die of something." Stone picked up a stack of papers on the counter and flipped through them. "Cameron Katz was a walking pharmacy."

Jake expected the news. "PEDs?"

"Full steroid stack," Stone answered. "Test, Tren, and Winstrol. HGH too. And he was medicating the fallout. Two different blood pressure meds. A diuretic."

"That's pretty unusual for someone in his twenties," Jake said.

"Not on this many 'roids," Stone said. "He was a heart attack or a stroke waiting to happen. And sure, all this would explain it if he were experiencing episodes of uncontrollable rage. Your working theory would have made sense. Only he didn't do it. He didn't shoot his wife. He didn't shoot anybody. Somebody just wanted to make it look like he did."

Jake's head started to pound. "Dammit," he muttered. "I've been asking all the wrong questions."

"Don't beat yourself up. Everything I saw on the surface? I'd have put all my chips on murder-suicide too."

Jake went over to Rianne Katz's body. He lifted the shroud far enough so that he could see her face. Like her husband, it was unmarred. Her eyes were still open. Still frozen in that look of shock.

She looked 'em dead in the eye, Stone had said.

"Who did this to you?" Jake whispered. He knew each hour that passed had made it harder to find the answer. And he'd already lost hundreds of them chasing all the wrong clues.

Ten

"How long before you think you'll have something for me?" Jake said. He had Agent Mark Ramirez on speakerphone while Meg and Birdie sat beside him.

"Fast tracking every single thing I can," Ramirez said. "We've been backed up for weeks handling some overflow from that charter plane crash outside Cincinnati. I should have phones and fingerprint data in the next couple of days. Blood and ballistics is gonna take a bit longer. I gotta be honest, this shuffled my cornflakes as much as yours. On sight, everything looked like a murder-suicide to me."

"I appreciate whatever you can do," Jake said.

"So do I, Mark," Landry said. "I'm gonna have to go out in front of news cameras here in a minute. There's no way to sugarcoat that I've got a killer out there somewhere."

"Copy that," Ramirez said. "The second I know anything, you'll know it."

"Day or night," Jake added. "I'm working this thing round the clock."

"You bet," Mark said. They ended the call. Landry didn't look well. She had bags under her eyes and her hair looked lopsided. Jake was pretty sure she was getting about as much sleep as he was. Next to nothing.

"Do you have any leads at all?" she asked.

"We're starting from scratch," Birdie said. "Every interview I did, I wasn't asking if anyone wanted to hurt the Katzes."

"We're starting re-interviews today. Now. Troy Pfeiffer has agreed to come in shortly."

"That's the business partner?" Meg asked. "The computer nerd?"

"Yeah. Both Katz's brother and Pfeiffer said they were having some money trouble. I didn't delve very hard into why. He mentioned something about Katz playing it fast and loose with his follower numbers. Some glitch in the software Pfeiffer developed. But none of that seemed like a motive for murder or suicide."

"Let me know when you know," Meg said. "I don't think I can let the day go by without making some sort of statement."

"Why can't you just say it's gonna take time?" Birdie asked. "We don't even have the report from BCI yet. Seems like a perfect reason to stall."

"Normally, yes," Meg said. "The trouble is, Cameron Katz is internet famous. It's shining a bigger light on this than we'd otherwise see. That Facebook group Darker Side of Blackhand Hills has run with it."

"They're trouble," Jake said. "I don't need armchair detectives on this one."

"Agree," Meg said as she stood up. "So work as fast as you can."

She left Jake and Birdie alone, closing the door to the office.

"You think this was a coincidence?" Birdie asked.

"What?"

"Like Ramirez said. That crime scene looked like a murder-suicide. That can't be an accident, can it? It's what someone wanted us to think. Which means this was calculated. Planned. Maybe not far in advance. Maybe in the moment. I don't know. Could it have been some sort of hit?"

"Anything's possible at this point," Jake said. "Stone also said Katz was loaded with steroids. He wasn't getting those at the local pharmacy. He had a dealer somewhere. Maybe that's a good place to start. We need to do some canvassing at his gym."

"How do you feel about me using Keith?" she asked. Birdie had been dating a gym rat for a while. Jake wasn't much of a fan of him. But that might not matter at the moment.

"It's a good thought," he said. "Does Keith use?"

"I don't think so," she said. "Certainly not now. He's pretty religious about what he puts in his body. And I've never seen anything lying around his apartment that shouldn't be there. But I'm not gonna get anywhere if I march into that gym asking where I can get my hands on PEDs."

"I trust your judgment," Jake said. "Work that angle."

His desk phone buzzed. That would be the civilian clerk telling him Troy Pfeiffer had arrived.

"You need me in on Pfeiffer?" Birdie asked.

"No, start figuring out who was supplying Cameron Katz. We'll compare notes later."

Birdie grabbed her jacket off the back of her chair and headed out. Jake grabbed a pad of paper and walked across the hall to the interview room.

Troy Pfeiffer sat with his back against the wall, sipping coffee from a paper cup. He gave Jake a genuine smile as he walked into the room.

"Thanks for coming in on such short notice," Jake said, shutting the door behind him.

"I was surprised you called me again," Pfeiffer responded.

Jake took the chair opposite Pfeiffer and tossed his pad on the table. "I'm going to be blunt. Every second that goes by makes my job that much harder. I need your help, Troy."

"Of course. I told you that the last time. Anything I can do."

"I was hoping you'd say that. How are things for you?"

"What do you mean?" Pfeiffer chewed his thumbnail.

"Well, I realized the bottom dropped out of your business the second Cameron died. So in addition to losing your friend, you have that added stress."

Pfeiffer gave Jake a grim nod. "It's been a shock. But I think I told you last time. Things had been starting to go downhill for a little while. I'm okay. I'm working. Making more than I was in the business, actually. And it's steady. Stable. I don't know that I'm cut out to be an entrepreneur."

"That's good," Jake said. "Last time you told me you had some investors drop out. You said they got spooked because of Cameron's activities. Misuse of the app. Who were these investors, Troy?"

"What difference does that make?"

"Why don't you let me worry about that? Can you answer the question?" He slid the legal pad across the table. "Better yet. Will you write down their names?"

Troy picked up a pen, but hesitated, not grabbing the pad. "I think I need to know why. Are you planning on talking to any of them?"

"Would that bother you?"

"What's going on? Cameron committed suicide. What business would any of that be to my investors?"

Jake regarded Pfeiffer for a moment. He didn't seem particularly nervous. He wasn't sweating. He kept his gaze steady and on Jake. He was calm. Generally cooperative. All other things being equal, he was asking a reasonable question.

"Can it just be enough that I need the names? You're winding the business down anyway."

Troy clicked the end of the pen a few times, almost absentmindedly. Then he grabbed the pad and wrote down three names, then gave Jake the pad.

"Are you going to talk to them?" Pfeiffer asked.

"Yes. How much do you still owe them?"

"I don't," Pfeiffer said. "That third name. Michael Kasper. He bought me out. He took on the debt and paid back Whit and Lea Roundtree."

"Lea Roundtree," Jake repeated. "That sounds familiar."

"She's a social media influencer too. She did segments on one of the morning shows for a while. You might have seen promos for it."

"Maybe," Jake said. "Look, Troy. I'm going to level with you. My investigation has taken a turn. This might be hard for you to hear.

But it's going to come out. I would appreciate it if you could keep it under wraps for now. Though I know I can't legally stop you from saying anything."

"Whatever it is," Troy said. "I can keep my mouth shut. What's going on?"

"It doesn't look like Cameron Katz committed suicide," Jake said. "Someone shot him."

Troy's color instantly drained. He blinked rapidly. It seemed like genuine shock, but Jake was no mind reader.

"Murdered him?"

"Yes."

"Rianne?"

"I don't think so," Jake said. "Her wounds weren't self-inflicted either. It doesn't appear that either of them fired a gun that day. Someone else was in that house."

"You think ... God. You think it was about money? People we owed?"

"I didn't say that. I'm just trying to understand all the facts. I'm trying to figure out who might have wanted to do Cameron or Rianne harm."

Troy shook his head vigorously. "I don't ... I can't ... This isn't happening. Murder? Because of our business? God. Am I in danger?"

"Just take a breath," Jake said. "I haven't said anything like that. I have no reason to believe anyone's targeting you. But I feel like I don't know the whole story about what was going on in Cameron's life. I'm trying to explore every angle. So, I'm asking you. You knew Cameron as well as anyone. You spent the most time with him besides Rianne. Money is often a motive for murder. You and Cameron were having trouble in that regard. Did he owe you money?"

"Me? You think this was me? I wasn't here. You can check my phone. Hook me up to a lie detector." Troy pulled out his cell phone and put it on the table.

"I appreciate this," Jake said. "It helps me a lot. And no. I don't have any suspicions about you. That's not what this is."

Now, Troy Pfeiffer began to sweat. "No," he said. "No way. Do I need a lawyer?"

"That's up to you," Jake said.

Troy shook his head. "No. I'm telling you. I have nothing to hide. I mean it. Check my phone. I insist. I was out of town when Cameron and Rianne were killed. Cameron was my friend. I'd never hurt anyone."

"Okay. Okay. But Troy, I need you to think about this. You know what Cameron was like. You talked to him every day, right? Does it surprise you that someone might have wanted to hurt him?"

Troy closed his eyes and dropped his chin. It was as clear a tell as anything. When he opened his eyes again, he reached for the legal pad and circled Whit Roundtree's name.

"Whit didn't pull his money because of business reasons."

"Okay?" Jake said.

"Look, Cameron had a good heart. And he loved Rianne. That's why this whole thing has seemed so crazy. God. I know this sounds awful. But a big part of me is relieved that he maybe didn't kill Rianne. I just couldn't wrap my head around it. I didn't think he would ever hurt her. Not physically. But Cameron had problems. Like an addiction. To women."

Jake sat back and crossed his leg over his knee. "Tell me."

"He couldn't help himself. Cam would screw a garden hose if he could have figured out how. I wasn't involved in that part of his life. But in college, everybody knew to keep their girlfriends away from him. He really tried with Rianne. I know it. He told me. He even tried to see a therapist right after they started dating. When I agreed to go into business with him, I made him promise that he wouldn't let his personal crap interfere with what we were trying to do."

"But he did anyway," Jake said.

"Yeah. We started going to fitness industry conferences. That's how we started generating sales. That's where we hooked up with Whit and Lea. Maybe a year ago, I found out Cameron was screwing Lea. I was furious. He promised me he was gonna cut it out."

"He was also with Rianne during this?" Jake asked.

"He was. That's another reason I was so angry. Rianne was amazing. And she was head over heels for Cam. Anyone could see that. It just didn't matter. Cam couldn't keep it in his pants. It ended though. That I'm sure of. Maybe six months before Cam and Rianne's wedding. He broke it off with Lea. He was trying. As far as I know, he wasn't sleeping with anyone else leading up to their wedding."

"But Whit found out?"

"Yeah," Troy said, defeated. "About two months ago. And look, we were already kinda circling the drain. Cam generated a lot of bad will when people figured out he was fudging his follower numbers. If things had gone on ... if Cam hadn't died ... I think we would have ended up where we are anyway. But yes. Whit pulled his money and wanted nothing to do with Cam."

"Do you think Whit might have physically hurt Cameron?" Jake asked.

Troy slid his hands across the table, then pulled them into his lap. "If you're asking me if I think Whit could have killed Cameron. Lord, I don't know. I have no information that he did. I don't know if Whit has ever been to Blackhand Hills. He and Lea live in Rocky River. We saw them frequently at cons. And I know Cam and Lea would meet up somewhere halfway. I suppose if you could figure out if Whit came to Blackhand Hills, that'd be a pretty big clue. But ... yeah. Physically hurt? Yeah. I wasn't there. But last year, at MPF Con. Muscle ProFit Conference in Myrtle Beach, Whit and Cam got into a physical fight. Like I said. I didn't see it. But it was a scene. And it was really bad for business. Not just because of Whit pulling his money. It was a bad look and drama I never wanted associated with the brand. And that's it. That's all I know. I swear it."

"Why are you just now telling me this?" Jake asked. "I asked you about Cameron and Rianne's marriage. You withheld all this. Why?"

"You said Cam killed Rianne. You said he committed suicide. Why would I think any of this would have mattered? Rianne's folks weren't fans of Cam. Would it have done any good for them to hear this too? My God. They think Cam murdered their daughter. Isn't that bad enough?"

"You should have told me," Jake said.

"You said it was a suicide," Troy shot back once more.

Frustrated as he was with the guy, he wasn't completely wrong.

Troy sat back hard. Jake picked up the legal pad and set it beside him.

"I appreciate it, Troy. You've been a great help." He tried to keep the sarcasm out of his voice.

"Can I ask you a favor?"

"You can ask," Jake said.

"I know you're going to talk to Whit and Lea. I mean, of course you have to. But can you leave my name out of it? I'd rather Whit not know I'm the one who told you. And you don't have to. A lot of people witnessed the fight between them. It could have been anyone. I think there was chatter about it in a couple of the fitness industry forums. But if Whit killed those people, if he's capable of that, I don't need him knowing I talked to you."

"Of course," Jake said. "I'm not in the habit of telling suspects the names of my sources."

"Okay," Troy said, visibly relieved.

"I appreciate your candor, Troy. This helps."

"But you still want my phone, don't you?" Troy said, his tone bitter.

Jake rose. He pulled a single sheet of paper he had tucked into the back of the legal pad. It was a waiver. He gave it to Troy.

Troy glowered at him, but picked up the pen and signed.

Eleven

Meg's press conference went about exactly as she predicted. Jake stood at her side while she did her best to keep people from panicking or speculating about a serial killer at large. In the back of Jake's mind, he couldn't be sure this wasn't one.

By the time he got back to his office to shut the lights off and finally leave for the day, he was bone-tired with a monstrous headache to match. He plopped down in his chair and searched through the piles on his desk for his keys. His foot knocked against the banker's box he'd brought up from the Crypt.

He slid it out. It was an odd thing to see his own name written at the top of it. Every reasonable brain cell he had told him to leave it. Send it back downstairs and forget about it. Instead, he picked it up, balanced it on his hip, and walked out to his car.

He popped the trunk with his key fob and placed the box inside.

"Jake!" Birdie called from across the parking lot. She'd just pulled up in her cruiser. Her personal vehicle was parked right alongside it.

Jake raised a hand to wave. He hit the button on his key fob and closed the trunk.

"Any luck with the gym?" Jake asked.

"Not yet," she said, breathless as she walked up to him. "Keith's got a friend of a friend over there he's pretty sure will know what we need. He's going to lay some groundwork starting tomorrow. It's not going to take long to find Cameron's dealer if he connected with him or her through the gym."

"Good," Jake said. He'd called her earlier and filled her in on Troy Pfeiffer's updated story. "I'm going to track down this Whit Roundtree tomorrow. Pfeiffer says he works from home and is always responsive to calls or texts. How do you feel about paying a visit to Rianne's parents? I called them earlier ahead of Landry's press conference. I wanted to give them a night to process around everything before coming at them again with more questions."

"I'll handle them," she said. "What about Cam's brother? I can hit his place too."

"That'd be a big help. It's not the greatest neighborhood. Why don't you take Bundy or Stuckey with you?"

She rolled her eyes. "You think I need a babysitter?"

"No," he said. "To be honest, I wouldn't go back out there alone again myself."

"All right," she reluctantly agreed. "I'll round one of them up in the morning. Go home, Jake. Get some sleep. Don't let this one eat at you too much."

He felt like she could see through his trunk. He could have told her about the box, but he didn't want another lecture about how close to home the Katz case was.

"Check in with me tomorrow after you've done your interviews. I'll let you know how it goes with Roundtree."

"You gonna interview the wife?"

"At some point. I'm hoping to get the husband alone first. I'm sure he's gonna want that too."

"Probably. Hey, a few of us are heading over to CIPS to grab a beer after work. You feel like joining?"

"I thought you said I look like I could use sleep."

"That too." She smiled.

"Nah. You go on ahead. Tell Gemma I'll talk to her tomorrow. And for the love of God, don't tell her you thought I looked tired. She'll be over with a thermos full of soup and a hot water bottle before my head hits the pillow."

Birdie laughed. She gave Jake a wave over her shoulder as she headed back to her car.

Jake felt pensive as he made the drive home. He got there in time to watch the sunset from his back porch. It had rained hard this morning. He could still smell a whiff of ozone. Birdie was right about one thing. He did need a beer. He went to grab a cold one from the fridge. The banker's box sat on his small kitchen table against the wall. Jake took a long swig of his ice-cold Coors Light as he stared at it.

He ran his fingers along the edge of the box. The thing smelled musty, having sat in a dusty corner of the Crypt for over thirty years. He knew Frank Borowski's fingers were the last ones to touch it before it was stored away with hundreds—thousands—of other boxes. His parents' lives, tucked in with old robberies, assaults, homicides.

Borowski had become like a second father to Jake after his own had died. He took him under his wing, coaching him throughout his entire wrestling career. Pushing him. Challenging him. Taking him on the fishing trips Jake Sr. no longer could. Giving him a place to hang out and hide out when everything just got to be too much. And it was Frank who inspired Jake to become a cop in the first place. Frank tried to talk him out of it. But when he made up his mind, Frank was the first one to cheer him on.

Frank, he thought. It had all ended so badly with him. He'd betrayed Jake. Kept secrets that could have cost Jake his career. Now, he was on the run, in hiding somewhere. Not for the first time, Jake prayed he would stay hard to find. He never wanted to have to be the one to arrest Frank Borowski for the mortal sins he'd committed when he crossed the line between justice and revenge.

Walk away, a voice inside Jake's head said. Maybe it was Frank's. Maybe it was his own father's from beyond the grave. He knew the second he took the lid off that box, there'd be no going back.

Leave it be. There could be nothing in there but ghosts and pain long buried. What difference did any of it make now?

Jake finished his first beer while standing in the middle of his kitchen, staring at that box. He tossed the bottle into the recycling bin and grabbed another from the refrigerator door.

He took a long swig and set his bottle on the table in the living room. He walked back over to the box. He slipped his fingers through the cut-out handles and picked it up.

It wasn't heavy, but the weight of it settled over him. He put it in the center of the living room table, took a seat on the couch in front of it, and took another long swig of beer. He felt the first slow flush as the beer did its job. Jake wiped his upper lip with the back of his hand and then set the beer down.

His phone buzzed in his back pocket. He took it out. A text from Gemma. There were four more unanswered. Jake put his phone on silent and set it on the table face down.

He reached for the lid. There was one last moment of hesitation as his hands hovered over the box. He took a breath and then lifted the lid and cast it aside.

A single sheet lay on top. A cover sheet. He picked that up and turned it upside down, laying it on the couch cushion beside him.

Frank's "suppy," his supplemental report, lay there as if it were staring up at Jake. Judging him. Taunting him. As he picked it up, he had the strangest sensation of something floating up around him. Not unlike kicking up a butterfly while walking in the grass. These were ghosts, maybe spirits. If you believed in that sort of thing. Jake never had.

His eyes went blurry as he tried to read Frank's copy. He squeezed them shut and then opened them, waiting for his vision to clear. It was as if his own brain were playing tricks on him, trying to give him one last chance to walk away from this.

But the words soon came into focus. The report itself was a dozen pages long. Jake flipped to the back of it, looking for Frank's conclusory findings. If he was going to do this, he didn't think he could do it all at once. He didn't think he could let himself get bombarded with all the terrible things he knew happened that day. Things he'd allowed to exist in his mind as fragments. Sterile words. It let him keep it all at a certain distance. But this? This was as close as he knew he'd ever get.

He found the summary on the second to last page of the report. Frank had typed this portion out in all caps, as if he knew Jake himself might look for it one day.

"After viewing the crime scene and both victims, conducting extensive interviews with the below listed witnesses, and referring to the findings of the ME, Dr. Ethan Stone, it can be concluded that Jacob Cashen shot and killed Sonya Cashen then shot himself. The disposition of this case is cleared: Murder/Suicide."

Jake's throat went dry. Clinical. Sterile. There was still a chance to leave it that way. Below the summary, Frank had typed his list of witnesses.

1.Max Cashen (father of victim one)

2. Ava Cashen (mother of victim one)

3. Gemma Cashen (daughter of victims)

4. Robert Arden (brother of victim two)

Each name went through him like an arrow. Beneath the list, Frank had noted that each interview had been videotaped. Beneath that, Frank had meticulously listed each item contained in the box itself along with its corresponding colored tab.

1.Crime Report (responding crew – Red)

2. EMS Report (Blue)

3. ME Report (Yellow)

4. Crime Scene Photographs (Pink)

5. Witness Interview Recordings (4 Labeled VHS tapes)

6. Lead Detective's Notebook (Orange)

7. Photocopy of Purported Suicide Note Written by Victim One (Green)

8. Lead Detective's Formal Supplemental Report

Jake's vision swam. It felt as if he were choking on his own heart. His hands shook as he read the list twice more, each time stopping at item number 7.

Photocopy of Purported Suicide Note Written by Victim One

Suicide note. Jake blinked hard, still not believing what he was reading in black and white.

Suicide note. Green tab. Damn Frank Borowski for his painstaking organizational skills. Jake reached into the box. Two large Tyvek envelopes held hard, bulky shapes within them. He knew these had to be the VHS tapes Frank referred to. God. Gemma had been just twelve years old. She would be on one of those tapes. Just a child. Being asked to describe the worst day of her life and the most horrible thing she would ever see. Growing up, she'd only told him what she thought he could handle. As adults, he'd only ever asked her what he thought she could handle. But this would be everything. Every detail. Frank would have had no choice.

Jake's hands shook as he put the envelopes aside. He peeled back each listed item, following the colored tabs Frank outlined. His fingers touched the green one. It was just a single small square piece of paper slid into a clear plastic sheet protector.

"Goddammit," he whispered. His father left a note. No one had ever told him he'd left a note. He couldn't be sure whether Gemma even knew about it. Slowly, carefully, Jake lifted the letter out of the box. He clutched it to his chest as if his father were somehow still attached to it.

Jake grabbed his beer and downed the rest of it. Then he laid the letter flat on the table and began to read.

TWELVE

I know you. I know you. I know you.

You don't see. You don't think I see. You call me a monster. I know it. I feel it. I am. I am. I AM. I AM. AM I. AM I.

This poison, it's eating me raw. Inside. Gnawing like worms. Through my bones. Through my bones. Into my skull! Deeper and deeper. I see what it is now. What they're doing. You say it's a vitamin. LIAR. You want to chain me up. Pump more more through my veins. I see. I know. Know more.

Sonya you are my heartbeat. My soul. But it's cut out of me. This poison cut it out of me and left me nothing. Not even blood. I'd give you that too. It's turned to dust.

The Gryphon is noble. I know why you want that. I bit the apple and it killed me. The Gryphon *slayed your dragons. I wanted to. God, I wanted to. I can't stand your eyes. The both of you. You think I don't see. I saw you waiting together. Gryphon had his arms around you. In the hallway. Under the lights. Holding hands. Saying yes to everything but I would say no. Why wouldn't you let me say no?*

They put something in my food. I haven't eaten in one hundred and three days. My heart won't stop racing. I can feel them inside me. Watching through the lights. I smashed every bulb in the house but they still see. I can feel it on my skin.

I'm sorry, Brother Rob. I should have listened to you yesterday. I know you tried to help. You knew about the poison and what you did was right. You saw the Gryphon too. Everything you said was right. It would have consumed her. Touched her. And she's too pure.

It won't stop. I can't make it stop. It will get worse. I can feel it growing like cancer. There won't be anything left but the monster. The monster is me. It will poison you too. I think you didn't know. This is how I keep him from you. So many times. Toppy told me. Toppy was the way. I wouldn't listen. I am now. This is how I make you safe.

I left the rabbit with the floppy ears for Jakey. He's not a baby anymore, but he can still love something sweet. Let him have the red toolbox too. I don't know what to do for girls. I bought earrings for Gemma but they're too much for a little girl, maybe. Red apples. Remember her cheeks when she was just a baby. They're in my bottom drawer. I couldn't teach her how to dance.

Dad. Momma.

xxxxxxxxxxxxxxxXXXXXXXXXXX

Thirteen

Jake read and reread the letter maybe twenty times that night. Words and phrases in it lost all meaning. If any of them had any meaning beforehand. Names. People he had never heard of. Monsters. Dragons and gryphons. He thought they were poisoning him. Jake knew very little about what help they tried to get his father. He only knew it had all happened so fast. And he knew how painful it was for everyone to talk about.

It was past four in the morning before Jake finally laid the letter back in the box and closed the lid. He hoped he had the strength never to open the thing again but still, it called to him. When he finally fell asleep on the couch in front of it, he had strange, vivid dreams. Spiders in the house crawling out of every corner. Grandma Ava was in the window, pressing her finger to her lips. And Gemma as a young girl, running through the woods, her light-brown hair trailing behind. He could never quite catch up with her.

When his phone rang at 7:23 a.m., he rolled off the couch to the floor, drool caked at the corner of his mouth.

"C-Cashen," he said, pressing the speaker button. He hadn't even bothered to check the caller ID.

"Hey, Jake," Darcy Noble, the head dispatcher, said. "Didn't mean to wake you. A guy showed up a few minutes ago asking for you. He said you had an appointment to meet with him in Cleveland this afternoon, but he decided to come to you instead. He says his name is Whitney Roundtree. Is he full of crap?"

"What? Uh. No. No. Geez, Darce, how early did you get in?"

"I'm here by six thirty," she said. "Flex timing it this month. I need to be home before three. I'm watching my grandkids."

"Got it. Okay. Give me twenty minutes. Is the guy antsy? Can you keep him there?"

"Oh, he's antsy all right. But I don't think he's going anywhere. And I can put a deputy on him to make sure he doesn't. Stuckey's on flex time this week too. He's already here."

"Okay. Yeah. Twenty minutes. I'm on my way."

Jake took a quick shower, combed his hair and put on a fresh shirt and pants. He threaded his holster through his belt and slid his service weapon into it. His right hip throbbed as he took a step toward the door. He, like most cops, would have constant back pain from carrying a three-pound hunk of steel and lead on his hip for decades.

As he pulled into the lot, he was glad of the distraction. Glad to get to work and put everything he learned last night behind him for now. God Bless Darcy, she waited for him with a steaming cup of coffee in her hand.

"Don't get used to it," she said. "Tessa made an extra cup."

Jake thanked her. Tessa Papatonis made the best coffee in town. She and her husband Spiros ran the diner across the street. He hadn't been in for over a week. He knew this was her way of sending up a flare for him. She treated him like a son.

"Interview room two," Darcy said. "One's occupied. Deputy … er … Detective Wayne has a suspect in the Dollar Kart robbery."

"She's here already too?" Jake asked, sipping his coffee.

"She said her power's out. Some jackhole ran into a transformer down her street at three a.m. Crews haven't even been out yet."

"I've been telling her to let me put in that generator," he grumbled.

"Sheriff wants you to come find her sometime today. She wants an update after you finish your interviews."

"Got it," Jake said.

"She's getting bombarded," Darcy said.

"Got it. I got it," Jake said, exasperated. He grabbed a pad of paper from his desk and headed up one floor to interview room two, just above him.

Whit Roundtree was huge. He rose as Jake walked in and towered over him by at least half a foot to Jake's five nine. He wore a tight tee shirt with a Roundtree Athletic Club logo on the left breast and drawstring track pants. He had thick, corded biceps that looked earned as opposed to artificial as Cameron Katz's were. Jake tucked his legal pad under his armpit and shook Roundtree's hand.

"Thanks for coming in," he said. "Have a seat."

Roundtree looked nervous. He tapped his heel furiously under the table and drummed his fingers.

"Do I need a lawyer?"

"That's your call," Jake said. "You understand why I wanted to see you?"

"You were gonna march right into my gym, weren't you? That was your plan?"

"My plan is to have a conversation with you, Mr. Roundtree. Or do you mind if I call you Whit?"

"Whit's fine," he said. "I don't care."

"Well, I'm Detective Jake Cashen. Jake's fine too."

"Great," Roundtree said bitterly. "Is this about Lea?"

"Just calm down," Jake said. "I want to ask you about Cameron Katz. Do you remember the last time you saw him?"

"I haven't seen him," Whit barked. "Not in weeks. Maybe a few months. I had nothing to say to him. Anything business related, I talked to Troy Pfeiffer."

"I see. I understand you were an investor in Troy and Cam's business venture?"

"We gave them a loan, yeah," Whit answered.

"But you called it in recently? Withdrew your financial backing?"

"They got bought out. I didn't pull anything from Troy directly. I just chose not to be a part of the business after the new management took over. They bought me out. End of story."

"It's not though, is it?"

"What do you mean?"

"The end of the story. You weren't disinterested in the business, right?"

"Look," he said. "You dragged me here ..."

"No," Jake said. "I believe I was going to come to you. Eighteen hours ago you were fine with that. I didn't ask you to come all the way down here, Whit. That was your choice."

"Whatever."

"What have you heard about what happened to Cameron and Rianne Katz?"

"I heard he went nuts. Offed her. Then himself. It's awful. A real shock. But why do I need to be having a conversation with you about it?"

Jake smirked. Roundtree wasn't an idiot, but he was sure acting stupid.

"Look," Jake said. "You're a smart guy. From what I've heard, a pretty successful one. What I've also heard is you're the brains behind your own business with Lea. You're the one who figured out how to monetize her fitness platform. She's the face of it, sure. But you're the promoter. And it wasn't an accident, her becoming a successful influencer. But in Cam's case, I think it very much was. An accident, I mean."

Whit pursed his lips with disdain, but didn't answer.

"I've seen some of his content," Jake continued. "Cam wasn't really in on the joke, was he?"

Still, no response.

"It's gotta be pretty frustrating dealing with guys like that. You've got Lea out there doing science-backed stuff. Working her butt off. And doing everything clean. Then Cam's out there, getting famous for all the wrong reasons. Pumped up with steroids. Giving bad advice. Borderline misogynistic. But people are lapping it up. Hate watching it, but racking up views and followers left and right."

"Which is bullshit," Whit said. "He fudged the numbers. You wanna know why I pulled out? Because I don't want my name associated with that crap. I ought to sue his estate."

"Not sure there is much of one. I heard the buyout was just enough to cover their debts. Cam was broke. Worse than broke."

"Doesn't surprise me," Whit said. "The guy was money dumb along with everything else."

"What's everything else, Whit?" Jake asked. He wanted to give Whit the opportunity to volunteer what he knew about his wife's relationship with Cam. If he lied or pretended he didn't know, that would tell Jake a lot about him.

Whit exhaled sharply with exasperation. "What are you fishing for?"

"Just your story."

"My story? *My* story? Come on. What's this about?"

"You. You and Lea. Lea and Cameron. You and Cameron."

Whit jerked back in his chair. "What have you heard? Who's telling you something?"

"Come on, Whit, it's all over the internet, right? You and Cam are on surveillance video fighting, right? Last year? Myrtle Beach?"

"What does that have to do with anything?"

"You tell me."

"Look," Whit said, pointing a finger at Jake. "This is crap. Lea doesn't have anything to do with Cameron Katz anymore. He's a joke. No conference committee would even allow him to attend anything anymore as of a few months ago."

"All right," Jake said calmly. "So here's what I want." He slid the pad and paper across the table. "I want you to tell me where you were on the night of June 28th from about seven p.m. to seven a.m. the next morning. Will you do that for me?"

Whit went pale. "What? What is this?"

"Just a question," Jake said.

"I don't ... That was weeks ago. I don't know."

"Check your phone, your calendar; think hard, Whit."

Whit put both hands flat on the table. "What's going on?"

Either he was guilty and playing dumb, or he was innocent, but hadn't bothered to Google Cameron Katz since Jake called asking to talk to him.

"Answer the question."

Whit shrugged. He did as Jake asked and pulled out his phone. "That was a Friday night. The Tuesday before that, Lea and I left for a conference in Chattanooga. We were there until Friday afternoon. Friday night? I was just home. Where would I go?"

"When was the last time you talked to Cameron Katz?"

"I don't talk to Cameron Katz. Not for months."

"What about Lea?"

Roundtree went from pale to beet red. "She hasn't seen him either. Oh shit. Has she? What do you know? Did you see her with him? No, no. If someone is telling you that, they're lying. You have this all wrong."

"How do I have it?"

"Look, I'm not going to sit here and say I'm sorry Cameron Katz is no longer on this planet. But I never wished him harm."

"Except for the time you punched him in front of witnesses."

"That's ... I wasn't ... That's got nothing to do with anything. Yeah. Okay? You obviously know. Cam was screwing my wife. He was probably screwing everybody's wife. When I read on the internet that he killed his own wife then himself, I'll admit, I thought you must have got it wrong. I could see why his wife would want to shoot him. But that's none of my business. None. I haven't seen Cam, I haven't talked to Cam, I haven't thought about Cam until you called."

"Would you be willing to sign a paper authorizing me to search your phone, Whit?"

"What? Screw you. No way. I don't have to agree to that. I know my rights."

"No," Jake said. "You don't have to agree to it. But if you really have nothing to hide, what's the harm?"

"I know how you people can twist things. Take them out of context. Get a warrant, man." He rose.

"Whit, I've got more questions."

"Well, I don't have any other answers. You said I could leave. I came in here voluntarily. In good faith. You're treating me like I've done something wrong. Cam Katz killed himself."

Jake sat back. "See, that's the thing. It turns out that is not what happened. Someone shot him."

"Then his wife did it. I told you. He was making a fool of her."

"Like he was out of you?"

"Naw. No way. I'm not falling for that. I didn't do anything to Cam except what I did in public. You said you saw a video. Then you know exactly what happened."

“Can someone vouch for your whereabouts on June 29th?”

“I was home! I told you. So was Lea.”

Jake nodded. “I’m going to have to talk to her too, Whit.”

Anger flashed in Whit’s eyes. “You do what you gotta do. I didn’t do anything to Cam. Neither did she. We live in Rocky River. That’s two hundred miles away. I don’t even know where Cam lives. I don’t have his address. The only reason I now know he’s from this crap hole is because of you.”

“Fine,” Jake said. “But you know, those are exactly the kinds of things your phone would validate. It’s a good way to end any negative speculation right now.”

“Tough,” Whit spat. “I’m done. You wanna ask me any more questions, I want a lawyer with me. That goes for Lea too.”

“Fine,” Jake said. “Call one. Because tomorrow, I’m gonna want to interview her too. I’ll come to you.”

“Whatever,” Whit said. He marched around the table and yanked open the door. Jake stayed seated while Whit Roundtree stormed down the hall swearing.

Two seconds later, Birdie walked in. She’d probably been watching from the observation room next door.

“Well,” she said. “That was a thing, huh? What do you think about him?”

“You saw. What do you think?”

She looked back toward the door Whit had just vacated. “Hard to say. Either he’s our killer and he thought he could play dumb. Or he’s innocent and actually dumb.”

Jake snorted. That had been his exact impression as well. She pulled a file folder from under her arm and set it on the table next to him.

"I got access to one of the Facebook groups for attendees of the Muscle ProFit conference in Myrtle Beach where this thing came to a head between Roundtree and Katz. It was quite the scuttlebutt. I took a bunch of screenshots. But the consensus is that Roundtree was the aggressor, and also that Katz had it coming. The organizers had banned him from ever attending again. Sounds like some others followed suit."

"Well, Roundtree said as much. We need to work on a warrant. I want his phone. His wife's too. I'll interview her tomorrow. Don't know how far I'll get if he makes good on his threat to get her a lawyer."

"How much longer until BCI has something on the crime scene?"

"Might be a week or so," Jake said. "Though both Ramirez and Dr. Stone predict we won't have much in terms of blood or DNA belonging to anybody else. You just never know."

"You okay, Jake?"

"What do you mean?" he snapped, more than he meant.

She put her hands up in surrender. "Sorry. It's just you look like you haven't slept in a week. And ... that was a good interview, don't get me wrong. But it felt a little rushed compared to your usual."

"Roundtree was never going to cooperate. The second he found out Katz was murdered, he was gonna figure out he was a suspect. I'm lucky I got as much as I did before he started getting serious about a lawyer."

To Jake, her expression seemed a bit patronizing.

"Okay," she said. "I was just asking. You wanna grab some lunch?"

He felt his shoulders sag. "I'm not trying to be a dick. Sorry."

"It's okay. I get it. It's this case. It's ... just ... yeah. I get it."

He should have told her what he'd done. What he'd seen in his parents' file. That he had the thing at all. But he didn't. He didn't want to see that look of concern on her face. He didn't want to hear her tell him he should see someone. Or ask to be taken off the Katz case altogether.

He made an excuse about why he couldn't grab lunch with her. Then he spent the rest of the day buried in reports.

FOURTEEN

Two days later, Lea Roundtree agreed to meet with Jake at a family restaurant in outside Columbus. As he walked in, she surprised him by coming alone. She picked a round booth in the corner, big enough to fit a dozen people. Jake had to scoot awkwardly around the table to get close enough to have a proper conversation. It was two o'clock, well past the lunch rush, but he counted at least ten other tables with diners.

"The fish basket is good," Lea said. She had a huge salad in front of her, picked off a pepper and popped it in her mouth. She wore a tank top with the Roundtree Gym logo as Whit had. Hers revealed sinewy arms and a deep, tanning-bed tan that almost made her look purple. She had high, pencil-thin black brows and dyed black hair piled into a ponytail on the top of her head.

"Good tip," Jake said. "But I've already eaten. I'm glad you agreed to talk to me. I'm sure you've heard by now what I'm investigating."

"Someone killed Cam," she said, stabbing her fork into her salad. She didn't have the nerves or the attitude her husband did. If anything, Lea Roundtree acted like this was a mundane business meeting.

"I'd like to know about your relationship with him."

She finished chewing her bite of salad and then wiped the corners of her mouth with a red cloth napkin.

"I've been open about it. Cam and I were intimately involved starting early last year. But he was single as far as I knew."

"You weren't," Jake said.

"Whit and I have a unique relationship."

"It's open?" Jake asked.

"Not exactly," she said. "But Whit and I haven't lived as a married couple in quite a long time."

"He didn't mention that."

"He doesn't like to. Whit's held out hope for years that I'd turn into this dutiful housewife that had his babies and cooked dinner every night. That's not who I am. I respect people who do that; please don't misunderstand me. My greater point is that it's okay for everyone to live their authentic lives. When we got married, I felt Whit understood that. But he wants something else."

"So why stay married?" Jake asked.

"Because it's too expensive to get divorced. It's not just matrimony. We're business partners. And I do love Whit. Very much. I don't have any desire to partner with anyone else. Cam Katz was a physical relationship. That's all."

"Did he feel the same way?"

She finished another bite of her salad. "I believe he did. Look, Cam was fun to be around. He was adventurous. Funny. Sweet.

Charming in his dopey way. And he was easy. He didn't make demands or want more of me than I wanted to give. But I didn't love him. I was only fond of him. Very fond of him."

"How did Whit feel about that?" Jake asked.

"You talked to him. Surely you asked him that yourself."

"I did," Jake admitted. "But I'm here to get your side of things."

She put her fork down. "I didn't kill Cameron. Neither did my husband. I know why that would be your first, most logical theory. But this wasn't what other people thought on the outside. We were consenting adults. All three of us."

"Lea, forgive me if I'm having trouble seeing it that way. I'm aware that Cam and your husband got into a physical altercation that resulted in Cam being thrown out of a hotel and barred from ever attending the industry conference where this took place. And I know it was all anyone in your circle could talk about for quite a few weeks after the fact."

"You're talking about social media?" she asked. "Keyboard gossip?"

"Sure."

"I'll admit it was embarrassing. And I was furious with Whit after the fact. But we weren't living together. We haven't been for more than a year."

"So you weren't with him the weekend of June 29th?"

She smiled and wagged her index finger. "Nice try. Just because we don't have the same legal address doesn't mean we don't spend a significant amount of time together. Yes. I was with Whit the night Cameron and his wife were killed."

"Whit won't let me verify that by the most obvious means. I'll have a warrant for his cell phone records probably by the end of the day."

"You want mine too?" she asked, pulling her phone out of her purse. She opened it and scrolled through a few screens. Then she turned it toward Jake and laid it flat on the table in front of him.

"Look for yourself," she said. "Open my text app. Scroll as far down as you'd like. You won't see anything between Cam and me since the beginning of the year. We weren't talking. I ended it after the incident at ProFit. It was mutual. Cam decided he wanted to make a commitment to Rianne, his girlfriend at the time. I was supportive of that. I think she was good for him. She could keep him grounded. He needed that."

Jake took her dare and picked up her phone. He scrolled down. There were no texts to or from Cameron Katz until January of this year. When he opened them, their last exchanges were about setting up a dinner date. Jake put the phone down.

"I'm looking for more than that," Jake said. "Texts can be deleted."

"Of course they can. And you want the cell tower data. You want to know whether Whit and I were in Blackhand Hills the night Cameron died. That's reasonable. If you have paperwork, I'm happy to sign it. I've told Whit that he should do the same. But I don't make his decisions for him."

Jake wasn't sure what to make of her. Either she was guilty and just cold as ice, or she was innocent ... and cold as ice.

"You wanna search my car? My apartment? DNA? You can have it all, Detective Cashen. I'm sorry for what happened to Cameron and his wife. From what I know, he was really trying to make a go of it with her. He loved her. When I heard rumors you were thinking it was a murder-suicide? I knew that wasn't right.

Cameron was by no means perfect. Far from it. He had a lot of issues. To be honest, if I were friends with Rianne, I would have warned her not to marry him in the first place. Cam could have probably been good for a while, but he was going to want to be with other women eventually. He wouldn't have been able to help himself. He needed to be with someone who could accept that. By the way, I told him that many times. Told him to be honest with this girl before he put a ring on her finger."

"Like you were with Whit," Jake said.

"Exactly."

"But you and your husband invested heavily in Cam's business venture. He was in serious financial trouble when you decided to withdraw your financial support."

"We're not the reason Cam's business went belly up. Cam was a fraud. He wanted people to believe he achieved his physique naturally. I knew it wasn't. Everyone in the trade knew it wasn't. Honestly? I think most of his followers knew it wasn't. They were watching him to laugh at him."

"Were you?" Jake asked.

She shrugged. "He was a sweet guy. It was so obvious what he was doing, I never thought it would do any harm. The hilarious thing is a lot of people thought Cam was just a marketing genius and his social media content was satire. The thing was, Cam wasn't that smart. A lot of people were laughing at him behind his back."

"Were you one of them?"

"No," she said. "Never. I told you. He was a sweet, good-hearted guy. He was never gonna catch on that he'd become a kind of joke among other fitness influencers. He was fun to be with. But I figured at some point he was gonna get hurt."

"By whom?"

"Just in general. If he ever realized why people followed him."

Jake pulled a folder out of his backpack and set it on the table. It contained waivers and authorizations for all the searches Lea had mentioned. He put a pen on top of it.

Without even blinking, she opened the folder, quickly scanned the paperwork, and then signed every last one. She shut the file, clicked the pen closed, and then slid it all back to Jake.

"Anything else?" she asked.

"Not for now.

"Are they okay?"

"Who do you mean?" Jake asked.

"Cam's family. I know his parents weren't in the picture. But surely he had to have someone, didn't he? And I know Rianne's parents are still alive. Cam often talked about them. He knew they weren't fond of him and were against the marriage."

"They're processing everything the best they can," Jake said.

"Well, I wish them all the best, for whatever that's worth. Probably not very much. And I wish you the best too. I want you to find out who did this to Cam and his girl. They didn't deserve it."

Lea pulled two twenties out of her purse and laid them on the table. "Sorry to eat and run. You really should try the fish basket. I don't eat things with a face anymore, but it was one of my favorite things when I still did. You know how to get ahold of me. Tell me when and where you'd like me to submit a cheek swab or however those things are done now. Or here."

She picked up her water and drank it down in one gulp. The glass was smudged with her fingerprints as she set it back down in front of him. She had a half-eaten roll on the plate. She picked it up, took another bite, and set it down next to the water glass.

She didn't wait for Jake to say goodbye. She simply heaved her purse onto her shoulder, gave him a quick salute, and left.

As if she could read his mind, Birdie's name and profile image came up on his phone screen with an incoming call.

"Are you still waiting for Lea Roundtree?" she asked.

"She just left," Jake said, still staring at the path Lea had taken.

"Anything interesting?"

Jake chuffed. "She agreed to every search I asked for."

"How'd she seem otherwise?"

"Strangest damn interview I've ever conducted. If she's guilty, she's got a pair of brass balls. How'd it go with the relatives?" Jake felt bad that he'd tasked Birdie with re-interviewing both Rianne's parents and Cam's brother.

"The Timineys are reeling. And they refuse to believe Cam's not the one who shot their daughter."

"Really? I expected that would be a relief to her father."

"I think they took comfort in hating him," she said. "It's odd. But there's also no rulebook for how any of this should go. As far as Cam's brother, he's just so beaten down by life. To him I think this was one more blow. Though he did ask about life insurance again. Said something about how this might make things easier to collect. He'd heard suicide is often an exclusion."

"Nice," Jake said. "It's a long shot, but I want to search his phone too."

"Already on it. He agreed and signed a waiver."

What the hell was going on with these people? Jake thought. He waved the server off when she came back to bring Jake a menu.

"Any luck with Keith and Cam Katz's gym?" Jake asked.

"Not yet," she answered. "Keith's putting more feelers out. He's pretty sure he has an idea of who Katz might have been dealing with. But these people are spooked now that it's public knowledge he was murdered."

"Just keep me in the loop," Jake said.

"Always," she said, then clicked off.

He immediately got another text. This one from Virgil Adamski.

> Better see you at breakfast tomorrow. Tessa said she'd hunt you down. I wouldn't like to be on her bad side.

Jake smiled. He missed those old farts. Tessa too. And maybe a small break from everything weighing on him was a good idea. No doubt that's exactly what Tessa Papatonis thought too.

Fifteen

For the first ten minutes after he walked into Papa's Diner, Tessa lectured Jake about how many ribs she could feel under his shirt. A wild exaggeration, she ignored his protests when she served him a stack of pancakes tall enough to lean under their own weight.

Virgil Adamski, Bill Nutter, and Chuck Thompson reveled in the whole thing from behind their coffee mugs. The three of them retired from the Worthington County Sheriff's Department years ago. Since then, they'd held weekly "staff" meetings back here on Tessa's round top. Jake held the honor of being the only working cop they'd allow to join them.

It was good to see them all in one place. And each time Jake saw Virgil, he looked better and better. It was hard to believe they'd almost lost him less than a year ago.

"I'm never gonna finish all this," Jake said, under his breath.

"Better figure out a plan," Chuck said. "She sees leftovers when she busses the table, she'll kill ya. And don't think you can get away with tossing anything in the trash. She'll look there too."

"Gonna have to stuff it in your pockets, kid." Bill laughed.

Jake took a bite. Tessa's pancakes melted in his mouth. But they were so thick and rich, three forkfuls and he was pretty much done.

The conversation was easy this morning. Jake's nephew Ryan and his best friend Travis, Birdie's nephew, were helping put in four new dock sections for Virgil out on Echo Lake. Chuck's son gave him his first grandchild last week. He had a dozen pictures to share on his phone. Bill bought a vintage Mustang convertible and held as much affection for it as Chuck did for his grandson.

By the time Tessa came back with another pot of coffee, Virg got around to asking Jake what the three of them had probably plotted before Virgil had sent him yesterday's text.

"This case," Chuck said as he poured more maple syrup onto his plate. "You any closer to finding your shooter?"

"Just working the leads I have," Jake said. The men knew he couldn't share details, even with them, and certainly not in public.

"I knew Cameron Katz's grandma a little," Bill said. "I took her to her senior prom fifty years ago. Lord. How the hell did that go by so fast?"

"Did you take a horse-drawn carriage?" Jake teased. Bill threw a pad of butter at him.

"The Timineys, Rianne Katz's family, are having a hard time accepting that their son-in-law didn't kill that girl."

"You're sure though," Bill said. "A hundred percent?"

"Yeah," Jake answered.

"I suppose it'd be a hell of a lot easier for you if the husband had done it," Bill said. Chuck and Virgil went deadly silent. A beat later, Bill's jaw went slack.

Jake put a hand up, gesturing to quiet Bill before he launched into a stream of apologies.

"It's okay," Jake said. "I hope you can understand, I'm getting kind of sick of people giving me the look you're giving me now. I get it. But it's not necessary. I'm fine."

It took a moment for the air around the table to settle. The three men kept passing knowing looks to each other, confirming Jake's suspicion about their ulterior motives today. Finally, he dropped his fork and threw his napkin on the table.

"It's okay," he said. "You can stop dancing around it. Say what you wanted to say."

Virgil clasped his hands in front of him, resting his elbows on the table. "We just like to keep an eye on you. And we don't care much if you mind."

Jake couldn't help but smile. "Yeah. I get that."

He meant to change the subject. This was his opening to do just that. But something shifted in his mind. It bubbled up and before he could think, he asked the question.

"Okay," he said. "So let's get into this. In all the years I've sat at this table with you, we've never talked about my parents' case. I know you had to have been involved in it back then. I know how hard it was for Frank."

Before there were three old men at this table, there had been four. Frank Borowski had been as close to Virgil, Bill, and Chuck as a brother.

"Is there something you wanna ask?" Chuck asked.

Jake shook his head. "No. I don't know." There was. It sat like a boulder on his chest. But if he asked it, then they'd know what he'd done. His throat ran dry. He took another sip of ice water. His wrist shook a little when he set it back down. On his right, Virgil saw it.

"First off," Jake said. "I'm fine. Okay? I mean that."

"We know," Bill said.

Jake took a breath and launched straight into it. "Did you know my dad left a note?"

Bill dropped his chin to his chest. It was an answer in and of itself.

"You knew," Jake said. "All of you?"

Virgil sat back and turned his chair so his knees pointed toward Jake. "Frank mentioned it. He never said what was in it. I never saw it myself. But yeah. We were aware. It was part of the summary findings."

"I have to be honest," Bill said. "I wasn't sure if you knew, Jake. Not exactly the kind of thing that would have ever come up in casual conversation."

"No," Jake said, wishing he had something stronger than coffee in his mug. "I didn't know."

"You've seen it," Virgil said. It wasn't a question. "Jake, what are you doing?"

There was something in his voice. A grim finality. Jake realized Virgil and the others already knew he'd taken his parents' case file.

"You know I went to the Crypt," he said.

"I heard something through the grapevine," Virgil said. "I don't think you have to worry. It's not common knowledge in the department. Just among some of us who worked with Frank. And there are damn few left of us."

Jake shook his head. "Why didn't anybody tell me? My grandparents had to have known about it. Frank would have told them."

"You're not doing yourself any good," Bill said. "Leave that file alone, Jake. Leave it buried where it belongs. If you have to, tell Landry you want off the Katz case."

"That's ridiculous," Jake said. "There isn't a single one of you who would pull themselves from this under the same circumstances. I know how to do my job."

"Frank knew how to do his too," Chuck said. "And as far as Max. I'm sure he had his reasons for keeping that from you. You were just a kid, Jake. A baby, actually. God. You don't know what that case did to Frank."

"What did it do?" Jake said, raising his chin and meeting Chuck's eyes.

Virgil put a hand on Jake's shoulder. "It tore his guts out. He loved your dad. He loves your grandfather. Then he loved you. He went on leave for a little while after. Did you know that? The stress of it got to him. Having to tell Ava she lost her son. She loved Sonya like a daughter too."

"I hate this," Jake said. "I hate that other people know things about my parents that I don't. I hate the look of pity everyone gave me then and still gives me now. So yeah. I took the box from the Crypt."

"To what purpose?" Chuck asked. "You know everything already. The only thing that stuff will do is torture you. Your dad wouldn't want that."

"He didn't know what he wanted. I read the note."

"Put it back," Bill said. "At least for now. You're right. None of us would have been able to pull ourselves off the Katz case either. But while you're working it, leave the box alone. If you wanna open it later, when you're not mired in this crap, do it then."

It made sense. He knew it when he put the box in his trunk. He hadn't been able to go back to it since he had read the letter. It still sat on his living room table.

"I can't," he said, both to the others and to himself. "I just can't. And you know you'd feel the same way if it had been your family."

A heavy silence fell. It occurred to Jake that neither Tessa nor Spiros had come out to sit with them as they normally did. They knew what this conversation was about. And they had known Jake's parents too.

"Yeah," Bill admitted. "You're right. I would do just what you've done. But it doesn't mean I won't try to keep you from throwing yourself in front of a moving train, Jake."

"I'm fine," he said, taking his last sip of coffee. He threw a twenty on the table.

"Just talk to him," Chuck said. "To Max. If you're angry about that letter, give him a chance to understand why. And cut him some slack. It was a terrible time for him too. God, he loved your dad more than anything. They were together all the time. They were as close as a father and son as I've ever seen. Then, he was gone. And your grandpa couldn't save him. No one could. You were so little. Gemma too. You had no parents. It fell to Max to try to raise you. He lost a lot of his wife during that time too. He was holding your family together with his bare hands, Jake. Never forget that. So if you wanna be mad at him. Just get over it soon, okay?"

"I appreciate the advice," Jake said, then realized it could have sounded sarcastic. Maybe part of it was. "I mean that. Really. I'd appreciate it if we could keep this conversation at this table."

"Of course," Virgil said. "You know you don't even have to ask."

"I know," Jake said. And he did. But everything felt so overwhelming just then. He couldn't let it be. Rianne and Cameron Katz needed his full attention.

He gave Tessa a hug before he left. To her credit, she didn't ask him any questions. Jake sat in his car for a moment. Part of him didn't want to go back to the office. He wanted to do what his grandfather did when his mind wouldn't stop spinning. He would head out to the woods and disappear. It would be okay. Just half a day.

But as Jake put his car in gear, his phone rang. Mark Ramirez's ID popped up. Jake pressed the accept button on his car's dashboard computer.

"Hey, Mark," he said.

"How far away are you from your office?" Mark asked.

"I'm across the street. Just leaving the diner," Jake answered.

"Okay. I'm about twenty minutes out. I've got phones and prints back on the Katz case. I know how anxious you are about this one. I'll bring everything straight to you."

The woods could wait. Jake's head was back in the game.

Sixteen

"You mind if I sit in on this one?" Landry asked. She caught up with Jake just as he entered the building. "Erica gave me a heads-up that Agent Ramirez is inbound."

Before Jake could answer, through the window to his right, he saw Ramirez pull into the closest visitor parking space. He turned back to Meg.

"Of course not. It'll save me from having to brief you later." Not that he would have tried to deny her anyway. Landry was exactly the kind of sheriff every cop wanted. She stayed abreast of major cases, but never got in the way of an investigation. If Jake needed more resources, she bent over backward to provide them. She trusted his judgment. It didn't mean she didn't question it at times, but she rarely pulled rank. Among the best of her traits, she kept the media away from him as much as she could.

Birdie was waiting in their office. She'd brought in another table and transferred all the Katz materials to it. When Ramirez came in, they had an uncluttered place to talk.

"Glad you're both here," she said. "I finally got a name from Cameron Katz's gym. It's looking strong that I found his PED dealer. He's coming back into town the day after tomorrow. I've got a meeting set up."

"Fantastic," Jake said, tossing his backpack onto his chair. Ramirez tapped on the doorframe. He had a backpack of his own.

"Come on in," Jake said. "We'll set up over there."

"I don't know how much you're gonna like what I have to say," Ramirez said. "Good to see you, Sheriff, Detective Wayne."

"It's Erica," Birdie said. "I think we've known each other long enough, don't you think?"

Ramirez gave her a sheepish smile. Jake wasn't entirely sure Mark didn't have a benign crush on her. He was married with six or seven kids.

"I'll take whatever you've got," Jake said. He and everybody else took seats at the table while Mark opened his pack and pulled out two thick binders. He was nothing if not organized. He handed one copy to Birdie. She scooted next to Meg so the two of them could read together.

Jake took his but didn't open it. He wanted Ramirez's highlights first.

"You wanna bottom line it for me?" Jake asked.

"Well, it's interesting. As crime scenes go, this one was pretty clean."

"Clean," Landry said. "I've seen the photos. It was a bloody mess."

"Clean in the sense that I'm not finding any evidence of anyone being there who shouldn't have been. But Stone's findings are rock solid. My guys agree. Victim two, Cameron Katz? He didn't shoot himself. I can't say for sure whether he shot victim one, the wife, yet."

"What do you mean?" Jake asked.

"We lifted fingerprints off seven individuals over the entire house. Upstairs, it's both victims. Downstairs is more of a mix. Tons of prints in the mudroom off the back door. Besides the victims, we matched a set to Marne Kowalski, the dog walker. Hers don't go much further into the house. Just a set on the kitchen counter near the sink."

"She would fill their dog's food and water bowls," Birdie said. "So that tracks."

"Handprint of hers on the back door glass. Footprints in victim one's blood about three feet away from where she was found. She never went any further into the house."

"Smart girl," Meg said. "That poor thing. She's a grade above Paige. Choir president when Paige was a freshman. She really likes her. And Paige hates everyone."

Jake smiled.

"Right," Ramirez continued. "I've got partial prints matching Deputies Stuckey and Bundy near the front door and foyer door. But they were careful after they entered. Nothing around the victim's bodies. You taught them well. They gloved and booted up pretty quickly. Then there's one more set of prints on the thermostat in the main hallway. Those took a little longer to match. But they belong to the heating and cooling guy."

"Katz had an invoice taped to the fridge," Birdie explained to Landry. "They had their furnace and AC serviced a week or so before. I tracked down the service person who came out."

"That's it?" Jake asked.

"That's it. They kept a pretty clean house. The upstairs in particular. We could still smell bleach when we did our main work."

"You don't think someone could have been trying to cover their tracks with that?" Meg asked.

"I don't think so," Ramirez answered. "We found traces of it in all the places you'd expect. Sinks, bathtubs, toilets. Nothing on any door handles or the flooring."

"What about the gun found in Katz's hand?" Jake asked.

"His prints only," Ramirez said. "It'll take a few weeks for ballistics to come back. I'm trying to rush that through as fast as I can. But they were at least able to tell me informally that the gun had been recently fired. They're working on the bullets Stone pulled out of the bodies, and the shell casings found at the scene. But it's not at all unusual that the others were more or less clean."

"What about the blood patterns?" Birdie asked.

"Victim one was shot from the front, facing the shooter. But you already knew that from Stone's report. On the couch with victim two ... spatter patterns are consistent with him being seated when the kill shot came."

"No sign of restraints or anything?" Jake asked. "Stone didn't find any ligature marks on the body. Or glue."

"We didn't recover anything like that. My guess, somebody pointed his own gun at him. But I have no physical evidence to back that up."

"And no way to know if he stood idly by while his wife was murdered," Birdie said.

"There were no defensive wounds suggesting he put up a fight," Jake said.

"As far as blood or DNA, no bingo there either," Ramirez said. "Only blood at the scene belonged to one or both of the victims. No other foreign biological matter of any kind.

"Phones?" Meg asked.

"I wish I could tell you I found some bombs," Ramirez said. "There just weren't any. We got victim two's call and SMS text history. Nothing that raised any red flags. There are calls and texts to his wife. Mundane stuff. Grocery lists. Scheduling. The most recent stuff was when they were in Barbados. She's on the beach; he's on a fishing charter. They're coordinating their plans. It's all normal stuff between the two of them. He texted Troy Pfeiffer quite a bit, but it's not contentious. Just business related."

"They were going under," Jake said.

"That's clear," Ramirez said. "But I don't see either of them losing it with the other. Transcripts of the most recent stuff are in your binder. There's nothing on his phone to your suspect. If they were in communication, it wasn't on his phone or Roundtree's. On business stuff, Roundtree was only communicating with Troy Pfeiffer. As for the wife? The one Katz was hooking up with? She's listed in Katz's contacts as Insurance Agent Todd."

"So he's trying to keep it a secret from Rianne," Birdie said.

"Yeah," Ramirez responded. "But there's no communication between them after January 17th."

"That tracks with what she told me," Jake said.

"Now," Ramirez said. "What there is before January 17th is some pretty raunchy stuff. She's sending nudes of herself to him. A lot of sexting between them. But I don't see anything that raised my eyebrows between Lea and Whit Roundtree with each other. Same deal. Mundane husband and wife stuff. Though it's clear, they're not living together. That's pretty much it."

"None of it makes sense to me," Landry said. "At least in terms of this affair Katz was having."

"It's certainly not a garden variety fling," Jake said. "She insists it was physical only and that her husband knew all about it."

"He didn't approve of it," Birdie said.

"He made threats," Meg said. "He assaulted Cameron Katz."

"All true," Jake said. "So far, I can't put him at the crime scene."

"I can't either," Ramirez said. "Her phone never got anywhere near Blackhand Hills. Neither did his. It's stationary on the 29th after four p.m. Consistent with the tower closest to his home."

"Which isn't what he told you," Birdie said. "He told you he was with Lea that night. At her place."

"He could have left his phone at home," Jake said.

"Or," Ramirez said, "he knew enough to leave his phone at home if he traveled down here to off Katz."

"I can't rule it out," Jake said.

"Will he submit to a lie detector?" Landry asked. "I know they're not admissible in court, but it might help you on a gut feeling level."

"I'd like to talk to Katz's dealer first," Jake said. "Mark, I appreciate you bringing all this down."

Ramirez got to his feet. He pulled out a lumpy envelope and set it on the table. "Flash drive with everything I've got on there. If you have anything else you want me to run, let me know."

"Thanks," Jake said. "But based on this, I don't have probable cause to search either of Roundtree's cars or residences."

"In any case," Ramirez said, "just let me know."

Ramirez showed himself out. Meg had a deep scowl on her face.

"He's still out there," she said. "Or she. Whoever did this. This really could have been random, couldn't it?"

"We don't know enough to make that jump," Jake said. "We just have to keep working it."

"Just keep me posted," she said, rising. "I can keep the vultures at bay for a while. But Roger Timiney has money. He's applying some pressure. He's talking about hiring a private investigator."

"He can do whatever he wants," Jake said. "But I'll plow over anyone who gets in my way or tries to impede this thing. I know he's grieving."

"You might want to talk to him again," Meg said. "It could do some good."

Jake nodded. "I'm fine with that. I'll head over there after lunch."

Satisfied, Meg left the room.

"You want me to ride shotgun for your trip to the Timineys? I've got a little rapport with the wife."

"It's okay," Jake said. "Keep working the gym angle. Scour his social media. Are we sure Katz didn't have a whack job or two following him?"

"I haven't found anything in recent posts, but he's had the account for almost two years. I'll keep digging."

"Thanks," Jake said. He hesitated, then turned to Birdie. "If I haven't said it, you're fitting into your new role seamlessly, Birdie.

You're a born detective. I don't think ... I know how much I need you on this one. If you see me going sideways, you'll tell me. Right?"

"Of course," she said. "And you're not, Jake."

He tapped his knuckles on the desk. "Yeah. I'll just be glad when this one's cleared."

She knew the look on his face. She knew what was on his mind. But to her credit, she didn't pry, and she didn't give him that look of pity he'd seen too many times from other people.

By the time Jake made it home that night, he felt bone-weary and thick-headed. His meeting with Roger and Pam Timiney had taken more out of him than he thought it would. Meg was right; they just needed a bit more hand-holding. More assurances that their daughter's case was his main priority. It was more than that; it was his only priority at the moment.

As he pulled into his driveway, one of Grandpa's goats stood in his side yard, chomping the grass.

"How did you get out?" Jake sighed. The goat blinked her slitted eyes but kept on chewing. "Well, you were smart enough to get yourself down here, you can find your way back."

The goat burped in response. Jake laughed and went inside.

He kicked his shoes off, loosened his tie and unstrapped his gun. It lifted his spine as he put the heavy thing on the kitchen table and grabbed a cold beer out of the fridge. He popped off the bottle top and tossed it in the garbage. He peered further into the fridge. He saw a Styrofoam container with a note on top. He pulled it out.

"Shrimp basket, on me. Fried pickles. They're better if you heat them in the air fryer. That's the big black thing on your counter I bought you. Put them in for five minutes. You're welcome. Also,

Grandpa says if you miss Chili Sunday he's going to find you and nail your pants to one of his kitchen chairs. Love you. You're welcome. Gemma."

Jake shook his head. He looked around. She'd been here for a while. The blankets were neatly folded on the back of his couch. Pillows fluffed. He smelled pine cleaner. She'd mopped the floors and taken his garbage out.

He walked into his bedroom and laughed. She'd put fresh sheets on and left two mints on each of his pillows. He walked back out. She'd left the closet door slightly ajar when she took his vacuum cleaner out.

Jake's heart skipped. The closet. He had put the banker's box with their parents' case file on the top shelf there. Gemma never missed anything. She would have noticed it was new.

He put his beer on the living room table and went back to the closet. The vacuum cleaner was tucked against the wall, its cord neatly coiled. But the box didn't look like it had been moved. It was still shoved back against the wall as he had left it. From this angle, you wouldn't know what it was as it had no label or writing on the sides, only the top.

Jake sighed with relief. If Gemma had found it, she'd have dropped everything and been waiting for him when he got home. She wouldn't have been able to help herself. All of her protective instincts would have kicked in.

Jake pulled the box down. He hadn't gone back to it since finding that awful note. He walked back out to the living room and set it on the table.

He sat down and lifted the lid. The note was still there, at the top of the pile. He'd left it facedown. It still was. Jake's heart lifted a little. She hadn't seen it.

He reached into the box and pulled out Frank's suppy again. His organizational methods reminded Jake of Mark Ramirez's. Everything tabbed and color-coded.

He shouldn't look. He knew he shouldn't. But like the last time, he knew he wouldn't be able to turn away. He lifted and turned to the pink tab labeled "Crime Scene Photos." As the contents of the box shifted, one of the bulky Tyvek envelopes slid sideways. He lifted it out.

"Witness Interview – Gemma Cashen – October 12, 1992."

Jake held the envelope to his chest.

She wouldn't have been able to help herself. All of her protective instincts would have kicked in.

Jake rose and walked into his second bedroom. He used it as a catchall and sometimes as a home office. But when Ryan was a toddler, Gemma lived here with him between marriages and careers. Grandma Ava had an old collection of cartoons on VHS that Gemma found and brought here along with the TV/VCR combo Grandma used to keep in her bedroom.

Jake didn't even know if it still worked. He left it on the floor in the corner behind some TV trays. He pulled it out, plugged the power cord into the wall, and sat on the floor in front of it. He ripped open the Tyvek envelope and pulled the black rectangular tape out. The air felt like acid in his lungs as he popped the tape in. The screen immediately flared to life, then filled with static.

Then, a moment later, a still image from a room Jake knew very well flickered on the screen. Interview room one at the Sheriff's Department. It was just across from his office. It looked exactly the same. Even the chipped paint near the door. The same table too. Same chairs.

A young girl sat in the one facing the camera. Small. Skinny. Light-brown hair. It was Gemma. And she was only twelve years old. Grandpa Max had his arm around Gemma and leaned in as if he were about to kiss her on the head.

Someone had taped the remote control to the top of the TV. Jake pried it off. He scooted back until he leaned against the edge of the twin bed he kept in here.

Then he hit play.

Seventeen

"Honey, are you sure?" Grandpa Max asked. He had his hands on Gemma's shoulders, sitting beside her. But she wouldn't turn to him. She kept her eyes focused on Frank, sitting at the opposite end of the table. Jake saw him in profile. He did the math in his head. Frank would have been thirty-eight years old. The same age as Jake was now. He still sported the same buzz cut. But he had color in his cheeks that had long since faded. He wore a blue polo shirt, the sleeves stretching around his hard-cut biceps. The year before, Frank Borowski, coach, had taken over the high school wrestling program. A position he would hold for over twenty years.

"I'm sure, Grandpa," his twelve-year-old sister said. That face. Those hard, determined eyes. Her straight back and pursed lips. Stubborn. She would get her way. She never backed down when she got like that. Not now. Not then.

Jake saw his grandpa shoot Frank a look. To Jake, Grandpa Max looked the same then as he did now. Always an old man. Always fierce. He would have been just past fifty.

"Okay, then," Max said. "But I'll be right outside."

"I'll be fine," Gemma said, crossing her arms in front of her. Pure defiance. Pure Gemma.

Max kissed her head and stared hard at Frank. Jake knew that look too. *Don't mess with this kid or I'll end you.*

But he walked out of camera range and Jake heard the steel door close behind him. It still made the same squeak just before it slammed.

"Gemma," Frank started. "You know me, right? You remember I came to your school? I had you in my D.A.R.E. Class."

"Yes," Gemma answered.

"Good. And what your grandpa said is absolutely right. If you want him to come back in, that's fine. If you want to take a break. If you want to stop, we'll do whatever makes you feel comfortable."

"You want to know what I saw," she said.

"Yes."

"Then, no. I don't want Grandpa here. I don't want him to hear anything. I can't tell you everything if he's listening. It will make him sad."

Jake's stomach dropped. She was protecting Max. She was just a little kid, and already she felt it was her job to protect the adults.

"I'm sorry," Frank said. "I can't imagine how scared you must have been yesterday. But you're safe here, okay? I promise."

"I know."

"Do you want a glass of water? It's almost lunchtime. I can have anything you want brought in. I think there are still some donuts in my office across the hall."

"I don't want anything," she said.

"Okay," Frank said. "Then we'll get started. See that camera up there? It makes it easier for me to do my job if we record when we talk. Is that okay with you?"

"I don't care."

"Good. Honey, if there's anything you don't want to answer, you don't have to. If there's anything you want to ask me, that's okay too."

Gemma nodded. She kept her arms crossed in front of her, shielding herself. Jake wanted to reach through the screen and hug her. Such an odd thing, seeing her like this. He felt a wave of paternalistic affection for that little girl on the screen.

"Okay," Frank said. "Do you want to talk about the hard stuff first? Get it over with?"

"Yes," Gemma gushed. "Please."

"That's fine. So why don't you tell me what happened when you came home from school yesterday. You rode the bus?"

"Yeah. I always ride the bus. I'm the last stop on the route. I move up to the front of the bus and sit behind Mr. Kirby."

"He's a nice man," Frank said.

"Yeah. I got off. Mom wants us to come through the side door through the garage. So we can take our shoes off in the mudroom and hang our backpacks. I tried to, but the door was bolted. I couldn't get in."

"That was strange?"

"Yeah. So, I went around to the front door. We kept a hidden key under a rock out there. I had to find it. Sometimes Jakey uses it and forgets to put it back. But the door was open. Like standing open. I knew that wasn't right."

Jake watched Frank's posture shift. He leaned back a little. Said nothing. He wouldn't have wanted to interrupt Gemma. He'd have wanted her to just get her story out without any prompting or interjections.

Gemma took a breath as if she were steeling herself for the rest of it. Jake found himself doing the same thing.

"I went in," Gemma continued. "The house was really quiet. And the smell was off. Mom was supposed to be at work. She always puts something in the crock-pot on days she won't be home. When I get home, I'm supposed to stir it and turn the heat down. But I didn't smell anything cooking. I noticed that right away. So I put my bag down and walked into the kitchen."

She stopped. Finally unclenching her arms from around herself, she put her hands on the table. The resolution was good enough, Jake could see her chipped pink nail polish. Gemma did, too. She pulled her hands back and started picking at the polish on her right thumb.

"I saw my mom," she said. Her tone changed. Her body went rigid. She sounded almost robotic. "She was on the floor, curled up. It was strange. I thought it was spaghetti sauce. I thought she was down there cleaning it up. But it wasn't. I got closer to her and I saw that it was blood. It was all over her. I tried to see if she had a pulse. She was looking at me. So, I thought that meant she was alive. But she wasn't. She was cold. I knew what that meant."

"I'm so sorry, honey," Frank said.

"It smells like metal. I've read books where it says that. I didn't get that. Blood is blood. I've had cuts before. When Jakey was a baby, maybe one year old. I leaned down to kiss him in his crib. He headbutted me and I had a really big gash above my eyebrow. I still have a scar, see?"

Gemma brushed the hair away from her forehead and pointed above her left eyebrow. Jake smiled. She still had that scar. It was silvery and very faint. But it was there.

"I had to get six stitches. My dad thought I lost an eye; there was so much blood. It didn't smell like metal. It tasted salty though. I remember that. But yesterday. My mom. It smelled like metal."

"Do you remember what you did?" Frank asked gently.

"Yeah. I knew you're supposed to call 9-1-1. I ran upstairs first. I don't know why I was thinking this. My dad's car was in the garage. I hadn't really paid attention. But it popped into my head and I thought maybe he was home. Maybe he was asleep or in the shower. He was gone though. So, I ran back downstairs to make the call. But she had the phone in her hand. We have a long cord on the wall phone. It stretches all the way down the hall. The end of the cord had blood all over it too. And she wouldn't let go. I had to pull it out of her hand. Then I called the police. I told them my mom was hurt. I think I told her she was dead. I don't remember exactly what I said. The lady on the line was worried if there was somebody else in the house. I knew there wasn't."

"You did the right thing," Frank said.

Gemma stared past Frank. He imagined the only thing she could see just then was the horror she'd witnessed at their house.

"She was yelling at me," Gemma said. "The lady from 9-1-1. Telling me I was supposed to stay on the line. But I couldn't. I kept thinking about my little brother. He was gonna come home. He rides the bus too. The elementary school lets out an hour after the junior high. I just started to panic about Jakey coming home and seeing Mom like that. I know she wouldn't want that. I know she'd want me to take care of him. So I tried to. I called Mrs. Wayne, Ben's mom. Ben and Jakey are best friends and they ride the bus together. I called her and asked her to pick Jakey up and not let him ride the bus."

"That was pretty smart, Gemma," Frank said. "Very grown up."

Jake's heart twisted. He hadn't known that. The day for him was a blur. He'd only been seven. Everything before that day he remembered in images, small vignettes. But the day Grandpa Max came and got him from Ben's house and told him his mother and father were gone was the beginning of his linear memory.

She protected him. In the middle of the worst thing she'd ever seen. In the middle of her own shock and grief, she had thought of him. She had made sure he was somewhere safe. Jake's eyes welled with tears. He clenched his jaw until it subsided.

"It's just all I could think to do," she said. "When I hung up, I don't know what made me think of this. Why it popped into my head. But I went to the backyard. I wish I knew why. That's what I keep thinking about. Why did I go there? But I did. And I saw Dad. He was leaning against the willow tree. The one he was gonna cut down. He had blood all down his shirt. And ... his head."

For the first time, Gemma choked up. She drew her knees up and hugged them against her.

"It's okay," Frank said. "We don't have to talk about that."

"I didn't have to go to him," she said. "I knew he was dead too. You could see it. He was kind of flopped over to the side but still sort of sitting. And I could see most of the back of his head was gone. Did he put the gun in his mouth? He had to have. How else do you get hurt like that?"

Jake shuddered. He held the crime scene photos in his lap, facedown.

"Gemma, were both of your parents there that morning, before you went to school?"

She shook her head. "Just my mom."

"Did she seem upset or anything? Did she talk about your father?"

"No. I don't really remember though. She was maybe a little extra impatient. I took longer in the shower than she wanted me to. My hair was still kinda stringy and wet when I had to get on the bus. But it was just Mom. She wasn't mad at me. She wasn't yelling. She made me Pop-Tarts for breakfast. Cherry frosted. Jake likes the blueberry ones but those are gross. And they turn his poop green. He thinks that's hilarious."

Jake laughed. He'd forgotten that.

"Was Jake up when you left for school?"

"No, Mom likes to get me going before she deals with him. He's a slowpoke. She has to drag him out of bed by his feet. She dresses him when he's still kind of asleep. She sits on the floor with him in her lap and pulls his shirt over his head. His undies. His pants. Sometimes he's even snoring when she does it. It's easier though. Cuz when he wakes all the way up, he's a squirmy worm. You can't get him to sit still for a single second. We were talking about that, me and Mr. Kirby, the bus driver. He said he knew Dad was going to put Jakey in wrestling. Are you gonna coach him?"

He would. Not then. But later. And Frank Borowski would become a father figure to him. A mentor. The one man besides his grandfather he always knew he could trust. Until he couldn't.

"I'm sure I'll watch him sometimes," Frank answered.

"Sorry," Gemma said. "I went to La La Land. That's what Dad says. He laughs when I talk too much. Not mad. He says I can't get to the point."

"You're doing just fine," Frank said. "What about your dad? Has he been sick lately? Or different in any way?"

Gemma grew quiet. She chewed her bottom lip. Then she sat straight again and wrapped her arms around herself.

"He's been kinda sick. He was having a lot of trouble sleeping. It was going on for a while. My mom was getting worried. I found him in the middle of the night sometimes. I'd wake up to go to the bathroom and hear him hammering stuff out in his workshop. And it's been all the time. For a long time."

"Has he seemed angry? Or sad?"

Gemma shook her head. "Not really. But they've been yelling. They do it after we're supposed to be in bed. But I've heard it sometimes."

"Do you know what they've been yelling about?"

Gemma rubbed her left eye. "I don't know. They go to the basement so I can't always hear what they're saying. And I'm not a spy. But I know some of it was about the medicine my dad was supposed to take. He said he hates it and it's not working. My mom was pretty pissed about that. Er ... sorry. I'm not supposed to say pissed."

Frank laughed softly. "Gemma, it's okay. You can use whatever words you want to with me."

"And he's been spending the night somewhere else a lot over the last few weeks. They said it was for work. Overtime. And even that he was gonna go to third shift. But for some reason I thought they were lying."

"Did you ever ask either one of them about it? The arguing? Or him spending nights outside the house?"

"Mom blows me off. She smiles and says Dad's just tired. I know it was more than that though. He just ... he was spending all his time in that workshop. And he wasn't sitting down to dinner. Then ... I started watching what he ate. I didn't tell anybody, but he wasn't eating. Like ever. His clothes weren't fitting him. I asked him what's wrong. He just said everybody needs to go on a diet sometimes. And there have been a few times I caught my mom in her bedroom crying. She chased me out right away. Told me not to worry about it. She said it was menopause. But I'm not stupid. My mom's not ... wasn't ... even thirty."

Jake had no awareness of any of it. God, Gemma knew something was wrong. She tried to get them to tell her what.

"I just don't know anymore," she said. "I don't know what happened."

"It's okay," Frank said. "And it's okay to be angry or confused. Anything you feel, it's normal. You don't have to hide it from anyone. Okay? Will you promise me that?"

Gemma didn't answer for a long time. Jake knew her so well. He'd seen her every day of his life until he was eighteen years old. He recognized the way she eyed Frank at this point in the video. Cool. Almost condescending. His sister had always felt she was smarter than anyone in the room. That she knew what to do when they didn't.

"You said I could ask you anything," she finally said. "Did you mean that?"

Frank put his pen down. He would have ended the interview there. Jake would have. She'd described everything she witnessed to the best she could. If he went any farther, he'd risk implanting things in her head he didn't mean to.

"Yes," Frank said. "I meant it."

"They won't tell me things. My mom and dad hid everything. Now my grandparents are trying to do the same thing. But I'm not a baby."

"No, you're not. What do you want to know, Gemma?"

"My parents," she said. "Will there be an autopsy?"

Jake watched Frank go stiff as a board. Jake felt himself go rigid too. The question caught him off guard now as much as it clearly had Frank all those years ago.

"Gemma ..."

"I want to know," she persisted. "I know what they are. I need to know what's going to happen to my mom and dad now."

It would have presented Frank with a dilemma. He would wonder whether it was his place to tell her something as heavy as that. Maybe it was Max and Ava's decision. At the same time, she was clearly precocious. Frank himself taught Jake that when you interview children, you have to meet them where they are. And they are more resilient than most people think.

"Yes," Frank answered. Jake would have told her too. "In situations like this, we have to do autopsies."

Gemma nodded, satisfied. "Okay. Thank you for telling me."

Frank stayed silent. Gemma tapped her fingers against the table, clearly wrestling with something in her mind. Then she focused that laser stare on Frank and asked him an even harder question.

"My dad did this," she said. "He killed my mom, didn't he? I know he killed himself. I know you can't get a wound like that unless you give it to yourself."

Jake watched Frank's head drop a bit. "Honey, I ..."

"I already know, okay? I know it. But somebody needs to say the words. You need to say the words. My grandparents are afraid to. Or they don't want to. They talk in whispers. They give me looks. Grandma won't stop crying. They aren't going to say it to me. They aren't going to say it to Jake. Someday he'll ask and I will have to tell him. So you have to tell me. You have to say it. My father killed my mother."

Seared. Gutted. In Frank's place, Jake didn't know if he could have held it together in front of this child. He would have had no choice. Frank had no choice. She was brave. He could not be a coward in front of her. You fall apart later. When no one is looking. You fall apart alone.

"Yes," Frank said. A single word, delivered with clarity and bluntness. A confirmation he knew this child needed. "Your father killed your mother."

Gemma kept nodding as she processed the information. As it crystallized in her mind, giving finality and definition to the chaos and horror she'd seen with her own eyes. He no longer remembered not knowing. But of course no one would have told him right after it happened. He was just seven. But someone, sometime, told him the truth about it being a murder-suicide. He knew she was right that day. He knew it had to have been Gemma who said the words to him when he finally asked. He had no recollection of it. Not when. Not how. It was simply part of the fabric of who he was.

"Thank you," she said. "For telling me the truth. I have one last question. And you might not know. But it's something else my grandparents can't bring themselves to say."

"What is it?"

"I get to decide, don't I? At least, I have a say."

"In what, Gemma?"

"Where we live. I know we can't ever go back to that house. Jakey's already asking. I don't really know if he understands what dead is. That they're gone forever."

He did though. While he didn't remember when he was told the circumstances, he remembered the day Grandpa sat him down and told him Mom and Dad were gone. They were dead. He always knew that meant forever.

"It's going to be on me," Gemma said. "I know that. My grandma can barely talk right now. Grandpa is keeping her away from us so she doesn't upset us. She just sits in her room staring out the window. My grandpa's worried. But he won't say that either. But do I have a say?"

"Gemma, that's one I can't answer for you. But from what I know about your grandparents, of course they're going to take care of you."

That look from Gemma again. It was hard to describe. A tilt of her head. A squint. But she did that when someone was telling her something she knew wasn't the complete truth. Or that she knew better than they did. Yes. Their grandparents would take care of them. But he also knew Gemma felt responsible for him the second their parents died. Jake had resented her for it sometimes. Felt smothered by it. And the day he turned eighteen and graduated from high school, he'd gotten as far away from Blackhand Hills as he could. He'd been so tired of being the kid whose father killed his mother. At eighteen, he still believed people thought about him more than they really did.

He couldn't regret it. But he wanted to take back so many mean things he'd said to his sister when he was a hot-headed teenager. He knew in the span of this video, and the eighteen hours that had happened before it, his sister had gone from a child to an adult. And he felt strongly he had just freeze-framed the exact moment when that gelled. It was right here. Right then. As she stared at Frank Borowski, the little girl disappeared.

The video ended just two minutes later. Grandpa Max came back in, put his arms around Gemma and took her out. Frank rose slowly, turned, and walked over to the camera. Jake saw the redness in his eyes as he was about to spill the tears he'd kept in check in front of Gemma. He reached up, pressed the power button, sending the screen back to static.

Jake closed his eyes. He still clutched the crime scene photo folder to his chest. Slowly, he opened his eyes and laid the folder in his lap. This was the thing his sister had tried to protect him from. He'd seen hundreds of crime scenes like the one she described. It was just like the Katzes' house. It had stirred the ghosts Gemma tried to bury.

He could have put the folder back in the box. But something made Jake open it. He felt strongly that he must bear witness to the thing that had altered his sister in the literal blink of an eye.

He looked down. His breath catching, he flipped through every photograph. His mother in the kitchen. The blood in the tile grout. Her bloody handprint on the mustard-yellow kitchen phone. Then, his father slumped against that willow tree Jake had forgotten all about until now. He had climbed it. He had loved it. Its roots now watered with his father's blood.

He'd seen worse things than this. Bloodier crime scenes. Victims in various gruesome stages of decay. He'd never been squeamish. He wasn't now. But as he stared at them, grief speared through him. He had forgotten what it was like to miss them so much he couldn't breathe. The puzzle of his life seemed to break apart and reform tonight. More sections fleshed out. More flashes of what life was like before that day.

He remembered being so sleepy, cradled in his mother's arms as she pulled his socks on. He curled against her, the shampoo she used making her smell like flowers and sunlight. His father putting him on a stool in his workshop, making him hammer nails in boards. Catching night crawlers near Grandpa's pond. Both of them getting in trouble for wearing their good tennis shoes and tracking mud back into the house.

God. Gemma. Part of this felt like an intrusion into a secret she had every right to keep. But it also felt like a history that belonged to Jake. He never should have opened that box. At the same time, he wished he had opened it long before.

Eighteen

Jake spent the morning reading Ramirez's cell forensics report in more detail. It was a good, mind-numbing distraction from everything he saw last night from his parents' murder file. Unfortunately, it told him nothing. Cam and Rianne Katz didn't appear to have any animosity toward each other or any idea that someone was about to kill them both.

Whit Roundtree's phone was no help either, other than to back up his alibi that he hadn't been anywhere near Blackhand Hills the night of the Katzes' murder. At least his phone hadn't. With no physical evidence tying him to the scene, he had no probable cause to arrest him. Or anyone.

A little after ten, Meg walked in looking grim. Jake leaned back and rolled his chair away from his desk. "You don't look like you have good news."

"Neither do you," she said.

"I have no news," he said. "Not a damn thing. Every lead I have goes to a dead end."

"I'm really beginning to hate this case," she said.

Jake couldn't argue the point.

"So what's up?" he asked her.

"Something just came across my desk. I thought it would be better if you heard it from me here instead of ... well ... anywhere else."

Jake felt a tingling sensation in his fingers. What now?

"9-1-1 call came in last night. There was some kind of library fundraiser at the Carlow Township branch. The Arden Foundation sponsored it. A children's literacy drive."

"Okaay," Jake said. He had nothing to do with his mother's side of the family. They'd disowned both him and Gemma right around the time their parents died. Other than his Uncle Rob, he hadn't seen any other Arden since he came back to Blackhand Hills more than three years ago.

"Your grandmother had some sort of incident. She collapsed. They're saying it was a heart attack. A pretty bad one. She's at Hope Hospital. I don't know much more than that but I can try to find out."

Grandmother. Sometimes Jake forgot he still had a living one. Grandma Cashen died almost twenty years ago of an aggressive, fast-moving form of ovarian cancer. It happened during his freshman year in college. He only remembered meeting his mother's mother once when he was a kid. He remembered her as cold and distant. And his grandfather, his mother's father, pulled her away from them as if they were lepers.

"Thanks for telling me," he said.

"You okay?"

"Yeah. I'm sorry. I know she's my grandmother, but you know I don't have any dealings with my mother's people if I can avoid it."

"Maybe I shouldn't have said anything. But someone was going to tell you or you would have found out from the local news. Of course I don't know the full details, but from what the paramedics were saying, she coded in the ambulance at least once."

"Got it," Jake said, turning back to his computer screen.

"Okay," Meg said. "I'll let you get back to work. I know you'll tell me something when you have something to tell."

Birdie walked in just behind Meg. She'd spent the morning running down her lead with Cam Katz's gym.

"Good," Birdie said. "You're both here." She had a file under her arm and slapped it on the table in the middle of the room. She opened it and pulled out a printout of a rap sheet and mugshot.

"Meet Benny Bellucci."

Bellucci had a wide red head and a neck just as thick. Another musclehead.

"Cam's dealer?" Jake said.

"In the flesh. Good news and bad news."

Meg closed the office door and leaned against it. "Give me the bad news first."

"Airtight alibi," Birdie said. "Bellucci's been in jail in Pike County for the last two months. Serving ninety days for possession. Seems he dabbled in cocaine along with illegal steroids. So, he couldn't have killed the Katzes."

"What's the good news?" Jake asked.

"Pretty much just that I found him. Oh, and I also confirmed he's the only one Katz had any dealings with. They had a signal. When Katz needed something from him. He'd turn in a workout glove to the lost and found at the gym. Bellucci would go to the desk and say he was missing one. If it was there, Katz and Bellucci would meet up about a block away."

"Great," Meg said. "Do you have anything tying employees or management at the gym to this?"

"Not so far," she said. "But it's worth turning over to vice. I haven't talked to the gym's owner or anyone else. I wanted to make sure you weighed in, Sheriff."

"Appreciate it. I don't want you two heading off on tangents on this one. Give your report to Detective McDonald."

"Roger that," Birdie said.

Meg opened the door and left Birdie and Jake alone. Birdie sat on the edge of the table. "Sorry," she said. "I was hoping that was gonna go somewhere. And it's not completely dead. Bellucci had a supplier. I've talked to the detective handling his case for Pike County. Filled her in on why I wanted to talk to him. If she kicks over anything else that might be related to our case, she'll let me know. I'm not optimistic. Bellucci's an idiot. I just don't get the vibe that he's part of some high-level organized crime syndicate. For whatever else he was, it looks like Katz was paid up. And he was being discreet. No rumors out there he was talking to anyone he shouldn't have been. Nobody's got him registered as a CI."

"He's also too high profile," Jake said. "Somebody had to know killing him was going to draw attention online. It just seems too sloppy to be a calculated hit."

"This thing's gonna go cold," she said.

Jake turned his chair and stared at the whiteboard Birdie drew up. She walked over to it and stuck Bellucci's mugshot under the tier she'd drawn for Katz's gym. Then she drew a big red X through both.

"The Roundtrees are alibied out. So is Bellucci. We don't have any physical evidence tying anyone else to that scene. The dog-walker never saw anyone coming or going who shouldn't have been," Birdie said. "What are we missing, Jake?"

He got up and stood beside her. "Money. Revenge. Silence. Heat of passion. Or some random nut job."

"We have no reports of any murders with a similar MO in the area. In the state, actually. No sign of forced entry. Nothing was taken from the house. Both victims died wearing their rings and jewelry," she said.

Jake walked up and took Rianne Katz's picture down. "Maybe we've been looking at this the wrong way."

"What do you mean?" Birdie asked.

"We've assumed Cameron was the target. He's the one who had possible enemies with clear motives to kill him. From the beginning, we haven't been able to understand why someone would have taken Rianne out too."

"She walked in on something," Birdie said. "Witnessed her husband getting shot. Like you said. Silence is a motive."

"No sign of a struggle. No defensive wounds on either of them. He's shot while seated on the couch. She falls to the ground in the kitchen. I don't know. I just feel it in my bones that Cameron watched his wife die. He was sitting in the direct line of sight of her body. I know it's just me speculating."

"I feel that too," she agreed.

"So what if Cameron was never the target?" Jake said. "What if Rianne was?"

"But why? There's nothing on her phone suggesting *she* was carrying on an affair. By all accounts, she was in love with her husband and looking forward to building a life with him. She wasn't doing drugs. No skeletons in her closet like Cameron had."

"When you talked to her friends," Jake said. "We were focused on what motive Cam would have had to kill her. We were still thinking of this as a murder-suicide. I want to talk to them again. We don't know enough about Rianne. Her parents think she was a perfect angel. Maybe she wasn't. Maybe now that they've had to time to absorb both victims were murdered, they might have more to say."

"I think so too," Birdie said.

Jake's phone buzzed. A text from Gemma.

> Come get lunch. I hired Smokin' Eddie for the week. Brisket melts in your mouth. I'm selling out.

He hadn't seen her. Hadn't talked to her since watching her interview tape. He wasn't planning on telling her about it. What would be the point? She knew him so well, she would probably suspect something was wrong the second he looked at her.

"You free for lunch?" Jake asked Birdie. "Gemma's got a smoker out there."

"Sounds delish," she said. "I've actually already got a date."

Jake raised a brow but resisted the urge to ask her if it was Kieth the musclehead.

"I'm meeting my nephew. Can you believe that? Travis has actually offered to take me out to lunch and pay for it. We're just going to Papa's Diner. Say hi to Gemma for me."

"Got it," Jake said. "When does Travis leave for West Point?"

Birdie's face fell. He knew she was proud of Travis, but dreading the day he left.

"Next week," she said. "He's heading down a week early to get the lay of the land. I offered to go with him but he doesn't want me to."

"He's a big boy," Jake said.

"That's the other thing I keep forgetting to tell you. My mom is coming in a few days before Travis leaves. He hates the idea, but I'm having a cookout. Just a small get-together. He wouldn't let me throw him a grad party for high school. So this is the compromise. You have to come. I'll text you the details."

"Wouldn't miss it," Jake said. "Can you set up a meeting with Rianne Katz's friends? As soon as tomorrow, preferably."

"On it," she said. "Now go see your sister. If you can snake me some brisket or pulled pork, I wouldn't hate it."

"I'll see what I can do," Jake said. The thought of Smokin' Eddie made Jake's stomach growl loud enough for both of them to hear it.

Smokin' Eddie's barbecue did not disappoint. Jake wolfed down two brisket sliders and a heaping serving of potato salad. He'd have loved a cold beer to wash it all down, but he was still on duty for a couple more hours.

Eddie's magic was a boon to Gemma's normal lunch crowd as well. She meant to sit with him while he ate, but had spent the last forty minutes zipping all around the pub helping the servers, bartenders, and bussers.

She managed them all with blistering speed and efficiency. His sister was in her element here. In charge. Barking orders like a drill sergeant. Catching disasters before they could happen. He'd always known her like this. Bossy. Brazen. Sometimes annoying as hell. Gemma thought things had to be her way or no way. The frustrating part was that she was right about that far more than she wasn't. And she'd been doing it all since that awful night. She would never stop. Never slow down. She'd be telling Jake what to do from her own coffin if she could swing it.

Finally, she caught a lull and made her way over to Jake's booth. Sweat beaded her brow. She had her bleach-blonde hair pulled back in a ponytail on top of her head. She'd sweated off most of her makeup. It made her look younger to Jake. It was hard not to see that twelve-year-old girl in Frank's interview sitting in front of him.

"You okay?" she asked.

Jake smiled. It was just as he knew it would be. She pegged him instantly.

"I'm fine," he said. "Just a little stressed from this case I'm working on." The truth, from a certain point of view.

"You work too hard."

"Ha. There's the pot calling the kettle black."

"I need to find my own Smokin' Eddie," she said. "This is great, but he's taking a huge cut. Not that he doesn't deserve it. You think Gramps would part with his barbecue recipe? I've got my eye on a Myron Mixon smoker. It'll set me back a bit, but look at this place? It'll pay for itself in three months or less."

"You gotta find somebody to cook it," Jake said. "Grandpa Max is a master, but he can't handle anything like this. And you can't mention it. Cuz he'll want to try. So you gotta have somebody in place before you even talk to him. Somebody he'll endorse. He'll fight you at first. But I think he'll eventually cough up his secrets."

"It's Cashen's Irish Pub," she said. "He can be the star of the show. I'll give him all the credit. He can sit at that copper top like a king as all his loyal subjects stuff their faces with brisket burgers. He can even help me tweak the menu items. It'll give him something constructive to do."

"I agree with all of that," Jake said. "Just don't drag me into it when you ask."

"Coward," she teased.

"I gotta tell you something," Jake said. "I heard because it came through as a 9-1-1 call. Grandma Del had some kind of heart attack. Sounds like it was pretty serious. I don't know the details, but the paramedics said it was grim."

Gemma's smile faltered. "What are we supposed to do with that?"

Jake shrugged. "Nothing, I guess. Landry told me because she didn't want somebody catching me off guard with it. I don't want someone doing that to you either."

"More than half the people in this town have probably forgotten or never knew we're supposed to be part of that family."

Jake drank his iced tea. "The Ardens have forgotten."

"Good old Uncle Rob has to be salivating," she said. "From what I hear, Grandpa Paul already has one foot in the grave. As soon as Del keels over too, everything they have will be free and clear."

"You really think there's much left?" Jake asked. Their mother's ancestors had been founding settlers in this region. A great-great-something grandfather had established the clay mill that employed most of the county at one time. They built Ardenville, the old company town where most of the early millers had lived. It was an abandoned relic now, except for the cemetery and the elaborate stone monument they'd erected for his mother. She had been the first person buried there in fifty years. She was also the last.

"Oh, I think Paul has squirreled away plenty of his millions."

It had been a sore point with his grandfather for decades now. The Cashens were never poor, but they lived modestly. Jake had to take out loans for college. Grandpa scrimped for Gemma's braces and the rest of their medical bills growing up. All on account of the crappy insurance Grandpa was left with after devoting thirty years and a lot of his mobility to the mill the Ardens owned and profited from. He felt that the least the Ardens could do was contribute to some of the expenses for their own grandchildren.

But no. Because Sonya Arden had sullied herself with the likes of a Cashen against her family's wishes. Got pregnant with Gemma at seventeen and chose Jake's father and her unborn child over her parents' bribes. He'd heard a rumor that they were going to pay her to have an abortion.

"Well," Jake said. "Anyway. I figured you should know. Do with it what you want."

"What are you going to do with it?"

"Not a damn thing," Jake said. "I don't wish the woman ill. I never did. Mom loved her. You're named after her."

Gemma's expression turned sour, as if she'd just smelled a pile of dog shit. "Not anymore. You know I dropped Adele as my middle name the first time I got married."

Jake's phone vibrated on the table beside him with a text from Birdie.

> Shantal Watson, Rianne Katz's bestie, is okay with meeting us at the library where she works tomorrow morning. I'll send the address. Pick me up at seven.

He gave her a thumbs up in response.

"Thanks for telling me, I guess," Gemma said.

"Do you think about her much?" Jake asked.

"Grandma Del? Uh, no. I make a point not to. Or any of them."

"No," Jake said. He took a breath, hesitant to tell her what he really meant. "I mean Mom."

Gemma cocked her head to the side. "Of course I think about her. What brings that up?"

"Nothing. Just talking about Del, I guess."

"Is there something you want to ask me?"

Yes, there were a thousand things.

"No," he said. "But I realize I never do. You're always asking me if I'm okay. I usually don't ask you."

Gemma smiled. She grabbed the towel she had stuffed in her apron and playfully swatted Jake's arm with it. "Don't worry about me, baby brother. It's my job to worry about you."

She got up quickly, leaned across the table, grabbed his face in both hands and placed a big, slobbery kiss on his forehead. Then she raced off to put out whatever kitchen crisis she sensed brewing.

"I love you too, sis," he said to her back as he watched her go.

NINETEEN

Shantal Watson agreed to meet Jake and Birdie at the library in Athens where she worked. She'd reserved a quiet study room. Lucy Vane, Rianne Katz's other college friend, ended up being too upset to make the trip.

"Thanks for making time for us," Birdie said after she introduced Jake. The study room had seating in the form of a long L-shaped couch that ran along two walls. Jake and Birdie sat next to each other and Shantal took the opposite corner.

"I have about thirty minutes before I have to start storytime for the five-year-olds."

"This shouldn't take long," Jake promised. "Are you aware of the current focus of our investigation?"

"Just that now you're saying both Cam and Rianne were murdered by somebody else?"

"We believe that, yes," Jake said.

"You think it was Rianne somebody was after?"

"We don't know," Birdie said. "But at this point we can't rule anything out. That's where we're hoping you might be able to help."

Shantal shook her head. "Were they robbed? I don't think either one of them had anything of real value. But people are crazy."

"I was hoping you could help me get to know Rianne a little bit more," Jake said. "I know when Detective Wayne talked to you a few weeks ago, we were more concerned with Rianne's relationship with Cameron. We still are. But I'd like to go back a little further. You've known her for a long time. Her parents told us you and Lucy were as close to her as anyone in the last few years."

"We've been tight. Yes. But less so in the last year, I'd say. Since she started getting really serious with Cam."

"Shantal," Jake said. "Can you think of any reason why someone would want to hurt Rianne?"

Shantal turned her palms up, shrugging. "Not really. Ri was as sweet as they come. Maybe too sweet."

"What do you mean?" Birdie asked.

"Ri was nice to everyone. She was the kind of person who always wanted to give people the benefit of the doubt, you know? No matter what kind of signals they gave off. She didn't like it when other people were catty around her. Sometimes it got annoying. Lucy and I are a little sassier. But that's why we loved her so much. Ri was one of the few truly good people I knew in my life."

"What about the men she dated?" Jake asked. "Did she have a lot of boyfriends before getting together with Cam?"

"Not really. She was engaged before. Maybe three years ago."

Jake took out his notepad. "What was his name?"

"Nate," she said. "Nate Parra. They met in college. Nate was a friend of a friend. A nice guy. But Lucy and I never thought it was a good match."

"Why's that?" Jake asked.

"I don't want you to misinterpret me. Nate isn't somebody I'd ever worry about hurting Rianne. He wasn't jealous. He didn't have anger issues. And I don't think he and Rianne had been in contact for a while. Though you could never tell with her."

"What do you mean?" Birdie asked.

Shantal let out a breath. "When I said Rianne was the nicest person you'd ever want to meet, I meant she really was too nice. She was the kind of girl guys could fall in love with easily. We used to call her a stalker magnet."

Jake and Birdie exchanged a look.

"She had stalkers?" Birdie asked.

"No. Ugh. I'm sorry. I'm not making sense. It's hard to explain. Like we'd go to a bar or the gym or something. Some guy would start checking Rianne out. Maybe ask for her number. She just wanted to be friends with everybody. So she'd go out with a guy once or twice, but she wasn't good at telling them when she didn't want it to go beyond that. I don't know how many times she had these hangers-on. Guys who didn't read the signals that Ri wasn't into them like that."

"Did she ever express any worry or concern about any of these men?" Jake asked.

"She wasn't afraid. But like Nate, for example. I swear, she never really wanted to marry him. But he asked. They'd been dating for almost two years. She didn't know how to say no. As time went on, she knew she had to break it off. So she did. But it wasn't clean.

She kept texting with him. Met him for lunch a couple of times. Lucy and I wanted to shake her. She needed to be a little harsher. Set a better boundary. I know there were some guys she dated that probably felt led on."

"Did Nate ever talk to you or Lucy about how he felt?" Birdie asked.

"A couple of times, yes. It was awkward because he was part of our extended circle of friends. It was pretty common for us all to be in social situations together. Once when Rianne brought another date, I knew Nate was really hurt. I actually kind of got into it with her after that one."

"How did she take it?" Jake asked.

"Not well. She started to cry. I backed off."

"Did you ever talk to Nate about it after the fact?" Jake asked.

"Lucy and I both did. Like I told you. He was a really nice guy. But we ran into him and sat down and told him he really needed to move on. Rianne wasn't interested in starting anything back up, no matter how nice she seemed."

"How did he take it?" Birdie asked.

Shantal's face dropped. "I want to be really clear here. In no way do I think Nate Parra had anything to do with what happened to Rianne. This all went down a long time ago. It's been over three years since she broke things off with Nate. I think he moved back to his hometown."

"Do you have contact information for him?" Jake asked. "I'd like to talk to him."

"Do you know if he's even aware of what happened to Rianne?" Birdie asked.

"I honestly don't know. It didn't occur to me to reach out. Yeah. I have a cell phone for him. I don't know if it's still good." She took out her phone, pulled up Parra's contact, and turned the screen so Jake could see it. He jotted down the number.

"You said there were other guys you thought Rianne might have led on," Birdie said. "Do you have any information on them? Names? Numbers?"

"No," Shantal said. "I really don't. I'm sorry. Ri dated Nate. They broke up. A year or so later, she met Cameron. They got pretty serious pretty quick. If she dated in between, it wasn't anything."

"Do you remember who that might have been?" Jake asked. "Anybody she dated in between?"

Shantal shook her head no. "We graduated. Lucy, Ri, and I. We went our separate ways. We're always in touch. But it got hard to plan things together in person. We tried to get together once a season. Just weekend getaways or meet-ups. In the last year, we didn't even really do that. Ri was busy planning her wedding and trying to save money."

"That's understandable," Birdie said.

"I wish I could give you something you could use," Shantal said. "Lucy and I both do. Ri was just about as normal a girl as I know. She didn't have enemies. She only had friends. Are you really sure about this? You really think it was someone trying to kill Ri and not Cameron?"

"No," Jake said. "We're not sure of anything yet. I just don't want to leave any stones unturned."

"And she never expressed any worries to you in those last few weeks or months?" Birdie asked. "About money? Her job? Anything?"

"No. And for the last six months, when we talked it was by text. You have her phone, right? You can see everyone she communicated with?"

"We can," Jake said.

"There wasn't much there," Birdie said. "I don't even think Nate Parra was listed in her contacts. Do you know why that would be?"

"I do, actually. Ri was on her mom and dad's cell phone plan until she graduated. Then she went and got her own plan. I happen to know it because I went with her to the store to help her pick out a phone. I needed one at the same time."

"That makes sense," Jake said. "Do you remember if she traded the old one in?"

"Gosh. No. That was years ago. I'm sorry. I can't remember."

"What about her wedding?" Birdie asked. "You and Lucy were her bridesmaids. How did she seem that night?"

"Good. Great, actually. Ri wanted to be a bride forever. And she was so gracious. Nothing Bridezilla about her. The only real tension I picked up on was from her parents. It was clear they weren't big fans of Cameron. That kind of made me sad, because he really seemed to make her happy. And it wasn't anything overt. Just looks I saw them give Cameron. The Timineys are hard to warm up to for anybody. They're just old-fashioned. Set in their ways. I think they wanted Ri to *marry up*. Which is crazy. She's not the Princess of Wales."

"Nobody showed up who shouldn't have been there as far as you know?" Jake asked.

"No. It was a low-key event. They got married at the state park. Outdoors. Then they rented space inside the pavilion. I wanna say she had no more than a hundred guests. Lucy was the only other person I knew. We were the only ones she invited from college. It was all her family and a few of the people she worked with."

"What about Cam's side?" Birdie asked.

"There were a couple of people from the gym. His business partner, that's who I walked with. His niece was the flower girl. His brother walked with Lucy. But I bet he had fifteen people there at most. Everyone else was Rianne's side."

Another woman tapped on the door and poked her head in. She pointed at her watch.

"I'll be right out, Loris," Shantal said, then rolled her eyes. Then she turned to Jake. "I'm sorry. I'm going to have to get back to work. I'm also sorry I can't be much help."

"You have been," Jake said.

"I'll talk to Lucy. See if she remembers anything I don't. It's been hard for her. We both loved Ri, but Lucy's taking this really hard. She said you can call her if you need to talk to her."

"I may," Jake said. "And if there's anything either of you can think of that might help, and it can be anything at all. Even something you don't think is important. Please give me a call. Day or night."

He pulled out a business card and wrote his personal cell on it. Shantal took it and slipped it into her back pocket. He and Birdie rose. Shantal walked them out to the parking lot. It was a bright, sunny day. Temps were approaching ninety. Jake slid on his sunglasses and then shook Shantal's hand.

He and Birdie walked to his cruiser. He blasted the A/C as they pulled out.

"What do you think?" Birdie asked.

"Not much. But I definitely wanna talk to Nate Parra."

"I'll run a background check on him," Birdie said. "It's probably a long shot, but like you said. No stone unturned."

"Good. Maybe we'll get lucky."

"Something has to break, Jake. This wasn't random. It couldn't be."

"You've seen the same thing I did on Rianne's phone," Jake said. "Nate Parra wasn't important enough to her to carry his contact info over to her new phone. That's worth pursuing. If she deleted him from her life altogether, I want to know why."

"Do you think we could pull records from her old cell number?"

Jake scratched his chin. "Unlikely we'd be able to get a text or call history going back that far. I suppose I could ask her parents if they happen to have her old phone. It's a long shot, but worth an ask."

"Good idea," Birdie said.

By the time they got back to the station, they were two hours into overtime. Jake wanted to head back into the office, but knew Landry was getting heat for overtime approvals. Plus, he needed to think. Or, more than that, he needed to try to shut his brain off, at least for a night.

"Will I see you tomorrow?" Birdie asked, standing near her car.

"Huh? Is it Saturday?"

"Jake," she said, unamused. "Travis's party. Four o'clock. He's expecting you. So am I."

"Wouldn't miss it," Jake said. Though it had completely slipped his mind. Thank God she'd reminded him. Birdie Wayne was the last person whose bad side he wanted to be on.

TWENTY

Travis Wayne looked more like his father every time Jake laid eyes on him. In the year since he graduated high school, Trav had filled out. Put on twenty pounds of solid muscle, and grown close to two inches taller. It happened like that a lot with kids his age after their wrestling careers ended and they stopped having to cut weight. It gave Travis a new tough, rugged look that made Jake proud as much as it awakened his grief for his best friend.

They'd already said their goodbyes two days before. Travis wanted today to be a happy occasion, not bittersweet. There'd been plenty of that for the past month and a half.

"I can't get over it," Gordon "Jolly" Byrne said as he walked up to Jake, sipping a Modelo. Jolly had also been close with Ben Wayne and a former teammate. Their heavyweight.

"It's a little shocking if you haven't seen him for a while," Jake agreed.

"Ben would be so proud. I mean, he'd be scared shitless about sending his kid off to join the military. But he'd be damn proud."

"It's good you came," Jake said. "Travis is hiding it well, but he misses his dad a lot today."

"Where's Ben's dad?" Jolly asked.

Jake looked across the yard. Birdie stood near the grill. Grandpa Max volunteered to man it and was churning out burgers and dogs. Jake and Gemma figured he couldn't get himself into too much trouble. Plus, Ryan stayed nearby ready to step in if the old man lit himself on fire. But a bit off to the side, holding court at a picnic table, was Judith Wayne, Ben's mom and Travis's grandmother. She had Alzheimer's but still recognized everyone she loved. She'd made the trip along with her health aide, a pretty red-headed woman who sat beside her holding Judith's hand.

"Birdie said the trip was too much for Rudy. He's declined quite a bit since his stroke a few years ago. He's in assisted living and the trip would have been too much for him."

"Man," Jolly said. "I had such a crush on Judy back in the day. Is she doing okay?"

Jake laughed. Jake thought of Judith as more of a mother figure. She'd stepped into that role plenty after Jake's mom died. She had been with him the moment he found out about the loss. It had been her shoulder he cried into when he finally accepted that his grandfather's words were true.

"She's all right," Jake said. "Birdie says events like this still bring her some joy. She can talk about old times."

Another of their classmates waved to Jolly. Jake stayed back as Jolly walked over to talk to him.

Aidan and a few of his little friends were playing basketball in the driveway. Temps were close to ninety today and Jake gave Ryan a look across the yard. In addition to keeping Gramps from burning himself to death, Ryan was making sure he stayed hydrated because he refused to come out of the sun.

"You okay?" Birdie seemed to materialize out of thin air. He'd been so focused on Grandpa at the grill, he didn't hear her come up.

"I'm good."

"You're kinda quiet today," she said.

"So are you. I should be asking you how you're holding up."

Birdie gave him a somewhat sad smile. He put an arm around her shoulder. "I'm not going to get to talk to him for a while after he gets there."

"He'll be okay."

"I know. And he's ready. I've had a long talk with him."

"So have I." Jake smiled. "And I think he's more than ready too."

"Still, it's going to be pretty lonely in that house all by myself. I'm actually thinking of moving. I was gonna talk to Gemma about that later. That is, if she still has her realtor license."

"I think she does. Where are you thinking you'd move to?"

"I don't know. They're putting those new condos in Lublin Township. Not far from you, actually. We could be neighbors. And I don't need all that house anymore. Four bedrooms. Two acres of yard to maintain. I'm over it. It was Ben and Abby's dream, not mine. It was important to me for Travis to have continuity after we lost Ben. Now? He's not coming back."

Her voice trailed off.

"He's not leaving forever, Birdie."

"He is though," she said. "Sure. He'll visit. And I'll have a spare room whenever he does. But he's never going to live with me again. You know it."

"It's been three years, Birdie," Jake said.

He squeezed her tight and stopped himself from giving her a brotherly kiss on her temple. If they were alone, he would have. But here, enough of the people they worked with could see. He'd been accused of playing favorites with her since the second she joined the Sheriff's Department.

Sensing his intentions, Birdie pulled away. It was a strange line they walked. Birdie was like family. She was Ben's little sister. He knew Ben would have wanted him to look out for her in the same way he would have wanted Ben to look out for Gemma had he been the one to take a bullet to the head.

"I better check on the ice situation," she said.

"Let me know if you need me to run out and get more," he said.

"Don't worry. There are twenty teenage boys over there. I've got enough grunts to boss around. Do me a favor though. Go talk to my mom. She's been asking about you. She's having a really good day. I was worried it would be too much for her today. But Lindy, her aide, says she's holding up really well. Mom's more talkative than she's seen her in weeks."

Jake gave Birdie a salute.

As soon as she disappeared around the side of the house, he noticed Judith Wayne was in a rare moment of solitude. Birdie and Travis's friends and family had been catching up with her all day. Lindy sat quietly beside her.

Jake grabbed a plastic cup and filled it with lemonade to bring to her.

"Jake!" Judith beamed as he walked up. "I was hoping you'd get around to me. Sit. Keep an old lady company for a while."

"Who are you calling old?" Jake said.

She waved him off. Jake introduced himself to Lindy. "I can sit with Mrs. Wayne for a while," he told her. "We're old friends, aren't we, Judy?"

"I used to change Jakey's diapers." Judith laughed.

"Are you sure?" Lindy asked.

"Absolutely," he said. "You haven't eaten anything. Go grab a plate. I'll holler if I need you. Promise."

"I'll just be over there, Mrs. Wayne," Lindy said.

"Go eat," Judith said. "You're too skinny. Let me catch up with this boy."

Jake sat on the bench opposite her and handed her the lemonade. Judith sipped it then guzzled down almost half the cup at once.

"That tastes so good," she said.

"Are you too hot?" Jake asked. "I can take you into the house ..."

"Shh. I'm fine. I don't want to be in the house with all the other old people. I like people watching out here just fine."

"Good," Jake said. "Me too."

"He looks so much like his dad, doesn't he?"

Travis was across the yard with a group of his friends. He threw his head back, laughing at one of their jokes.

"He does," Jake said.

"I don't know where he's gotten off to," she said. "I told Benny this morning to help Max with that grill." Birdie had warned him about this. Judith often forgot that her son had died. Jake wished he could. It was one blessing of her dementia. She had crafted a different world in her head. One where Ben was just around the corner.

"Benny loves you so much."

She reached across the table and put her hand over his.

"How are you feeling?" Jake asked.

"Hot," she said. "But it's good to be out in the sun. I'm pasty white."

Judith didn't let go of his hand. "Erica's worried about you. Are you taking care of yourself?"

The question took him off guard. But Birdie warned him of that. Judith could snap back in and out. She could be completely lucid and present one moment, confused the next.

Judith Wayne eyed him. She wasn't buying a word he said. "I saw on the news this morning. That poor couple who died. That's your case? You and Erica?"

"It is," Jake said.

"She turned it off. Didn't want me to be upset. Are you? You know I think about Sonya and your dad a lot."

"Really," he said. "Yeah. I mean, of course. But I'm okay. Really."

"I miss them too," she said. "I remember everything like it was yesterday."

He gave her a side-long glance. Birdie also said his mother's recall of distant past events was crystal clear. Better than it had been before her dementia progressed.

Jake was torn. He didn't want to upset her. And yet, Judith Wayne might be the one person he could safely ask about what she knew about those awful days.

He'd told no one about the suicide note except for the Wise Men. He hadn't yet been able to confront Grandpa Max about it. Part of him harbored anger about it toward his grandfather, even though he knew that probably wasn't fair. He also knew the safest thing for him to do with Judith was change the subject.

He didn't.

"Did you know how sick he was?" he asked.

Judith put her cup down. Her eyes cleared as she stared at Jake. When she spoke next, it was as if a switch had flipped.

"No. I knew he was struggling. Well, I knew your mother was struggling. But she didn't confide in me. I wasn't her best friend back then. It was you and Ben who connected us more than anything. So we talked a lot. Yes. And I could see how bad your father looked. Skinny. Gray skin. Agitated. I knew he wasn't sleeping and I knew they were having trouble between them. But God, no, Jake. I didn't know how sick he was. It was a shock to everyone."

There were parts of his father's letter that gnawed at him. Most of it made no sense. He talked about voices. People he'd never heard of before. But he talked about "Brother Rob."

"He was paranoid," Judith continued.

"About what? My grandfather said something about him having a bad reaction to the medication he was taking."

Judith raised a brow. "I don't know if that's what made him paranoid or not. But ... there was an incident about a week before he died."

"What incident?"

"It just wasn't right," she said. "What happened at your mother's funeral? That's something I always wanted to tell you. To make sure you knew. What your uncle and your grandfather did ..."

"There was an incident at the funeral?" Jake asked. "I don't remember, really. I know there were two of them. One for her. A separate one for him."

"I went to both," she said. "The one for your father was so beautiful. Just his closest family and friends. The spot your grandmother picked out was just so lovely, overlooking that stream. Do you go there often?"

"He does," Jake said, gesturing toward Grandpa Max. "Every weekend. I have to take him down sometimes. His eyesight isn't what it was. But ... I don't really remember my mother's funeral. Just that abomination of a monument her parents erected for her in the Ardenville cemetery."

Judith spit out a laugh. "You know, I thought the same damn thing. I just never wanted to say anything. Sonya would have hated that. She wanted to be cremated."

"She did?" Jake asked, shocked. "How do you know?"

"It's funny the things you remember," she said. "But maybe two months before she died, Sonya and I went to a funeral together. One of our grade school teachers passed away. Mrs. Henderson. Boy, was she a battle-ax. Anyway, we went. The poor woman looked so terrible in her casket. She'd suffered from cancer for a long time and Melvin Chalmer, the old undertaker, could work miracles. But Livia Henderson looked ghoulish and gray. Anyway, I walked up to the casket with your mom. When we walked back, she told me she hoped when her time came they would just put her in an urn and spread her ashes out on Echo Lake. Your dad taught her how to fish out there."

Jake felt a lump in his throat. He'd never heard that either. Was this all true? Was she remembering accurately? But everything she said *felt* true.

"I didn't know that."

"Well, she said it. I tried to tell Paul and Adele that. They wouldn't hear of it. And I know they were grieving something awful. But the way they conducted themselves at your mother's funeral. Well, it's hard to forgive."

"I don't remember that either. It's all just such a blur."

"Of course it is," she said. "And your grandfather was so dignified. That just sticks in my head. He put on his suit. Went to the barber. He looked so handsome. He had his arm around your grandmother. I think he was holding her up. Gemma had you by the hand and the four of you walked into that chapel. Paul caused such a scene."

There were flashes of memory. Both of his grandfathers standing nose to nose.

"They didn't want us there," he said. "Did they ask us to leave?"

Judith squeezed his hand. "Your Grandpa Max wouldn't allow it. He marched the four of you right up to the front and knelt in the pew. It took my breath away."

Rage burned in Jake's heart. He'd forgotten. Gemma had cried. It was the first time he'd seen her do that since they heard about their parents. But in the pew, holding his hand so tight. She cried.

"Thank you," he said. "I'd forgotten. I should have remembered that."

"Honey, you can ask me anything about them. I know it's sad, but it warms my heart to talk about your parents. I loved them both."

"You said there was an incident before they died. What did you mean?"

She gave him a tightlipped smile. "Your father wasn't well. You asked me if I knew. I did. But I thought he was drinking too much. I didn't know until later that he wasn't drinking at all. But there was a day I went over there to drop you off after you'd spent the night at our place. Your mom was home by herself. I don't know where Gemma was. We sat at the kitchen table to just chit-chat while you and Ben were in the backyard playing in that old tree house."

The one my father shot himself under, Jake thought, but didn't voice.

"Your father came home and he was so angry. He said ... he said some terrible things to your mother. Things that weren't true. Oh, Jake. I'm sorry. I don't even know why I'm bringing this up."

"Because I asked you. I don't mean to upset you. But I think I need to know."

She nodded. "Jake, please understand your father wasn't in his right mind. We all know that now. But he got it in his head that your mother was ... that she was stepping out on him. And she wasn't. She damn well wasn't. Griffin Malley was his best friend at the time. There was nothing going on between them. I'd swear that on my life."

Judith's words echoed through him. Griffin Malley. Griffin. His father had mentioned the "Gryphon" repeatedly in that note. Jake brushed it off as nonsensical ramblings. He'd mentioned another name too. Toppy.

"I don't remember him," Jake said, barely above a whisper.

"You don't remember your Uncle Griffin?"

He shook his head.

"Well, he moved away. Not long after we lost Sonya and Jake Sr. I just assumed he stayed in touch with your family."

"No," Jake said.

"Mrs. Wayne?" Jolly walked up, his voice booming. "Lady, you are still one hot mama."

Judith looked at Jake with sympathy for the interruption.

"Sorry," Jolly said. "I didn't mean to barge in."

"It's okay," Jake said, standing. He'd pressed Judith far enough. He felt selfish for it. "We were just catching up. She's all yours."

He leaned down and kissed Judith Wayne on the cheek. "We'll talk again soon," he said. She touched his face. Then he left Jolly to charm her.

Jake kept walking. He couldn't leave. Not yet. But he had to find somewhere he could breathe better.

Griffin Malley. Uncle Griffin. His father killed his mother because he thought she was cheating on him? Or had Judith concocted a fantasy like thinking Ben was still alive? Jake knew in his bones that wasn't it. It was her short-term and recent memory that was impaired, not the past. Her recollections cast his father's suicide in a very different light.

Brother Rob was right?

What in God's name had happened that day? What hadn't he been told?

"Jake?"

Gemma called after him. Jake had made it to the end of Birdie's driveway.

"You okay?" his sister asked. "You look like you've seen a ghost."

Jake curled his fists at his side. He had. But he couldn't tell her. He couldn't reopen a wound he knew his sister had fought her whole life to heal. So he squared his shoulders, found a smile for Gemma, and walked with her back to the party.

Twenty-One

Nate Parra was easy to find. He and his uncle ran a microbrewery just outside of Dayton. Birdie had the day off as she took Travis to the airport. He promised to take her out for a drink at Gemma's after his shift. She was going to need it.

Jake waited in the parking lot of Orville & Hops Brewing. A neighboring business owner tipped him off that Nate worked a second job as an EMT three nights a week and usually came straight to the bar to open. He pulled Parra's driver's license to get an idea what he looked like.

Parra was tall, trim, and muscular. He looked a little like Cameron Katz, actually. Tanned. A thick head of dark hair, and a swagger to his walk. Jake got out of the car.

"Mr. Parra?" he called out. Jake wore a suit and his badge on a chain around his neck. He'd left two unreturned messages for Parra detailing exactly who he was and what he wanted to talk to him about. So Parra wasn't exactly surprised when Jake walked up. He was, however, agitated.

Parra had a small duffel in his hand. He was still wearing his uniform from last night's run. Navy-blue cargo pants and a tee shirt emblazoned with the township fire department logo.

"You wanna do this here?" Parra said.

"You wouldn't return my calls," Jake said. "And I'm in the middle of a murder investigation. You think you could spare me fifteen minutes?"

Parra looked nervously back toward the bar entrance. There was another car, a small candy-apple-red vintage Mustang, parked next to his. Two seconds later, the bar door opened and a petite, pretty young woman with a scowl walked out. She had black hair, teased high, big hoop earrings, and a nose ring.

"Sophie, go back inside," Nate barked. "I'll be there in a minute."

Sophie ignored Parra's orders and walked up to Jake, her nose in the air.

"What's your business here?" she asked. Jake noticed a wedding ring set on her left hand. Parra too wore a wedding band.

"Mrs. Parra?" Jake guessed.

"Who's asking?" she said, staring straight at Jake's badge.

He reached into his pocket and handed her a card. "I just need to ask your husband a few questions about ..."

"Sophie, I said go back inside!" Parra shouted. "I'll handle this. Petey's going to be here in ten minutes. Finish inventory and I'll be back."

Sophie stared at Jake's card, scoffed, then turned on her heel and did as Nate asked.

"Not here," Nate said. "We can go for a drive. There's a gas station on the corner. You probably passed it on your way in. We can park there."

Parra didn't wait for a response. He walked around to the passenger side of Jake's car and got in. Jake climbed behind the wheel and did as Parra asked. He pulled into a spot in the far corner of the gas station lot and killed the engine.

"I'm not here to cause you any trouble," Jake said. "You really should have returned my calls."

"I'm here now. What do you want from me?"

"You understand what I want to know about. You've heard what happened to your ex-fiancée, Rianne Katz."

Parra bristled at the name.

"Did you know she'd recently gotten married?" Jake asked.

"No," Parra said. "I knew she was seeing somebody, but I haven't talked to Ri in almost three years."

"Was that your choice or hers?"

Parra didn't answer. He simply stared out the windshield.

"Will you tell me what happened?" he asked.

"That's what I'm trying to figure out. But Rianne and her husband were shot. They were murdered. So far, I can't figure out why. I understand the two of you were close for a while. Do you know anyone who might have wanted to hurt her?"

Parra snapped his head around and glowered at Jake. "You think I did?"

"I didn't say that. But you've been pretty jumpy since the second I walked up. And you've been dodging my calls. So why don't you tell me what I'm supposed to do with that?"

"You met Sophie. The subject of Rianne isn't a popular one with her. She doesn't like the idea that I've had anyone in my life before her. It's her fiery Italian blood."

"When was the last time you talked to Rianne?" Jake asked. His first attempt was to see if Nate Parra could stick to a consistent story.

"I told you. Almost three years ago. It was a bad breakup. She wasn't someone I wanted to have anything to do with again."

"But you loved her. You were going to marry her," Jake said.

"Yeah."

"How far did that go?"

"We told my folks," he said. "We were going to tell Rianne's. We had a date picked out. She went shopping for wedding dresses. She asked our friend Lucy to be her maid of honor. We weren't just engaged. We were planning a wedding."

"Then what happened?" Jake asked.

"Rianne just dropped it on me one night that she wanted to call it off. I don't know why. She never really told me. Just that she wasn't ready. That she loved me, but she couldn't be my wife."

"Sounds sort of cold," Jake said. "I understand from a couple of your mutual friends that you'd been exclusive for a while. Through most of college. You all went to Wright State?"

"You talked to Lucy and Shan," he said. "Shan called me. She's the one who told me Ri got killed. She was worried about how I'd take it. Things were pretty awkward for a while. When Ri and I broke up, she got custody of most of our friends. I hadn't heard from Shan or anyone from that crowd in years. I'd moved on. But it still hit me like an anvil to the chest. Ri and I were together for a long time.

Almost three years. I thought I was going to spend the rest of my life with her before she pulled the rug out from under me. But it's like I told you. We didn't stay in contact after it was well and truly over."

"Shantal said that was a big part of the problem. She indicated Rianne might have led you on for a while. That she had a hard time with breakups."

Parra snorted. "I guess you could say that. Yeah. Ri was the master of mind games. She'd say she didn't want anything to do with me. Then, two days later, she'd call me in tears and wanting me to come over. Or I'd run into her somewhere and she'd kiss me. Send me these texts where she'd pour her heart out. Then she'd go cold again. It took me a long time to figure out how messed up that was. She said it was because she'd always love me and wanted me in her life still. Just not as a boyfriend."

"That's rough," Jake said.

"Like death by a thousand tiny cuts. Isn't that what they say?"

"That would have driven me out of my mind," Jake said. "I had a girlfriend like that once. Dated for years. Then she kept showing up every time she got lonely. Like I was her backup."

"That's exactly it," Parra said. "We went away one weekend. I took her to Chicago. I thought we had a good time. She'd just moved to Blackhand Hills. Took a job with a design firm. I was upset about that because she never discussed it with me. Not that I wasn't supportive. But she just packed her stuff and moved almost two hours away without even mentioning she was gonna do it. So, I went down there the next weekend to see if we could talk about it. I knock on her apartment door and some other dude opens it in his boxer shorts. I mean, Jesus, I texted her and told her I was on my way. She didn't stop me. She didn't tell me not to come. It was like she was throwing this dude in my face. That was the last straw for me. That's when I blocked her number. That was the last time I had any contact with her."

"Who was the other dude?" Jake asked.

"I don't know. Somebody she met through a dating app. This was after we graduated from college. Probably six months after the Big Breakup when she called off the engagement. But we hooked up on and off for all those months. She was working the same job she had in college at a department store. She was trying to find something in her field. She was staying with me. Then the weekend trip. Then she packs her stuff and moves. Then I see her hanging all over some other guy. It was a wake-up call, that's for sure. I had my pride."

"But you were still in love with her?" Jake asked.

Parra frowned. "I don't like where this is going. Are you accusing me of something?"

"No," Jake said. "I'm just trying to get a picture of what Rianne's life was like in those last months and years. Do you know if she dated online a lot?"

"No idea. I tried to get answers from her friends but they froze me out too. Rianne made it seem like I was the asshole."

"That's not the impression I got from her friends at all," Jake said. "It was the opposite. It sounds like they were frustrated with Rianne for leading you on. They said she never wanted to hurt your feelings so she sent a lot of mixed signals."

Nate barked out a laugh. "Yeah. That's an understatement. But that one was a pretty damn clear signal. I practically caught her straddling this guy."

"Did you argue?"

Parra pinched his face and shook his head. "No. I never said another word to her. I just turned and walked away. She tried to chase after me. Saying she was sorry. She threw her arms around my neck. I was calm. I was gentle. But I was firm. I peeled her off of me, got in my car, and never looked back. She tried to text me and I blocked her number. That was it."

"Did you ask about her after that?"

"Not at first. But it's like you said. We did have the same circle of college friends. So I heard things through the grapevine. I don't think she dated the boxer shorts dude very long. A few weeks. I don't know. Then, all of a sudden, she's with this other guy. The one she married. From what I heard, she did to the boxer shorts dude what she did to me. With him one weekend, with Katz the next."

"Do you remember his name? The boxer shorts dude?" Jake asked.

Parra shook his head. "Nope. Never asked. Didn't care. Figured let him have her. Now, I know I dodged a major bullet ..." Parra's voice trailed off. He flushed red. "Oh my God. I didn't mean it like that. Shit."

He started to tremble and buried his face in his hands. "I didn't mean it."

"I get it," Jake said. "It's just a figure of speech."

"I don't know. I swear to God, I don't know. You can check my phone. I don't care. I wasn't talking to Rianne. I met Sophie a year and a half ago. Fell for her hard. She's nothing like Rianne. She's direct. Says what she means. Hell, she's the one who asked me to marry her. More like demanded it."

Parra's face split into a smile.

"She's something," Jake agreed.

"She's everything," he said and it read sincere to Jake.

"What did the guy look like?" Jake asked. "Mr. Boxer Shorts."

Parra shrugged. "I don't know. Big guy. Muscular. That's what Rianne likes. Liked. Brown hair. Tan. About my height. Six foot two. I know that's the way I could describe about a million guys. But I honestly wasn't studying his face or anything. I was trying to keep myself from breaking his damn nose."

"Do you think you could find out who he was?" Jake asked.

"No," Parra answered quickly. "I don't want to be involved in this. It's not good for me. It's certainly not good for my marriage. I've got a great thing going. Sophie's the love of my life. For so long I thought Rianne was. But Sophie ... she like woke me up, you know? Got my head back on straight. She's pregnant. We're not telling people yet, but we found out a week ago."

"Congratulations," Jake said.

Nate went quiet, then he turned to Jake. "Did you come here thinking I had something to do with Rianne's murder?"

Jake didn't answer.

"Here," Parra said, pulling his phone out of his pocket. "Check my phone. You'll see I haven't been talking to Rianne. I don't even know her number anymore. When did she die? Like what day?"

"June 29th, around midnight," Jake said.

Parra squeezed his eyes shut. "Was that a Sunday?"

"Saturday."

"I pull overnights for the county three nights a week. Friday to Saturday, Monday to Tuesday, Thursday to Friday. Then I'm here every day. I'll give you my shift supervisor's name. You can check. I haven't had a weekend off in six months. I wasn't anywhere near

Rianne. I don't even know where she was living except in Blackhand Hills. Search my car. Take my DNA. Whatever you want."

"I appreciate that," Jake said. "I don't need to take you up on that right now."

"Are we done?" Parra said, opening the car door.

"For now," Jake said. "I might have a few more questions later. Maybe you could answer if I call you again.

"Yeah," Parra said.

"I can drive you back."

"Nah, I'd rather walk. Give Sophie a little more time to cool down. She's gonna grill me when I walk in. And it's better you're gone before I do. Like I said. Fiery Italian blood. Though, her passion has advantages." Parra blushed and smiled wide again.

"Got it," Jake said. Parra got out, closed the door and started walking back to his bar.

His alibi would be easy enough to check out. He had a fleeting thought that maybe he should check Sophie Parra's as well. Though if her husband were telling the truth, Sophie wouldn't have a motive to hurt Rianne Katz either. And why would either of them want to kill Cameron in any event?

He pulled out his phone and called Birdie. She answered right away. She'd just dropped Travis off and was leaving the airport. Jake decided to take her mind off it and quickly filled her in on his conversation with Parra.

"He says it really felt like Rianne was trying to throw this rebound guy in his face. Maybe her other friend, Lucy Vale knows more about who this guy was?" he said.

"I think we for sure need to find out," she said. "I didn't like that Vale was a no-show when we re-interviewed Shantal Watson."

"I didn't like it either. And if this was Rianne's pattern, having relationships that overlapped, Boxer Shorts/Rebound Guy is someone I want to talk to."

"I'll see if I can pin Lucy Vale down for a second interview," Birdie said. "We still on at CIPS later?"

"How did it go at the airport?" Jake finally asked.

Birdie went silent for a moment. "It's done," she said. "He's nervous but excited. So am I. Plus, Lindy, my mom's health aide, just texted. She got her safely back to the nursing home."

"It was a good visit," Jake said.

"She loved talking to you," Birdie said. "You wanna let me know why I caught her crying in the bathroom after you left?"

Jake didn't know what to say. Guilt speared through him. He hadn't meant to upset Judith Wayne.

"Relax," Birdie said. "You don't have to tell me all your secrets. But it's been a rough day. I could use a beer and a friend."

"I've got you for both," Jake said. "I just need to grab a shower and a change of clothes. If you get there before me, save us a table. I'll be designated driver."

Birdie thanked him and clicked off.

The drive went quick. Jake enjoyed the solitude. But he couldn't get Rianne Katz out of his head. Parra had called her the master of mind games. She had cheated on him, any way you sliced it. Maybe she'd done the same to this mystery rebound guy too when she hooked up with Cameron Katz.

Jealousy was a motive for murder. Jake walked into his house. His parents' case box sat on the dining room table, almost beckoning him.

Jealousy was a motive for murder. Judith Wayne's words pulsed through him.

Griffin Malley was his best friend at the time. There was nothing going on between them. I'd swear that on my life.

He picked up the copy of his father's awful letter.

Gryphon had his arms around you. In the hallway. Under the lights. Holding hands.

Uncle Griffin, Judith had called him. Jake had no memory of him at all.

He sat on the couch and slid the box toward him. Were there more answers in here?

Jealousy was a motive for murder. In his father's case, he knew it was a delusion. He didn't need Judith Wayne to tell him that.

But had his father told anyone else? Had they missed the signs?

He pulled out another Tyvek envelope, with another bulky VHS tape inside. He had an hour before he promised to meet Birdie at Gemma's bar. He found himself walking to the spare bedroom and sliding the tape out of the envelope. The label on the front of it read:

Taped Interview – Max and Ava Cashen

Squeezing his eyes shut and taking a deep breath, Jake popped the tape into the player.

Twenty-Two

Based on the grainy timestamp in the left corner of the video, Frank had waited until late in the evening the day after his parents were found to interview his grandparents. Gemma had been first. Jake guessed Frank spent the day dealing with the scene, talking to Dr. Stone, their neighbors, maybe even his father's doctors.

Grandma Ava had been a formidable woman. Toward the end of her life, she'd dyed her hair jet black. Jake remembered her as plump, with soft brown eyes and big, enveloping hugs. The woman on the screen looked nothing like her. She looked so young. Her hair was still black, but natural, with not a gray hair to be seen. And she was slender, not skinny, but she wore a sleeveless navy-blue shirt showing off toned arms, no doubt from working in her beloved gardens.

Jake did the math. Grandpa would have been fifty years old. Grandma, maybe forty-eight or forty-nine. Young grandparents who'd had his father when they were both barely twenty years old. Then, his own parents were only seventeen when Gemma came, entirely unplanned but loved.

"How is Gemma doing?" Frank asked. "She held up pretty well during her interview. She's a tough kid."

"She'll be okay," Max said abruptly. "She'll keep her head up."

"We took her to Judy and Rudy Wayne's," Grandma said in a voice Jake didn't recognize. Quiet. Timid. Shattered. "Gemma would probably rather be with one of her own friends, but she doesn't want to leave Jakey. He spends so much time with the Waynes; it's good for him to be there. We'll get them in the morning."

"I'm glad," Frank said. "There are a lot of people in this community who want to help. I'm one of them."

"What did she tell you?" Max asked. "What didn't she want me to hear?"

"I'm going to leave that for her to tell you herself if she feels like it. I promised her that much. But I suppose it's nothing you don't already know or couldn't guess. For now, I need to ask you some questions about your son and your daughter-in-law."

Grandma sank against Grandpa. He put an arm around her and held her close. She blew into a tissue and pressed her fingers to her brow as if she had a headache. The quality of the video had degraded with time, but Jake could still tell his grandmother's color wasn't good.

"How was Jake feeling, acting over the last couple of days?"

"I hadn't seen him," Max said. "Not since last Friday. He came over to help me put one of the fences back up. Damn billy goat keeps kicking it down."

Jake smiled. He knew exactly which section of fence he meant.

"How did he seem then?" Frank asked.

"Kinda quiet. A bit jittery. He kept dropping his hammer. I asked him if he was okay. He was a little short with me. Said he didn't want to talk. So, I left him alone and worked on another section of the fence. We had dinner that night. He was quiet then too."

"The whole family?" Frank asked.

"No." Grandma Ava sniffed. "It was just Jake. He spent the night with us. I didn't ask why. Sonya said he'd been having trouble sleeping. I knew it had been going on for a while. And he'd gotten skinny. But he was fine. There was nothing wrong with him."

Grandpa Max bristled at this. He frowned at Frank.

"He wasn't fine, Ava," Max said gently. "He'd been real nervous for a while. On edge."

"Did you talk to him about it?" Frank asked.

"I tried," Max continued. "He didn't want to talk about it. So I talked to Sonya."

"When was this?" Frank asked.

"I wanna say six, seven months ago. That's when I knew my boy was having trouble sleeping. I make chili on Sundays. Jake comes with Sonya and the grandkids every week. A couple weekends in a row, they didn't come. Sonya said something about Jake not feeling well. That didn't sit too good with me so I went over there. Jake was gone. Sonya was sitting at her kitchen table crying her eyes out. When I asked her what was wrong, she said Jake didn't want her to tell me. That she knew she was breaking his confidence, but she was at her wit's end. Said he wasn't sleeping. He was pacing all over the house at night. Going in and out. Going out to his workshop in the garage. Running his drill and table saw all hours of the night. I went down there. He had all kinds of unfinished projects thrown all over the place."

"That was unusual?" Frank asked.

"Completely. I taught Jake to keep a clean workstation. He knows better."

"Did you talk to him about it?" Frank asked.

"Tried to. Jake got real defensive. Mad at Sonya for talking to me behind his back. I told him it wasn't like that. Didn't help. My boy was just hopping mad and stormed out of the house. So I backed off. Sonya thought that was best too. She didn't want to agitate him anymore."

"Do you know when he got help?" Frank asked. "We found some prescription medication in the trash can in the garage. Quite a bit of it. The bottles were open and the pills were all spilled out."

"Sonya took him to a doctor," Max said. "Some kind of shrink. They prescribed him a whole bunch of stuff."

"What are you talking about?" Grandma shouted, pulling herself away from his grandfather. "You're making it sound like my son was crazy. He was not crazy. He was just under some stress at work. That's why he wasn't sleeping. I knew I should have kept him at home. Made him stay with us."

"Ava," Grandpa said, his voice measured and calm. "Jake was not fine. He got sick. I think that's pretty obvious."

"What are you saying?" she said, jumping up from her chair. "What are the two of you implying? This was an accident. The gun must have gone off by accident. He was cleaning it. I know that's what it was."

"Ava, sit down," Max said.

"I will not. I will not listen to another word of this. I will not sit by and keep my mouth shut while you talk about Jake like he was some lunatic or criminal. I will not."

"Honey," Max said. "Why don't you wait for me outside then? This shouldn't take long."

"Mrs. Cashen, I can ..." Frank started. Grandma Ava turned her back on him and stormed out of the interview room, slamming the door. Grandpa Max buried his face in his hands.

"Do you want to take a break?" Frank asked. "Go after her?"

"No," Grandpa said. "It's better we get this over with. And it's better if it's just me. You can see for yourself my wife is struggling with this. Jesus. Of course she is. You wanna ask me how this all happened. God. I don't know. But I know it wasn't a damn accident. I blame those pills. They got Jake all mixed up. Not thinking straight. I don't know what he was thinking in those last minutes. I think maybe those pills made him hallucinate or something. I told Sonya. I told her I thought they were making it worse. I don't trust any of that stuff."

God, Jake thought. His poor mother. She was trying to get help. His grandmother was in full denial. His grandfather had old-fashioned ideas about psychiatric care. And it was neither of their faults. But it could have been different.

"Max," Frank said. "I know this is going to be hard to hear. But your son left a note. I'm trying to make sense of it. Maybe you can. But I have to warn you, it won't be easy to read."

Grandpa sat back, his jaw hanging slack. "A note? A suicide note? Did Gemma see it?"

"I don't think so," Frank answered. "It was found underneath Sonya's body. She may have been holding it and dropped it."

She read it, Jake thought. His mother had read it before she died.

"Let me see it," Max snapped.

Frank had a file folder beside him. He pulled out a copy of the note. Likely the exact one Jake found in the banker's box. It was sheathed in a clear plastic protector.

Grandpa grabbed it and started reading, his lips moving as he pored over his father's rambling words. When he finished, he hung his head and shoved the paper back across the table.

"He thought we were poisoning him," Grandpa said. "He got it in his head that the medicine was Sonya trying to kill him."

"Did he express that to you?" Frank asked.

"Not in so many words. But it's pretty clear from what he wrote, isn't it? I don't know. I just don't know. Maybe he heard me talking to Sonya about it. Maybe he knew I wasn't crazy about the stuff. Did I make this worse?"

"Max, you can't think like that. You're right that Jake was sick. It will take a day or two before the autopsy is finished. That'll answer some questions. And I'm talking with the psychiatrist who was treating your son. Did you know he'd been diagnosed with schizophrenia?"

Grandpa's face contorted with pain. "Sonya tried to tell me. But they were both so private about it. I think that was Jake. He wouldn't have wanted her to tell me something like that. Ava's right. We should have stayed home this week. When Jake came to us, we never should have let him go back to that house. God. The kids weren't safe, were they?"

"I think you'll drive yourself crazy if you ask too many what-ifs. I think you did the best you could. Your wife is right that this looks like it was a horrible accident."

"He loved her," Max said. "You have to understand that. Jake loved Sonya with his whole heart. He wouldn't have hurt her on purpose."

"I believe that," Frank said. "Can you shed any light on what he was trying to say in this note? Who's Toppy?"

Grandpa chuffed a bitter laugh. "He was a stuffed bear. Jake got it for Christmas from Ava's mother. The last Christmas she was with us. Jake was maybe two years old. He named it Toppy and carried it around with him everywhere until the stuffing fell out. Ava tried to sew it up. She put it in the washing machine and it just fell apart. Jake was maybe six or seven by then. We had to throw the thing away. For a while, he talked to Toppy like an imaginary friend. You know. How some kids do. It was nothing. He outgrew it. You think that could have been a sign?"

"I think it's like you said. It's what some kids do. That's all. Max, what about Griff? It sounds like Jake thought maybe Sonya was cheating on him. Did he tell you that?"

"No. And it's nonsense. I don't want that spread around. This is crazy!" Grandpa said, picking up the letter and shaking it. "I don't want Ava seeing this. You hear me? I don't want anyone else seeing this."

"I have no intention of showing anyone but you. It'll be part of the case file though. It's evidence."

"So be it," Grandpa said. "I have to go. I have to check on Ava. I gotta get her through this somehow. I've gotta figure out what to do about the kids."

"We're finished," Frank said. "I'm going to talk to your daughter-in-law's family."

"When can I have my son and daughter-in-law back? I need to plan a funeral."

"A couple of days," Frank said. "After the ME's done with his full report. I can have someone help you contact the funeral home."

Grandpa rose. "I can take care of all of that myself. We'll just want something simple. They'll go in the family plot down by the creek. It's where Ava and I are going when our time comes."

Frank rose. "Of course." He came around the table and extended a hand to his grandfather. When Max clasped hands with Frank, Frank drew him into a hug. From this angle, Jake couldn't see Frank's face, but he saw his grandfather's. He squeezed his eyes shut so tightly and trembled. He sobbed silently against Frank Borowski's shoulder before finally letting him go.

As far as Jake knew, it was the only time he'd ever seen his grandfather cry. When Grandpa walked out of the room, the tape ran for a few moments. Frank had his back to the camera but braced himself with both hands on the table.

It killed him, Jake thought. What had happened to his parents had cut a hole in him like the worst cases do. Jake knew it would shape the rest of Frank's life in its own way. He would take Jake under his wing. He would guide him. And it all started in this small, unguarded moment captured on a grainy VHS tape.

"Jake?"

He jumped; the voice startled him. He whirled around.

Birdie stood in the hall, her face sheet white. Jake looked back at the television screen. It had gone to static. But Birdie had been standing there long enough to have seen what he was watching. Her expression couldn't mean anything else.

"Jake," she said quietly, as she walked further into the room. Her eyes surveyed the mess he'd made. His parents' case box was open. Stacks of paper, copies of evidence, lay everywhere. The top of the box with the file name sat perched on the edge of the spare bed. Birdie slowly leaned down and picked it up.

"I was worried," she said. "You were supposed to pick me up. You never made it to Gemma's bar."

Jake got to his feet. He couldn't explain anything away. There was no good excuse he could make.

He glanced at his smartwatch. He'd lost track of time. It was past nine o'clock. He forgot to pick Birdie up.

"I'm sorry. I just ..."

"How long have you had this?"

"I was just ... a while."

Birdie put the box lid down. She walked out of the bedroom and into the living room. Steeling himself for a lecture, he followed her.

"The Katz case," Birdie said, turning back to face him. "It's stirred all of this up. I've been so worried about that. Jake, you should just let me handle it. Everyone will understand. You shouldn't have to deal with this."

"I'm fine. And I'm doing my job."

"Of course you are. But this? Jake. This isn't good for you."

Jake took a seat on the couch. "I don't care."

"I do." She sat next to him, their knees touching. "I care a lot. Does Gemma know you're doing this to yourself?"

"No," he snapped. "And you can't tell her. She's been through enough."

He had more pieces of the file laid out on the table. Birdie picked up one stack. They were copies of the crime scene photos. She put her hand to her mouth. He knew it wasn't the scene itself that shocked her. She'd been a cop long enough and served in Afghanistan before that. Jake knew she was thinking the same thing he thought when he saw those photos. Gemma had found them. Gemma had only been twelve years old.

"You asked my mother about it," Birdie said. "I got her to tell me. She remembers everything from the past in exacting detail."

"I crossed a line," Jake said. "I'm sorry. But she didn't seem upset by it."

"She wasn't," Birdie said. "I understand why you felt you had to ask. But to what purpose? You know what happened. You've always known."

"You'd be no different," Jake asked. "If you had unanswered questions about what happened to Ben, you'd pull his case file. You know you would."

"And you'd tell me not to."

Jake gave her an ironic smile. "I suppose I would."

"What unanswered questions, Jake?"

There was a moment when he could have made a different choice. Made something up. But somehow, Birdie felt part of this too. More than just walking in on him. Her family had practically adopted him on weekends growing up. Her parents had been a stabilizing influence on him as much as Frank was. As much as his grandparents tried to be.

He reached for the plastic sheath and handed his father's letter to Birdie.

She read it. When she finished, she slowly closed her eyes and exhaled. She handed the page back to him.

"I never knew he wrote that," Jake said. "My grandfather never told me."

"Can you blame him?" Birdie asked.

"I don't know. But your mother explained some of it. She didn't even know she was doing it. She can't have known about this letter either."

"Frank Borowski swore he'd never show it to anyone else," Birdie said. "I was standing in the hall for a minute or two. I saw the end of that tape."

"Your mom said my dad thought my mom was cheating on her with this guy Griffin. I don't remember him. But I think the Gryphon he mentions in the letter is Griffin the man."

"Your father was ill, Jake. This letter? It's exactly the kind of thing I'd expect someone suffering from schizophrenia would write. You've encountered people like this. The paranoia? It's pretty classic. And it's not real. It's a delusion. All this does is tell you what you already knew. So what's the point of torturing yourself?"

"I want to talk to him. I want to know what he knows. I want to know why this guy seemingly disappeared after my parents died. Your mom said he was my dad's best friend. I don't remember him. He was nowhere when I was growing up. There's no mention of him in Frank's report except for this letter."

"You think your mother was cheating with him?"

"No," Jake said. "I don't know. And I know that part doesn't matter. It's just. This is mine. I don't know how else to explain it. This? This box. This history. It belongs to me. It's this giant chunk of me I've never understood or known. Now I want to. Now I'm ready."

Birdie shook her head. "It just doesn't matter, Jake."

"It does to me. I hope you can understand that." He felt something break inside of him. Like his heart split open. He hadn't given voice to any of this. Not even to himself. But he knew it was true. Maybe people who find out they are adopted feel something similar. Like a part of your existence that's been hidden from you. Or maybe it was more about his parents. He remembered so little.

"I can feel them," he whispered. "In every page of this file. Those videos. As horrible as it is, the people I love are talking about them. Unfiltered. Candidly. They never do anymore. It just hurts too much. It's like this is all I have."

Birdie put a hand on his thigh. "I understand."

"You can't," he whispered.

"But I can. I had Ben for much longer than you had your parents. I don't want to remember him how he died. But it still haunts me. He was all alone in those woods. I go there sometimes. I've never told anyone. But I walk up to that tree where he was found. I touch the ground where he bled. And I swear to God, I still feel him there."

Her voice broke. Jake's protective instincts flared. He wanted to take her pain away. He touched her face, caressed her cheek and then ran his fingers down her jawline. She did understand. She didn't judge him. And she knew. She grew up as a witness to his grief just like Ben had. She'd seen him as a young boy, crying into a pillow while her mother had stroked his back and sung him to sleep in those first few terrible days.

She was Birdie. And she knew.

He froze. So did she.

"Jake ..."

She was *Birdie*. Jake pulled away and got to his feet. He shook his head to clear it.

Birdie stared at the wall for a moment. Then she too came back into herself.

"So what now?" she asked.

"I don't know," he said. "But I'm not done with this. Can I trust you won't mention this to anyone?"

"Jake," she said, rising. "Of course not. You know I've got your back. I still don't think any of this is good for you. But I want to help if you've made your mind up."

"I think it's enough for tonight. I can walk away from it for now. Focus on the case in front of us."

"Good," she said. "Because Rianne and Cameron's wedding photos came in. Pam Timiney sent me the link the photographer sent her. She went through and wrote out the names and relationships of everyone she could. She said Mia Casey, Rianne's third bridesmaid, can fill in the rest from Rianne's friends. Mia's willing to meet us at the office tomorrow morning."

"Thanks," he said. "For ... all of it."

"We're partners," she said, emphasizing the word. Partners. She was Birdie. She was his partner. And he knew how lucky he was to have both.

Twenty-Three

Birdie brought in one of the bigger monitors and set it up in the conference room down the hall. She and Jake had combed through Cameron and Rianne Katz's wedding photos for a couple of hours first thing in the morning. It was standard fare. Shots in front of the preacher. Posed pictures of the wedding party in a small outdoor pavilion. An outdoor reception at one of the state parks. As Rianne's parents said, no more than a hundred people.

Mia Casey was Rianne's third bridesmaid. As Lucy and Shantal described, she had no partner on Cameron's side. She walked alone down the aisle wearing a pink strapless dress and carrying a bouquet of cut wildflowers.

Mia walked into the conference room accompanied by her father, a personal injury lawyer. A strange choice, but Jake appreciated that this trip was upsetting for Mia. She'd never seen the inside of a police station let alone served as a witness in a double homicide.

"There's nothing to worry about, Mia," Birdie said. Mia took a seat at the table. Her father did his best to fade into the wall, choosing a chair in the corner where he could see his daughter, but not the monitor.

"I don't know how I can help you," she said. "I have no idea who might have done this to Rianne."

"It's okay," Jake said. "We don't expect you to. I'm just trying to identify the guests at Rianne's wedding."

"You think one of them killed her?" Mia asked.

"No," Jake answered. "But I need to talk to as many people who knew Cameron and Rianne as I can. Maybe it's to our advantage that she had her wedding so recently. Everybody she cared most about would have been there, right?"

"I guess," Mia said. She looked at her father for reassurance. Jim Casey was a portly man with thinning black hair he combed over. A pair of horn-rimmed readers perched at the end of his nose. But he looked as uncomfortable being there as Mia did. He nodded to her.

Birdie queued up one photo of the entire wedding party in front of the altar.

"I know all of these people," Jake said. "Cameron's brother, his business partner, Rianne's sorority sisters. I've spoken to all of them except you. I think you might have unique insight into Rianne's last couple of weeks. You're the only one of her friends who lived nearby."

"We met when I interned for Delilah Grossjean. We overlapped by a few months. Rianne had just moved here and didn't know anybody. I took her for drinks a few times. Introduced her to some of my friends. Showed her around town. She was nice. But we weren't best friends or anything. I was actually surprised she asked me to be in her wedding. But I was her only local friend."

"That's understandable," Birdie said.

"And you knew Cameron too?" Jake asked.

"A bit. It's a small town. I'd seen him around. And I knew he got sort of famous on social media. He was a few years above me grade-wise, but he graduated with my older brother, Mal. I knew *of* him, is how I'd describe it."

"Did you have any opinions about him when Rianne told you she was going out with him?" Jake asked.

"Not really. I didn't think he was into anything bad. Like drugs or anything. And we went on a couple of double dates. Not recently. Last year. Cam seemed nice. He was polite. Treated Rianne well."

"So I have access to Rianne's cell phone," Jake said. "I've seen a few texts between the two of you. It didn't look like you two texted very often."

"We didn't. And I wasn't as close to her in the last couple of months as I had been when I still worked at Delilah's. We were starting to fall out of touch. She asked me to be in her wedding like eight months ago."

"Were you surprised they got married so fast?" Birdie asked. "From what we understand, they'd been dating less than two years."

"Kind of. I didn't realize Rianne was looking to settle down. It wasn't something we talked about. But she was happy. And I told you Cam seemed to be treating her well. It's just that my boyfriend didn't have a lot in common with him. Braden doesn't dislike Cam, but they just weren't into the same things. Braden's working on his doctorate in biochemistry. He's a gamer. Cam was more of a jock. Way into nutrition and fitness. So as couples, we didn't mesh all that great."

Jake turned her attention back to the wedding photos, this time focusing on guests at the outdoor reception. Many were family members of Rianne's. Roger and Pam Timiney had already identified those for Jake. Most of them lived out of town and left right after the reception. Rianne invited more people from college and their dates. No high school friends. Other than Mia and her date, she identified only six other people local to Blackhand Hills. Two of them were clients whose homes Delilah and Rianne worked on.

"I'm sorry," Mia said after flipping through the last photograph. "I just don't know much about any of those people."

"What was Rianne's mood like during the reception?" Birdie asked.

"Fine. She got a little drunk. Her mom didn't like that. But people kept giving her shots. She was having fun. There was no harm in it. She wasn't sloppy or anything. I mean, there were a couple of times things got a little raunchy. When they did the garter thing. Cam dove under her dress and made a big deal out of it. A joke. Pulled stuff out. Props. A toothbrush. A pair of fuzzy handcuffs. Granny panties. Everybody was laughing. Her parents just stood to the side scowling. Oh, and he pulled out a dildo. That's when it got kind of icky. The thing was huge and did this swirly vibrating thing. He pulled it out with it turned on. It was just kinda crass. But whatever. It was harmless. I'm sorry. That probably doesn't have anything to do with anything. But you asked me about Rianne's mood. That's the only thing that was a little tense. Her dad stormed off for a while. I think it was an overreaction. But by the time they cut the cake, it was all fine again."

"Mia," Jake said. "What about other people Rianne might have dated? Was there anyone before Cameron that you know of?"

"I knew she had a fiancé a while back. I never met him. But she talked about him. Neville? Nate?"

"Nate," Birdie answered.

"Yeah. That's it. I think it was kind of ending when she moved to Blackhand Hills. I got the impression that's one of the things that ended it. But yeah. She started seeing some guy just about as soon as she got here."

"Do you know his name?" Jake asked.

Mia shook her head. "No. Or if I did, I don't remember. I only know that at all because one week Rianne's car was on the fritz. She was living in those duplexes off County Road Eleven. The dumps. She didn't stay there long. Anyway, I had to pick her up and drop her off that week. One of the mornings I got there a little early. When I walked up to her door, this guy was coming out. It was obvious it was a walk-of-shame situation. He was tucking his shirt in when he came out."

"What did Rianne say about him?"

"I got a strong impression she hadn't meant for me to run into him. Like that's why he was sneaking out so fast. Like maybe she lost track of time or overslept and tried to kick him out before I got there. I tried to joke with her about him. She shut down pretty quick. Seemed irritated. I let it go."

"Do you remember what he looked like? This guy?" Birdie asked.

Mia shrugged. "He was cute. Tall. Maybe six feet. Light-brown hair. He had some stubble. Oh, he was muscular. He had on a nice pair of shoes. Brown leather. Polished. But he didn't say a word to me. He was all sheepish."

"Do you think you'd recognize him if you saw him again?" Jake asked.

"Maybe. But this was maybe a year and a half ago. The following weekend, she went out with Cameron for the first time. I remember that because she asked me about him. Like you did. Said she met him at the gym and he told her he went to Stanley High School like I did. I told her just about what I told you. That he was more my brother's age. And I remember because the week before I ran into her sneaky link."

Jake scowled; Birdie tapped his arm and whispered, "Booty Call." Nate Parra's words stuck in his head. If Rianne had dumped this rebound guy the same way she had Nate, he could see why someone could get pretty angry with her.

"I'm sorry," Mia said. "I really don't know anything else. I never saw the first guy again. I did try to ask her. I asked her why it didn't work out with him. Rianne just blew me off. She said he was nobody. That was that. If anything, I'd say she was embarrassed about it. I didn't judge. What do I care if she hooked up with some guy one weekend?"

"I appreciate it," Jake said. "You've been helpful."

"I don't see how," Mia said, sliding her purse over her shoulder as she stood. Jake had almost forgotten her father was in the room. He got up and walked to Mia's side.

"Thank you for your time," Jake said. He handed a card to both of them. Mr. Casey put his arm around his daughter and led her out of the room.

Jake sat back down, letting Mia's interview marinate in his brain for a moment. Birdie pulled the flash drive out of her laptop and pocketed it.

"It's not much," Jake said. "But maybe it's something."

"Except her physical description of this guy matches about eight hundred people in town."

"It also matches the description Parra gave, if it's the same guy. There's nothing in Rianne's phone," Jake said. "No dating apps. No texts of a dating or romantic nature except from Cameron."

"But that's twice now. Both Nate Parra and now Mia Casey have described a situation where they walked in on Rianne with some guy she clearly didn't want them to know about."

"We don't even know if it was the same guy," Birdie said. "Jake, I'm really starting to feel like we're never going to solve this one."

Jake wouldn't let his mind go there. Not yet. But Birdie's gut instincts could be spot on. They usually were.

Twenty-Four

Jake woke up choking. He clawed at his face but couldn't draw air. Something slimy. Something wet blocked his nose. He sat straight up and pulled a sopping wet kitchen towel off his face. His heart raced and instinct drove him to reach for the loaded gun he kept on his nightstand.

"You're not quick enough," Grandpa Max snarled. "Doesn't give me much faith that the streets of Blackhand Hills are very safe, Jake."

Jake blinked hard, letting his eyes focus. It was still mostly dark out of his bedroom windows. Max stood in the doorframe, hands on his hips, frowning.

Jake picked up his cell phone from the charger. It was just past seven a.m.

"What the hell is wrong with you?" Jake asked, tossing the wet towel far enough that it hit the adjoining bathroom floor.

"Get up," Max barked. "Got some work for you to do."

"What?" Jake felt nine years old. Grandpa would often wake him from a dead sleep on the weekends to handle some chore he thought up. Back then, the old man would drag him halfway out of his bed by his feet. The wet towel was at least a minor improvement.

"Oil in that tractor needs changing."

"Now? At the crack of dawn on a Saturday?"

"Dawn was almost two hours ago, Sleeping Beauty. I let you sleep in."

Jake threw his legs over the side of the bed. He wore nothing but a pair of boxer shorts.

"Meet me out front in five minutes," Max ordered.

Jake grumbled in protest but knew his grandfather well enough to understand arguing was pointless. He pulled on a pair of jeans, found his work boots, and grabbed an old tee shirt from the drawer. He took sixty seconds to brush his teeth and slap on deodorant.

As promised, Max was leaning against the four-wheeler, arms crossed and impatient.

"Did you drive down here?" Jake asked. "You know you're not supposed to be behind the wheel of anything. Much less when it's still half dark out."

"I'm fine," he said. "I know these trails blindfolded and nobody's telling me what I can or can't do on my own damn property."

He was in a rare mood this morning. Jake wondered what had him so roiled. He walked up to his grandfather and snatched the keys out of his hand. "I'll go with you, but you're done driving for the day. Get in."

Grandpa growled, but relented. He climbed into the passenger seat. Jake threw the vehicle in reverse and then roared up the trail to the top of the hill. Grandpa kept his equipment in the pole barn next to the Big House.

Grandpa left the big door open when he got the four-wheeler out. His John Deere tractor was halfway out of the barn with the hood detached.

"You wanna tell me why this is a damned emergency?" Jake asked.

"Because the grass needs cutting. I got eaten alive by mosquitos last night when I was just trying to enjoy the sunset off my back porch."

"Yeah," Jake said. "And Ryan cuts it after lunch. And he's fully capable of changing the oil if it needs it."

"Can't rely on him yet," Max argued.

"Yes, you can," Jake said. He grabbed the oil can off the shelf and stormed over to the tractor. His grandfather was right that the oil gauge read a little low, but nothing that couldn't have kept until after Ryan finished his chores. Jake let the old oil drain out of the tractor while he went back to the shelf and found a new filter.

Grandpa sat on a rusted old bench stool watching and occasionally barking out the obvious. Man, he was feisty today. Jake knew better than to ask why or he'd get an earful.

Fifteen minutes later, Jake had the oil changed. He slammed the hood down and put his supplies neatly back on the shelves.

"Come on," he said to his grandfather. "Let's go up to the house. I'll make you breakfast. Did Aidan milk those goats yesterday?"

"Don't know," Grandpa said. "He was walking around in circles up there. That's all I know."

Jake smiled. If he had a penny for every time his grandfather had said the same thing about him growing up. Jake closed the garage door and started to walk to the service door. Grandpa didn't budge. He sat with his hands crossed, one leg on the bottom rail of the bench stool.

"You coming?" Jake asked. "Or are you just planning to sit here sulking?"

Grandpa looked straight at him. "That depends on you."

"On me?"

"You got something you wanna talk to me about?"

Jake did a double take. "What's under your skin, Gramps? You're talking in riddles."

"Let's go," he said, popping up from the stool. He walked past Jake and climbed back into the passenger seat of the four-wheeler.

"We can walk up to the house," Jake said. "It's twenty steps."

"We're not doing this in that house. Take me down to the creek."

Jake felt an electrical current go through his arms. The creek. There was only one reason Max Cashen ever went down to the creek. To put flowers on Grandma Ava's grave. There were no flowers in the ATV.

Jake let out a sigh, but climbed behind the wheel. They drove in silence down to the cemetery. Max hopped out and took his seat on the bench he'd built facing Grandma's headstone and his father's right beside it.

"Sit," Max ordered.

Jake had half a mind to leave him there. If the old man knew the trails cold with half his eyesight gone, let him prove it. Except he knew he would never do that to him. So Jake reluctantly sat beside him and stared at his own name on a dusty headstone.

"Something you wanna ask me?" Max started.

"I think it's the other way around, isn't it?" Jake responded. "Who have you been talking to?"

It didn't matter. Max had ears everywhere. Jake knew Birdie would never have told a soul about the files tucked away behind a locked door in his spare bedroom. But Jake had asked questions out in the open at Birdie's cookout. Maybe it was Judy Wayne herself who had told Max.

"Do me a favor and don't insult me," Max said. "Not here. Not in front of him or her."

"They're gone, Grandpa," Jake said. "They're not listening in."

Max clenched his fists. But he didn't take the bait. Jake felt momentary guilt for throwing it. This was a sacred place to Max Cashen.

"Yeah," Jake said. "I was asking questions. I talked to Judy Wayne about my mom and dad. I didn't want to upset you with it."

"Is it this case you're working on?" Max asked. "I know a lot of people in town have been talking. They go quiet around me in a way they haven't in over thirty years."

"I'm not trying to stir things up for you," Jake said. He felt himself falling into an old pattern. Avoid the subject. Protect his grandfather. His grandmother. Don't ask. Leave it behind. There was nothing anyone could do about what happened. Leave the living to the living. But something shifted inside of him. What he'd said to Birdie was true. Some kind of dam had burst. Once he started, he knew he had to see it through.

"He wrote a note," Jake said.

Max dropped his head. He relaxed his fists.

"You never told anyone," Jake continued. "Not Grandma. Not Gemma. Not me."

Max turned to him. "That was my business."

Anger sparked in Jake. "Your business? It's not yours alone. He's my father. I had a right to know. I had a right to talk about it."

"I've never stopped you from doing that! Were we not just sitting here a couple of weeks ago with you asking me questions? You weren't being honest, were you? It wasn't just some out-of-the-blue, spontaneous question. You had an agenda."

"I didn't have an agenda," Jake said, but stopped himself from digging his heels in too far on that. He let out an exasperated sigh. "I mean, when I was growing up. Grandma would leave the room if anyone mentioned either of my parents' names. You changed the subject. Had me changing oil in a tractor at some godawful hour of the morning. Fixing fences. Avoiding it."

"So what? What good would it have done to let you wallow in it?"

"It wasn't wallowing. It was grieving. It was facing what happened."

"You think I didn't face it?"

Jake took a breath. He didn't want to come at this with anger. With accusations. "The letter," Jake said. "Why didn't you tell anyone? Why didn't you tell me?"

"And when was I supposed to do that, Jake? You were seven years old. You were a baby when they died."

"No," he said. "But I'm thirty-eight years old now. I grew up."

"Sure," Grandpa said. "When you were older. What? When you turned eighteen? Happy birthday? When you were twenty-one and building your own life? It doesn't matter. It wasn't my son. That was ... that was nothing. Borowski should have burned it. And how do you know about it now?"

"Because I've read it," Jake said. "Because I have their case file. And I think you already know that. That's why you brought me out here. To make me admit it."

Max rubbed his eyes. "You shouldn't have done that. What was the point?"

"This," Jake said. "I think this. Right now. This is the point. And I need to know what it means."

"There was no meaning," Grandpa said. "God. You were so young. You don't remember. And thank God for that. I would have given anything for Gemma not to have been the one to walk into that house that afternoon. Anything."

"I know," Jake said. He put his hand on his grandfather's knee.

"But what did he mean?" Jake asked. "That letter? Judy Wayne said Dad got it in his head Mom was cheating on him."

"That's an absolute lie. Not Judy. But your mom. She did everything she could for my son. She didn't cheat on him."

"I know that," Jake said. "Dad was sick. I know that too. But Judy said the guy was his best friend. Where is he? What happened?"

"I don't know," Max said. "I didn't ask. It didn't matter. It was a lie. That's all. If you wanna blame somebody, blame me. I think your mother was right. I think your father should have been in a hospital. One he couldn't get out of. She talked about getting the court involved. I didn't want to hear it. I wouldn't do it. I would not stand in open court and tell some judge my son was crazy."

"He wasn't crazy," Jake said. "But he was very, very sick, Gramps."

“He wouldn’t want this for you,” Grandpa said. “You having that file. Looking at all that ugliness. She wouldn’t either.”

Jake said nothing. He was too young to know what either of his parents would have wanted for him. That’s what burned the most.

“And she wouldn’t want to be buried under that damn monstrosity out in Ardenville. She’d want to be right here. With all of us.”

“Judy said something about that too,” Jake said. “That Mom told her she wanted to be cremated and have her ashes spread out here. They went to some other funeral together and Mom said it.”

“I tried.” Grandpa sighed. “*That* I would have gone all the way to court for. To be able to put Sonya where she belonged. I talked to a lawyer. He said we had a good case. But your grandmother talked me out of it. She didn’t want any more ugliness. And she said Adele was a mother who lost her child too. If it brought her peace to have Sonya closer to her, so be it.”

“I never knew that,” Jake said. “Judy said ... Gramps, she said the Ardens didn’t want us at Mom’s funeral. She said you got into it with Grandpa Paul. I guess I remember that a little. You were talking to him but didn’t want us to hear. I remember waiting to go in. Standing outside on the church steps. I was holding Grandma’s hand. Gemma held my other hand. Did the Ardens really try to throw us out?”

Grandpa bristled. It was an answer. “Never mind them,” he said. “Some of that goes way, way back before you were born. Some of it was before I was even born. Your great-grandfather on the Arden side hated my dad. It went both ways. My dad was part of the gang that organized and fought to unionize the clay mill workers. Boy, did Jake stir up trouble when he got together with your mom.”

Grandpa laughed to himself with a twinkle in his eye. "She was something. This little bitty thing with too much hair. She took one look at my son and decided he was for her and she wasn't gonna let anyone tell her otherwise. Not even him. I was wrong about her. Didn't think she'd last a season out here. She grew up with maids cleaning up after her. Never held a shovel in her life. But she was right there alongside your grandma on her hands and knees helping her plant the garden. Up to her arms in chicken shit raking out the coop in the mornings. The chickens were her favorite. They followed her all around the yard. Then she'd run after that damn flight risk of a billy goat. She loved it here. Took to it like she was born here. Ava was wrong to stop me from fighting to keep her here."

It was the most Jake had ever heard his grandfather say about his mother. His love for her came through in the passionate way he spoke of her.

"Everyone says Gemma's like her." Jake smiled.

Grandpa laughed. "That's true. But Gemma's even feistier."

"Everyone says I'm more like him," Jake said, giving voice to the fear that clawed at him sometimes.

"You're exactly like him," Grandpa said. "The good parts, Jake. You have to trust me on that. I know."

"Thank you for telling me," Jake said. "Now you understand why I did what I did."

"Leave it be, Jake," Grandpa said. "Pack up that file. Put it back in whatever moldy, dank corner they keep it in at that station. Better yet, burn it. It's like poison. Will you promise me?"

Jake couldn't make that promise. His grandfather's face grew weary, but he didn't ask again.

"Did you ever tell Grandma about that letter?"

"No," Grandpa whispered. "Jake, you don't understand. Your mother and father weren't the only ones who died that day. Ava did too. Inside. She looked like my Ava. Talked like her. Did her best to act like her, but she was a shell. Dead behind the eyes. She was good at faking it for everyone else. For you. For Gemma. But not for me. I saw everything. Some joke that is, huh? It would have done me good to be half blind back then. Maybe she could have snowed me too."

"She was in denial," Jake said. "She wanted to believe it was all an accident."

Grandpa nodded. "I thought she would snap out of that after a while. She never did."

"That's why you didn't want us to talk about it. Because you wanted to protect her."

Grandpa didn't answer. He didn't have to.

"It killed her, Jake. She hung on as long as she could. She raised you and Gemma. She wasn't perfect, but she loved you and she was there. Then you went off to school. Left home. And don't get me wrong. It's good that you did. But it was the last thing. She knew her job was done."

"She had cancer, Grandpa," Jake said. "She didn't will herself to die."

"Didn't she?" Grandpa said. "She could have fought. She was young enough. Strong enough. There were more treatments. The doctors were optimistic. But she wanted to let go. Deep down in a place she'd never speak of, I think Ava was relieved she got sick. I think she knew it was her way out. Or even that it was something God sent to her so she could go be with Jake. A gift."

Jake's heart twisted. He'd never known sadness like that. Grief that strong. Of course, he missed his parents. He ached for them. But they'd been gone for so long. He grew up learning how to be without them. He couldn't imagine what it had been like to lose a child. Then, for his grandfather to watch the woman he loved go through so much shared pain. To be helpless beside her as she withered away. Then, to find a way to go on without her.

He put an arm around Max, laid his head on the old man's shoulder.

"I love you," Jake told him. "And I know what it is you did."

Max shuddered. He put his hand over Jake's where it rested on his shoulder as they sat among the ghosts.

Twenty-Five

On the day Rob Arden lost his sister, he was only twenty-five years old. Thin, fit, freshly barbered blond hair that would later fall out. He wore a green polo shirt and khakis as if he'd come to Frank Borowski's interview room straight from the golf course.

It was odd to see him like this, Jake thought. He had no family pictures with the Ardens. Had heard no stories about any of them growing up. There was only the cool distance they kept. The open hostility Uncle Rob, now a county commissioner, showed him. An attitude Jake never understood. But the thirty minutes Rob gave Frank on a crisp fall day in 1992 made certain things more clear.

Grandpa Max's words burned through Jake. He'd begged him to leave the rest of this box alone. Stop digging for answers his grandfather said would never come. But Max Cashen knew his grandson. He could never let this go.

Jake texted Meg that he'd be late coming in this morning. Birdie was busy trying to track down Rianne Katz's mystery rebound guy. Mia Casey called her late last night and told her she remembered Rianne once told her she was meeting a date at a bar in Zanesville. That seemed strange to Mia at the time. Why go to a bar an hour and a half away? When Mia asked, she remembered Rianne saying her date was friends with the owner. It was a long shot, but worth pursuing because they had nothing else so far.

"Will your parents be joining us?" Frank asked as the static on the tape faded away showing a fairly clear picture this time. Young Rob sat straight up, his hands folded and resting on the table as if he were a student about to take an exam.

"They most certainly will not," Rob said. "They're in no condition to be grilled by you."

"I'm not going to grill anyone," Frank said. "I just want to make sure I understand what happened to your sister and brother-in-law."

"You must not be very good at your job then. So I'll make it easy. That scum terrorized my sister. Ripped her away from her family. Turned her against us. Didn't take care of her. Then he murdered her. That's what happened, Detective."

Jake felt every muscle in his body go tense. He'd heard that vitriol spewed from Rob Arden's mouth his whole life. He'd held his grandfather back from taking a swing at him more than once.

"Okay," Frank said, showing more restraint than Jake would have. "I understand how upsetting this must be for you and your whole family. I'll try not to take up too much of your time. Are you comfortable if I record this interview?"

Rob looked straight at the camera, contempt clearly written in his tightly narrowed eyes.

"Fine," he said. "For the record, my name is Robert Paul Arden, twenty-five. I live at 924 Eaton Circle in Hart Lake."

"This isn't a court of law, Rob," Frank said. "You're not under oath. This isn't formal testimony. This is a conversation. That's all."

"What could you possibly want to know?" Rob asked.

"For starters, when was the last time you spoke to your sister?"

"I don't know," Rob said. "Maybe a week ago. Maybe less. She hadn't visited our mother in a while and I called to ask her about that."

"How did she sound to you then?"

"Alive."

"Were you aware of any difficulty she was having with Jake? That he might be ill?"

"We didn't talk about Jake," Rob answered.

"It was a sore subject, I gather."

"Sore subject? That's putting it mildly."

"How so?" Frank asked, sitting back in his chair, crossing his ankle over the opposite knee. Jake imagined what Frank was thinking. That they were going to be there for a while.

"It's not a secret," Rob said. "I've never pretended otherwise. My family did not approve of her relationship with that man. I warned her. Over and over. She wouldn't listen. He'd brainwashed her. Raped her."

Jake vaulted to his feet. He wanted to rip through the screen and wrap his hands around Rob Arden's neck.

"What do you mean rape?" Frank asked.

"My sister was only sixteen years old when Cashen made her go to bed with him. That's statutory rape."

"He was sixteen as well," Frank said. "From what I've heard so far, she was in love with him, Rob. They were married. They have two children."

"You really want to sit here and argue with me about that? He ruined her life. Now he's taken her life and ruined ours. I don't know if my mother is going to recover from this. She's in the hospital right now. Did you know that? My father was worried she might try to hurt herself; her grief is that strong."

"I'm very sorry to hear that," Frank said evenly. "I really can't imagine what your family is going through."

"That's right. You can't."

"So your sister didn't mention that her husband was struggling with mental illness?"

"She didn't have to," Rob said. "It was obvious. He was practically speaking in tongues the last time I saw him. That was maybe two weeks ago. I ran into them in town. She was going into the pharmacy and he was sitting in the passenger seat of their car. He wasn't making any sense. Rambling about people who weren't there. I don't know."

"Did you ask Sonya about it? Did you offer to help?"

"Are you accusing me of something?"

"Absolutely not. I am only trying to understand what was happening with your sister and her husband over the last couple of weeks."

"Jake Cashen was not a good man," Rob said. "He got my sister pregnant because he thought she'd be a meal ticket. That's all the Cashens have ever been. Looking for handouts. Thinking the world owes them something. Trying to take things they haven't earned."

Jake couldn't believe what he was hearing. His sister was dead. He had a niece and nephew out there who were still young children. Jake Cashen Sr. was dead. He had so far not asked a single question about where he and Gemma were.

"I understand your frustration," Frank said. "But if we could focus on the events of the past week or so. Did you speak to Jake at all other than this encounter in front of the pharmacy?"

"No," he said. "I never talked to Jake. I purposely avoided it. There were times he tried to block me from communicating with my sister. He isolated her from her own family."

"Rob, I'd like to show you something. I'll warn you, it might be disturbing. But it involves you in a way. I'm hoping you can maybe shed some light on its meaning."

Frank opened the file folder on the table. Like in his interview with Grandpa, he had that same copy of his father's suicide note in its plastic sheet protector. He slid it across the table to Rob.

Rob picked it up. His eyes flicked over the page. He rose to his feet while he read, then threw the paper on the table.

"What is this? Why would you show this to me?" Rob demanded.

"Jake left it," Frank said. "Clearly, he was suffering from some delusions. But he mentions you. That part about Brother Rob being right. Do you know what that could be referring to?"

"I have no idea. I told you. I avoided having any contact with that scumbag. Maybe in the back of his sick, twisted mind he started to realize he wasn't good enough for my sister."

"Maybe," Frank said. "You're certain you didn't talk to him the day before? He says he talked to you yesterday in the note."

"That note is nonsense. What the hell are you accusing me of?"

"Nothing. I'm just trying to understand what might have set Jake off."

"He. Was. Crazy. I told you. I hadn't seen him for weeks. And I do not talk to him. Do you hear me? I don't talk to Jake. Not yesterday, not last week. He was a lunatic and now everyone knows it. Too bad it's too late for my sister. Are you going to put this out there? Because if I see this leaked to the media, I will sue your ass so fast. You'll be writing parking tickets the rest of your life if you're lucky."

"I have no intention of releasing this," Frank said. "You can lower your weapon, Rob."

"They knew!"

"Who knew?"

"The whole lot of them. The Cashens. They knew that man was sick in the head. They did nothing. They threw my sister to the wolves. I should sue them for wrongful death. Drive them back to the hole they crawled out of. Take every measly little thing they have. They will not see one penny from my sister's estate."

"Rob," Frank said. "Shouldn't all of that be for her children?"

He didn't answer. He simply scowled at Frank. Then he leaned forward and jabbed a finger on the table.

"They knew. And they did nothing. This?" He picked up the letter, crumpled it, and threw it against the wall. "This is the rambling of a crazy person. What are you even talking about? Let me tell you something, I better not hear that you've tried to talk to either of my parents. They don't need to be dragged down into this. They deserve peace. They deserve to have their daughter back. Where is she? We would like to make sure she's buried in consecrated ground. Back where she belongs."

"That will be for the families to decide," Frank said. "The medical examiner will be in touch when Sonya's remains can be released."

"Fine."

"Rob. What about the Gryphon Jake mentions? Does he mean Griff ..."

"Enough! I don't want to hear another word of this. Who knows what that lunatic meant? My sister gave up everything for him. Everything. And this is what he did. He made it so that no one else could ever have her. Could ever love her. We were talking again, Sonya and me. Not often. But we were starting to communicate. That must have pissed him off. He wanted to control her. Well, he sure did, didn't he?"

"Rob ..."

"No. No more. I'm done with this. I'll take my sister home where she belongs. Then, I never want to hear the name Cashen again. You tell those inbred hillbillies that. We'll have nothing to do with them. Their name won't even be on her headstone."

Frank rose. Rob turned his back on him and stormed out of the room.

Jake heard his front door open and close. He'd lost track of time again. It was after ten a.m. He knew it was Birdie. Gemma would already be at the bar by now, opening for the lunch crowd.

Birdie walked into Jake's spare room. She held a thin silver book under her arm.

"Look at this," Jake said. He rewound the tape to the final seconds. He played Rob's last tirade for her. Where he called his family inbred and swore to erase his mother's name.

"He's an asshole, Jake," Birdie said. "At least he's stayed on brand all these years."

"I should have let my grandfather strangle him in Gemma's parking lot last year. Now I understand why Max was so furious."

"Did he say anything useful in that interview? Or was he just spewing lies and hatred?"

"Mostly lies and hatred," Jake said. "But Frank started to ask him something about the Gryphon. He said Griff and Rob ended the interview. Any luck out in Zanesville?"

"No," she said. "The bartender vaguely remembers Rianne as a customer. Said she came in a couple of times with a date. They sat in a dark corner booth. He recognized Rianne from the picture I showed him. All he could tell me about her date is that he was white, tall, with brown hair. But it wasn't Cameron. And it was the same guy both times she came in with him. If Rianne told Mia this date was friends with the owner, she was either lying or mistaken. Nobody would validate that story."

"We may never find this guy. And if we do, the odds of him having anything useful to say ..."

"I did find something," Birdie said. "Come sit down with me."

He followed her out into the living room. They sat side by side on the couch. She set the book on her lap. It was the Stanley High School yearbook from the early nineties.

"I talked to Mom again," she said. "Asked her about Griff again."

She opened the yearbook to the sports pages. She had one in particular marked with a sticky note. It was a team shot of the men's varsity wrestling team. His father was sitting in the front row, with a mean look on his face. Beside him, another boy about his size sported the same glower.

"Griffin Malley," she said. Then she pointed to a candid shot on the opposite page. His father and this Griffin Malley were sitting in the bleachers together, laughing.

"Your mom said they were best friends. That they'd known each other since high school. I never got far enough with Max to ask him. He shut me down on that."

"I found him, Jake," Birdie said. "He lives three hours away in Port Clinton. He's a retired plumber."

Jake stared at the picture. The Gryphon. Griffin. A man who had become so close to his father. Knew him better than Jake ever could.

"I've seen him," Jake said. "There's a picture somewhere. A scrapbook my grandmother kept. My parents eloped so she never had formal wedding photos. But she threw a party out in the backyard. I remember a picture of my dad sitting next to this same guy, laughing just like this." He pointed to the candid photo on the bleachers. "I forgot about it until just now. We didn't take that book out very much. It would make my grandma cry. I don't even know where it is now. But this guy, he was there. At the party. Laughing with my dad. I think I remember him. God. I remember him. Just bits and pieces. But yeah. When I was a little kid. We had this cookout. I think for my dad's birthday. This guy was there then too. It might have been my dad's last birthday before my parents died."

Jake sat back. His mind was spinning. Griffin. Griff. He couldn't remember the name. But the face. Vaguely familiar. And he remembered the man having white teeth and a dimple. Griff.

"I talked to him, Jake," Birdie said quietly. Jake snapped his neck back, then turned to her.

"I told him we work together. I told him about you. If you want to talk to him, he's willing. He said he figured someday you or

Gemma might come looking for him. He said he'd meet us halfway in Delaware. Five thirty. We'll go right after work."

"We?" Jake asked.

"You've done enough of this on your own," she said. "You need a friend. And I'm not taking no for an answer. Either you take me with you or I won't tell you where he wants to meet."

Stubborn women, Jake thought. He was surrounded by them. But when she said it, he felt relieved.

Twenty-Six

Birdie spent the morning knocking on doors near Rianne Katz's old duplex. Jake hoped she could find someone, anyone, who had seen Rianne with another man. The tenant who had shared the other side of the duplex when Rianne had rented there had moved out almost two years ago. Jake got his name from Rianne's ex-landlord but he'd been so far hard to find.

After lunch, Birdie came back to the office, defeated. "I don't know if this is even worth our time anymore," she said. "Did you have any luck with the neighbor?"

"Not so far," Jake said. "The guy's name is Adam Smith. So it's gonna be like looking for a needle in a haystack. The landlord in Blackhand Hills didn't keep copies of his driver's license on file. The forwarding address he gave hasn't panned out yet. It's another rental property in Athens. But ... that landlord *did* keep copies of his application and credit report. Paper ones. They're in a storage unit and her husband's driving out there to see what he can find. They'll get back to me sometime tomorrow."

Birdie plopped into her desk chair. She unbuttoned the top button of her blouse and fanned herself with a file folder.

"It's ninety out there. My A/C is on the fritz."

"You want me to take a look at it?"

"Nah. I've got a guy coming out. Keith recommended him."

"Forget Keith's guy. Call Howard's. Lance took over the business from his dad."

Jake reached into his desk drawer and rooted around for a card. He found it and tossed it to her. "Tell Lance you're working here now. His old man always used to give discounts to cops."

"If you say so," she said. "Keith was pretty glowing about his guy too."

"How's that going?" Jake said, regretting it as soon as it spilled out of his mouth.

Birdie's face dropped a little. "It's not," she said. "We broke up."

"Again? Is this like the third time?"

"Second, smartass," she said. "Oh, I saw Landry in the hall. Told her we're both punching out around three thirty. It'll give us both time to change before we meet Malley."

Jake noted the subject change. He debated telling anyone else about his plan. Gemma still had no idea he'd been poking around in their parents' case. Grandpa was better off thinking he'd backed off. He'd decide what to tell them after he talked to the guy.

"Knock knock." Mark Ramirez stood in the doorway, his hair slicked back from sweat. He stepped inside and stood directly under the air-conditioning vent.

"You stink," Birdie said, wrinkling her nose.

"I've been wriggling around in a crawl space over in Logan for the past two hours. Kid offed his grandma and stuffed her down there. It's an ugly one. You don't want to know."

"You want something to drink?" Jake asked. Mark walked over to the table and sat down. Birdie was right; he did smell ripe. Jake reached over and opened the small fridge they kept for lunch leftovers and cold drinks. He tossed Mark a bottle of water. Mark rubbed the cool plastic across his forehead.

"What's the bad news?" Jake asked. "You wouldn't be here if you didn't have some."

Ramirez cracked open his water and chugged it down. He smacked his lips and set the bottle down. "Ballistics came back on your murder-suicide." He reached into his pocket and pulled out a thumb drive. He tossed it to Jake. Jake caught it one-handed.

"It's a long one," Ramirez said. "I can give you the Cliff Notes. I figured you'd have a lot of questions after you saw it. I thought I'd save us both some time and just pop in. I would have been here sooner but Grandma's crawl space was a bigger job than I thought it was going to be. Don't have the ME's report, but it looks like the kid fed her rat poison over the course of two weeks."

"That's awful," Birdie said. She brought her laptop over to the table. Jake got up and popped the flash drive into the port.

"What have you got?" Jake asked.

Ramirez leaned forward and pressed a couple of keys on Birdie's computer. Thirty seconds later, he had two sheets of paper. Copies of his report summary.

Birdie skimmed it, frowning.

"Here's the gist," Ramirez said as he scrolled down the PDF of the larger report on the computer. "Victim one. White female. Two bullets were recovered from the body and acquired by us from Dr. Stone. Both hollow points. We did microscopic analysis and 3D imaging."

Ramirez hit the page down key several times then turned the screen toward Birdie and Jake. He pulled up a close-up image of the two bullets side by side.

"Both showed the same microscopic striations. Meaning they were both fired from the same gun."

"Makes sense," Birdie said. "I wouldn't have expected anything different."

Ramirez put a finger up, indicating for her to wait. He continued. "The two spent cartridges were found on the kitchen floor near your female victim. We examined those under a comparison microscope. Both showed the same unique tool marks from the firing pin and ejector. There were no prints found on the cartridges. Both cartridges were from the same 9mm Federal. Chrome in color."

"Dammit on the lack of prints," Jake said. "This thing's getting harder and harder. Give me some good news, Mark. Something I can use."

Ramirez cocked his head to the side and took a breath. He went back to the screen and scrolled further down. "So, victim two, your white male. A single bullet was recovered from the body and acquired by us from Dr. Stone. I also got a single shell casing on the living room floor near the body of victim two. Rolled under the couch. We went through the same process on that bullet and casing as was done for victim one."

He scrolled down until another image popped up. A close-up of a single bullet. "The lab found one noticeable difference from the bullet in victim one. See it's rounded at the tip. It's more something you'd find in target or range ammo."

Birdie scooted closer and squinted at the screen. "I don't see any difference."

"It's subtle," Ramirez said. "But trust me. It's there. You got a 9mm Taurus laying right next to victim two's dominant hand. The gun had a full ten round magazine. The significance there was that the bullet and casing from this gun were most likely in the chamber already. All rounds found were 9mm Federal range ammunition."

"You're losing me," Jake said. "I saw all that with my own eyes."

"The lab test-fired the gun. Then they compared the bullets to the one pulled out of your victim. The kill shot. Bullets and casings from the test firings and the one found in your guy and under that couch were a match."

Ramirez loved this stuff. He could go on for hours talking about microscopic analysis.

"Here's the deal though," Ramirez continued. "When the test-fired bullets and casings from the Taurus were compared to the bullets and casings pulled out of victim one, they didn't match. The shell casings showed different tool marks from the test fires. The test-fired bullets had totally different striations."

"They were two different guns," Jake said.

"You got it in one," Ramirez said.

"There were two different guns," Birdie repeated.

Jake actually shook his head, trying to wrap his mind around the impact of Ramirez's conclusions.

"The Taurus, the one found next to Cameron Katz. It was Rianne's gun. That's not in question."

"It was registered to Rianne Timiney," Ramirez said.

"Somebody shot Cameron Katz with his wife's gun," Birdie said.

"But Rianne was shot with a different gun."

"Anything in your crime scene analysis that would indicate two shooters?"

"No," Ramirez said. "I mean, I can't rule it out. I can tell you with scientific certainty that the female victim was shot with one gun, the male victim was shot with a different one."

"Then it had to be two shooters," Birdie said. "Right?"

"No," Jake said. "I don't think so. Cameron's murder was staged to look like a suicide. Of course they'd want to use his own gun to do it."

"She was already dead," Birdie said. "Rianne had to have already been shot dead before the killer got to Cameron. If the killer was trying to make it look like a murder-suicide, he'd use the same gun on both. Their gun."

"Cameron might have walked in on something," Jake said. "Then staged Cameron's death like a suicide to cover his tracks."

"He did a good job of it," Ramirez said. "But only by the looks of it. By the science of it, this was sloppy as hell."

"I think it just proves our working theory," Jake said. "Rianne Katz was the target. Cameron Katz might have just been in the wrong place at the wrong time."

"We have to find that rebound boyfriend, Jake," Birdie said.

"That's all I got," Ramirez said. "If you don't mind, I need to get out of here and get in a shower."

"Hurry," Birdie said as Ramirez walked past her, leaving a stink trail.

Jake combed through the ballistics report a few more times. The science didn't lie. Two guns were used. One was the Taurus registered to Rianne Katz. The other was still out there somewhere. Another needle in a haystack, but if he could find his suspect, the bullets he fired would damn him.

"Jake," Birdie said. "It's after three. Are you ready to cut out of here?"

Jake stared at the blown-up image of the two bullets pulled out of Rianne Katz's abdomen. A tantalizing clue. One he would have to put aside until tomorrow.

Now, he had a meeting with the Gryphon of his father's tortured mind.

Twenty-Seven

"Here?" Jake asked. Birdie had pulled into the parking lot of a small township park outside Delaware, Ohio. A copper dinosaur stood sentry in the center of it next to a jungle gym and a giant slide. Two toddlers posed next to it, waiting for their mother to snap a picture of them. A group of older kids, maybe fourth graders, sat in the picnic area eating snacks, their parents at a different table, talking and laughing.

"He said this place is within walking distance from his daughter's house," Birdie said. Jake scanned the park. At the far end, a man sat alone, smoking a cigarette.

"I suppose that has to be him," Jake said.

"There's a walking trail through the woods over there. I'm going to check it out."

Jake caught himself from asking her why she wasn't coming with him. Instead, he gave her a simple thanks and started walking across the park. As he passed the jungle gym and the picnic tables, the man rose from his bench and snuffed out his cigarette. He looked nervous. Terrified actually.

He had thick silver hair and a grizzled face with deep lines around his eyes. A strong jaw. About Jake's height. Still fit with a trim waistline and bulky biceps. He stood with a wide stance, his center of gravity held low. A wrestler, Jake could spot one anywhere.

"Mr. Malley?" Jake asked.

Malley trembled a bit, then held out his hand. "Griffin," he said. He blinked rapidly, his eyes shining with unshed tears. When Jake stepped forward to take his offered hand, Griffin took one unsteady step backward, practically tripping over the bench behind him.

"I'm sorry," he said, his voice cracking. "It's just. I didn't ... You're ..."

"I look like him," Jake said. "Everyone who knew him tells me that."

Griffin shook his head. "No. Not like him. Not similar to him. You could be his twin, Jakey."

Jake blanched.

"I'm sorry." Griffin smiled. "I don't suppose anyone calls you that anymore."

"No," he said. "I can't even tell you when they stopped. But not even Gemma calls me that."

Griffin's face fell. "Gemma. She's not with you?"

"No. She doesn't know I'm here. I haven't told her I've been pursuing any of this."

Griffin sank back down onto the bench. Jake paused, then took a seat beside him. They could see the walking trail from here. Birdie had stopped to pet another hiker's yellow Lab.

"Is she your wife?" Griffin asked.

"She's my partner," Jake said, then realized that could mean something else. "My work partner. She's a detective. She's the one you spoke to on the phone. Erica Wayne. Her brother Ben was my best friend."

"Rudy's little girl?" Griffin asked. "You're kidding. That's Birdie? I didn't make the connection."

Jake had forgotten. Both his parents had called her Birdie too after he gave her the nickname. If they were friends, Griffin would have known that.

"Yes," he said.

"Well, she sure grew up well. My God. She's stunning. I remember her with skinny little scabby knees. You and Benny used to chase her off when Judy would come to pick you up at Jake and Sonya's."

"You remember a lot," Jake said. "I'm sorry. I forgot who you were. I didn't know you and my dad were close."

Griffin let out a bitter laugh. "Your dad was like a brother to me for a time. We grew up together."

"You were teammates," Jake said.

"Yeah."

"Were you there when he met my mother?"

Griffin's face split into a wide smile. He still had those white, straight teeth Jake remembered from that old scrapbook photo. It was so familiar, but also so foreign.

"One of our other friends dared me to go up and talk to her. Sonya was so ... she was like this princess. Untouchable, we thought. There was a light about her. We thought she was so serious. She went to St. Iz. She and a group of her friends started showing up at this drive-in we all went to. That shows how old I am. That had to be '79, maybe '80. I think we were fifteen or sixteen. I had to be sixteen, I guess. Jake was the only one of us with a license. He stole his dad's truck one weekend. I knew he was gonna catch hell for it, but he didn't care. I walked up to Sonya. I told her that my friend had a crush on her. I thought Jake was gonna kill me. You know what she said?"

Jake shook his head.

"She said good, because I have a crush on him too. Tell him to stop being such a wimp and come over here and talk to me."

Jake laughed. It was something Gemma would have done. "What did he do?"

"Your dad was no dummy. So he marched right up there and he and Sonya walked off together. That was it. From that point on, they were together every chance they could get. And it wasn't easy. Her folks weren't actually giving their blessing. Ardens never had a high opinion of us Stanley High kids. Which is a joke. They've lived in Blackhand Hills longer than any of us."

"Not much has changed about that," Jake said.

"I wouldn't think so. But for that whole year, Jake and Sonya would find ways to sneak off. It was like a movie sometimes. He'd go to her bedroom window and throw pebbles at it. She'd climb down this rose trellis. I thought she was gonna break her neck."

Jake tried to imagine it. He'd been raised with the story of how much his parents loved each other. Generically, as a point of fact. Through Griffin's words, a different picture emerged. It wasn't just love. They had to have been desperate for each other to go through all of that.

"Then her folks found out," Griffin continued. "That was a scene. We were all out at the fairgrounds. Jake and Sonya were walking down the thoroughfare holding hands. Sonya's dad and brother drove up in a golf cart, furious. Her dad grabbed her and tried to shove her into that cart. I thought he was gonna throw her over his shoulder like a caveman and hit her over the head with a club. Yelling and screaming. They drew a crowd. The sheriffs showed up to break it all up. Rob took a swing at your dad. The rest of us were on him pretty quick. He got off easy. Just a shiner and a fat lip. His dad was threatening to press charges against Jake. Cops talked him down."

"I didn't know any of that," Jake said.

"I don't think your grandparents ... your dad's parents ... knew anything about it. It got harder for them after that. Your dad was miserable. They were making plans to run off together. I know that. Jake wanted to quit school over it. Your grandpa helped screw his head back on. Then, Sonya was pregnant."

"Do you think they did it on purpose?" Jake asked. He'd never thought of it before.

"No, God, no," Griffin said. "I told you. Your dad was no dummy. That was just one of those things. But they made a decision. They were going to keep the baby and get married. Sonya moved into your grandparents' place. They both got their GEDs. Jake took a job at the mill. God, he never wanted to do that. He wanted to open his own carpentry shop."

"Thank you for telling me," Jake said.

"How are you?" Griffin looked at him. "And your sister."

"We're okay," Jake said. "Gemma's got two sons of her own. She owns a pub. Used to be the End Zone."

"No kidding? Good for her. And you're a cop. I think your dad would have liked that. Probably would have scared Sonya to death."

"Griffin, the reason I came here. The main one, anyway. I have to know what happened to my dad."

Griffin reached into his pocket and pulled out another cigarette. He lit it and took a long drag. "It's a bad habit. I've tried to give it up a few times. I had lung cancer about ten years ago. I know it's crazy. Just can't stop."

"My dad left a note," Jake said.

Griffin nodded. "I know."

"How could you know? It was part of the case file. My grandmother never even knew about it. Just Detective Borowski, my grandfather, and Uncle Rob, as far as I know."

"Frank showed me," Griffin said. "He asked me about it."

"You're not mentioned in the case file," Jake said. "He videotaped every interview."

"He came to my house," Griffin said.

"My dad thought you were having an affair with my mom, didn't he?"

Griffin dropped his head. When he lifted it and stared at Jake, his eyes had gone cold. "That's not true. That was never true. Your dad was in a really bad place. None of us really understood how bad it was. Except for Sonya. And we all failed her. That I didn't do something sooner ... Jake, it's the biggest regret of my life."

"What could you have done?" Jake asked.

"He wasn't sleeping. He wasn't eating."

"That's what everyone says."

"But he was doing okay? I thought so anyway. He was showing up for work. Doing his job. People get depressed sometimes. I tried to talk to him. He was like a brick wall. He was a lot like his father. When Jake decided to dig his heels on something, that was it. It's what he did with Sonya. He'd have burned the whole damn town down if that's what it would have taken to be with her."

"Then he wasn't," Jake said. "He got delusional."

"Yes," Griffin said. "We tried an intervention of sorts, Sonya and me. She asked for my help. She figured I was one of the only people who he'd listen to. Who'd tell him the truth. We managed to get him to see a doctor. We thought it was okay for a while. They gave him Haldol. It really helped calm him down. Helped him sleep. Then, he stopped taking it. Sonya didn't realize it. Neither did I. When she figured it out, she confronted him. I backed her up. He went apeshit. Said we were trying to poison him."

"It's in the letter," Jake said.

"Then Rob got in the middle of it."

Jake cocked his head.

Griffin finished his cigarette. "Rob and his family, they made things really hard on Sonya. Whenever she tried to talk to her mother, her dad and Rob would put a stop to it. Told her she had to choose. That she couldn't be an Arden if she were a Cashen. Really nutso stuff."

"He said the opposite," Jake said. "My Uncle Rob says it was my dad keeping her from having any contact with her family."

"You've known him your whole life, haven't you? Your Uncle Rob?"

"Yeah."

"Which version of events rings more true to you?"

"I take your point."

"That was a big point of stress for your mom. And your dad felt really guilty about it too. He hated being the reason she was feuding with them. But that went on for years and years."

"Birdie's mother told me a story about my dad confronting my mom about you."

"Is this something you really have to know?" Griffin said. "You really think it'll help anything?"

"I don't know. I just know I need to have the truth."

"The truth," Griffin said. "Your dad couldn't see reality anymore. That's the thing. He had it in his mind that the people who loved him were trying to hurt him. Had turned against him. And Rob ..."

Griffin dropped his head again.

"What?" Jake said. "Rob what?"

"He saw an opportunity, okay?"

Brother Rob was right. Jake could see the line written in his father's handwriting.

"That stuff about me and your mom? It started because Rob told him. He told him she was cheating on him with me."

Jake felt like his heart had been torn from his chest. The air got thin.

"How do you know that?" Jake asked.

"Because he told me. Your dad told me. He showed up at my house in the middle of the night. Just absolutely out of his mind. Broke through a window. I swear to God if he'd had a gun, he would have shot me. It keeps me up at night sometimes wishing he had. Because things would have turned out a lot differently."

"My father told you my Uncle Rob said you and my mother were having an affair?"

"That's what he told me," Griffin said.

"The Gryphon," Jake said. "In his letter, he wrote that my mother would be better off with the Gryphon. He said Brother Rob was right. It's because Rob told Dad that you, Griffin, were sleeping with my mom."

"I wasn't. And deep down, I know your dad knew that. God, I hope deep down he knew that."

He knew. Jake thought. Rob knew his father was having a mental health crisis. He knew he was paranoid. He fed into it.

"Rob thought he could break my parents apart."

"Something like that," Griffin said. "Yeah. I'll never forgive him for that."

"It wasn't your fault," Jake said. "You didn't do anything wrong. Rob is a liar. He said he hadn't talked to my dad in weeks before they died."

"That," Griffin said, rising, "is a damn lie. Rob was there all the time. Stopping by to try to guilt Sonya into coming to visit her folks. Sonya would tell him she wasn't coming to the house unless the rest of her family was welcome too. He'd show up when your dad was at work. It went on and on."

"He might as well have loaded the damn gun," Jake muttered. "But it's still not your fault, Griffin."

"It was!" he shouted. "Goddammit, it was! I sent her there alone!"

"What are you talking about?"

"Your dad just took off. Disappeared. He left a message on my answering machine saying that he was going to kill himself. That there were worms in his head. Crawling into his brain. Just absolutely insane stuff. Said I could have Sonya. That he'd make it easy for us. Then he called your mom and told her pretty much the same thing. That he was gonna kill himself. She was so scared. Out of her mind with worry. We both were. And we couldn't find him. For like a day and a half. We looked everywhere. She couldn't get ahold of your grandparents. They went on some overnight anniversary trip. This was before any of us had cell phones. But we looked all over town."

"Did you call the police?" Jake asked.

"Sonya didn't want to. I begged her. But she was afraid it would make things worse. That if he did have a gun, he wouldn't listen when they approached him. Then they'd have to shoot him. I know now it would have been better that way."

Jake's head spun.

"I had to go to work. I couldn't take another day off. Sonya was trying her best to just keep everything normal for you guys. I thought maybe she should send you both to stay with someone for a while. She thought she could handle everything. I mean, it was Jake."

"I don't remember," Jake said. "I don't remember my dad being missing. Or her being frantic."

"Because she didn't let you see. Either of you. She protected you. You guys were everything to her. But that day, she went to work. I told her she should. That it wouldn't do her any good to sit around worrying. So she did. But she got another call from Jake. Eerie. He told her goodbye. She knew he meant it. She called me. Told me to get over to the house and she was gonna go to Jake's dad's. I talked her out of it. I thought for sure if Jake was gonna make good on that promise, he'd do it out in the woods. If anything happened, I didn't want her to be the one to find it."

"He went home," Jake whispered.

"I sent her there," Griffin said. "Me. I thought she'd be safe at home. I thought I'd be the one trying to talk him down. Or ... finding him dead. I was wrong. You understand? If I'd let her do what she wanted, go to your grandpa's, she'd still be alive. Maybe your dad wouldn't be. Maybe I'd be dead. I would have preferred it."

"The phone was in her hand," Jake said, seeing the crime scene photo in his mind's eye.

"I think she tried to call me," Griffin said. "That haunts me. Maybe she tried to call me. Or call over to your grandparents' house because she knew that's where I went. But she walked in on him, I think. God, I don't know what happened in that house. I don't know if he startled her? Or if she said something about his medication and it set him off? Or maybe he was so far gone he thought she was me. That's what I think it was. What it had to be. He had it all mixed up in his head and it was me he wanted dead."

"Stop," Jake said. "Everyone keeps telling me that digging through this doesn't do any good. It's the same for you. You're only right that my dad was out of his mind."

"He wouldn't have killed her. Please know that. He never would have hurt her."

"I know," Jake said. "It's okay, I know."

"I didn't know. I walked your grandparents' property for a couple of hours. I was sure he'd be out there. I just knew it. Because he knew he'd be alone. By the time I got back and tried to get ahold of Sonya, it was too late. It was all over. I didn't want Sonya to find him. But it was Gemma, God. It was Gemma."

Griffin Malley broke down. He doubled over and sobbed into his hands. Jake put an arm around him and held him until the storm subsided.

"You did everything you could," Jake said. "Everyone did. It was an accident. It was the disease."

Griffin straightened and nodded.

"You were gone," Jake said. "You left."

"I had to," Griffin said. "I couldn't stay in that town afterward. It was too much. Too heavy. Too sad. And there were rumors starting. I always figured Rob was behind that too. People looking at me. Glaring. Maybe thinking I really was sleeping with Sonya. So I left. It was better for everybody."

"I forgot," Jake said. "I think I knew you. But I forgot. Gemma must remember. She's never mentioned you. My grandparents didn't either."

"It's okay. What were they supposed to say?"

"I don't know," Jake said. "Answer questions, I guess. Like you are now."

"I've tried to keep track of you," Griffin said. "I still know a few people back home."

"You shouldn't have had to leave."

"It was better. Trust me. People were talking. It was causing problems. I didn't need that. Your grandparents for sure didn't need that. They needed to focus on you guys and their own grief. I knew the only way to kill the rumors was to leave. The fact that you're only now learning about them, some thirty years later? That just means it was the right decision."

"It doesn't mean it was a fair one," Jake said. "Where did you go?"

"I needed a fresh start. My grandparents were still alive then, living in Ireland. That seemed far enough away. So, I moved in with them for a few years. Helped both of them through their final illnesses. I met my wife there. Bridget. We started a life. When she got pregnant, she wanted our kids to be born here though. She had some family in Port Clinton. My sister at the time didn't live too far from there either. She was in Findlay. I've never been back to Blackhand Hills since. But I never stopped thinking about you guys. I always hoped you and your sister were okay."

"We are," Jake said. "But I think she'd like to meet you too. Maybe it's time for you to come back for a visit."

Griffin's face went hard again. "Does he still live there?"

Jake knew immediately who he meant. "He does. Rob Arden is a county commissioner now."

"I'd like to meet Gemma and see you again too. But I can't be near your uncle. You understand? Because I think I'd have to kill him."

"Jake?" Birdie walked up. Jake rose. It was time to go. Time to find a way to process everything Griffin Malley had told him.

"You don't remember me," Griffin said, standing. "I knew your parents. And Jake's. It's nice to see you again, Birdie."

Birdie gave Jake a quizzical look. Then she smiled, stepped forward, and gave Griffin Malley a hug.

Twenty-Eight

Jake was late coming in the next morning. It had taken him some time to do what he knew had to be done. Birdie sat at her desk as he walked past her carrying the banker's box containing his parents' case file. He set it on the floor in the corner of the office.

Birdie swiveled her chair toward him, her pen in her hand. "Do you want to talk about it?"

Jake stacked two other boxes on top of his parents'. He could close it, shove it to the side, but he wasn't yet ready to put it back in the Crypt.

"No," he said. "I don't think there's anything left to say."

Birdie regarded him, her eyes holding questions. "Okay. But you know you can with me. Anytime. We're partners. But I'm your friend, Jake."

"I know. Thank you for coming with me yesterday. I didn't want you to. But you were right that you should."

She smiled. "Haven't you figured out yet I'm always right?"

He had a smart retort. Before he could make it, his desk phone buzzed. Melanie, one of the civilian clerks, was handling reception this morning. "Jake," she said. "I've got a guy on the line who says he heard you were looking for him."

Jake narrowed his eyes, not immediately knowing who it could be.

"Says his name is Adam Smith," Melanie said. Birdie rose to her feet and grabbed a pad of paper off her desk. Jake pointed toward the second desk phone sitting on the table behind her. She went to it, poised to answer it.

"I'll take it," Jake said.

"Line two," Melanie told him, then transferred the call. Birdie pressed the speaker button.

"Mr. Smith? This is Detective Jake Cashen." He took a seat at the table. Birdie joined him.

The caller cleared his throat. "Hi. Um. I ... uh ... I got a call from my landlord. She said you were calling and asking about me. Is there a problem? Can you tell me what this is about?"

He didn't know. It made sense. If Jake's information was correct, Smith lived in Athens now. News from Worthington County might not have reached him.

"I'm really glad you called," Jake said. "Do you think you could meet me somewhere so we could talk in person?"

"I don't think that's possible. I'm in Sacramento for a work conference for the next week. Can we do this now?"

Jake raised his chin at Birdie. She had her pen ready to go.

"If that's all you can do, Mr. Smith. First, I want to confirm you're the right Adam Smith. Did you live at 3425 Fincher Street in Stanley?"

"A couple of years ago, yeah. When I was working at TopCell Wireless. Now I'm working for a data analysis firm."

"Okay," Jake said. "Was Rianne Timiney your neighbor?"

"Rianne? Sure. She lived in the unit next to mine."

"Good," Jake said. "Then yes. You're who I need to talk to. Are you somewhere quiet where you can give me some time?"

"I'm in my hotel room. I don't have to be anywhere for about an hour," Smith answered.

"Perfect, Mr. Smith. I'm working a homicide here in Blackhand Hills. Rianne Timiney was one of the victims."

Momentary silence. "Oh my God. She was murdered? Someone killed Rianne?"

"Yes," Jake said. "Along with her husband, Cameron Katz. Did you know him as well?"

"I didn't. I knew she started to date some guy named Cameron. That was right about the time I was getting ready to move out. I didn't know they got married. What happened?"

"That's what we're trying to figure out. You said you knew about Cameron. Did you talk to Rianne a lot?"

"I mean, sure. We were neighbors. I'd see her coming and going. Same with me. We were pretty friendly. God. I'm just trying to process this. She's dead? Man. I had no idea."

"I understand," Jake said. "Mr. Smith ..."

"Adam, just call me Adam."

"Thanks. Listen, I don't want to take up a lot of your time. But I'm trying to piece together some things that were going on in Rianne's life before she started dating Cameron Katz. Did she date frequently? Did you ever meet anyone else she was involved with?"

"I don't know if I'd use the word meet, exactly. But yeah. She had a boyfriend before that. I can't say I really liked him. Jesus. I'm really sorry. I didn't know this had happened. Or that you were looking for me. I would have called sooner. I would have called as soon as I heard."

Jake and Birdie exchanged puzzled looks. "Why is that, Adam?"

"You're asking about guys Rianne dated. Do you think that's what this was? One of her ex-boyfriends?"

"We're exploring every lead we can. Yes."

"She had shitty taste in guys," Adam said. "I'll say that right upfront. Yes. This boyfriend she had when I lived there. You know, I don't know if I'd even call him a boyfriend. There was this maybe two- or three-week period I saw him around. It got intense. He was bad news."

Birdie started writing furiously.

"Tell me about him," Jake said.

"He was over all the time. I think he would show up unannounced. A couple times when I was leaving for work, he'd be knocking at her door. I'd see her answer in her pajamas. Clearly surprised to see him."

"Did she seem upset by this?"

"Yeah, actually. That's what I'm saying. It seemed to me like some guy she had just hooked up with one night. And he couldn't take the hint that she wasn't interested in something serious with him."

"Did she tell you that?" Jake asked.

"Kind of. I mean, for a few weeks, he was over almost every night. Then she told me she broke up with him. But for a few more months, he'd show up at all hours of the day and night. And there were a couple of times she'd pretend she wasn't home. I knew she was, but she wouldn't answer the door. He came up to me a couple of times asking where she was. Seeming pretty agitated. Every time I asked Rianne about it, she'd tell me everything was fine. She didn't want me involved."

"Do you know his name?" Jake asked.

"No, I'm sorry. If she told me, I don't remember it. But he was a real leech."

"Can you describe him?"

"White guy. Tall. Muscular. Brown hair."

Birdie wrote it down. But her face fell, just as Jake's did. It was the same nondescript description he'd gotten from Mia Casey.

"What about the car he drove?" Birdie asked. "Adam, I'm Detective Wayne. Detective Cashen's partner."

"Oh. Hey. Yeah. It was a dark-colored truck. Maybe charcoal. It could have been navy blue. I wanna say a Chevy. I'm not a car guy though. Ohio plates, but I couldn't tell you the number."

"What can you tell me about it?" Jake asked.

"That's it. But more than once, I caught him parked across the street watching Rianne's apartment. Like waiting for her to come home. Or waiting to see when she'd leave. He was catching on to the fact that she wasn't answering the door when she was home. I approached him a couple of times. Asked him what his business was. One time he just sped off. Another time he tried to get all charming. Told me Rianne asked him to wait for her. I didn't buy it. That's about the time I tried to talk to Rianne about it."

"How did she respond?" Birdie asked.

"Same way. Uncomfortable talking about it. She kind of blew it off. Saying he was harmless. That she'd handle it."

"And you don't remember his name?" Jake asked.

"I really don't. Sorry. But he was some kind of security guard, I think. One of the times I saw him picking her up, he was wearing a uniform. I couldn't tell you what kind. What it said. I didn't see it real close. I was pulling out and he was pulling in."

"Do you at least remember what color?" Jake asked.

"Tan, I think. Maybe brown?" Smith answered. "It was hard to tell. He was wearing a thin zip-up hoodie over the shirt. I could see his uniform pants and his gun belt. That's one of the things I said to Rianne. When I told her maybe she should watch out for him if he carried a gun for work. She kept saying not to worry. Said she had her own gun. She said he was the one who taught her how to shoot it."

"Did she happen to mention where?" Birdie asked. "Like at a gun range? Outdoors somewhere?"

"I didn't ask. Rianne's whole attitude was just very nonchalant. You know, casual. Kind of laughing me off in a way. I really felt like she didn't want me to bring it up or talk about the guy. She kept trying to change the subject. But I don't know. If she were my sister, and some guy was acting like that around her, you better believe I'd have had words with him. More than words. I just didn't feel like it was my place. We were friendly, but we weren't friends. She never had me over. We didn't hang out socially. I'm sorry. That's really all I remember. If you can find that guy, he'd probably be worth talking to."

"That's really helpful, Adam," Jake said. "Is there anything else you can think of about this guy?"

"That's it. But like I said. Had I known this had happened to her, I would have called. I think you should try to find him. I don't know if he was still into her or what. This was a couple of years ago. I was getting ready to move and Rianne said she was dating somebody else. Cameron. I hadn't seen the other creep for a while and I moved. I heard later she moved out not long after me. So I just assumed it had all worked itself out."

"Okay," Jake said. "If you think of anything else. Particularly a name. You've got the number here. You'll call?"

"Of course."

"Do you think you'd recognize this guy if you saw a picture of him?" Birdie asked. Jake gave her a thumbs up.

"I might," Adam said. "I never got real close to him. Only saw him in passing or when he was sitting in his truck. But sure, if you've got a lineup or something, I'd be happy to try."

"We'll keep in touch," Jake said.

"You bet." Then Adam Smith clicked off.

"We need to find this guy," Birdie said. "Jake, Rianne's friends said she was a stalker magnet. Nate Parra said she was the master of mind games. If this guy felt led on, and he was unbalanced to begin with, he'd have the perfect motive for killing her and Cameron. But with two guns?"

"He staged it," Jake said. "He goes over there to talk to Rianne. She rejects him again. It gets out of hand. Or maybe he went there with the plan to kill her. Your classic, if I can't have you nobody will."

"Then Cameron shows up. Maybe he even walks in on it," Birdie said.

"Rebound Guy knows Rianne has a gun cuz he's the one who taught her how to shoot it," Jake said.

"There were no signs of a struggle," Birdie said.

"Rebound Guy could have controlled Katz by keeping his gun pointed at him. Made him show him where Rianne kept *her* gun. Set him up on the couch. Shoots him with it to make it look like a suicide."

"He probably couldn't get Katz to shoot himself," Birdie said. "Why would anyone comply under those circumstances? You have a gun pointed at you. You're not gonna volunteer to off yourself. Dr. Stone agreed that this thing was sloppy. The shooter's making it up as he goes along because he didn't expect Katz to walk in on him."

"No foreign fingerprints in any other part of the house," Jake said. "No struggle."

"If Smith is remembering right, this guy had his own gun."

"A security guard," Jake said. He was on his feet, pacing. He went to the photos of the crime scene he had stuck to the whiteboard. Rianne on the kitchen floor. Phone in hand. Katz on the couch in the next room, the gun he was shot with on the floor beside his right hand.

Jake tried to imagine it. Rianne was shot in the chest from the front. She was facing her killer. Katz either walked in from the front door or through the mudroom in back. Either way, all the shooter would have had to do to control him is point the weapon at him. According to her father, Rianne kept her gun in the bedside table.

Jake went through the motions, shaping his right hand into a gun. The master bedroom was just down the hall from the kitchen. The shooter could have walked Katz down it, kept his own gun pointed at him while he retrieved the second gun. Then marched Katz back to that living room couch.

"What are you thinking, Jake?"

"Security guard," he said. "Birdie, can you think of any place in the county that employs armed private security guards?"

"No," she said. "They project us out."

Adrenaline shot through Jake's body.

"Us," he said.

"Smith said the guy was wearing a hoodie over his uniform. Jake, I did the same thing as a uniformed cop. If I had to make a stop on my way home from work, or before I came in. Otherwise, too many people would come up to me asking questions or complaining about something."

"So did I," he said.

"Most of us do," she said.

"Us," Jake repeated.

He sifted through the piles on the table. He pulled the copy he'd made of Ramirez's initial crime scene analysis.

"No foreign prints," he said. "Jesus, Birdie."

She rose and stood beside him. As Jake reached the relevant line in the report, Birdie found it too.

"Jake," she said.

"Stuckey and Bundy," he said. "They walked in ungloved. That's standard. You expect that. They had to clear the house first."

"Prints on the back door leading in from the mudroom. Both of them," Birdie said. "Stuckey's prints in the kitchen. A partial from Bundy on the doorframe leading to the living room. Jake ..."

He took his own service weapon out of its holster. He popped out the magazine and thumbed out a round from the top of it.

"Federal 9mm hollow point, chrome colored," he said. "Same ammo we carry, Birdie."

"Jake, they were first on scene."

"What do you know about either one of them? Outside work."

She threw her hands up. "Not much. Most of the time I partnered with Chris Denning. But they're both solid cops. I know you think so too. I'd see them out the same way you did. If a bunch of us got together for drinks. Retirement parties. Weddings, sometimes. I think I remember seeing Stuckey a couple of times with a date. But I couldn't describe her."

"Me either," Jake said. "Brown hair. Muscular. Tall. That describes both of them."

"We need to get two photo arrays together. Send one to Smith. And to Mia Casey."

"Birdie, I wanna be careful. You know this place has eyes and ears everywhere. Before I start rattling witnesses and throwing their pictures around, we need to be damn sure. Because it's gonna get back to both of them pretty quick."

Birdie slid more papers around until she found a small stapled stack. She flipped through it. "Bundy and Stuckey canvassed as a two-man," she said. "They talked to three of the Katzes' neighbors between them. Stuckey wrote up the report."

She handed the stapled papers to Jake. Jake skimmed their supplemental report. None of the neighbors saw or heard anything.

"It's mostly older people in that neighborhood," Birdie said.

"Retirees. The kind of people who have time to look out their windows."

"Before we do anything," Jake said, "I want to re-canvas. I want to talk to everyone Bundy and Stuckey interviewed."

"We can go tomorrow morning," she said.

Jake put the report down. His stomach flipped over as nausea set in.

"We're talking about cops, Birdie. Our guys. If we get this wrong ..."

"We won't," she said. "We can't."

"Say nothing to Landry. Or anyone. This is between you and me for now."

"Of course."

"Hey, guys!" Jake jumped. He'd been so hyperfocused, he'd forgotten they'd left the office door open. Birdie noticed it at the same time he did. She mouthed a four-letter word.

"Sorry," Deputy Denning said. "Didn't mean to interrupt. But it's five. A bunch of us are heading over to the Union Hall. There's that retirement party for Jerry Lenders. You're coming, right?"

Jerry Lenders was one of the longest-serving firemen Worthington County had seen. Everyone called him Jerry-tol, a play on Geritol, the vitamin supplement targeted for seniors.

"Yeah," Birdie said. "Thanks for the reminder. We'll be over in a few."

"You want me to wait?" Denning asked.

"Go on ahead," Jake said. He was trying to think of an excuse to get out of it. He wasn't sure he could be around every deputy and fire personnel just now. But Jerry Lenders was a good guy. His absence would be noticed. Particularly by Landry.

"We'll catch up," Birdie said. Denning smiled and kept on walking.

"We'll make an appearance," Birdie said. "Just act normal. Stuckey and Bundy will both probably be there."

"Good," Jake said. It was a ridiculous thought. But Jake wondered if he could see the truth in either one of their eyes.

Twenty-Nine

Birdie and Jake walked into the hall just in time for a group toast to Jerry-tol. Jerry was a big, burly guy who always volunteered to play Santa Claus when the cops and firefighters toured the pediatric wards at Christmas. Jerry sat in the middle of the crowd, sobbing. His wife stood next to him, beaming with pride. Two younger men stood behind her, looking like Jerry's clones. His sons. He knew one of them had followed his dad's footsteps and joined the fire department.

But Jake didn't focus on them long. Matt Bundy and Tom Stuckey stood at the bar together. From behind, it was difficult to tell them apart. Tall. Brown hair. Muscular. Both traditionally handsome. Both men Jake routinely requested when he needed support. Both good cops. Could one of them be a killer?

"Jake," Birdie whispered at his side.

"I need a drink," he told her, brushing her off. He walked up to the bar right next to Stuckey.

"Cashen!" Stuckey beamed, slapping Jake on the back. By the glaze over his eyes, and the smell of bourbon on his breath, he figured

Stuckey was at least three drinks in. Bundy locked eyes with Jake, an unspoken gesture, assuring Jake that he had Stuckey under control. Bundy sipped a soft drink.

"We were just talking about you," Stuckey said.

"All good, I hope." Jake smiled. Lieutenant Beverly was serving as bartender tonight. He poured Jake a draft beer and slid it over.

"We were saying how much we appreciate you letting us give you a hand on Katz," Stuckey said. "We were saying how glad we are that Ed Zender is outta there."

Beverly raised a brow as he poured another beer for Chris Denning at the other end of the bar.

"Zender woulda closed that case by now," Stuckey said, his volume about one level too high. "Woulda called it a suicide and clocked out. Lazy. Selfish. Matt wasn't thrilled."

"Stuckey," Bundy snapped. "Enough, man. Drink your bourbon."

"Wasn't thrilled about what?" Jake pressed.

"Ignore him," Bundy said. He made a C with his hand and tipped it up toward his mouth twice, simulating drinking.

Stuckey slapped a hard hand on Bundy's back, pushing him slightly. "Matt was hoping he'd get promoted. He thought ..."

"Tom, enough!" Bundy shouted.

Jake smiled. "It's all right. I meant what I said to both of you. You're both doing a great job. When the time comes, you'll be top of the list if you want it. I'll vouch for you."

"See?" Stuckey said, swaying sideways. "I told you Jake's solid. Not everybody thinks so, you know."

"All right," Beverly jumped in. "You're cut off, Tom. Bundy, you gonna make sure he gets home?"

"I got him, Lou," Bundy said.

Stuckey seemed oblivious of being the topic of their conversation. "Denning!" he shouted upon seeing Chris and Birdie at the other end of the bar. He swayed forward out of Bundy's grasp and headed toward Birdie. Jake mouthed "sorry" when she caught his eye.

"Don't pay him any mind," Bundy said. "He's had a rough week. We got a domestic violence call a couple of days ago. Rough one. Kids involved."

"That's tough," Jake said. "You okay with it?"

"Sure," he said. "As okay as anybody can be with it. Stuckey's got some vacation he's gotta use up before the end of the year. I'm gonna make him take it."

"What about you?" Jake asked. "When's the last time you had a day off?"

"I think I should ask you that question. Every time I walk by your office, you're in there."

"This one's been a bear," Jake said. "Every time I think I'm somewhere, I hit a dead end. I really think this one might end up going cold."

No reaction out of Matt Bundy. Behind him, Stuckey was making a nuisance of himself to Birdie and Denning.

"I better get him out of here before he does something stupider. I wasn't out for Zender's job. Er ... your job."

"But you did put in for the one Erica got. I know that ruffled some feathers."

"Not mine," Bundy said. "Let me be clear on that. But it means a lot to me that you've noticed the work Tom and I put in. A lot of other people wouldn't. But I suppose you know that as well as anybody."

"Matt!" Stuckey shouted. "You ready?"

Bundy looked relieved. "I thought that was gonna be harder."

Jake smiled. "Better get while the going's good. He could change his mind."

"We don't need Landry paying attention," Bundy said.

"Don't worry about it. He's off duty. She'd never make an issue out of something like that as long as he doesn't try getting behind the wheel."

Bundy dangled his keys in front of him. "On it."

Jake raised his beer mug to Bundy and watched him walk over to Stuckey, put an arm around him, and lead him out the front door.

"He was drunk when he got here," Beverly said. "Good kid. But I'm wondering if that's a problem. This isn't the first time he's been like that at a work thing."

Jake laughed. "I think I've seen you like that at a couple of work things, John."

Beverly whipped a towel at Jake, but didn't argue. Jake finished his beer and set it on the bar. He checked his smartwatch. He'd been seen by enough people. It was a good time to go.

He walked over to Birdie and Denning. "Stuckey do anything he can't undo?"

Denning shook his head. "He's all right."

"I'm gonna head out," he told Birdie. "You drinking tonight?"

"I got it," Denning said, raising his glass. It had clear, bubbly liquid in it. "Club soda with lime. I promised Landry I'd DD for anybody who needed it."

"I'm just having the one," Birdie said. "You sure you wanna head home so early?"

"I'm fine," he said. Denning didn't realize they were having a different conversation. Birdie kept a hard gaze on him.

"I'll see you first thing in the morning," she said. "We'll re-canvas together, okay?"

Jake saluted her, shook Denning's hand, then headed for the exit.

It was an unusually cool August evening. He had two unanswered texts from Gemma. She wanted him to bring groceries over to Grandpa Max before work tomorrow. He texted back an "okay" emoji and slipped his phone in his back pocket.

He weaved between a couple of vehicles parked at an angle and fumbled for his keys in his other pocket. For just that split second, he wasn't looking where he was going. He took another step and walked straight into someone.

Jake looked up, ready to apologize. Then he realized who he'd made contact with.

Uncle Rob.

"What the hell are you doing?" Rob shouted. It was dusk, but the man's expression was clear to read. Contempt. He curled his lips and narrowed his eyes as if Jake smelled like rotten fish.

"Get out of my way," Jake said, all inflection out of his voice.

Rob blinked, sensing pure menace from Jake. Rob took a step back. Jake felt like his feet were encased in cement. He wanted to be anywhere but in Rob Arden's presence. And yet, he couldn't make himself move.

Brother Rob was right.

Griffin Malley's grief-hardened face swam before him. *I can't be near your uncle. You understand? Because I think I'd have to kill him.*

Then Jake replayed Rob's words to Frank Borowski all those years ago. *I hadn't seen him for weeks. And I do not talk to him. Do you hear me? I don't talk to Jake. Not yesterday, not last week.* All lies. Griffin confirmed Rob had been taunting his father right up until the end.

"You're drunk," Rob spat. "Typical. You planning to get behind the wheel? That's perfect. Then what, your buddies in there think they'll cover for you when you plow into somebody? I don't think so."

"Get. Out. Of. My. Way," Jake growled.

Something came over Rob. The man's lack of situational awareness stunned Jake. Jake stood with his fists tightly clenched at his sides, his head down, as if he were a bull about to charge. It was taking every ounce of self-restraint he had not to deck Rob Arden. He didn't know what he must have looked like to Rob. He felt his face flush. Turn purple, maybe.

He thought of his mother. Trying to hang on to the man she loved while he descended into madness. And this man, standing in front of him, his face filled with raw hatred, had cut the very thin rope his father must have clung to.

I can't be near your uncle. You understand? Because I think I'd have to kill him.

"What the hell is wrong with you?" Rob asked. Why didn't he leave? Why didn't he just move past Jake like Jake had asked? And why did he hate his sister's son so much?

"There's nothing wrong with me," Jake said. "There's nothing wrong with my sister. There's only something wrong with you."

Was it his tone? The flash of anger in his eyes? But it was as if Jake lit a match and threw it onto a line of gasoline. Rob ignited.

"You're crazy," he said. "Just like him. Aren't you? Only worse because they gave you a gun and a badge."

Jake tried to do a mental ten count. Rob took a step closer. "Her heart has been broken for thirty years. Did you know that? And he did it. That lunatic. That scum."

"Whose heart?" Jake asked.

"Whose heart? Whose heart! My mother. Your grandmother. This is on your family too. She's sick. She's dying. You don't even ask about her?"

Jake took a step back as if Rob had slapped him. "My grandmother? Now she's my grandmother? *My* only grandmother was Ava Cashen and she died twenty years ago."

Rob raised a hand, then slowly put it back down. "You know what? You're not worth it. I told you. You're just like your father. Batshit crazy. And dangerous."

The flaming line of gasoline seemed to engulf Jake instead. He imagined the scene between Griffin and Rob. He would have been smug. Proud of himself as he claimed victory by feeding his father's disease. His paranoia.

"You might as well have pulled the trigger yourself," Jake said. He was calm at first. But then it was as if a dam burst inside of him.

No, more than that. It was as if both of his parents had taken hold of him. Spoke through him.

"You lied," Jake said. He jabbed a finger into Rob's chest, pushing him backward. Rob's face turned white. His mouth formed an O.

"You lied to him. You knew he was sick. You didn't care. You saw your opportunity and you poisoned his mind with your lies. I met him. You didn't know that, did you? I met Griffin Malley. He told me what you did. You tried to ruin his life too."

"How dare you," Rob managed to croak out.

"She loved you. My mother loved you. You were her little brother. You turned on her. You betrayed her. It was your words my father had in his head. You used my dad as a weapon against her. What for? Did you hate her even though she loved you? Was it the money? Get her out of your way. Get us out of your way, then you could have it all to yourself. What did you tell my so-called grandmother to get her to go along with it? Huh?"

"You don't deserve a penny!" Rob shrieked. "None of you. How dare you throw that in my face? I knew it. I knew someday you were going to turn into a monster just like he was. My sister didn't love him. She was trapped by him. I warned her about what was going to happen. Then it did. There's nothing of her in you. You're all him. And he's right where he belongs, in the filthy ground where he was born."

"You ever speak her name to me, or his, I'll ..."

"You'll what?" Rob spat. "Say it. Right here. Show me who you really are. Show everyone."

Jake took a step back. He came into himself for a moment. From his periphery, he realized they weren't alone. A handful of Jerry's guests had come out into the parking lot. Stuckey and Bundy were there.

"You're a piece of crap, Cashen," Rob shouted. "You see this? You see who he is?"

Rob took a step toward Jake. Jake's vision tunneled. He wanted Rob to hit him. He found himself praying for it. *One shot. Take it. Lay a hand on me.*

It was Matt Bundy who got between them. Jake knew he was cold sober, but Bundy took an exaggerated stagger sideways and put his hand on Rob's shoulder.

"Thass my friend. Thass, Jake."

Rob pinched his face in disgust. "Get off me. Take your hand off me!" Bundy didn't. Instead, he put a heavy arm around Rob's shoulder, pretending to need him to stay upright. Rob shoved him sideways, hard. But it was enough. Rob backed down.

But there was one other spectator, her face gone gray. Her eyes sparking with fury.

Sheriff Landry.

"Jake," she said, toneless.

Jake couldn't look at her. At anyone—he kept his eyes locked on Rob.

"Stay out of this," he said. "This is a family matter."

"We are not family," Rob said. "Sheriff, your detective just threatened me. I'm sure I can count on you to handle it appropriately."

"Go home, Commissioner Arden," she said.

Shock registered on Rob's face. "Figures," he said. "You'll take his side."

"I'm not taking any sides. I'm defusing a situation. Go home. Detective Cashen is going to do the same."

Finally, Jake turned to her. He didn't think he'd ever seen her that angry.

"He made a physical threat to a fellow public servant in this community. In front of the town sheriff. And you're going to do nothing? I don't think so."

"Go. Home," Landry said. This time, Arden heard her. He sneered at Jake one last time, then turned and got back into his car.

Jake stayed frozen until Rob sped away. When he turned to Meg, the rest of the bystanders had made themselves scarce. It was only Jake and Meg facing off. Bundy got ahold of Stuckey and pushed him down the row of cars and out of Jake's eyeline.

"Jake," she said.

"Don't," he answered. "You have no idea what you walked into."

"I don't know if I care," she said. "You were going to threaten to kill him, weren't you?"

"I didn't," he said.

"Because he cut you off! Because Bundy's conveniently hammered. Or wisely pretending to save your ass."

"Meg. I can't talk about this right now. I'm going to do what I came out here to do. What you ordered Rob to do. I'm going home."

"Have you been drinking?"

"I had one beer," Jake said, resisting the urge to shout. "Ask Beverly if you don't believe me."

"Fine," she said. "I want you in my office first thing in the morning."

"I have a murder to solve first thing in the morning," he said. He was angry. Though he knew it wasn't at Meg. He couldn't yet tell her what Birdie and he suspected on the Katz case. She had no idea he was protecting her right now.

"Jake ..." she started.

"You're just going to have to trust me," he said. Then he turned his back and walked to his own car.

Thirty

Jake used his hip to nudge his office door open, his hands full with a coffee cup from Tessa Papatonis and his leather folio. Meg was waiting for him, seated at the desk in front of all the Katz case materials. She wore her sternest expression. Her normally curly hair was wilder today as she lost her fight with the humidity.

Birdie wasn't at her desk. That could only mean Landry sent her away. Birdie always beat Jake in.

"Can I at least get a cup of coffee in me before the inquisition?" he asked, walking to his desk and setting the folio down.

"No. And this isn't an inquisition. Do you know how many phone calls, texts, emails I've had to field since last night? The *Daily Beacon* has completely crawled up my ass for a comment. The mayor even called."

Jake sat down hard in his desk chair. "I told you last night. That was a family matter between me and dear old Uncle Rob."

"He's telling anyone who'll listen that you threatened to kill him."

"The Hall has cameras out front that capture the entire parking lot. Be my guest. Have them pulled. I laid a single finger on him. That's all. Under the circumstances, I think I showed Herculean restraint."

"What's going on, Jake?" Meg asked, her eyes softening. "Forget me as your sheriff for one second. Talk to me as your friend."

Jake didn't want to go through it all again. He didn't want yet another person telling him how he'd crossed some line. That digging up the past did no good. But the fact that Meg was asking meant that Birdie had kept his confidence. He knew damn well Meg had to have grilled her too before he got here.

"You're not going to respect what I'm telling you? That this is a personal matter between me and my uncle?"

"Not when it results in your having a very public altercation with a pretty influential county commissioner who has been angling for your badge since the second you got it. Not when it takes up a good part of my day trying to volley questions from people fully capable of stirring up a scandal that could derail a lot of the things I'm trying to do for this county."

Jake took a sip of his coffee. "Behind you," he said.

Meg looked confused. Then she turned. She was sitting directly in front of the stack of banker's boxes he put there. The Cashen box was at the bottom, clearly labeled.

Meg walked over to it, squatted down to read it. Then slowly rose and turned to face Jake again.

"Before you say it," Jake said. "I haven't broken a single departmental policy. I'm not subject to any disciplinary action. Me looking at that, or having that file doesn't expose you or this department to anything."

She shook her head, flapped her hands, and then plopped back into her chair. "Something in that file is the reason you looked two seconds from murdering Rob Arden last night?"

"Yeah. And for the record, he started it."

"Is that what my official statement should be?"

"That's your call."

"He's threatening to file a formal complaint. If he does, this is going to IA whether you like it or not."

"I can guarantee you he's not gonna do that," Jake said.

"How?"

"You're gonna have to trust me that this thing, if it's made public, is gonna be a lot worse for Rob than for me."

"You know what, fine," she said. "It's bullshit. I can admit that. You're right. You weren't on duty. You weren't carrying. But you've been off the last few weeks, Jake. I've been concerned. Erica's been concerned. And before you ask, no. She hasn't come to me with anything. I just know both of you pretty well by now. I see the way she looks at you. And I'd have to be an idiot not to put together how the Katz case could stir some very dark stuff up for you."

"I'm so sick of explaining myself about that."

"I'm not asking you to. But I am asking you to make sure you take advantage of the help that's available to you. If you need it."

"A shrink?" Jake asked. "EAP? Yeah. No thanks."

"Fine," she said, rising. "So I'll change the subject. Where are we on Katz? I'm getting a lot of pressure about that one too."

As if she were psychic, Birdie opened the office door and hesitantly walked in. "Coast clear?" she joked.

"Haven't pulled the pin out of any grenades just yet," Meg said. "I was asking for a status report on Katz."

Birdie's eyes flicked to Jake.

"We're working on a lead this morning," Jake said. "So if you don't mind, I'm gonna have to cut this conversation short."

"What lead?" Landry asked.

"Let us see if it pans out, then I'll let you know."

"Jake ..."

He grabbed his keys off the desk. "Another thing you're gonna have to trust me on. Right now we're operating on a hunch. A good one. But one I need to button up before bringing it to you."

Meg frowned. "I get the feeling I'm not gonna like what you tell me."

"Don't worry about it," Jake said. "Yet." He grabbed his suit jacket off the hook by the door, stabbed his arms into it, and ushered Birdie back out, leaving Meg alone in their office.

Jake was silent for most of the trip back out to the Katzes' neighborhood. Birdie had gotten adept at sensing his mindset. It was the same with him about her. They were settling into the groove of being partners. It was only when Jake turned down the road leading to Cameron and Rianne Katz's house that she spoke up.

"I called Nadya Louden, one of the neighbors Bundy and Stuckey interviewed. She's a little curious about why we're coming back, but seems totally cooperative. She's a retired paralegal."

"Good," Jake said. "I'm gonna park one block over. I'd rather the other neighbors didn't see my cruiser parked in her driveway."

"You really think Bundy or Stuckey is watching that closely?"

"I think I don't want to take any chances."

Jake did as he said. At nearly ninety degrees before ten o'clock, they were both sweating by the time they got to the Louden residence. Nadya swung her screen door open just as they walked up. Jake guessed she was in her mid-sixties. Tight curls dyed reddish, almost maroon. She wore a tracksuit and had a single earbud in her right ear. She pulled it out as she invited Jake and Birdie inside.

Her house smelled clean, but it was in complete disarray. Clutter everywhere. Old magazines. Stacks of green plastic tubs going as high as the ceiling. They passed two bedrooms and a bathroom to get to the kitchen. Each room was filled with more junk than the others. The kitchen, however, was immaculate. Jake and Birdie sat at the table and declined Nadya's offer of more coffee.

"I don't know that I can help you much," she said. "Everything I remember I told to that other policeman."

"We're just trying to be thorough," Birdie said. "And this shouldn't take too long."

"Of course," she said. "I'll do anything I can to help. Rianne was a good neighbor. I didn't see Cameron too much. I know he worked from home in their basement. But he kept odd hours. And I knew they were out of town. The week before this all happened. Marne, the little girl who walks their dog, I recommended her to them. Such a sweet kid. She's having a pretty rough time with all of this."

"I can imagine," Jake said.

"You're not going to talk to her again, are you? Oh. I hope you don't. I mean, if you have to. Of course. But she's just not been the same since this all happened. I know her mother is pretty worried."

"Mrs. Louden," Jake said. "You said you were home all Friday night and into Saturday morning, the weekend the Katzes were killed?"

"Yes. There was a marathon of *The Thorn Birds*. All ten hours of it. I was hunkered down watching. Almost got to the part with Cardinal de Bricassart's death scene. I cry my head off every time. That's when I realized Gunther wasn't around—that's my kitty-cat. He's always right there if he thinks I'm sad. So I paused the show to look for him."

"And you didn't see or hear anything?" Birdie asked.

"Nothing that I thought was unusual. That's what I told the other cop. Not at first, anyway. I'd talked to Rianne the day before. They'd just gotten back from their honeymoon. She was out getting her mail and I walked up to her and asked her about it. She was just beaming. All tan. Glowing. She said Cameron had some sort of meeting that day and wasn't gonna be home until later. I asked her if she wanted to join me for dinner. She said she thought she might. She was gonna call and confirm later. When she didn't, I really didn't think too much of it."

"Did you see Cameron at all that day?"

"No. Like I said, I was inside most of the day watching that marathon."

"The medical examiner thinks the shootings happened around midnight that night. I think when the other deputies talked to you, that hadn't been established yet. Does that change things?"

Nadya frowned. "No. I don't think so. I told your associate I never heard anything that sounded like gunshots. But that was a Friday night. Our neighbor on the other corner, he's got a couple of teenagers. They were having kids over. They had one of those boom boxes going. It might have covered up anything like that."

Jake raised a brow at the word boom box. He could see Birdie suppressing a smile.

"It was just that truck," she said. "The one parked across the street from Rianne's."

"Truck?" Jake asked.

"Yes, Gunther got out. I told you. It was odd he wasn't on my lap the minute that funeral scene started. He's an indoor cat. I'm responsible about that. But sometimes he'll dart out when I open the door. Don't worry, he's neutered. But he's wily anyway. He's a good boy. He comes when I call him. So I walked out that night. Called for him. This was about eleven thirty, maybe a little later. The show was almost over. I stood out there for maybe five minutes before Gunther came running back. He was hiding under the back wheel of that truck parked in front of Rianne's."

"Can you describe it?" Birdie asked.

Nadya shrugged. "It was just a truck. The streetlights were on, but it was still dark. So I can't tell you what color. Dark though. Not red. Not white. And I don't think black either. But maybe a dark gray or a navy blue."

"Do you remember the make or model?"

"Yes," she said. "I told the other officer. It was some kind of Chevy. I could see that logo on the back. I don't know what model. I'm not a truck person. My daughter laughs at me. But I like my PT Cruiser."

"Do you remember which deputy you spoke to?" Birdie asked.

"There were two of them," she said. "Real nice fellas. Polite. Very sensitive about making sure I was okay. This was upsetting, as you can imagine. They took turns knocking on doors around here. I'm sorry, I can't remember which one it was I talked to. They both looked alike."

"Does this help?" Birdie asked. She showed her phone to Nadya Louden. She had department ID photos of both Stuckey and Bundy on it. Nadya took the phone, squinted and then swiped back and forth between the two photos.

"Maybe this one," she said, giving the phone back to Birdie. She'd picked Matt Bundy. "Maybe. I don't know. Or the other one. I'm sorry. Why does that matter? Did one of them do something wrong?"

"No, not at all," Jake said. "I'm just making sure my report is as detailed as it can be. Was there anything else distinguishing about the truck? Like a bumper sticker? Any dents or dings or rust you might have noticed?"

She shook her head. "He asked me that too, your deputy. But no. I only noticed it at all because Gunther ran out from under it. It scared me. If he'd stayed there, he could have gotten run over."

Jake's pulse quickened. Birdie asked Nadya Louden a few more basic questions. Then, there was nothing else she had to add. They said their goodbyes, thanked her, and walked one block over back to the car.

Jake reached for his tablet under his seat. He turned it on and opened the file containing the Katz materials.

"Jake," Birdie said. "I don't remember anything in those supplemental reports about a truck being parked in front of the Katz's house."

Jake found the witness statement Stuckey wrote up. They worked as a two-man that day. Just as Nadya Louden remembered, they took turns canvassing different neighbors. They submitted a joint report that Stuckey wrote up. He'd made no distinction about who spoke to whom. That in and of itself wasn't unusual.

"It's not here," he said. "No truck. Just that Nadya Louden walked outside with her cat but didn't hear anything."

"She was clear," Birdie said. "She specifically remembered telling them."

"Whichever one of them talked to her either didn't report it, or if it was Stuckey on Bundy's recall, he left it out."

"I mean, it could have just been an oversight," she said hopefully. Then she met Jake's eyes.

"No," they both said together. With every loop they closed, it became clearer one of their own may have committed a double murder.

THIRTY-ONE

"You're not going to like it," Jake said. He stood with his hands on his hips in front of Meg Landry's desk. Birdie had taken a seat on the couch along the wall. Meg was at her desk, leaning far back in her chair, nursing a headache with an ice pack on her forehead.

"Well, I wasn't really expecting you to tell me this is a double homicide, but the fun kind."

"Fair point," Jake said.

"Rianne Katz's neighbor remembers her having a creepy ex who would sit outside her house at all hours of the day and night, watching her from his car. After they supposedly broke up. He said the guy was a security guard, but it doesn't track. He wore a gun. He had a hoodie over the top of his uniform so the neighbor couldn't tell me what agency the guy was from."

Meg pulled the ice pack off her head and tossed it on her desk. She opened a drawer and popped three ibuprofen, washing them down with her bottled water.

"We've got another neighbor reporting seeing a dark-colored truck parked outside Rianne's house the night of the murder. Description matches the one the first neighbor gave belonging to the creepy boyfriend. Rianne's ex-fiancé and her best friend said she had a pattern of bad breakups. The kind where she'd lead the poor guy on to the point of driving him a little nuts. Not saying it's her fault. Don't get me wrong. But if she hooks up with someone who's already unhinged."

"It's a good motive," Meg said. "What else?"

Jake looked at Birdie. "There are two sets of prints at the scene belonging to two men who don't yet have alibis for the night of the murder."

"What," Meg said, sitting up. "Since when? I didn't see that anywhere in the report. Ramirez specifically said no foreign prints and no signs of forced entry."

"No foreign prints," Jake said. He put a page of Ramirez's report on her desk, having highlighted two names from the list of identified prints.

"Jake," Meg said. "These are my deputies. This is Stuckey and Bundy."

"Yeah."

Meg looked at Birdie, then back at Jake. "Bundy and Stuckey. Jake, explain this to me like I'm five."

"There's nothing to explain. Both Bundy and Stuckey fit the physical description given by Nate Parra, the ex, and Adam Smith, the neighbor. They both saw Rianne with a guy matching their physical characteristics."

"Come on. They're tall, white, ripped guys with brown hair. Cameron Katz fits that description too."

"Then there's the ballistics report," Jake said. "The bullets taken out of Rianne's gun are the same kind that we carry. And yeah, I know half the cops in the country use the same ammo. Still, it's another piece of the puzzle."

"You still don't have it," she said. "Is there any witness who can say they saw either Matt or Tom with Rianne?"

"No," Jake said. "But one of them fudged the suppy."

"How?"

"Nadya Louden, the across-the-street neighbor. The one who described the truck outside the Katzes' house. None of that was written in the report they handed in after canvassing."

"Who talked to her?" Meg asked.

"We don't know," Birdie answered. "She couldn't ID either one definitively when I showed her their photos. She recognized them, but couldn't remember which of them she had told about the truck. They submitted a joint report. Stuckey wrote it up. But if Bundy were the one to actually talk to Nadya, he could have left that out. Or Stuckey could have intentionally left it off the write-up."

"If he did," Jake said. "No reason why Bundy would have reviewed the report before Stuckey submitted it to me. If Erica wrote up a report incorporating my notes or oral statement, I wouldn't necessarily go over her work on the official report. If we all did that, it'd take twice as long to get anything done. It's inefficient. Either you trust your partner or you don't."

"I'll admit. This looks bad. Certainly enough to have a conversation with both of them. Tie up their whereabouts the night before. You could tell them it's a formality. They might not buy it, but if they're innocent, they're not going to balk at it," Meg said. "You know you don't have probable cause."

"No," Jake said. "I want to search both of their phones. I can't do that without a warrant."

"Hell," Meg said. "I'm not sure you've got reasonable suspicion for even that."

"I disagree," Jake said. "But I want more before I pull that trigger. And I think I've got an idea how to get it."

He hadn't had a chance to run this part by Birdie yet. She was hearing it for the first time along with Meg.

"Let me guess," Meg said. "I'm going to hate this too."

"You let me set a trap," he said. "Make Bundy and Stuckey think I've got new evidence that should break the case. Give them access to it. See what they do. One of them's already tampered with evidence by burying Nadya Louden's full statement. If one of them's guilty, I think they'll bite."

"What new evidence?" Meg asked.

"I haven't figured that part out yet," he said. "It has to be something tangible. Something that could just conveniently go missing or be tampered with to render unusable."

"You've already got the murder weapon," Meg said. "At least one of them. You can't very well lie about the other one. One of those two has that strapped to their hips, presumably."

"I'm working on it," Jake said. "I'll get there."

"You don't have a lot of time," Meg said. "But really? God. Could this really be one of our guys? Because think about it."

"I have," Jake said. "I've done nothing *but* think about it. I think the killer went over there that night to confront Rianne. Her neighbor, Nadya Louden, said Rianne told her Cameron was going to be out of town overnight. If Bundy or Stuckey were watching the house, they'd have figured out Katz wasn't coming home that night. So whichever one of them goes in to talk to Rianne. Or try to hook up with her. Or maybe even with the specific intention of killing her. Only Katz shows up just before midnight, according to his cell phone data. After Ms. Louden took her cat back home. Stuckey or Bundy was already there. One of them kills Rianne. Maybe it was premeditated, maybe it was in the heat of the moment. Either way, he went over there armed. Things went sideways. He shoots Rianne twice. Killing her. Maybe Katz walks in on it."

"Bundy or Stuckey turns his gun on Katz," Birdie picked up the narrative. "Assume he knows where Rianne keeps her gun. Adam Smith, her other neighbor, said she told him this mystery boyfriend taught her how to shoot it. Which also means he knows exactly what kind of ammo is in it. Or he points a gun at Katz and forces him to go get the gun."

"He puts him on the couch," Jake said. "Shoots him at point blank range with Rianne's gun. Does his best to stage it like a suicide by putting the gun in Katz's hand. Getting Katz's prints all over it."

"Nobody reports the crime until over twelve hours later," Birdie said. "When Marne Kowalski, the dog walker, shows up. She finds the dog in its crate, barking like mad. She said Zephyr sleeps crated. So the poor thing's been in there for something like fourteen hours."

"Bundy and Stuckey get the radio call," Meg said. "That can't be a coincidence."

"I checked the log," Birdie said. "They were running a two-man, assigned to Arch Hill Township. 9-1-1 call came in at three, a half hour before their shift was set to end. Unit 21, another two-man with Chaplin and Holtz, was closest. But Stuckey and Bundy responded first. They poached it. Chaplin and Holtz didn't argue.

They were about to end their shift too. They both knew that whoever took that call was going to end up working a boatload of overtime. It was a Saturday evening and a gorgeous, eighty-five-degree day with pure sun. If it were me and Denning, we'd have handed that off in a heartbeat."

Meg rubbed her temples. "This is crazy. Isn't it?"

"I don't think so," Jake said.

"Jake, even if you figure out a way to run whatever sting operation you're planning, there's still a plausible reason for Stuckey and Bundy's physical evidence to be at that scene. A half-assed defense attorney can make reasonable doubt out of that. You're gonna need more. You're gonna need a way to tie Stuckey or Bundy's gun to this crime. You know that's what Boyd Ansel's gonna say."

Jake felt like punching a hole in the wall. Meg was right. Everything about the crime scene itself was circumstantial. He did what he always did when he was frustrated and trying to work something out. He paced.

Fingerprints. No DNA. Stuckey or Bundy had to have been wearing gloves when he killed the Katzes. Which meant he had to have gone there with the intention of killing Rianne Katz and getting away with it. The bullets came from two different guns.

"We can test-fire their guns, can't we?" Birdie asked. "The same way BCI figured out two separate guns were used. A bullet fired from Stuckey or Bundy's guns will have the same striation patterns as the ones pulled out of Rianne Katz."

"Which is another thing that will need a warrant," Meg said. "I think it's worth an ask to the armorer. If either one of them reported their weapons stolen or defective in the last month, that would be telling."

Birdie's words reached Jake's ears as if they were in an echo chamber.

A bullet fired from Stuckey or Bundy's guns will have the same striation patterns ...

"We don't need a warrant," he said. "And it won't matter what either of them have done with their weapons since Rianne Katz's murder."

"Explain please," Meg said.

Jake took his own weapon out of its holster and laid it on Meg's desk. "The sample bullet. Every single deputy in this department has a sample bullet on file before they're issued their weapons. If there's any officer-involved shooting, it's how we prove whose weapon was fired. Both Stuckey and Bundy have theirs on file."

"Jesus," Meg said. "Jake, get ahold of the armorer. Now. Make the request."

"It'll take time," Jake said. "BCI is going to have to do a comparison analysis. But I can get the ball rolling. In the meantime, we need to eliminate one of them as quickly as we can."

"Fine," Meg said. "So figure out this trap you wanna set."

"I have an idea," Birdie said. "About the evidence."

Jake took a seat on one of the chairs in front of Meg's desk. "How about a nanny cam?"

"Where?" Meg asked. "Isn't that something Ramirez's team would have absolutely grabbed?"

"Abby, my sister-in-law, she used to have one for Travis when he was a baby. It was in this little purple stuffed bear. She kept it on a shelf in his room with the rest of his toys. For a while, she had a babysitter. She was a new mom. Super nervous. But when I was overseas, she'd send me videos from it. Baby Travis when he popped out of his crib the first time. She'd catch him playing peek-a-boo with himself. Anyway, it's still at the house."

"Does it still work?" Meg asked.

"It doesn't have to," Jake said. "Stuckey and Bundy just have to think it does. That's kinda brilliant, Bir—Erica."

"We tell them the thing got wedged between the washer and dryer or something. Fell off a shelf in the mudroom. We went back to the crime scene and just found it. We don't know what's on it because we have to turn it over to BCI for analysis, but it appears it's been running non-stop since before the murders. That it was definitely recording something that night."

"We tell them tonight," Jake said. "Just before their shifts end. Casually. I'm taking it down to the night property room. Sarge will log it in the morning. We have to turn it over to BCI to have the SD card analyzed. Ramirez is gonna pick it up by ten o'clock or something."

"How will you know if they tamper with it?" Meg asked. "We don't keep cameras down there."

"I've got a cheap $50 trail cam I put up on Grandpa's barn," Jake said. "It runs on a rechargeable battery. Tiny thing. But it takes good-quality videos and has a motion detection setting. It'll be easy to hide. Easy to stick somewhere that'll catch anyone coming into that cage."

"That's a lot of what-ifs," Meg said.

"If it works, it works," Jake said. "If it doesn't, it doesn't. But it's a cheap, easy plan."

"I'll get the bear cam," Birdie said. "I can be back in twenty minutes."

"Same on the trail cam," Jake said. "It'll only take me ten minutes to set it up down in the property room."

"You don't think Bundy or Stuckey will be suspicious when you lay this little story on them?"

"No," Jake said. "They've both expressed interest in the case. You know that. And I can think of a dozen reasons why I'd casually run into either one of them."

"Stuckey has lunch at Papa's every day," Birdie said. "I was planning to pick up carryout for Jake and me today anyway."

"I have a reason to seek out Matt," Jake said. "You know he kind of had my back at the Union Hall with Rob."

"All right," Meg said.

"Nobody else can know about this," Jake said. "Only the three of us. We cannot risk tipping either of them off."

"Get it done," Meg said, reaching for her ice pack again. "Then come find me the minute you know anything. If it doesn't work, I don't see how there's any way to proceed without a warrant. We better be damn sure what we're doing before it comes to that."

Jake nodded. "You look awful, by the way. You should take a sick day. Maybe it's better if you're not in the building for any of this."

"You know," she said. "That's not a half bad idea. Just ... be careful. Both of you. If this is one of those guys, they already killed Cameron Katz to keep him quiet about what he did to Rianne. That's some pretty dark, desperate shit. Watch each other's backs."

"Copy that," Jake said.

Thirty-Two

Jake's little $50 trail camera worked better than he thought it would. He tucked it into a shadowy corner of the ceiling, aimed right at the shelf where Birdie's decoy teddy bear would sit. He used a tiny piece of black electrical tape to cover the indicator lights on the camera. No one would ever spot it. He half wondered if Meg shouldn't put in a budget request to install the real deal down here.

He checked the app on his phone. The camera had a strong signal. He'd theoretically get a motion alert when someone walked in. It didn't always accurately send a notification when he had the thing out at the barn. But the SD card recorded and stored thirty seconds of video anytime there was movement. It had kept Gemma's goats and Grandpa's chickens safe from coyotes a few nights ago.

He got his chance to set up Matt Bundy about ten minutes after he left the property room. Bundy had just clocked out. Birdie texted him twenty minutes ago that she'd caught up with Stuckey as he was leaving. She said he'd been wearing a blue hoodie over his uniform shirt because he wanted to stop at Dollar Kart on his way home.

“Hey, Bundy,” Jake said. “You got a sec?”

Bundy waved to Darcy, the civilian dispatcher, down the hall.

“You owe me two crullers!” she shouted.

“What’s that about?” Jake asked.

“Lost a bet. Long story.” Matt smiled. “Come on. You can walk out with me. You heading out too?”

“Yeah. Promised Gemma I’d stop by the pub on the way home. She brought in some Pineapple IPA she wants me to taste test. I mostly hate that crap. Give me a Coors Light draft.”

Matt laughed. “I get it. Well, if you want to get out of it, a bunch of us are meeting up at Wylie’s later tonight. What’s up?”

Jake waited until they’d walked out of the building. Clouds gathered. The weatherman called for rain later tonight.

“I just wanted to thank you for stepping up the other night. Out at the Hall. That stuff with my uncle, it shouldn’t have happened.”

“Look,” Bundy said. “It’s none of my business. Plus, everybody knows what a tool Rob Arden is. He’s been riding your ass for years. Frankly, whatever you’d have done to him, he probably had coming.”

“Are people still talking about it?” Jake asked.

“Not to me. And I’d tell them the same thing I just said if they did. You’re good, Jake. Landry give you a hard time?”

“Nah,” Jake said. “Just a little schoolmarm lecture. I think she’s got the same opinion of my uncle as everybody else. But she’s gotta stay on his good side for us as much as she can.”

“Right, right,” Matt said. “This is me.”

He hit his key fob. His truck beeped. He drove a metallic gray Ford F-150. Jake guessed it was seven or eight years old. Certainly, the same one he would have been driving if he'd dated Rianne Katz a couple of years ago. At the same time, he scanned the lot and spotted six other trucks that looked pretty similar. Including his own, four spots over.

"Hey, Matt," Jake said, just as Bundy opened his door. "I also wanted to thank you again. The work you and Stuckey did on Katz has really made my job easier."

Bundy cocked his head slightly. "I appreciate that. But we haven't done anything amazing. That's you and Wayne if this case ever gets solved."

"I told you before. It means a lot when I can trust you guys to turn in solid canvassing. You know more than anyone, we've got a lot of bare minimum deputies in that building. I meant what I said. You or Stuckey put in for the next slot in the detective bureau, you'll have my backing. Now, don't tell anybody you heard this from me, but I think Gary Majewski is finally gonna retire pretty soon."

Bundy laughed. "That guy's been on more medical leave than he's worked over the last couple of years."

"No lies there," Jake said. "Hey, I also wanted to tell you. Geez, I can't believe I almost forgot. I've been so hyperfocused on this case. I think we're onto a major break on Katz."

Jake studied Bundy's face. His eyes. He saw no unusual reaction. He barely saw a reaction at all.

"Wayne and I went back to the scene this morning. Kind of a Hail Mary. Just looking for anything BCI or we might have missed. I wasn't expecting anything. Wayne found this stuffed animal wedged between the washer and dryer in that mudroom.

Bedraggled purple bear or something. Anyway, it was one of those nanny cams. We talked to the dog walker who found the bodies again. She said the Katzes kept it on a shelf. That way they could see their little dog when they weren't home. They kept it penned up in the laundry room there so it wouldn't crap in the house."

"Huh," Bundy said. "Was it working?"

"We won't know for sure what's on it until BCI can have a look. But there's a damn good chance we'll have audio from the night of the murder at the very least," Jake said. "Anything that happened in that kitchen ten feet away should have been picked up. I just keyed it into the night property room. BCI's gonna pick it up by ten tomorrow morning. Agent Ramirez thinks he'll have something for me by the end of business tomorrow or early the day after tomorrow at the latest."

"That's great," Bundy said. "Yeah. Let me know. But that seems like a pretty big thing for BCI to have missed."

"It was really wedged back there. I don't even know what made Wayne think to move that dryer. I told Ramirez I'm not too happy. It was still plugged in and running when we found it. There was enough memory on its SD card to store a couple of weeks' worth of data. I'm really hopeful whatever's on that card will solve this thing. Ramirez sounded pretty certain it has that potential."

"Wow," Bundy said. "Well, yeah. Let me know what you find. It'll be good for those families to have some justice."

"Will do," Jake said. "See you tomorrow. Hopefully with some good news for a change."

Bundy got into his truck. He adjusted his mirror, plugged his phone in, and pulled up a hard rock playlist. He gave Jake another casual wave as he backed out. If he was ruffled by the news Jake shared, he was one hell of a good actor. Jake had witnessed that firsthand the other night when Bundy pretended to be drunk and de-escalated his confrontation with Rob Arden.

Birdie was waiting for Jake in his favorite booth at Cashen's Irish Pub. Gemma was slammed. She'd made good on her promise to bring Grandpa's smoker out. She hired a pit boss. She'd done a soft launch of Grandpa's secret recipe brisket last night. So far, people had been asking for more.

"She's gonna need to hire more people if this keeps up," Birdie shouted over the crowd. She'd already ordered a pitcher of Miller Lite. "How'd it go with Bundy?"

Jake gave her the highlights, also his impression of Bundy's cool demeanor.

"Same with Stuckey," she said. "I don't know, Jake. Gun to my head right now, I'd say neither of them is acting guilty. I hope we're wrong. As much as I want to solve this thing, I think I'd almost rather it go cold than end up being one of those guys."

"I don't know how I feel," he said. "We're just gonna have to wait and see."

"All set with your motion detector?"

Jake slapped his phone on the table. He pulled up his app and turned it toward Birdie. She clicked on the screen, showing the live feed running to the night property room.

"My pulse is going a mile a minute," she said. "How can you stay so calm?"

"There's nothing else we can do."

"There's a sight for sore eyes!" Gemma came up, grabbing Jake's head and planting a huge, sloppy kiss on top of it. Then she licked her hand and tried to smooth down a small cowlick he had back there. He needed a haircut.

Gemma forced Jake to scoot over as she hopped into the booth. "Are you seeing this? They were lined up around the building when we opened."

"That's great," Birdie said.

"Though I could really use Ryan and Travis for another couple of weeks. You heard from Trav?"

Birdie shook her head. "Just a text when he got there and settled into his dorm. But I know they'll be keeping him busy morning, noon, and night for a while. No news is actually good news. What about Ryan?"

Gemma sighed. "There was nothing for me to do this year. He just packed up his car and drove to campus by himself. He's got an apartment with two of his teammates. Though there's a good chance it's all a ruse. I think he's really living with that girlfriend and they don't want her parents finding out."

"You don't know that," Jake said. "Give him the benefit of the doubt."

"As long as you did what you said you were going to do," she said.

Jake pointed at Gemma with his thumb. "My sister here thought Ryan needed a lesson on how to wear a condom."

"Yeah, sorry, Gemma." Birdie smiled. "I'd say odds are that ship has already sailed. I caught Travis and Violet Welsch on the basement couch about a month ago."

"Ouch," Jake said. "How'd that go over?"

"I mean, what am I gonna do? I can't even play the card that it's my house. I'm holding it in trust for him until he's twenty-five. He's over eighteen. But he at least had the decency to be embarrassed and sort of apologized."

"You still planning on moving out?" Jake asked.

"She is!" Gemma answered for her. "That's one of the things I wanted to tell you, Birdie. The sellers made a counteroffer on the condo in Golden Oak. It's not bad. They just want an extra ten days to turn over the keys. And no inspection contingency. It doesn't mean you can't walk away if you get a bad inspection. They're just saying they won't pay for any defects out of the purchase price. It's an almost brand-new unit. Two years old. I think you're gonna be fine."

"Golden Oak?" Jake asked. "That's only a mile and a half from me."

Birdie looked shell-shocked. "Wow," she said. "That was fast. That's the first offer I've made on anything."

"It's perfect," Birdie said. "Ground floor unit. Golf course side. It comes with a free membership to the Blackhand Hills Fitness Club. Low HOA, only $200 a month. Three bedrooms. Two bathrooms. Way more storage than you usually see in condos. The owners put in all new appliances six months ago because the wife wanted all stainless steel."

"Gemma, thank you."

"I'm paying for the next round," Jake said. He clinked his beer mug with Birdie's. "What are you gonna do about Ben's place?"

"I talked to Travis about that," she said. "He's okay with me packing up Ben and Abby's things. We're renting a big storage unit. Then I'm going to rent it out until Travis comes back. If he wants to live in it, it'll be there. If he doesn't, he can sell it and move wherever he wants."

"Wow," Jake said. "It's kinda hard to think of those boys as adults now. Time went by so fast."

"Tell me about it," Gemma said. "Aidan's the next one you're gonna have to have a talk with, baby brother. Not quite eleven years old and he's figured out his pecker is a fun toy. Let's just say I'm teaching him how to do his own laundry."

Birdie wrinkled her nose. Jake chuckled.

"Back to work," Gemma said. "You two gonna be good to drive? Carly gets off in an hour. She'd be happy to drive either of you home."

"I'm just having the one," Jake said.

"Oh!" Gemma said. "Forgot to mention. Nice try not filling me in on your attempt to rearrange our uncle's face. I got ambushed about it at the butcher shop this morning. You wanna let me in on what's going on this time?"

Jake cleared his throat. "Nothing exciting. He just had the nerve to give me trouble for not asking about, as he put it, *our* grandmother."

Gemma's color went a little pale. "She's not dead, is she?"

"Not that I've been told," Jake answered.

"Well, good, I guess. Just do me a favor, will you? Stay away from that asshole. You're never able to hold your temper around him. One of these days he's gonna push your buttons enough you'll do something that could get you fired. You know that's what he wants."

"I can take care of myself," Jake said. Gemma gave him the same sideways look she always did when he said anything like that.

"I think it's time for me to cash out," Birdie said, using her most diplomatic tone.

"On me tonight," Gemma said. "You're about to earn me a nice commission. You? Little brother, you pay full price."

Jake rolled his eyes as Gemma sashayed back to the bar. He was about to pull two twenties out of his pocket when his phone vibrated on the table. His eyes locked with Birdie's. She grabbed the phone before he could. She quickly plugged in his passcode. He'd ask her later how the hell she knew it. Or how many times she'd used it before.

"It went off," she said, breathless. "It's live. There's ... I can see someone's back. Jake. There on the shelf. The bear."

"Let me see!" Jake insisted. Birdie turned the screen so they could both watch. She was right. The picture was crystal clear. A man. Brown hair. Wearing a black hoodie pulled up over his head. He reached for the purple bear. Jake couldn't see what he was doing with it, but was certain he was pulling out the SD card. They saw him reach into his pocket and pull out something else.

"That son of a bitch is swapping the memory card," Birdie said.

"He's wearing gloves," Jake said.

"So he's stupid, but not that stupid."

The man looked left and right, but was still only showing his back to the camera.

"It's not going to work," Birdie said. "If we can't see his face. If there are no prints."

"Relax," Jake said. "He still had to sign a key out."

"You think he's stupid enough to sign his own name?"

Jake was about to tell her to calm down again. But he had the same secret fear. What if after all this trouble, they wouldn't be able to get a clear shot of who this was?

The man leaned down, picking up something he'd dropped on the ground. For a moment, he went out of frame.

"Dammit!" Birdie shouted.

"Shh," Jake said, not wanting her to draw any attention to their table.

The man turned, his face still hidden by the dark hoodie.

"Shit," Jake said. "It's the wrong angle. How the hell did I rig it up at the wrong angle? I tested it."

"Shhh!" It was Birdie's turn to silence him.

One second. That's all they got. Just one second when the man turned, almost by accident, and looked directly at the camera. There was no mistake. It was a clean, clear shot of his face, straight on.

And Jake knew in that instant he'd have to do everything he prayed to avoid.

"Jake, I think I know where he might be headed. Denning told me a group was getting together at Wylie's tonight. He invited me to come."

"Shit," Jake said. "I heard that too. This has to happen now. Get Denning, find out who's there. Don't let on why you're asking. I need an hour to get everyone together. There can't be any mistakes. Somebody's gonna have to drag Judge Cardwell out of bed tonight for my warrants."

"Jake," Birdie said. "There will probably be at least eight other deputies in that bar. A fair number of second shifters are still armed."

"I know," he said. "I need to call Landry. And we need SWAT involved."

Thirty-Three

It took an hour to gather the team. SWAT Sergeant Tim Grady and six members of his team would be staged a block and a half away behind a now vacant furniture store. Deputy Amanda Chaplin would be their inside woman, texting Birdie a play-by-play.

"I can do this," Chaplin said, her eyes cold, her face expressionless. "Just give me five minutes."

"Amanda, you cannot do anything to tip anyone off," Jake said. "You understand?"

"I understand. I can do my job."

Birdie glared at Jake. She knew Chaplin better than he did. Jake nodded and stepped back. Chaplin closed her eyes and exhaled, flaring her nostrils. Then she put her game face on and walked into the bar through the front entrance.

"Stand by," SWAT Sergeant Tim Grady said into his radio.

One minute. Two. Sweat formed under Jake's collar. Three minutes. Four.

"We need to get in there," Grady said.

"Give her a chance," Birdie said.

As soon as she finished her sentence, Birdie got her first text from Chaplin.

"Bundy's at the bar with Chris Denning. Stuckey just got up to go to the men's room," Birdie said.

"Let me take him," Jake said. "I'll go in the back and walk Stuckey out."

Grady nodded. "Tell Chaplin to stay on Bundy," he said. "I don't want him anywhere near Stuckey or anybody else."

"Understood," Birdie said. She stepped away from the group to text Chaplin her instructions.

Jake walked around to the back of the bar. One of the line cooks was taking a smoke break next to the dumpster. He waved to Jake as Jake opened the screen door and let himself in.

No one questioned him as he cut through the kitchen and came out into the short, dark hallway where both restrooms and the manager's office were located. As soon as he turned the corner, Tom Stuckey walked out, still zipping up his pants. He noticed Jake at once.

"Hey!" he called out. "What are you doing back here?"

"Stuckey," Jake said. The man froze, his smile fading. He knew instantly from the tone of Jake's voice that this wasn't going to be a casual conversation.

"What's going on?" Stuckey asked.

"Take a walk with me," Jake said.

"Jake?"

"Just take a walk with me."

Stuckey looked back toward the bar. Then he frowned at Jake. There was a moment of hesitation. Jake's hand started to move toward the heel of his weapon. Stuckey shook his head but started walking toward Jake.

Jake waited, letting Stuckey pass him. Then he walked behind him back through the kitchen and out the service door. The line cook scooted past them both on the way back in.

"We're gonna take a ride," Jake said. His car was parked just a few yards away. Again, Stuckey hesitated. But he let Jake lead him to his car and got in the passenger side. As Jake walked around to the driver's side, he called Birdie.

"Stuckey's with me," he said.

"Copy that," she answered, then clicked off.

Jake got in, closed the door, and started the engine.

"You gonna tell me what this is all about?" Stuckey asked.

"I absolutely am," Jake said. He pulled out of the parking lot and headed downtown toward the Sheriff's Department. It was only a two-minute drive. They could have walked. Jake pulled into the lot, cut the engine, and turned to Stuckey.

"I have to tell you something," he said. "Sorry about the cloak-and-dagger shit, but I wanted you to hear this from me. I think I owe you that much."

"Jake, what the hell is going on?"

"We're making an arrest in the Katz murders. It's going down now. It's Matt Bundy, Tom. He killed Cameron and Rianne Katz. We're sure of it."

Stuckey's face went through a series of changes. First he smiled, as if Jake were joking. Then his eyes widened. Finally, it was as if someone had released a valve and all the air went out of his body. His face went slack.

"Come on," he said. "It's going to be a long night. I'll answer any questions I can. But I have a few for you."

Stuckey moved like a zombie, shuffling his feet. At one point, he grabbed hold of Jake's hood to keep himself from staggering forward. Then, he followed Jake into his office and nearly collapsed in a chair at the table.

Jake's radio squawked. "Go ahead," he said, holding it up to his face.

"All clear. All safe," Tim Grady said. "Beverly's going to oversee booking."

"Copy that," Jake said.

A second later, Birdie called him on his cell. "You okay?" Jake asked.

"Okay as any of us can be," she said. "I've got a half a dozen pissed-off cops in front of me."

"You need help with that?"

"I got it."

"Okay. Let me know when Deputy Holtz comes back with our warrants. Then head straight over to Bundy's. Have a crew sit on his truck until we get the word."

"Understood," she said.

Jake set his cellphone on the table. Stuckey sat with his head in his hands.

"I don't understand this," he said. "Jake. Are you sure?"

Jake nodded. He laid out what they had. The prints. The ballistics. The altered statement from Nadya Louden. Finally, Jake played the video of Bundy switching out the SD card from Birdie's decoy nanny cam.

Stuckey held Jake's phone in his hands, playing the recording over three times. Trembling, he put the phone down.

"He didn't tell me Nadya Louden saw a truck parked out in front of that house, Jake. I swear to God."

"I believe you. But I need you to think. Hard. Did Matt say anything to you? Grill you for info about the case. Anything out of the ordinary."

Stuckey kept shaking his head. "No. God. Jake, you know what that scene was like. You, of all people. That one was a gut punch. I couldn't shake it. Matt knew that. We talked about it. Hell, we commiserated about it. He said it was hard for him too. Two nights after we took that call, it really got to me. I kept seeing Rianne Katz like she was. It was a bad one, Jake, Christ. I slept on Matt's couch! I went over there so we could talk it out. He consoled me. My God."

"I'm sorry," Jake said, putting a hand on Stuckey's shoulder. "I really am. I wish this were anything else."

"He knew her," Stuckey said. "He dated her?"

"That's what it's looking like," Jake said. "Obviously, I've got a lot more evidence to collect. I should have my search warrants within the hour. Bundy's being booked as we speak."

"Can I see him?"

"You know you can't."

"I want him to tell me to my face. I want to see his face."

"There will be time for that later," Jake said. "Right now, I need your statement, Tom. Did Matt ever talk about a girlfriend? Did you know he was seeing someone?"

"No. Shit. I tried to fix him up with a friend of mine a few months ago. He said he wasn't interested. He ... Jake, that day. Matt insisted we take that call. Like he jumped on it. I told him it wasn't ours. Unit 21 was closer. It was odd to me, but why the hell would I think Matt killed those people?"

"What do you remember about when you got there? Tom, I need to know every step you took. Everything you saw Matt do."

"I don't ... nothing. We followed crime scene protocol to the letter, Jake. We secured that scene by the book. You know that. You commended us on it."

"Who was the first one to go to Cameron Katz's body?"

"He did," Stuckey said.

"Was there ever a time Matt was alone in that house?"

"I don't ... maybe for thirty seconds. He had me radio it in to dispatch. I walked away, stepped out on the back porch and made the call. But like I said. Thirty seconds at the absolute max. And ..."

"What, Tom?"

"It's just. In the weeks since it's happened, Matt's been obsessed. We've driven by that house maybe a dozen times. He said it just haunted him. And I got it. It's like that for me too. I just thought ..."

"I need you to write it all out, Tom," Jake said, sliding a fresh legal pad and pen across the table. "Everything you remember about

Matt's actions when you walked into that crime scene. Everything he said. Everything you can remember about what he's said since. All of it. Take as much time as you need. You understand? This needs to be thorough. I know this is a tough one to process. But I need you to try to put your personal feelings aside and think like the good cop you are."

Stuckey stifled a sob. But he recovered quickly. He picked up the pen and started writing.

Twelve hours later, Jake and his team finished their preliminary sweep of Matt Bundy's house and truck. Jake drank coffee by the pot. He had photos of everything relevant from the searches. And Mark Ramirez called with the most damning evidence of all.

"It's a match," Mark said. "Bundy's sample bullet matches the ones taken from Rianne Katz's body. They were fired from Matt Bundy's service weapon. I've got some quick results on the phone. I'll text them to you. She's all over his camera roll. Some early stuff on his GPS. His phone didn't move from his house the night of the murder. But there were other hits before that. He was in the area of her house as much as twenty times in the week prior. And we found a box of treasures under his bed. A lot of testing yet to do, but he's got dozens more photos of Rianne. Some are pretty disturbing. I'm sending photos of everything we found."

Jake squeezed the phone against his ear. Some part of him still wished it would be a different answer. "Got it," he said. "Thanks for all of it. Let me know when you have the full report."

He clicked off, slid his phone into his pocket. He stood outside interview room one. Deputy Denning had just brought Bundy up from his holding cell. He'd had all night. Twelve hours to stew in this alone. Jake turned the door handle and went inside.

Thirty-Four

Jake brought four things into the interview room. A tablet, pen and paper, and a printed Miranda waiver. He set the pen, paper, and waiver in front of Matt Bundy.

Bundy looked rough. A day's worth of uneven stubble grew along his jaw. He had bloodshot eyes and unruly hair. His clothes were rumpled. He stared at Jake, expressionless, his chair back against the wall.

"Let me be clear about a few things," Jake said. "This is not an interrogation. I'm not looking to catch you in a lie. I'm not expecting a confession. You can sit there and stare at me the whole time. I don't care. You can spill your guts. I don't care. If you're looking for any help from anyone in this building, we're beyond that. There will be no union rep called. You forfeited all that when you went into that property room and tampered with evidence. You're on tape for that. That's the first thing. Here's the second."

Bundy didn't move. Didn't even blink.

"Do you want a lawyer?" Jake asked. "Say the word. Right now. I'll even make the call for you. My advice? You should have one. Let me repeat, you'll get no help from anyone in this building. Make your choice."

Still, nothing from Bundy. Jake pushed the Miranda waiver closer to Bundy and set the pen on top of it. He recited Bundy's rights. He also knew he'd been read them by John Beverly as they put him in the squad car in Wylie's parking lot.

"If you understand, sign it," Jake said. "Or don't. This interview is being recorded."

Bundy didn't hesitate. He picked up the pen and signed his name on the Miranda waiver. Then he sat back, crossing his arms in front of him.

"Good," Jake said. "So, one more time. Now's the time to call your lawyer. Do you want a phone? Do you want to write his or her name down for me? Do you want a public defender?"

Bundy, stony silence.

"You know how this works. This is your window. Your only chance to help yourself out. What you do with it is up to you."

"I'm aware," Bundy said.

"Great. I imagine you're sitting there thinking I don't have it. You might be thinking worst-case scenarios about what I do have. As I said when I sat down. My intention is to be absolutely clear. Your job here is over. You'll never wear a badge again. This is you."

Jake opened the tablet and played the recording of Bundy in the property room. Bundy glanced down, but showed no reaction.

"Nadya Louden has given a second statement," Jake continued. "I know you failed to report evidence. She told you she saw a vehicle matching the description of your truck parked outside the Katzes' house right before the shooting happened, according to the ME's death timeline. Stuckey backs that up. You never told him Mrs.

Louden's full statement. He also says you had up to a minute unattended at the crime scene and you got to Cameron Katz's body before he did."

Bundy crossed one leg over the other.

"The bullets pulled out of Rianne Katz came from your service weapon. That's confirmed. They've been matched to your sample bullet from the armorer. I'm gonna take a wild guess you didn't know they're kept on file for all of us before we're issued a gun."

This time, a tiny flicker in Bundy's eyes.

"Just got a text from Detective Wayne. She's got positive IDs from Nate Parra, Rianne's ex-fiancé, and Adam Smith, her former neighbor. They both say they saw you with Rianne two years ago. You were in a romantic relationship with her over a two-week period. Smith signed an affidavit that he saw you sitting outside Rianne's apartment. Watching her comings and goings for days on end. Stalking her. Rianne's co-worker, Mia Casey, also confirms she saw you coming out of her apartment after a hook-up."

"I've heard enough," Bundy said.

"You don't get to decide that. I do. Your prints are at the house. You can't hide behind your badge on that one anymore. BCI did a prelim on your phone."

Jake picked up the tablet again and scrolled to an album of pictures Ramirez pulled off Bundy's phone. He had seventy-two pictures of Rianne Katz. Some she posed for. Many, it appeared she was unaware she was being photographed. One, Bundy caught her naked in her own bathroom, shielding her face as if she hadn't consented to the photograph.

"We're going to scrub your truck," Jake said. "You might have cleaned it. But you shot two people at close range. Are you absolutely certain I won't find trace blood evidence? Because nobody is that good, Matt. Everyone thinks they are, but you can't be."

Bundy ran a hand down his haggard face. Jake flipped to a different file on the tablet. Here, he'd stored photos taken during the late-night search of Bundy's home. He pulled out the tablet's stand and propped it up in front of Bundy.

"Recognize this?" he asked. "You've got a storage bin under your bed, Matt. Not too smart. But then, I guess you thought you'd outsmart us all. We'd never come looking. Never suspect you."

Jake scrolled to the next photo. It showed the contents of a clear plastic under-bed bin. It contained another stack of photographs of Rianne Katz. Some were the same as the ones found in his camera roll. He'd printed them out. Blown up one of Rianne in the nude. Two pieces of women's jewelry. A necklace. A ring. Two tee shirts. A pair of red lace women's panties.

"You know we'll run those for DNA," Jake said. "Hair and fiber. You wanna guess what we'll find?"

Bundy didn't break his stone mask. Not until Jake scrolled to the very last photo from the bin. This item had been removed. The photo showed it in Jake's gloved palm.

"That's a safe deposit box key," he said. "What's it doing among things you stole from Rianne Katz? Huh? What does it go to? Better yet, why did you hang on to it?"

It was then that Matt Bundy began to sweat. He chewed his fingernails and tapped his heel on the floor.

"We're going to figure it out, Matt," Jake said. "Maybe you couldn't, huh? Did you take it from Rianne's house? Was it on her keychain? We found that on the floor in the corner of the kitchen near her body. I'm thinking either she's got her own treasure trove on you somewhere, or you've got more on her. Something you didn't even want in your house."

"No. No way, man," Bundy said. "You wanna make it like I'm some psycho. That's not how this went. She was the psycho. You know the kind. And she was all over me, not the other way around. Practically jumped me the first night I met her. Never let go after that. Needy. Wanting attention. But passionate. Insatiable. Almost frantic about it. Two or three times a day. Every day. She wanted more and more attention. Yeah. That was great at first. But I figured out pretty quickly she'd never be satisfied. I can tell you right now, if I hadn't broken it off, she was gonna either trap me with a baby, or lie about one. The only thing I'll admit to is being turned on by some of it. At least in the beginning. I told you. She was passionate. God. She was sexy as hell. I was weak. Yeah. Can you blame me? I mean, you've seen her."

Jake went rigid. "Yeah. Yeah, Matt. I've seen her." Jake couldn't get the image of Rianne Katz lying on her own kitchen floor. Waxen white from the loss of so much blood.

"I said enough," Bundy shouted. "I know how this goes. You're right."

Jake sat back. "You want a lawyer now?"

"No," he said. "I want Boyd Ansel. I know he's probably already out there. You bring me the prosecutor. I don't talk unless he's in the room."

Of all the things Matt Bundy could say, that's the one that shocked him. It was as good as a confession in Jake's eyes. Bundy knew what this was. He knew he could be facing capital murder charges. Jake rose. He turned his back on Bundy and stepped into the next room.

Bundy was right. Four people sat in the observation room behind the one-way glass. They'd heard and seen the whole interview. Meg Landry. Birdie. Dean Lowell, the union rep. And Boyd Ansel.

"You ready for him?" Jake asked Boyd. Ansel's face was purple with fury.

"He thinks I'm gonna offer?" Ansel said.

"He thinks he's going to be slick enough to weasel his way down to second degree," Jake said.

"No way," Landry said. "Boyd, I know you understand the political fallout that would bring for both of us. Plus, those people had families, for chrissake."

"It's a no go," Boyd said. "I'd rather take it to trial."

"I think the families would too," Jake said.

"He's got one card to play as far as I'm concerned," Ansel said. "He can keep a needle out of his arm."

Jake nodded. "Are you satisfied with his waiver of rights? You'll talk to him without his own lawyer present?"

"I'll give him another chance to call one," Ansel said. "But as far as I'm concerned, this ends today. Right now."

Jake held the door open so Boyd Ansel could walk through. He watched Ansel from the window as he sat down in front of Matt Bundy. Jake felt bone-tired. Like his legs might not work much longer. He sat down between Birdie and Sheriff Landry. Lowell looked like he was about to be sick. He got up and walked out of the room. Then they listened to Matt Bundy as he tried to explain how he could murder two people and try to get away with it.

Thirty-Five

Dear Mom, Dad, and Cameron,

If you're reading this, I know something bad happened. I am so sorry for putting you through it. Please know I tried everything. I did everything I was supposed to do.

But if I get hurt someday. If I go away someday. Matt Bundy will be responsible.

I know you'll be angry with me for not telling you sooner. I know you'll want to kill him. Please don't. Please don't ruin your own lives for my mistakes. I wish I could lay it all out. Tell you the whole story so that you could understand why I've done some of the things I've done. I've started this letter at least ten times but always end up tearing it to pieces. So, I'll start again. Maybe this time, I'll be brave enough to save it.

Let me be clear about something. I don't sleep

around, no matter what Matt tries to say. I cared about him. I still do. Even after the last two years of hell. I even thought I loved him for a little while. But when I met Cameron, everything changed. I saw what Matt really wanted from me.

Cameron, I'm so worried about you being angry with me. Or you being so angry that you'll do something that will get you in trouble so deep, I can never get you out. I know you've tried to help. Tried to take care of my problems. I know I've pushed you away. I just never wanted anyone else to get hurt. I know what Matt is capable of.

God, I'm rambling now. I meant to be clear and direct. So here is what I want you to know. Matt thinks he loves me. He doesn't know the meaning of the word. He wants something to own. To control. That's not me, and never will be.

I'm sure this is me overreacting. Here I am, ready to rip this letter up again. I don't know. But just in case.

I've clipped two notes to this letter. Matt left them on my windshield. There were more. A lot more. These are the only two I've kept.

Matt is a police officer. I'm not naive and I know what happens if I try to turn him in. He told me himself. His brothers take care of their own. No one is going to believe me. He's right. I know it. I don't want any of you to get hurt.

Please. He promised he'd hurt anyone I tried to talk to about him. I believe him.

I'm so sorry that this will all be hard for you to see. So don't even look. Please. Don't open the envelope I've stapled to this letter. Just give it to someone you trust.

I love you.

Your daughter, your loving soon-to-be wife,

Rianne.

Another copy of another letter slipped into a clear plastic sheet protector. Jake laid this one on top of the box. He had copies of what was inside the envelope Rianne Katz had attached to it. All of it tucked away in a safe deposit box under her father's account at his credit union in Terrace Park.

Jake slipped the copies of the other items into their own plastic sheaths. Two scraps of paper. The words on them were written with a black Sharpie.

"I'm here, Rianne. Always here. I have eyes everywhere and they're trained on you. Never forget that."

And

"You think he's better than me? Can satisfy you the way I do? Sooner than you think, I'm going to show you again. I know how to make you bend for me. Remember that."

Then there were three photographs Rianne took of herself in her bathroom mirror. She had bruises in the shape of clear handprints along her left arm. A split lip. An eye nearly swollen shut.

Jake laid those on top of the box and closed the lid.

"Ansel just finished up at the courthouse," Birdie said. Jake startled. He hadn't heard her walk into the office. She moved the hand truck he'd brought up away from the doorway and walked over to the table.

"How'd it go?" Jake asked.

"No surprises. He pled to second degree on Rianne. First degree on Cameron. The lesser charges. Obstruction. Witness tampering. Though none of that really matters. The judge set formal sentencing for next month. But it'll just be a formality. Bundy's going away for life. It's done."

Jake felt a wave of relief. He expected nothing else, but still, it was good to hear the official word.

"Boyd's heading over to the press room. Landry's there now. They go live in five minutes. You better hurry."

Jake leaned back against the table. "They don't need me."

Birdie eyed him. "I don't think it has anything to do with need, Jake. You have to take your victory lap on this one."

"Victory? Strange word."

"You know what I mean. The families are down there. Rianne's parents. Cameron's brother and his niece. They're doing okay, those two. I talked to Keeley Katz's social worker. He passed his home visit with flying colors. And it sounds like Rianne's folks aren't going to fight him over the house. It was in Cameron's name alone. Without a will and without Rianne to survive him, it goes to the brother."

"It's a good neighborhood," Jake said. "It's a better place for Keeley to grow up. If her father can keep his demons in check."

"You want me to take that down to the Crypt?" Birdie asked, putting her hand on the Katz box.

Jake picked it up and placed it on the hand truck. "That'd be good."

"This one stings, I know that," Birdie said. "But this was good work."

Jake smiled. "And you know none of this would have happened without you. I mean that. You've been a rock star on this case. And for me. I know you helped keep me from heading into some very deep waters."

Birdie reached for him. She squeezed his hand. "That's what partners are for. I'm sure it won't be long before you need to do the same thing for me."

She stepped forward. Jake wasn't expecting it, but Birdie slipped her arms around him and hugged him. He hesitated for just an instant. Then his heart gave out and he hugged her back, smelling her hair.

When they broke apart, he went to the corner of the office. He shuffled three more boxes around, turning with just one in his arms.

"Can you take this one back to the Crypt for me too?"

Birdie's eyes flicked to the lid. It was his parents' case file.

"Sure," she said. "I'd be glad to."

Jake walked slowly over to the hand truck and stacked it on top of the Katz files.

"Jake," she said. "There's something I should have told you yesterday. I was debating even telling you at all."

Jake raised a brow. "That doesn't sound like good news."

"No, it's fine. It's just. Well, I intercepted a message Darcy took down for you. She's going to have my ass if she finds out I haven't given it to you."

Birdie reached into her pocket and pulled out a crumpled pink sheet from Darcy's message pad. She handed it to him.

"Don't shoot the messenger," she said.

Frowning, Jake read the note. It was from someone named Simon Furlong. Below his name, Darcy had written in parentheses, Adele Arden – Assistant. Below that, she'd jotted down the message.

"Adele Arden wants to see you and sister. Room 1453. Hope Hospital. Call Furlong before you go."

Jake crumpled the note back up. He thought about tossing it into the nearest garbage can.

"I take it you read it," he said.

"It's why I've been holding on to it. I knew you'd try to throw it away. Maybe you should. I heard they called hospice last week. I don't think she's got very much longer."

Jake slipped the note into his pocket. He didn't have an answer for Birdie. And he didn't have one for himself. Not now.

Birdie grabbed the handles and turned the cart toward the door. "You're late," she said, pointing to the open laptop on Jake's desk. He had the livestream from the press room up. Though it was muted, Sheriff Landry was speaking to the media with Boyd Ansel at her side.

Jake wanted to be anywhere but down there. But Birdie was right. He owed it to Rianne and Cameron Katz's families to be there.

Birdie rolled the boxes out of the door. Jake watched as she turned the corner, heading for the elevator all the way down to the basement.

"I think the message is clear," Sheriff Landry spoke into the microphones. "We will deliver equal justice, no matter who the perpetrators are. I want to thank Boyd Ansel for his swift and decisive handling of this case. As he's just told you through his competent advocacy, the families of this tragedy will be spared the ugliness of a trial. I have full faith and confidence that the victims in this case will get the justice they deserve. Even though I know it can't bring them back and their loved ones will forever have to carry their loss. I hope it's at least some small consolation that we've achieved a final and decisive resolution to this matter, thank you. Now I'd like to hand it over to the lead detective in this case, Detective Jake Cashen. Then we'll stay to answer any questions."

Jake glowered at Meg. He hadn't agreed to say anything. She smiled at him and put a hand on his back, gently nudging him toward the microphones.

Jake adjusted the microphone, sliding it up to accommodate his height. Meg was eight inches shorter than he was. He caused a screech of feedback for a moment.

"Sorry," he said. "I really don't have much to add to Sheriff Landry or Mr. Ansel's remarks. I'll just say unless there is any doubt. There isn't a single cop in this town, myself included, who wanted this outcome. But make no mistake. Matt Bundy is not one of our own. We do not protect people like him. He is a disgrace to the badge. I don't care who you are. Every citizen in this county should feel safe in reporting the bad actions of anyone who would cause them harm. Whether they wear a badge or not. That's all I have to say."

As soon as he stepped away, the questions came from all sides. Meg and Boyd answered them deftly. They began to wind down. Then, one reporter stepped forward. "I have something for Detective Cashen directly."

Jake felt a tingle of apprehension as Meg made way for him at the lectern.

"Yes."

"Detective Cashen, would you care to comment on reports of a public and violent confrontation you had with Commissioner Arden during the investigation of this case?"

"No," he said.

"Sources are telling us Commissioner Arden was going to file a formal complaint against you regarding your conduct in this case. But that he was pressured to withdraw it. He is accusing you of attempting to cover up the real killer in this case. And that it was pressure from him that forced your hand to go public and arrest Deputy Bundy. Can you explain that?"

Jake felt heat rising in his face. Meg put a hand on his arm.

"That," Jake said, "is patently false. Why don't you go ask Commissioner Arden what he's trying to hide by spreading more false rumors?"

"Jake," Meg said through gritted teeth. Then she pulled the microphone toward her. "As Detective Cashen said, those accusations have no truth to them. We have been open and transparent at every stage of this case. The right man is going away for the rest of his life. That is one hundred percent due to the tireless investigation and determination of Detectives Cashen and Wayne."

He opened his mouth, ready to unleash a tirade. Meg locked eyes with him. She put her hand over the microphone. "Not here," she whispered. "Not this day."

Jake saw Rianne's parents and Keeley Katz in her father's arms at the back of the room. He took a deep breath, then stepped aside.

"Thank you," Meg said. "That's all for now. I've been told it'll be open court for Matt Bundy's sentencing next month. Save your feeding frenzy until then. And please respect the privacy of the families during this incredibly difficult time."

She grabbed Jake's arm and dragged him with her into the staging area through a side door.

"Go home," she said. "You've earned it." It surprised Jake. He expected her to rip into him.

He holstered the sharp words he had in his mind if she had. "Thanks," he said. "I think I will. Good work, Boyd. The families are gonna wanna talk to you."

"I think they might want to talk to you too," Boyd said.

"My job's done. This is your moment now."

Boyd tried to persuade him to stay, but Jake had already started down the hallway. Back home, he had an unopened bottle of Blanton's Black, a fresh cigar, and the Reds were playing tonight. He felt the crinkle of the note in his pocket as he made his way to the parking lot. That too could keep for now. He'd decide whether it was worth telling Gemma about tomorrow.

As he pulled up his long gravel driveway, one of Gemma's goats had gotten loose again. It casually munched grass in his side yard. Jake got out, went to it, and gave it a gentle swat on the rump.

"Go on home, Bernie," he said. "Your girlfriends are waiting."

The goat gave him a dubious eye, then toddled off toward the creek. Jake walked up to the porch and stopped. There was a package on his doormat.

He reached down and picked it up. The label had his name and address, but no information about the sender. He shook it. It was lightweight, but something rattled inside.

He took it inside and set it on the table. His cell phone rang as he peeled his gun belt off, feeling the relief of the weight off his lower back. He silenced his phone. After pouring himself two fingers into a rocks glass, he grabbed the package and sat down heavily on the couch. He kicked his shoes off and took a slow sip.

He stared at the box. He hadn't ordered anything. Wasn't expecting anything. And most of his deliveries went in the deck box Grandpa Max kept closer to the road.

He reached over and grabbed a pocket knife he kept on the side table. Slicing through the tape, he peeled open the box. A phone fell out. It was a prepaid cheap flip phone.

Jake tossed the box aside. He gripped the phone, squeezing it hard. He knew he should toss it in the trash. He also knew he wouldn't.

He flipped it open. One message blinked in the inbox. Jake hesitated, then clicked it open.

The text read, "Call me." A phone number was hyperlinked beneath it.

"Shit," Jake muttered. His eyes went to the ceiling. He bit his bottom lip. Then he looked at the phone screen. He clicked on the phone number and made the call.

Thirty-Six

"Hello, Jake."

Jake walked outside and sat on a porch chair. The quarter moon looked orange tonight due to Canadian wildfires.

"Hi, Frank," he said. For three years, retired Detective Frank Borowski had been on the run after murdering a very bad man. But murder is murder.

"Big day today," Frank said. "But a tough day. It's never easy arresting a fellow cop."

"He's not a fellow cop," Jake said. "Matt Bundy's a cold-blooded killer. The only thing he's done right is plead out so those poor families don't have to relive the horror of this at trial. Arresting him was easy."

Jake could hear seagulls in the background. Of course, Frank would be near water somewhere. Maybe some beach in Venezuela. Certainly a place where he could get on a boat and fish.

"What do you want, Frank?"

"I thought you might want to talk. I thought you might have some questions for me."

Jake rubbed his brow. "I don't know, Frank. I feel like any answers you have you should have given me a long time ago."

"You were just a kid for most of the time I've spent with you."

"That's a cop-out. You've known me for over thirty years. I've been a man for twenty of them."

"You're right. But what did you want me to say?"

Jake sighed. "Who called you? Was it Virgil? Bill? Certainly not Chuck."

He knew Frank would never answer. He'd never admit that any one of the Wise Men were aiding or abetting his run from the law. He also knew Frank could never completely go no contact with them. Their bond was deep and old.

"I just wanted to make sure you didn't lose yourself chasing after ghosts. I know what that's like. It can destroy you. It destroyed me. You know that more than anyone else."

"Then stop chasing them. Stop running from them. Come back to Blackhand Hills."

Frank laughed. "And you know if I do that, I'll either spend the rest of my life in prison, if I'm lucky enough not to get the needle. Or end up at the bottom of a gorge courtesy of Rex Bardo. My preference for one over the other changes day by day. I think I'll stay right where I am. And you also know that's not why I called. Ask your questions, Jake. You might not get another chance."

"Are you planning something?"

"Nah. Plus the day I die, you'll know it. And the house will be yours."

Jake shook his head. "The day I hear you died, I won't believe it. And I never wanted that house."

"It makes me happy you'll have it. That you're watching over it. We spent a lot of good days there. You can't live in your grandpa's cabin forever."

Crickets chirped under the porch. Jake heard something scurry through the brush at the end of the driveway.

"You should have told me," Jake said. "You should have told me Rob Arden's the reason my father thought my mother was the enemy. He was probably the reason my dad got as bad as he did. You should have told me he left a note."

"And you know all of that was for Max to decide. My opinion, not that you asked for it, is he did the right thing. That note wasn't your dad. It was his disease. As far as Rob? There was no point. He showed his colors pretty quick, just like I knew he would. You already had enough reasons to hate him. If he'd tried to be some sort of surrogate father to you. If you had started to get close to him, I might have made a different choice. He never wanted anything to do with you. That wasn't your fault. But you figured out for yourself what kind of man he is by the time you were fourteen, Jake."

"He might as well have killed her," Jake said. "He stoked my dad's paranoia. He might as well have been the one pointing the gun at her."

"Except he wasn't," Frank said. "And I know that's the hardest part of this to accept. You've been looking for answers and excuses for what he did your whole life. You've wanted there to be some other villain so you didn't have to accept that it was your father, and your father alone who pulled that trigger on her and himself. And I know why. I know it keeps you up at night wondering whether that same demon is inside you. It's not, Jake. It's just not."

Jake felt hot tears sting his eyes. He held them back.

"It's not," Frank said again, quieter. "You're not the worst parts of your father. You're the best. Trust me. I've known you both."

"Why didn't you put it in your report?" Jake asked. "You knew what my dad meant in that note when he talked about the Gryphon. I thought he was talking about some mythical creature. But he was talking about his own best friend."

"You met him?" Frank asked. "You talked to him?"

For an instant, Jake wanted to deny it and he wasn't sure why. But something told him Frank already knew the answer. "Yes," Jake said.

"Then I think you know why he wasn't in the report. There was no reason for it. Rumors didn't kill your parents. And Griffin Malley is a good man. He was a decent, loyal friend to both Jake and Sonya. And he almost became the third victim on that awful day. Did you know that? Did he tell you? He tried to kill himself a few weeks later. Racked with guilt about how he thought it should have been him that Jake Sr. shot. That he sent Sonya to her death because he insisted on looking for your dad at Max's house. There were enough rumors flying around. Enough people in town started to believe he *did* have something to do with it. That, above all, is the worst thing Rob did. If I had put Griffin in that report, everybody at the Sheriff's Department would have known about it. They'd speculate as to why I questioned him. I wouldn't do it. I wasn't gonna help Rob Arden destroy him."

"But you could have told me," Jake said.

"For what purpose?"

"I don't know!" Jake shouted. "So I could know him. Talk to him. He was important to my mom and dad. He loved them. And I think he loved Gemma and me too."

"Those things are all true about his loving your family. But you found him without me. Maybe enough time has passed for both of you that you can have a relationship that isn't so damn tragic."

Jake didn't know what else to say. Everything Frank said made sense in its way. And he knew if he were in Frank's place, he might have made all the same choices. And yet, none of it helped. He still felt raw and angry.

"You have to let it go," Frank said. "There are no more answers. You have them all. And not one damn thing has changed now that you've seen that file. You knew Gemma went through hell and survived it. So did you. You knew your grandparents would probably have given up, checked out if they didn't have you and your sister to look after. As for the Ardens? You're already angry at Rob for that and have been your whole life. He deserves your hatred. Just don't let it drive you. Don't even give him the satisfaction of entering your thoughts."

"She's dying," Jake said. "Adele Arden. She sent me a note. Says she wants to see Gemma and me. I don't know why."

"Maybe you should find out. Not for her. But for you. I'm not defending her. The way the Ardens have treated you and your sister is deplorable. But Paul and Rob Arden are the driving forces behind that. Rob's been terrified since the day Gemma was born that she and later you would get half his money. He wasn't going to let that happen. It was easy for him to fan the flames of an old, stupid family feud. Maybe she was weak? Maybe her husband and son exerted undue influence over her, but Adele Arden went along with it. Maybe she wants to apologize."

It was Jake's turn to laugh. "Great. Only I'm not the one who needs it. She didn't break my heart. I never had a relationship with her even when my mom was still alive. That was her doing. But she hurt my mom. Apologizing now won't take away Mom's pain."

"Maybe not," Frank said. "But it might take away some of yours. You'll do what you want. And I know I have no right to give you any advice. But maybe go. See what the old bat has to say."

Clouds moved over the sliver of moon, turning the sky inky black. "I'm glad you called, Frank," Jake found himself saying.

"Me too. I'm still here, Jake. I still care what happens to you, even if you don't care what happens to me."

"Of course I care," Jake said. But it was as far as he could go.

"Maybe we'll talk again someday," Frank said.

Jake didn't answer. He knew it would always be on Frank's terms if they did.

"I know you tried to take care of them," Jake said. "My sister when she was twelve and in the deepest trauma of her life. My grandma, who wasn't strong enough to survive what happened in the end. Grandpa Max too."

Frank stayed silent for a moment. Jake checked the phone screen, thinking maybe he'd already hung up. The call timer kept running.

"I love you, Jake," Frank said. "Take care of yourself."

He didn't give Jake a chance to respond. The screen went blank as the call ended. Jake stared at it for a moment. Then he stood. He walked into the garage and picked up a hammer from a hook on the wall. He slid the phone's battery out and tossed it in the trash. Then he set the phone on his workbench and smashed it with the hammer.

Thirty-Seven

"Now that we're here, I don't know if I can go in, Jake."

His sister sat in the passenger seat of Jake's truck. She hadn't taken her seatbelt off even though they'd been parked for almost five minutes. She kept staring at the building.

Hope Hospital was only twenty-five years old. A three-story brick building with a giant marble water fountain in front of the main entrance. At the foot of it, there was an ornate, bronze plaque. A tribute to his grandparents, whose patronage had built this place.

"It's so stupid," Gemma said. "Everybody knows you don't come to Hope for anything but stitches and maybe a colonoscopy. But even that's a stretch. You don't come here for critical cardiac care. County has the level one trauma center and the best doctors."

"But this place has the plaque." Jake pointed. Gemma rolled her eyes.

"I'm not saying she could be saved," Gemma said. "How much can they do for an already frail, eighty-five-year-old woman, no matter how much money she's got?"

"I don't know, Gemma. But we can't sit here all day. If you don't wanna go, I'll turn around. Maybe this was a bad idea."

"No," she said. "No. We're here. Despite all of it, I'm damn curious. And she's never asked to see us in thirty years."

"You didn't tell Gramps, did you?"

"God, no," Gemma said. She finally unsnapped her seatbelt. She looked stunning today. Her hair was meticulously styled, curling around her face. She wore a pale, lime-green suit with three-inch matching heels. Her makeup looked like something Jake had only seen in magazines. She smelled good too. Some kind of new perfume. And he knew all of it was her armor. People named Arden had been calling them hicks and trash their whole life. Today, Gemma looked ... expensive.

He got out, walked around the back of the truck, and then opened the door for her. Gemma took his hand and hopped out. She looked him up and down. Jake hadn't dressed specially for the occasion. He wore a work suit, his badge already clipped to his belt and his weapon in its side holster. After they were done, he was dropping Gemma off at home and heading straight into work.

Gemma reached up, licked her finger and tried to smooth down his cowlick.

"Hey!" he protested, unsuccessfully dodging her reach.

"Come on," she said. "Let's go before I lose my nerve."

Her heels clacked on the sidewalk, but she moved surprisingly fast in them. She was in full "Gemma mode" as she stormed up to the front desk, demanding to be directed to Adele Arden's room. The volunteer at the desk widened her eyes in surprise.

"We're her grandchildren," Gemma barked.

"Right," the girl said. "You can go on up. She's in the VIP suite in the cardiac wing."

"Of course she is," Jake muttered. Gemma backhanded him in the chest. Then she grabbed him by the sleeve and charged full steam ahead to the elevators.

"What do you expect me to do if we run into Rob?" Jake asked.

"Behave yourself," she said. "If he needs decking, let me do it this time."

Jake smiled. Honestly? At this point, he'd put his money on his sister if it went to hand-to-hand combat with Rob.

The elevator deposited them on the third floor. It was well marked. The VIP suite was at the end of a short hallway to their left. The double doors were open and a young, pretty nurse stepped out. Jake knew her. Karma Dorman. They'd gone to high school together.

"Jake!" she smiled and whispered. Karma had always been cheerful. She'd served as class president and captain of the cheerleading squad. He once heard she had a crush on him. Though Jake had never really believed that. Today though, she threw her arms around him and hugged him. Jake cast a puzzled look at Gemma, over Karma's left shoulder.

"We're here to see Adele," Jake said as Karma let him go.

"Oh, I know. She's been asking. She wanted me to call you. I told her how I knew you. Hey, Gemma. You look amazing."

"Thanks," Gemma said.

"How is she?" Jake asked.

Karma's face fell. "It probably won't be too long. She's still talking. Goes in and out. But she stopped eating yesterday. That's usually the first sign. Her family ... er ... sorry. Her son gave consent to administer palliative care only. But we're managing her pain pretty well. She's comfortable. And surprisingly upbeat. You can go on in. I have to warn you though. She's with it most of the time. But that's getting iffy now too. She's starting to see loved ones she lost. I walked in on her talking to her father this morning. It was very sweet, actually. And it's very common with end-of-life patients. I just wanted you to be aware."

"I appreciate it," Jake said. Karma touched his arm, smiled, then walked back to the nurse's station.

"You should ask her out," Gemma said through clenched teeth. "I know she's not seeing anybody. She was married a long time ago. But not for very long. Never had kids."

"Thanks," Jake said. "I don't need a matchmaker."

Gemma snorted. "Right."

Jake began to open the door. "After you."

Gemma's face went white. "I ... not yet. Jake, you go first. I'll be in in a minute."

Jake frowned. "Gemma, if you don't want ..."

"No, go in. I mean it. I'll follow in a few minutes. I swear."

He grumbled but didn't argue. He gave his sister one more stern look, then walked into his grandmother's room.

Adele Arden sat up in bed. She looked out the window with a dreamy expression on her raw-boned face. Jake had always remembered her with cottony white hair. She still had that. She wore it pinned in a neat, thick bun. Jake knew if she pulled it loose, it had to hang down to at least her waist. She had tiny wrists, a single IV line taped to her paper-thin skin. She wore a white nightgown with puffy sleeves and trimmed with lace.

Jake didn't know what to call her. Mrs. Arden? Grandmother? He stepped forward and used the only name he remembered his mother ever saying around him.

"Hello, Grandma Del."

She turned from the window, her blue eyes clouded, but she smiled when she saw him.

"It's Jake," he said. "You sent a message that you wanted to see me?"

She held out her gnarled hands. "Come closer," she said. Her voice was pleasant, melodic. She had rings on almost every finger. A giant wedding set with a white gold band and a diamond as big as Jake's thumbnail. He wondered how she could even hold it up, as delicate as she was.

He went to her. He didn't take her hands but pulled up a stool beside her and sat so he was close enough for her to see him clearly.

"You grew up so handsome," she said. "You look a little like my father."

"Everyone tells me I'm the spitting image of my own," he said. Her face didn't fall as he expected it to. If the mention of Jake Cashen Sr. caused her any distress, she didn't show it.

"I suppose I see a little of him. Around the eyes maybe. If you bring me my purse, I can show you a picture of your great-grandfather. I keep one in my wallet."

"It's okay," Jake said. "I believe you. And I don't want to tire you out. How are you feeling?"

She drew her shoulders up to almost her ears, then dropped them. "Well, outside of dying, I feel pretty good." She delivered the line with such dry, deadpan wit, Jake waited a full beat, then burst into laughter.

"I'm glad you came," she said. "It's been too long."

"Yes," he said. "It has."

"I suppose that's my fault," she said. "It's been very upsetting for your grandfather."

Jake felt his jaw tighten. Upsetting? For his grandfather?

"I wanted to see you because I think things have gone on long enough. I still pay attention to what's going on out there. I understand you and my son had some cross words the other day."

Jake shook his head to clear it. Had she just said what he thought she'd said?

"I can assure you; it wasn't my intention. But like you said. Things have gone on for too long. It's your family that hasn't wanted anything to do with mine."

"Oh," she said. This time she reached out and grabbed Jake's hands. Her skin was warm; her grip was surprisingly strong. "That's not true. Not the way you think. I've thought of you so often. But I always knew you were better off with the Cashens. It looks like I was right. I follow the news about you, though. I can't understand why anyone would want to be a police officer these days. But I know you've done good work. I'm proud of you."

He felt a flicker of rage. As if her pride meant she thought she owned some part of any success he achieved. Is this what she wanted? To gaslight him? Only now, she was right about one thing. She was dying. What good would it do for him to unload on a frail old woman? It wouldn't make him feel better. He'd probably hate himself afterward.

"Well, thank you for saying that," he said. "I really am sorry you're ill. I should let you get your rest."

"Is Gemma with you?" she asked. "I thought I heard more voices outside. Karma is a sweet girl, but she doesn't know how to mind her own business."

"Gemma's ..."

Before he could finish, the door opened. Gemma walked in, taking slow, hesitant steps. Her face was flushed, and Jake knew instantly that she'd been crying. This was a mistake. He never should have told her about Adele's message. He never should have brought her here.

"Hello," Gemma said, then stepped forward until she stood at the end of Grandma Del's bed.

Something came over the old woman. She sat up straighter. Her eyes clouded even more. Her lips trembled. Then she broke into a beaming smile.

"Sonya," she said, breathless. "You look so beautiful. Come here to me."

Gemma was paralyzed. She looked desperately at Jake. He rose to his feet, ready to put his arm around his sister and walk her right back out.

Then Gemma recovered. The mask she'd worn since they walked inside dropped. Gone was the plastered smile and the armor she wore. She walked around the bed and sat carefully on Adele's side, letting her rest her hands on Gemma's thighs.

"Oh, honey," Adele said. "I'm so glad you got here. My beautiful girl." She reached up and laid her hands along Gemma's jaw. "And what a pretty suit. I always liked you in green."

"Thank you," Gemma said.

"I wanted to tell you. I have something I want you to give to your children. I know you've been telling me not to. But I simply won't hear of it anymore. Darling, reach over there. My purse is on that chair. Bring it to me."

It was surreal. Gemma stared at Jake, giving him a shocked look. But she did as Adele asked and handed the woman her purse. Adele's fingers shook as she unzipped it and rummaged through the contents. She pulled out several envelopes, stuffed them back in, then finally settled on one. A small manila mailer sealed with a string.

"Here," she said. "Take that with you. But cash it soon. It's from my personal account. Your father won't know. Your brother can't touch it. Use it for your house. Use it for my grandchildren. I trust you to do the right thing with it. Promise?"

"Uh ... s-sure," Gemma said.

"Good. Now that's settled. Tell me why you haven't visited me in so long. That was very selfish of you. It hurt my feelings."

Gemma slid off the bed. "I'm not Sonya, Grandma Del. I'm Gemma."

Del squinted and leaned forward. She blinked, then sank back into her bed, pulling the covers up to her chin. She looked at Gemma, then at Jake. Her frail brain was trying to process what was right in front of her.

"I know who you are. Don't treat me like I'm crazy."

"You're tired," Jake said. "We're going to go now. Let you get your rest."

"I meant what I said. I've been worried about both of you. Your grandfather and my son have only tried to do what's best."

"What's best?" Gemma said. Jake shook his head. This needed to be over. It was time to leave.

"Take care of yourself, Grandma Del," Jake said. "It was nice to see you."

"You aren't leaving me now, are you?"

"I have to go to work," Jake said. "So does Gemma. Maybe we'll stop by later."

She settled then. Her smile returned. "I'd like that. You could stop downstairs and have the cook make us some chicken noodle soup. They do it special for me."

"Sounds great," Jake said, putting his hand on Gemma's back.

"I hope that helps," Adele said. She pointed to the envelope in Gemma's hand. As they walked out, Karma stood there with a syringe in her hand.

"Morphine," she said. "She gets it every two hours now."

"You were right," Jake said. "She's not all there anymore."

"That?" Karma said. "I'm sorry. I wasn't spying. But whatever she gave you, she's been telling me about it for days. She even told me to make sure you got it if she passed before you came. So whatever that is, she means it. I'll back you up if her son wants to take you to court for it."

Jake thanked her. He and Gemma walked to the elevators. She clutched the envelope to her chest.

"You gonna open that?" Jake asked.

"Oh," she said, seeming to forget what she was holding. Gemma unwound the string sealing it shut. She pulled out a single piece of paper.

"Jake," she said. "It's a cashier's check. It's a hundred thousand dollars."

"You should cash it," he said. The elevator opened. They walked out into the sunshine. Gemma went to the bench overlooking the marble fountain. There was a plaque there too, dedicated to Paul Arden.

They didn't talk for a while. Gemma just stared at the zeroes on Adele Arden's check. Then she folded it and put it in her lap.

"Jake," she said. "Are you going to tell me what you and Rob were arguing about outside the Union Hall the other day?"

He looked at the ground. "Are you going to pretend you don't already know? At least twenty people heard us."

She said, "You went through Mom and Dad's police file." It wasn't a question.

"Who told you?"

She didn't answer. He knew it could have been anyone. He thought only Birdie and Meg knew. But Deputy Altman, the new records clerk, knew he signed it out. It had been sitting in their office, clearly labeled for days. And if it was Birdie, out of concern for him, he knew Gemma would keep her confidence.

"I'm sorry," he said. "I know it's been tough for you. I knew what it was. At least, I thought I did. I've been to a hundred scenes like that and worse. But ... I didn't know, Gemma. I do now. I understand everything you did. And I love you."

"I love you too, dummy," she said. "But will you promise me that it's over now? You can put it behind you? I don't care what that woman said up there. I guess I don't even care that she's dying. We know what she did to Mom. If it eases her last days a little to think I was Mom, fine. She's a human being and I'm glad to bring her comfort."

"At what cost to you though?"

"Jake, I'm fine. Really."

Jake smiled. "I think you might be the toughest bitch I know, Gemma."

She nudged him with her shoulder. "Don't forget it. Come on. Enough of this dreary crap. Let's get out of here. I've had enough of Ardens for a while."

"Gemma," he said. "There was something. In that file. I never knew about it. Neither did you. I was angry about that. I'm sitting here thinking I shouldn't even tell you. But that's the thing that made me angry. That nobody told me."

"What is it?"

Jake took a breath. "Dad left a note. It was nonsensical, mostly. But he said some things. Rumors that Rob started to make Dad's paranoia worse. If you want to see it, I have a copy."

Gemma stared at the fountain. She closed her eyes. When she opened them, they were clear as she looked at Jake.

"No," she said. "Burn it, Jake. Whatever he said, it doesn't matter. And it didn't matter to Mom. She loved him. He loved her. He loved us. And you aren't him. Neither of us is. We're safe, Jake. I know you know it."

"Okay," he said, pointing to the check in her lap. He took her hand. "I don't want a penny of that. You keep it. You could make better use of it than I could anyway."

Gemma held up the check. She let go of Jake's hand and tore the check in two.

"Gemma! You should keep it. You could put Aidan through college with that."

She ripped it again and then walked up to the fountain. She let the pieces flutter into the water. "I don't want it either," she said. "It's insulting. She thinks a hundred grand is enough to absolve her sins. Or maybe she's even more sinister than that. Maybe she thinks she's paying for our silence for what we know about Rob. And maybe that whole thing with her thinking I was Mom was a con. A way to keep us from challenging her. To keep me from saying what she deserved to hear. No, I don't want anything of theirs. I already have the most valuable thing that came from them. I have you. And my boys. I have myself. That money came from the worst of them. From the broken backs and diseased lungs of our grandfathers. The Ardens got rich by exploiting the people of this town and robbing it of some of its resources. They think they can build a crappy hospital. Or put up monuments to themselves. That everyone should worship them. I don't want it. Let Rob have all of it. Let it rot him from the inside out. It already has. He can die alone, surrounded by all their blood money."

He walked up to her. He kissed her. "I have the best parts of them too then."

As they walked toward his truck, Gemma cast one last look over her shoulder. Jake helped her into the truck and climbed behind the wheel. He turned to her.

"Gemma...those interview tapes in Mom and Dad's file, I knew... but I didn't know. What you did and saw." He fumbled over his words, not knowing quite how to express what he meant. He took a breath. "I know it was you. How brave you were. How strong. You got us through it. You got me through it. Sure, we had Grandma and Grandpa and a lot of other people. But it was you."

Her eyes glistened, but she smiled and looked skyward before meeting his eyes again. "Don't you get it? Are you gonna make me get all sappy too and say it?"

Jake narrowed his eyes in confusion. Gemma reached for his hand and squeezed it.

"It was you, silly," she said. "You're the one who got *me* through it, Jakey." She hugged him hard, and he let her. Then he put the truck in gear, eager to put Ardenville behind them.

She was something, his sister. She had their mother's heart, but Cashen steel in her bone marrow. Their father's legacy. He had tried to run away from it for almost twenty years. As they passed that old cemetery with their mother's monument rising tall, giving Ardenville its own skyline, he knew Grandpa Max was wrong about one thing. Sonya wasn't there. She never was. She was with him. She was with Gemma. And so was his father. He could feel him in a different way now. He could begin to let go. Frank also told him he had the best parts of his father, not the worst. For the first time in his life, Jake felt like maybe he could believe it.

Keep reading for a preview of The Coldest Ground, the next book in the Jake Cashen Crime Thriller Series.

https://declanjamesbooks.com/cold

Forty years ago, seven-year-old Michael Adkins vanished on a frigid winter morning. His remains were found two years later—mere yards from where he disappeared—raising more questions than answers. Now, a disturbing letter arrives with details only the killer could know, and Detective Jake Cashen's investigation rips open a cold case, exposing corruption, conspiracy, and secrets long buried beneath the coldest ground.

https://declanjamesbooks.com/cold

TURN THE PAGE FOR A PREVIEW

Exclusive Preview of The Coldest Ground

She stared at the wall, clutching a feather pillow under her head. Her least favorite rooster crowed outside the window. He did that every morning even though he had fourteen acres to free range and the coop was on the far end of the property. No, that bastard Rhode Island Red marched himself up the porch and perched on top of her grandmother's old cane chair belting out his screechy call with enough amplitude to wake the dead.

"Keep it up and I've got a stew pot big enough for you," she said. She inherited that phrase from her mother. Today's rooster descended from the one that used to drive her mother to chase it off with a frying pan or a spatula.

The white lace curtains billowed from the open window. It felt cool on her skin, but that gentle sensation was just enough to bring the stinging pain back to her arms.

She rose and padded to the bathroom down the hall. It was so hot that the wood floors were warm beneath her feet. She flipped on the switch. The bulb flickered, then flared to life, bathing her in harsh light.

Carefully, she unwrapped the bandages from her arms, pausing to hiss through her teeth as one piece of cloth stuck to the newly forming scab just below her elbow.

Fresh anger rose as she surveyed the damage. Three long trenches dug into her left forearm where he'd raked his nails across her tender flesh. The skin around it started to bruise. Her right arm wasn't as bad. For some reason, he liked to chew the nails on his left hand. Though it irritated her, it had brought her an unexpected blessing. He hadn't broken the skin on that arm, just scraped it lightly, though he'd gotten hold of the thin skin under her wrist and pinched it until she cried out.

He said the vilest things. Called her names. Threatened to leave her. She had screamed in his face that she's the best thing that ever happened to him. She tolerated it as long as she could. More than most women would. For months, she tried to placate him. Distract him. Keep the house and his meals the way he said he liked them. But his behavior just got worse and worse.

She washed her face and applied fresh ointment to the marred flesh of her arms. She re-wrapped the left one, hoping none of the wounds became infected.

She walked to the front door and opened it. The paperboy had missed the porch again. She spied the long yellow plastic bag in the dirt at the bottom of the steps. Sighing with exasperation, she walked down to get it. As she rose, she turned toward the root cellar on the side of the house.

The yelling had stopped. He pounded on the door for an hour last night after she finally got the upper hand. She relished the look of shock on his face as she pushed him hard enough for him to lose his balance and pitch backward down the uneven steps. Her strength had surprised her as well. She knew he'd gotten so used to her just doing everything his way. Giving in. Until last night, it had just seemed easier. But everyone has their breaking point.

She walked over to the Bilco doors. She'd wedged the steel pin through the heavy metal loops. It had shifted some but held. She'd heard him banging on those doors last night for just a few minutes. Then he settled, understanding it was no use. She finally drew the courage to handle things the way her mother had when she'd taken all the abuse she could stand.

"Have you learned your lesson yet?" she called out. He didn't answer. He probably fell asleep on the stack of old burlap sacks against the cool stone wall. The bastard had probably gotten a better night's sleep than she did. She only had her grandfather's antique fan to cool her off.

The rooster hopped off the porch and eyed her. He began to strut toward her, but something made him stop. Maybe he also realized she'd put up with as much as she was going to. The bird puffed out its feathers, then chose the wiser course of action and ran to the other end of the yard.

She took a step toward the cellar doors and paused. It was a full hour before sunrise. Let him sleep it off a little longer. He'd be easier to deal with after she had her caffeine.

She slipped the newspaper under her arm and headed back to the house. Two minutes later, she poured herself a cup of instant coffee. She slapped the paper on the table and read the headline.

> **Reagan Vows Strong Defense in Policy Speech, Has Strong Words for Soviets**

Let's hope so, she thought as she looked out the window at the tall, tasseled corn husks growing in the field across the road. The kitchen phone rang, startling her. She decided not to answer.

Instead, she went to it, lifted the receiver, then slammed it back down into the cradle as hard as she could. She picked it up and set the receiver on the kitchen counter. Let everyone hear a busy signal today.

She finished her coffee, folded up the paper, and rinsed her cup in the sink. She took her time getting ready for him. Showering. Brushing her teeth. Picking out her favorite sundress, the cotton one she'd made from Butterick 6024. She liked it so much she made four of them using different patterns of fabric for each. Today, she chose the red one.

"All right," she said, staring back at the mirror. "Let's see if you've learned your manners."

She twisted her hair into a bun and went outside barefoot. The grass felt cool on her feet. She kept an eye out for chicken shit. That was another thing he was supposed to stay on top of.

It took some doing to wriggle the pin out of the cellar door lock. She left it dangling from its rusted chain and then heaved one door open. It was dark inside. Either he'd pulled the chain to turn off the single light hanging from the ceiling, or the bulb had burned out. She felt along the wall as she descended the stone steps. It was so much hotter down here than she remembered it being. Stifling. Reaching up, she found the chain and pulled it, illuminating swirling dust motes. She breathed some in; they tickled the back of her throat, and she coughed into her hand. She looked toward the stack of burlap, expecting to see him stretched out, enjoying his chance to sleep in. But the wall remained in the shadows. She couldn't make him out.

What kind of smart mouth would he have for her this morning?

"Get up," she said. She picked up the broom she kept against the wall, just in case he decided to charge her. She wouldn't put it past him to lie in wait, ready to pounce.

No answer. She edged toward the pallet. He wasn't there. The light reflected in the dusty row of Ball jars she had lined up on the shelves. They were intact. It occurred to her it would have been like him to smash them all. Give her something else to clean up.

She took a step and tripped over something. Pitching forward, the broom flew out of her hands. She landed hard on her outstretched wrists, scraping the heel of her hand on something sharp.

She rolled over. There he was. Lying on the floor beside her. His lips were blue. His tongue bloated and grotesque, sticking out of his mouth. His eyes were wide open and opalescent.

She scrambled to her knees and reached for him.

"Baby?" she shouted. "Oh my God!"

She shook him. He was cold to the touch. Rigid.

No. No. No. No. Not this. This wasn't real. It couldn't be real. She hadn't meant this.

But little boys had to be punished. She could not let him treat her like that. How many nights had she spent in this same root cellar as a little girl, sleeping on those same burlap sacks?

"Oh," she cried out. "I'm sorry. I'm so sorry."

She did the only thing she could. She pulled him onto her lap and rocked him. He felt so small and light. Just forty-seven pounds the last time she got him to step on a scale.

"It's okay," she whispered. "It's all going to be okay."

She kissed his forehead. Smoothed back his hair. Then sang him the sweetest lullaby.

https://declanjamesbooks.com/cold

Catch Up with Jake Cashen

Have you read them all? Is this the first book you've read by Declan James? Check out the Jake Cashen series page on Amazon. From there, you can:

- make sure you haven't missed a book;
- reserve your copy of the next book; or
- find the recommended reading order.

CLICK HERE
DECLAN JAMES SERIES PAGE

Stay in Touch with Declan James

For more information, visit

https://declanjamesbooks.com

If you'd like to receive a free digital copy of the extended prologue to the Jake Cashen series plus access to the exclusive character image gallery where you can see what Jake Cashen and others look like in the author's mind, sign up for Declan James's Roll Call Newsletter here: https://declanjamesbooks.com/rollcall/

About the Author

Before putting pen to paper, Declan James's career in law enforcement spanned twenty-six years. Declan's work as a digital forensics detective has earned him the highest honors from the U.S. Secret Service and F.B.I. For the last sixteen years of his career, Declan served on a nationally recognized task force aimed at protecting children from online predators. Prior to that, Declan spent six years undercover working Vice-Narcotics.

An avid outdoorsman and conservationist, Declan enjoys hunting, fishing, grilling, smoking meats, and his quest for the perfect bottle of bourbon. He lives on a lake in Southern Michigan along with his wife and kids. Declan James is a pseudonym.

For more information follow Declan at one of the links below. If you'd like to receive new release alerts, author news, and a FREE digital bonus prologue to Murder in the Hollows, sign up for Declan's Roll Call Newsletter here: https://declanjamesbooks.com/rollcall/

Also by Declan James

Murder in the Hollows

Kill Season

Bones of Echo Lake

Red Sky Hill

Her Last Moment

Secrets of Blackhand Creek

Lethal Harvest

The Whisper Girl

Their Deadly Truth

The Coldest Ground

With more to come...

Made in the USA
Las Vegas, NV
26 August 2025

26947016R00229